CW00430563

HEALING OF THE WOLF

CHERISE SINCLAIR

VanScoy Publishing Group

Healing of the Wolf
Copyright © 2020 by Cherise Sinclair
ISBN: 978-1-947219-25-0
Published by VanScoy Publishing Group
Cover Art: Hot Damn Designs
Edited by Red Quill Editing, LLC
Content Editor: Bianca Sommerland

ACKNOWLEDGMENTS

Everyone pitched in to get this book published.

So many thank yous go to my crit partners Monette Michaels and Fiona Archer.

And a huge thank you goes to Bianca Sommerland, my content editor.

Hugs to Ekatarina Sayanova and her Red Quill editors, Rebecca Cartee and Tracy Damron-Roelle. Y'all are amazing—especially Saya who worked even when in and out of the hospital and having surgery. Thank you so much!

My amazing beta readers: Barb Jack, Marian Shulman, Lisa White, and Ruth Reid caught all sorts of errors.

(I should post some of my bloopers they've caught. Or not. So *embarrassing.*)

Yep, I'm incredibly grateful for my awesome team. Thank you all!

PROLOGUE

Seattle, Washington – *waning crescent moon*

All she'd ever wanted was to belong. To help the ill and injured. Instead, she was a captive, barely existing.

Completely *useless*.

A cell of four white walls, a solid door, and this bed made up her tiny world. Margery slammed her fist into the thin mattress with a muted thump. Because the weak gesture was all she could do. That *sadistic* guard. What she'd give to be able to kill him.

Tears stung her eyes with the memory of Gallia's bruised face. The bloody welts on her back. Because the gangly fourteen-year-old girl had accidentally bumped into the Scythe guard. The most brutal one.

1

Pressing her face to the lumpy mattress to muffle any sound, Margery growled. She'd been so *useless*. There'd been times she could intervene to calm an angry guard and keep him from hurting one of the younglings.

Not this time. Instead, Huber had backhanded Margery to the ground, kicked her half-unconscious, then returned to beating on Gallia.

She rubbed her aching face against the rough sheet and fought the urge to cry.

The first few years she'd been a captive, she'd hoped for rescue. Managed to endure. Clung to the fantasy of escape.

Eventually, hope died.

The Scythe were too powerful. The clandestine organization of wealthy, influential humans manipulated world events to gain even more power. Over a decade ago, they'd discovered the shifters, decided they'd be of use, and attacked Margery's tiny mountain village.

They'd been disappointed when all the adult Daonain died but had cut their losses and sent the young males off to train as covert operations soldiers. The young females— their sisters like Margery—remained imprisoned here in the compound to ensure the shifter-soldier's cooperation.

To the Scythe, the shifters were freaks. Animals to cruelly mistreat. And they did. The Scythe had no compassion, didn't hear pleas. Rarely responded to reason.

She kept trying, though. Once in a while, she could save a young one some pain.

But every time she spoke to a guard, hatred squeezed her lungs. And gut-wrenching fear froze her muscles.

At least today, there had been no broken bones. In the tiny clinic, Margery'd done her best to patch Gallia up while whispering comforting words and giving quick hugs. Something every young captive needed so badly.

She blinked back tears. *I need a hug, too.*

With a sigh, she pulled the light blanket closer. Her thin T-shirt and sleep shorts didn't lend much warmth, and November in the human city of Seattle was cold and damp. Rolling onto her back, she tried to ignore the nagging ache in her bruised face and ribs. Her ankle throbbed where the fractured bones had never healed right. Exhaustion dragged at her.

She was dying, slowly, but ever so surely.

Shifters didn't survive captivity.

When the Scythe had captured her village, her littermate, Orson, died while charging a soldier. Grandmama's body was tossed into her burning clinic. Mama died in wolf form, fighting in the streets.

Margery's other littermate, Oliver, was taken away to be a shifter-soldier.

Imprisoned in Scythe cages, the babies and the adults—all those who had shifted once—died quickly.

Now, the rest would follow them into death.

In their early twenties, after eleven years in captivity, the females were failing. Trapped by walls, so far from the forests and unable to shift. Beaten down, half-starved, filled with despair, the oldest of the hostages were losing their grip on life.

At the end of September, as the leaves were falling from the trees, Barbara had simply faded into death.

I miss you, my friend, but I'll join you soon.

Margery's miserable thoughts wouldn't allow sleep. If she could only sit in the moonlight... No, even that wouldn't help. Tonight, the night sky was empty of the Lady's glow.

Pushing her tangled hair from her face, Margery wiggled into a cross-legged position and closed her eyes. There it was, deep inside her—her haven. Fragrant, green forest surrounding a peaceful mountain lake. The water was no longer blue; each year, the Mother's waters grew grayer. The Scythe compound was so, so far from the lands of the Daonain.

But the lake still refreshed and calmed Margery's soul.

A creaking sound broke into her peace.

She turned her head. The cells around her were quiet— no one wanted to risk a beating. She could hear the low hum of nighttime traffic in the city and the scuff of a guard's boots outside as he patrolled the grounds.

Not that he was patrolling against a shifter trying to run. If a captive escaped or died, the Scythe would kill her brothers. Love for littermates made tighter shackles than any metal ones.

A creaking, groaning noise—the distinctive sound of the heavy door to the hallway of cells. Was there trouble?

Margery lay down and pretended to be asleep.

Keys clanked. A door somewhere unlocked and opened. Someone whispered, "Into the hall. We're getting out of here."

What? That was *Darcy's* voice.

Margery jumped off her bed.

Her friend was alive? Last September, she'd escaped. Like Margery, she'd been rail-thin, fading, dying. Margery had thought that was why Darcy had run—to taste freedom before her death. Soon after, the Director announced she'd been caught and killed.

Do dead people whisper?

Leaning against her cell door, Margery held her breath in hope—and listened.

Movement. More whispers.

Another door creaked open. Then the lock on her own cell turned. The door opened.

"Darcy." Margery's voice was almost inaudible because her friend stood there, healthy and strong. As joy filled Margery, she reached out.

Darcy squeezed her hand, tugged her out into the hall, and moved to unlock the next door.

When the last door was opened, the captives gathered —ages ranging from thirteen to twenty-four—silently crying and hugging.

"The Director said you were killed," Idelle whispered.

Darcy snorted her opinion of the lie. "I escaped and found other shifters. We're breaking you and our brothers out at the same time. You need to do what I say." Fear and determination radiated from her.

Margery stared at her in disbelief. Darcy should've stayed safe, not set herself up for certain death. One person might make it out. All of them? Past armed guards, powerful spotlights, machine guns in the bunkers. Over ten-foot stone walls.

We'll all die.

Yet hope rose within her like a painful, burning brand.

Darcy moved closer, her whisper barely audible. "Go to the ground floor, out the back door, and hide behind the building."

Little Alice, barely thirteen, tangled hair falling over her cheeks, tugged at Darcy's shirt. "What about the alarms? The floodlights? The guards? We'll—"

"The lights will be gone; trust me." Darcy held up a broken-off mop handle stained with blood. "I'll handle the guards."

But if we're caught trying to escape... Terror froze Margery's muscles. Fear fogged her vision at the memory of her worst beating. *The tearing gut-wrenching pain as her arms and legs broke, then her ribs. The backhand across her face—the guard's ring ripping her face open. Her blood hotter than fire. The huge boot crushing her ankle. Her screams...*

The metallic taste of panic choked her as she fought her way out of the memory. She ran a finger down the long scar on her face to remind herself it was over. In the past.

Darcy's eyes met hers. "Can you bring up the rear and make sure everyone stays together?"

No, no. The guards are out there. Will catch us. Hurt us.

The other females looked at Margery with hope, with fear. Waiting for her decision.

Her gaze fell on Gallia's bruised face. There was...a chance. It would be worth any torture to get the younglings out of here.

Reaching deep, Margery found some courage. She lifted her chin. "I can."

A few minutes later, she trailed the others down the narrow staircase. Every soft footstep echoed; every sharp breath sounded like a shout.

Each time the cubs turned to look at her, she nodded reassurance and held her finger to her lips.

Her heart thumped like a wild thing inside her ribs. Every nerve screamed for her to flee before the Scythe found them. The cold sweat of fear trickled down her back.

She kept her feet moving.

She wouldn't fail the others.

At last, the stairs ended, and she followed the group out the back door into the dark night. Darcy motioned for them to hide behind the privet hedge at the rear of the building.

At yelling from the front, everyone dove into the bushes.

Huddling down, Margery peeked around the dense foliage. The compound's floodlights were dark. Not even the generator-run emergency lights were on. Shouting, weapons out, guards ran past, and Margery cringed as her body remembered the brutal canes, the boots, the fists.

"Stay down." Darcy stripped and shoved her clothes under a bush. The air around her shimmered...and she trawsfurred into a panther.

Oh, Goddess. Darcy had *shifted.* None of the imprisoned females had ever managed to trawsfur.

Margery held her breath as awe mingled with an instinctive longing so deep it was carved into her bones.

I want to shift, dance in the moonlight, feel the breeze in my fur.

Inside the building, gunshots snapped. Men yelled. The door burst open, and two panthers sprang out, blood streaking their golden fur.

One shifted to human. Even as Margery blinked at the sight of a naked male, he bent and hugged the purring panther beside him, whispering, "Vicki, Vicki, Vicki, by the Gods."

The huge, shaggy-haired male's love for his female was almost a visible glow.

Training brought Margery back to common sense. The blood on Vicki's fur—was it hers or someone else's? Margery looked closer. As a pup, she'd seen shifters whose stomach fur and skin had sagged like that.

The female had recently given birth.

At the front of the compound, something crashed so

hard the ground shook. Metal screeched. A pistol barked, then more guns fired in a torrent of noise.

Margery's hands turned to ice. The guards were alerted. The captives would never get out.

The back door opened again. A dark-haired male emerged with arms around several bundles. "Hey, Alec. I think these cubs belong to you."

When the huge male didn't move, the dark-haired male looked around and spotted Margery in the bushes. He jerked his head. *Come here.*

She pulled in a breath, drew on her waning stock of courage, and stepped forward.

He handed her a baby, one of three.

Like the clear waters from a sacred spring, wonder welled up through the cracks in her soul. She held new life, a spark from the Mother of All. Her heart turned to mush, before fear blossomed again. This was no place for a newborn.

Her lips raised in a silent snarl. Nothing would hurt this kitling.

The male handed another baby to Alice. Idelle took the third.

When the male named Alec moved toward the infants, the dark-haired one blocked him. "Cubs come later, Cahir. We need to get everybody to the garage."

The garage. Where the cars were. Yes, yes, please.

"Dammit, Owen," Alec said under his breath, looking with longing at the babies. Then he sighed and raised his voice enough so all the captives could hear. "Aye, let's get them out of here. I'll take the lead. Vixen, stay by the cubs. Owen, left flank. Darcy, you bring up the rear. Let's go."

Darcy shifted to human, yanked on her black tank and tight sweatpants, and spoke to the females hiding in the bushes. "Come on. It's time to move to somewhere safe. Hurry."

No one budged.

Margery's mouth was so dry, she couldn't even swallow. But they couldn't stay here. Guards, gunfire... None of that mattered. The infants must be saved. She forced her feet to move forward.

No one else stirred. Just stared at the huge, naked male.

No one trusted males.

Seeing the frozen captives, Darcy shook her head. "Alec, I'd better lead."

"Aye," he agreed after a second. "I'll take rear guard."

As Darcy started across the lawn, Margery turned to the others and jerked her head, conveying an order of her own. *Let's go.*

Silently, the others rose and followed her. Behind Margery, Idelle carried the second cubling, Alice the third. They moved in a line across the soft grass, staying in the shadows.

Suddenly, Alice's baby began to cry.

Loudly.

Eyes wide as a fleeing deer, the girl froze.

Oh no.

Margery hurried back and took the babe in her free arm. Cuddling it, she rocked side-to-side, calming herself and the kit. "Shhh, shhh, shhh."

It quieted, staring up at her, pink lips pursed. Silent. Margery's talent for soothing had won.

Too late.

"What the fuck!" a man shouted. "What was that?" Guards charged around the side of the building—straight at them.

Their flashlight beams spotlighted Darcy in the front.

"There's the freak that escaped!" It was the worst Scythe guard—Huber.

If he caught Darcy, he'd kill her.

Instinct drew Margery forward to shield her, but she stopped mid stride. The *babies*. The babies in her arms were helpless.

In a flash, Darcy dashed forward, luring the men away. They chased her like a vicious pack of dogs. More guards cut across the lawn, fanning out. Shooting at her.

Margery turned to the captives. "Move farther back." With babies in her arms, she couldn't motion, but they heard her and faded back into the deepest shadows.

A guard spotted her before she could follow. "Stop right there!"

She froze. Arms full, she couldn't run fast enough. If she tried to hide, the guard would see the others.

Looming over her, he grabbed for one of the infants she held.

She spun, keeping the babies out of his reach.

"Freak bitch." His cane struck her shoulders. "Give me that monster."

Blow after blow rained down on her, and her shoulders hunched under the agony.

He will not get the kits. In captivity, all the babies had died; these newborns wouldn't stand a chance. As fury rose inside her—all those deaths—she kicked backward with all her might. Her bare foot hit his knee.

He shouted in pain and staggered back.

A screech like ripping metal filled the night as the mother panther, Vicki, sprang on him—and tore out his throat. Without pausing over her kill, the cat raced across the grass toward more guards.

Margery hurried into the shadows with the others.

All over the compound, pistols barked, the sharp snaps louder than the yelling guards. Panthers were golden blurs across the dark lawn as they attacked the Scythe around Darcy. Shrieking and yelling, the guards died under the werecats' fangs and claws.

In the center of it all, Darcy collapsed.

No!

Owen and another big male ran to her. Held her.

Darcy didn't move.

Loss sliced through Margery, and tears pooled in her eyes. If not for the warm weight of the infants in her arms, she would have dropped to her knees.

After speaking to Owen, Alec turned and bounded in

cat form back to her and the captives. He shifted to human. "Let's go."

The females stared at him, many in tears, others frozen with fear.

"Come on." Motioning for them to follow, Margery moved toward him, breaking their paralysis.

He led them around to the front and into the huge garage where the Scythe's black SUVs sat in a long line. One of the three garage doors was open to the black night, showing flashes of gunfire, men running, animal shapes. A fire blazed across the compound, painting the darkness like a nightmare come to life.

A gray-haired male rasped out a greeting to Alec. "That all of them?"

"Yep. Gawain and Owen are with Darcy. She was shot." Alec turned toward the door. "Vicki's alive—and out there fighting. Joe, can you—"

"Stubborn female." The older male's face was as harsh as his voice. A torn-off sleeve served as a bandage over a bloodied left forearm. "Aye, I've got this. Go fetch her."

"Thanks." Alec turned to the captives. "Once your tracking devices are removed, we'll get you out of here."

Margery felt her muscles loosen a tiny bit. The Scythe had said a tracking device was implanted in each hostage—a way to locate them if they ever tried to escape. Of course the devices needed to come out. How could she have forgotten?

As Alec shifted and disappeared out the door, Joe yelled, "Donal, the females are here."

"Coming." From the rear came a tall, lithely powerful male with black hair past his shoulders. Olive skin covered cheekbones as sharp as the peaks of the Olympic Mountains.

Donal looked at the huddle of females. "I'll start with the youngest. I'm afraid you each have two trackers to remove." The rich, resonant timbre of his voice tugged at something deep inside Margery.

"Two?" she asked.

"Aye, arm and leg." Donal motioned for Alice to come forward. "Come, cub. Sit on the bench here.

Alice took a step back. Her voice wavered. A male in authority wasn't to be trusted. "Margery?"

"Yes, sit down. This is good." Pushing away pity, Margery kept her voice firm to quell the youngling's panic. "We want that Scythe nastiness out of our bodies. The sooner the better."

Biting her lip, Alice sat, but gave Margery a pleading look. "Please?"

"All right." Margery looked around.

With Alec's help, Vicki had shifted to human and was dressing. The babies would have her care soon.

Margery handed the infants she held to the females who looked the most stable and settled beside Alice on the long, wall bench.

She took the girl's cold little hands. "I've got you,

lambkin." Pulling in a breath, she nodded to the patiently waiting male. "We're ready."

Donal crouched in front of Alice with the deadly grace of a panther shifter. His expression softened at the girl's fear. "I took the trackers out of everyone's brothers, little one. I'm getting quite fast at it."

"You saw my littermates?" Alice squeaked. "Are they all right?"

"Tynan said all the shifter-soldiers made it here."

As the male pulled out a scalpel, Alice gripped Margery's hands harder.

Blade in one hand, the male ran his other hand over Alice's upper arm, made a tiny cut, and popped the device out. Alice only squeaked once. Donal tossed the tiny tracker into a nearby trash bin.

Pushing the leg of Alice's sleep shorts up, he traced his fingertips over her thigh and made an irritated sound. "The one is deep and will hurt more, lass. I'm sorry."

He looked at Margery. "Can you—"

Knowing what he needed, Margery wrapped her arms around the girl, immobilizing her in a hug. "We'll both hold really still."

The male was quick; she had to give him that. One swift —deep—slice, and he tweezed the tracker out.

Tears ran down Alice's cheeks, but her sobbing was quiet. They'd learned to suffer in silence.

"All done, sweetie," Margery whispered. "All done."

"Thorson," Donal called to the older one. "Can you bandage her up, please?"

The grizzled male scowled. "You're not going to heal the youngling?"

"Goddess help them, I can't. We're not in territory, and I've barely enough power left to locate the trackers." Donal motioned to Gallia to sit on the bench a few feet down.

Power? What kind of power did he have?

"Herne's hooves, I hadn't realized." Thorson motioned to Alice. "Come, cub. Let's get that bleeding stopped."

Alice cringed away from him. She'd been captured so young that the only males she'd known were her brothers—and the brutal human guards. At least Margery could—sometimes—recall that most males weren't like their captors.

"Sir." Margery braced for a blow in case the tough old male reacted badly. "I can bandage Alice and the others."

"You know first aid?" Thorson growled the question.

Having given Vicki her infant, Idelle took a timid step forward to address both males. "Margery is..." She hesitated —smart captives didn't volunteer information. "Our young are comfortable with her."

"Makes sense, Thorson. Remember how Darcy was terrified of us?" Donal patted Alice's hand and nodded to Margery. "The help is appreciated."

His eyes held a silver hue, so like the moon she'd dreamed of, mesmerizing. Beautiful.

He moved down the bench to Gallia, breaking the spell.

A bit stunned at the impact of the silver-gray eyes, Margery shook her head and smiled at Idelle. "Will you help hold the younglings for him?"

"I will." Idelle settled beside Gallia on the bench.

"You'll need this." Thorson set a backpack of medical supplies next to Margery. As she rummaged for saline and dressings, he gave her a nod of approval and walked away.

One by one, as Donal finished with them, the younglings came to Margery, bleeding and shaking, and she bandaged the incisions. Afterward, each settled at her feet, crowding tightly around her legs. Taking comfort like little chicks from their mama hen.

"Thorson, the front gate is cleared. Load 'em up," a male yelled.

Thorson opened the door of the closest SUV and pointed to the youngsters around Margery. "Youngest cubs first." He turned and motioned to the new mother. "Vic, you and the babes, too."

Hope rose inside Margery. Maybe, maybe, they'd all get free. Not willing to court disappointment, she shoved the emotion down and turned to the cubs around her. "Alice. You go. Gallia and..." She picked out enough to fill the van.

They rose, oh, so reluctantly, unwilling to leave the safety by her side.

"Younglings," she told them firmly, "that new mother over there has three little babies. She needs you to help her."

"We will, Margery," Alice promised.

Given a task to accomplish, the others chorused their agreement. Surrounding Vicki, the small group climbed into the van.

The SUV started up, and Margery smiled in relief. Some would make it out.

As Thorson started loading the next vehicle, older teens settled down around Margery's legs. And she resumed her bandaging job.

Farther down the bench, Donal was removing Idelle's tracking devices. No more captives waited in line.

"Done. Go get bandaged." Still on one knee, the black-haired Donal needed a couple of tries to rise before he could stand.

Idelle dropped down beside Margery on the bench, silently pointed to her bleeding arm, then blinked. "I can simply ask for help, can't I? No one will hit us if we talk? I think I've almost forgotten how."

Bitter chuckles sounded from the females sitting in a circle around Margery.

"I know. Me, too." Margery patted Idelle's shoulder, then bandaged the incisions.

"Donal, are you finished here?" A male with short brown hair walked over, pulling on a shirt. Broad-shouldered, big-boned, and tall, he radiated authority like heat from a bonfire.

Like a Scythe guard.

Margery froze. The females around her clustered closer.

Gaze on Donal, the male didn't notice them. "We've got injured over there in the back."

"All done here, Tynan. Take the—" Donal saw Margery, and his black brows drew together. "No, I missed one. Come here, lass."

His deeply masculine voice made everything inside her want to comply.

But...move? Exhaustion had turned her legs to jelly, and her damaged ankle burned like a shackle of fire enclosed it. "Idelle, help me up," she whispered.

Rising, Idelle offered her hands and pulled Margery to her feet.

After testing her ankle, she found her balance, and everyone scooted back to let her pass.

The intimidating male—Tynan—stood a few feet away, strapping on a big black weapons belt. Gun, black baton—all the gear needed to destroy someone.

He was a guard.

No, Margery. He was a shifter, not a Scythe brute. Yet past screams echoed through her head, and she couldn't pull her gaze from the brutal weaponry as she limped past him.

Taking a seat in front of Donal, she clasped her trembling hands in her lap.

"I'll be quick, lass. It's not that painful." His eyes narrowed when he realized she wasn't looking at the scalpel. "No...you're not afraid of being cut, are you? Perhaps of me?"

Her gaze flickered past him to the armed male.

"Of Tynan? Really?"

She braced for the blow.

Nothing happened. His gaze took in the bruise on her face, the older ones on her legs and arms from the guards' canes. "Ah, I see. Those maggot-ridden humans."

His softened gaze showed his understanding, and she relaxed.

"Paws on the path, lass." His baritone softened to a compelling velvety smoothness. "You're almost at the end of the journey. Let's get this done so you can be on your way." The scalpel flashed over her arm, and the first tracker popped out.

So quick. She had skill, but nothing like his.

He touched her thigh and moved her sleep shorts out of the way, his fingertips barely on her skin.

She frowned. How could he find the tracker if he didn't touch her?

His fingers grazed her skin, up and down, sideways. His gaze met hers, the strain in his face obvious. "Sorry. I'm running on empty."

Empty? He did look exhausted. His skin was pale; his lean, careful fingers were cold.

"There." His hand curled around her thigh and held her firmly as he cut.

The splitting pressure was followed by burning pain. Gritting her teeth, she held perfectly still. Really, this was nothing compared to broken bones.

"Good lass. Almost done." As he picked up the tweezers, she studied his face. Too sharply chiseled, too stern, yet as mesmerizing as jagged lightning against a black sky. On his right cheekbone was a silvery scar shaped like a crescent moon, and her eyes widened at the mark of a healer—a shifter called to serve the Goddess.

"One more second." A brief pain jolted her as he pulled the tracker out. "Done. Let's get you bandaged."

He set the tweezers down. His gaze met hers—and held. The shaking inside her disappeared under a wave of warmth. A breath brought her his scent—the fresh green of softly growing grass beside a lake. It was a masculine scent, and suddenly she realized a *male* had his hand on her leg.

His fingers were lean. Slightly callused.

Suddenly, he swayed slightly, and his gaze went unfocused. His hand dropped, and he started to fall sideways.

Margery grabbed him around the shoulders. "Help!" Gently, she eased him down onto the concrete floor.

"By the Gods, Donal." Tynan hurried over, crouched, and set his fingers against Donal's neck.

Margery scrambled away from the guard—no, from the male shifter. Not a Scythe. Yet she couldn't breathe until she'd reached what she felt was a safe distance away.

Without acknowledging her reaction, Tynan patted Donal's cheek, getting no response. "Overdid it, didn't you, boyo." With a grunt of effort, he scooped up the healer and carried him to where several injured males lay near the garage wall.

Legs not cooperating, Margery stayed on the bench.

Gunfire still sounded outside. Yelling. Screaming. Someone shouted orders. The scent of blood and fear and sweat mingled with the stink of oil and gasoline inside the garage building. The shaking inside her grew.

Most of the captives were gone. The rest waited quietly near the older male, Thorson.

"Margery. You're still bleeding." Idelle hurried over, grabbing up the medical bag. Kneeling, she helped Margery wrap the incisions. "Where are they taking us? Do you think they'll let us see our brothers? Are they here, do you suppose?"

"Here?" Margery stared at Idelle, then at the nightmare outside. Was Oliver out there? The Scythe had trained her littermate to be a shifter-soldier, but that wasn't who he was. Quiet and sweet, the werebear should have been an artist—not a killer. The battle outside was no place for him. *Please, don't let him be out there.*

Thorson's rough voice echoed in the garage. "Any females left, load up in this van."

With Idelle beside her, Margery limped toward the SUV at the far end of the garage.

Across the compound, a flickering light grew in one of the brick buildings. Were their rescuers burning everything down? *Good.* The bitter rage inside her flamed along with the wood. Those cells, cages, and laboratories had heard the screams of an entire village of shifters, had witnessed the torture and death of her family, her friends.

Burn it all.

Fighting against the shaking fury, she turned away and saw the injured.

Lines of them, lying on blankets near the back wall. Being Daonain, they'd insisted the females leave first.

The healer lay near the end, still unconscious. Two younger males were tending the wounded, and one called frantically to the big uniformed male, Tynan. "I can't get the bleeding stopped."

Putting a pressure dressing on another bleeder, Tynan shook his head. "Do what you can. I'll be there in a minute."

Margery frowned, looking more closely.

Another injured male had froth on his lips, and each labored breath made a whistling sound. A pierced lung? The other young male stood over him, obviously at a loss for what to do.

Dear Goddess. The healer was down. And the helpers weren't trained.

She took a step forward. Would they be angry if she offered to help?

Her chin went up. Too bad. The males had been injured saving the Dogwood villagers. Some might be brothers of the hostages. They might die here, bleeding out from lack of skillful tending.

She walked over, still carrying the bag of dressing supplies.

Stopping beside the lung injury, she said to the uninjured young male. "Let me take care of him."

"You?"

Irritation with his surprise shoved away her fear. "Yes, *me*. You need assistance, and I can do it."

He hesitated, then called, "Tynan, this female wants to help."

The big male in charge looked over. His clear blue eyes held hers in an impersonal assessment that made her shiver. Every instinct told her to back away, but the wounded shifter was fighting for every breath. He needed her.

"Let her help." Tynan turned to Thorson, who was standing by the loaded SUV. "We'll bring her with us when we leave. Get the rest of them out of here."

"Aye." Thorson gave her a thin, appreciative smile.

She didn't bother to respond. Kneeling close enough that the injured shifter could feel the soothing warmth of her leg, she dug through the supplies for an occlusive dressing. "Easy there, it's going to be all right. Breathe out for me," she said and applied the dressing, pressing down the three sides.

Once he was cared for, she moved to a gunshot wound, a dislocated shoulder, a stab wound. More injured appeared.

As she splinted a fractured arm, a pair of wolves padded into the garage and changed into human forms.

Wolves. Mama had been a wolf.

As she watched them, she remembered that Darcy had been able to shift. Would leaving the prison mean the rest of captives might be able to trawsfur, as well?

Will I?

The question stayed with her, even as she knelt beside the next injured male.

And somehow, despite the blood and smoke and screams in the night, hope rose inside her, as irrepressible as the rising of the moon.

CHAPTER ONE

Ailill Ridge, Rainier Territory, Washington - day before full moon

A bitingly cold wind off the high mountains ruffled Margery's fur as she ran the trails with the other wolves. The light from the golden moon streamed over her in a palpable caress from the Goddess.

Every breath she took brought her new information, and after nearly five months of freedom, she could identify each scent.

There—that was the luring fragrance of prey. Deer had used the path in the last few hours. The musty odor of fowl was from an owl perched high on a branch. The metallic tang of blood came from a spot where a coyote had killed a rabbit in a clearing. Every sniff and every sound held meaning.

Finally.

The month following her first shift in December had been overwhelming, painful, and often embarrassing. Her ears and tail had operated independently. Her legs had tangled when she tried something new. And her messed-up ankle still caused problems, especially when running on uneven ground or leaping over logs or boulders.

After her first trawsfur, while in an Elder Village to re-learn Daonain traditions, she'd stumbled over her forepaws and almost knocked over a frail centenarian. So embarrassing.

Yet being in wolf form was...amazing. Despite her unreliable hind leg, she felt as if she were dancing on the forest duff. Four legs were so much better than two. More importantly, she was strong now. Healthy.

All her fellow captives had recovered once out of the city. Getting the birth control implants removed had probably helped, although the medical person said the implants were almost empty.

There had been no one to give them new ones.

Sadness slowed Margery's paws, and she stopped on the trail.

After the hostages arrived at the Scythe compound, the nurse practitioner, Phyllis, discovered thirteen-year-old Margery could calm hysterical younglings and care for the ill and injured. In Dogwood, Grandmama, a *banfasa*, had tended the villagers' health, and Margery had been in the clinic every day, learning and helping out.

After taking Margery as her assistant, Phyllis taught her human medicine—and they became friends. A few years ago, Phyllis grew too outspoken, insisting the captives weren't animals. The Director called her into his office, and she never came out.

Grief—and guilt—flattened Margery's ears. In a way, her friendship with Phyllis had caused her death.

A twig hit Margery's tail, making her jump.

Chittering came from up in a tree.

Yanked from the ugly memories, she looked up.

A scowling tree fairy swung on the end of a high branch. Margery huffed a wolfy laugh and got another twig thrown at her. Pixies were grumpy as bears when awakening after hibernation.

The winter had been long. Now, in April, the mountain valleys were beginning to lose their blanket of snow.

In bounding leaps that hurt her leg but still felt great, Margery caught up with the rest of the wolves. Shoulders brushing against the others, surrounded by the scent of pack and forest, she lost herself in the joy of feeling like she belonged.

Eventually, the alpha wolf led them back to Ailill Ridge. Some wolves veered off to the pack house where they'd left their clothing. More headed for their own homes. With two others, Margery trotted toward the south of town where she lived with several shifters in the territory's communal house. Forest surrounded the back yard, and they did a quick check to ensure they were unobserved. After trawsfurring to human, Margery dried the mushy snow off her feet, dressed in the clothing she'd left in a storage case, and followed Jens through the back door.

"By the Gods, Margery, I thought you'd never get back." Stomping into the kitchen, Portia shoved both her babies into Margery's arms. "They've been bawling their heads off, and I'm ready to claw them."

A werecat, Portia was so self-absorbed, it was surprising she'd even learned Margery's name. However, she used it often enough when demanding help.

As Margery cuddled the cublings, her nose told her what the problem was. "They're both wet and dirty. That's why they're crying."

Coming in, Jens growled under his breath. "Even I can smell it. You're the dam, Portia. You should change them."

The werecat gave a dismissive sniff. "That's why Margery gets free room and board. She's supposed to work for it."

A growl escaped Margery. "I get free room and board for cleaning the house as well as working as a banfasa. You get room and board for being a mother, which means you're supposed to tend your cubs."

Portia lifted a hand in a *yah-yah-yah* gesture and walked out of the room, leaving Margery with the cubs.

Lost that one, didn't I? Margery ground her teeth together.

But she was stuck. Unlike Portia, she wouldn't leave kits in need.

A few minutes later, with one cub all washed, she wiped the second. "Honestly, this wasn't what I thought life would be like when I left Seattle," she whispered to him.

Two months old and adorable, he gurgled and chewed on his fingers. Freed, his little fat legs kicked up in the air. The tiny pink toes made her smile, despite her dissatisfaction. "I love being a wolf—and you will too when you're twelve or so—but I wanted more than this."

Housed in Ailill Ridge for a time after their release, the Dogwood villagers had come to her as usual with their health problems and injuries. The local shifters followed. She thought her childhood dreams were coming true. She would tend the sick, be part of a community, make a difference. Would be loved and needed like Grandmama in Dogwood, whose grateful patients were always bringing edible gifts—apples, tomatoes, a rabbit. Cookies were the best. The villagers had loved their wise woman.

Margery's hope of belonging had died all too soon.

Last fall, a quorum of Cosantirs decided that keeping the Scythe's ex-hostages in one location was dangerous. As the Cosantirs were the God-called guardians of their territories, their word was law—and the Dogwood villagers were relocated to various towns.

Pete, the Cosantir of Rainier Territory, insisted on keeping Margery in Ailill Ridge.

Trapping her here.

Was it wrong to be discontented when her life was so much better than as a captive? She had adequate food, a warm bed, a wolf pack. No one hit her. It was just... The shifters in town didn't value her, perhaps because she wasn't a God-called healer, but merely a banfasa. Banfasas had no magic, only skilled hands, and the knowledge of what to do for injuries and for health.

In the Scythe compound, the captives had been grateful for her care. Here in Ailill Ridge, the townspeople treated her like a slave.

Like a slave, she received only room and board. Other shifters had paying jobs. Why didn't she get paid for what she did?

When rescued, the villagers had been given secondhand clothing, but that was the last clothing Margery had received, aside from a coat when it started to snow. With a sigh, she ran her hand over her faded, patched flannel shirt. Her jeans were ripped at the knee. She had no money to buy anything else.

Trying to take control of her life, she'd told the Cosantir of Rainier Territory that since being a banfasa didn't pay, she would find something else to do. Pete's face had turned dark with anger. He said tending to injuries and cleaning the communal house was her job, and she should be grateful to get a free place to live and free food. The conversation went downhill from there—and she left his house feeling guilty.

Her lips twisted. He'd manipulated her.

He'd also left her at a loss for how to escape this new prison.

As she carried the babies out of the nursery, the front door burst open. The wolf pack alpha, Roger, rushed in, shoving Jens out of the way.

Jens hit the wall with a low yelp of pain.

Margery growled under her breath. The alpha and his two betas were as violent and uncaring as Scythe guards. *I hate this place.*

Shoving his unkempt, yellow hair out of his face, Roger looked around the living room. "Where the fuck is Margery?"

"Here." Holding the two cubs, Margery didn't move from the nursery doorway.

"We've got wounded coming in. Get prepared," he snapped.

"What happened?" Portia called.

"Bunch of our young wolves brawled with a couple of fucking cats." Roger's dislike of werecats was well known. "All the injured are coming here."

It sounded like there were quite a few. As her adrenaline kicked in, Margery handed the cublings to their mother. "They're all changed."

Holding the babies to her chest, Portia scowled. "I suppose you'll take over the entire living room. Make every-thing bloody and dirty, and I'll miss my TV show." The female's self-absorption was appalling.

Margery half-smiled. "You're right—this house isn't a

good place for sick and injured. You should tell Pete to give me my own place."

Being in the communal house made sense when she first arrived. She'd needed to learn independent living—cooking, washing, shopping. But that'd been months ago.

Portia sniffed and walked away.

Hearing car doors slamming, Margery hurried into the laundry room to fetch her bag of medical supplies.

When she got back to the living room, the injured were being settled on the floor and the chairs. Whining, growling, crying. Young males weren't nearly as stoic as older shifters.

Pulling in a breath, she studied the situation. *Before beginning, determine who needs you the most*, Grandmama used to say.

That one by the wall was bleeding heavily. As was the one next to him. One was groggy and throwing up. She turned that young male onto his side so his airway would stay clear.

"Banfasa..." Gretchen, a statuesque blonde, grabbed Margery's arm. "Help Caleb right now!"

Margery looked at the beefy male who was one of Roger's betas. Parallel slashes cut across Caleb's upper and lower arm. Shallow. Nothing spurting. "Help him wash off the wounds in the bathroom sink. Then use these." She handed gauze packets to Gretchen. "Others need my help more."

Gretchen threw the packets into Margery's face. "You help him, you scarred-up bitch."

The insult barely registered as Margery finished formulating her triage plan.

She knelt beside an unpopular shifter who was bleeding out. Even as she worked on him, she snapped orders to the uninjured. Pressure to the wounds, blankets to prevent shock. Cleaning. Although the Daonains' immune system was far better than humans', infections occurred if debris remained in a wound.

Shifter after shifter, she cleaned and closed slashes with stitches or glue. The werecats had been savage. She also treated the cats who were suffering from deep wolf bites. It had been a nasty battle.

She talked with Roger about one wolf with a gut wound. He needed a hospital if he could be trusted not to trawsfur when in pain. Since a dazed shifter in pain would always trawsfur to his animal, he'd need an escort to ensure no sedatives were used.

After she'd handled the seriously injured, she moved to the less damaged.

Approaching Caleb, she saw Brett, Roger's second beta, had joined Gretchen. The beta snapped his teeth at Margery as if he was in wolf form and told Gretchen, "Fuck, she's slow."

"I know, right?" Gretchen curled her lip at Margery. "About time you got here, gimpy."

I don't care what these stupid people think about me. Yet she did, and humiliation formed a cold, hard stone in her chest. This was her pack; nevertheless, to them, she was just a crippled, scar-faced wolf who was only useful once in a while.

She knelt beside the injured male. "Caleb, I'm going to clean the wounds and get them closed up." She spoke low and soft until the shifter relaxed.

Ignoring the slighting remarks from Brett and Gretchen, she concentrated on her job.

A little while later, she finished with the last injured shifter.

Jens and an elderly female were handing out broth and raw beef to help with the blood loss. Some of the wounded had already left. One older male who lived alone would spend the night so she could keep an eye on him.

With an effort, she pushed to her feet, wincing at the painful throb in her ankle...and at the work still to be done. The living room was a mess and had to be cleaned.

She started collecting bloodied gauze and rags.

The last two wounded stopped on the way out. "Thank you for the tending, banfasa."

His littermate nodded. "Aye, thank you."

Warmed, she smiled at them. The rest had left without any thanks. It wasn't surprising, since that was how the Cosantir and the alpha of her pack treated her. No matter how much she did, she had no value.

As she stepped outside to dump the rags, the cool, fresh

night air whipped around her, blowing away her frustration, leaving her free to think clearly.

This wasn't who she wanted to be. A frustrated, unhappy person. But if she stayed, they'd continue to treat her like a stray cur. Because they could.

No, it was time to make a change. To find out how much more she could be.

CHAPTER TWO

A ilill Ridge, Rainier Territory - full moon

"I don't want that stupid banfasa living here..."

Ignoring the complaints coming from the other room, Margery smiled at the older shifter who'd spent the night and unwrapped the dressing on his arm. "Bleeding has stopped. No sign of infection. It's going to heal up well."

Having come to help the shifter get home, Roger and Brett were in the kitchen getting coffee—and had been cornered by Portia. Bits and pieces of their conversations drifted out.

"...hurt shifters showing up all the time...missed my TV show..." Typical Portia complaints.

Margery sighed and picked up a fresh roll of gauze. "Hold your arm out, please."

Portia's voice rose enough to be clear. "Give her someplace else to stay."

"Pete said no," Brett growled. "The banfasa stays in communal housing so she'll get room and board without any money. If she's broke, she can't take off like the healers did."

Margery's mouth dropped open. They didn't want her to have money? Was that why Roger had snapped at a shifter who'd tried to pay her?

"Fucking high and mighty healers." Roger growled. "It sucks that all we got now is a stupid banfasa. An ugly crippled one, no less."

She knew better than to take his insult to heart, yet...it still hurt.

Beside her, the older male heard. "Margery, Roger doesn't mean—"

Margery shrugged, trying to push away the ache. "I've heard worse." A decade's worth from the Scythe guards and staff.

She hadn't expected to be eviscerated by her own people.

His sympathetic look spurred her to ask, "I don't suppose you'd drive me to a different territory?"

He shook his head. "I won't go up against our Cosantir. I don't got a car anyway. Sorry, banfasa."

"Me, too." Seeing his regret, she patted his hand. "It's all right."

An hour later, with everyone gone, she considered going for a run, but her ankle still hurt. Instead, she took a cup of coffee onto the front porch and settled in a wooden chair. On a Thursday, the end of the small cul-de-sac was quiet.

Coffee in hand, she inhaled slowly, closed her eyes, and sank into the sense of the Mother. Here in the land of the Daonain, the presence of the God and Goddess was as close as the air she breathed.

Eventually, when her heart was peaceful, she opened her eyes. In the deep blue sky, puffy clouds drifted slowly toward the mountains. A breath of a breeze teased the tree branches. The squirrel-ear-sized light green leaves indicated spring had arrived.

It didn't feel like spring in her heart. Not after what she'd heard inside. Her shoulders sagged.

During her argument with the Cosantir, when she had said she'd leave Ailill Ridge, Pete told her flat-out she wasn't allowed to leave.

Now, considering what Brett and Roger had said in the kitchen, she had a few questions. Like...had Pete lied to her? Surely a Cosantir wouldn't be dishonest. Yet the betas said their healers had moved away. Possibly healers or males were allowed more flexibility.

Or maybe Pete had lied to her.

She took a big gulp of her coffee. And her determination crystalized. "I am leaving this place."

She'd go somewhere—anywhere—else. Out of Pete's territory. When she found a new town, she wouldn't tell people she was a banfasa. There were other jobs in the world, ones that let a person be normal. *She* would be normal.

Well, mostly normal. She'd still have a weak ankle and—she drew a fingertip over the long scar on her cheek—a less than attractive face. But she'd be like other shifter females who worked at jobs and got paid and lived where they wanted.

Or would leaving be stupid? Anxiety tugged on her nerves like stitches being removed. Food and a place to live were necessary for survival. If she left, she might starve. Die.

The Cosantir was clever the way he'd trapped her in this cage. She growled. "I'm a shifter. I don't do cages."

A female laughed. "That's good to hear."

Margery's head snapped around so quickly her neck muscles protested. A lanky redhead stood at the foot of the steps.

Caught talking to herself, she could only grin ruefully. "Hey, Heather. What brings you to Ailill Ridge?"

The wolf ran a business in a nearby town and occasionally showed up for pack runs. "I was visiting my littermates' ranch and swung by to say hi to your neighbor." Heather gestured to the house next door.

"Oh. Well. Want some coffee?"

"Nope, I'm good. But I'll join you for a minute or two." Heather came up the steps and took the chair next to Margery. "So, what cage are you in?"

"Um..."

"Yes, I'm nosy as a werecat." Heather grinned. "No, I'm not ashamed of it."

Margery hesitated. Should she ask Heather for help? No, that would be unwise. Heather's loyalty was to the Cosantir and the pack alpha, not a newcomer. Giving up the momentary hope of escape, Margery settled for a bland response. "I guess you could say we're all in cages when it comes down to it, right?"

"Wrong. There are cages and there are *cages*. I'm guessing whatever one you're in is making you miserable." Although Heather looked to be in her mid-thirties, her assured manner said older, maybe fifties. The Daonains' slower aging made it difficult to guess.

"I can't promise I have answers," Heather added, "but I can promise what you say will go no further."

"I..." The longing to be heard was impossible to resist. "It's like this: Although I work as a banfasa and clean the communal house, I only get room and board. No money." Her mouth twisted. "I don't even get to choose what I eat." Not since Portia had arrived.

"Room and board and no money?" Heather straightened. "And you're stuck cleaning *and* being a banfasa. Girl, that comes to less than even minimum wage."

"What's a minimum wage?"

"Oh boy, I forget sometimes that you were a captive." Heather shook her head. "We'll discuss minimum wages another time. What I'm saying is that your recompense seems unfair. Have you talked to the Cosantir?"

"Yes. He disagreed and..." Margery pulled in a breath, unsure how much she should share.

"Keep going."

"I overheard Roger say that not paying me is deliberate. It's a way to ensure I can't leave."

"A crow-cursed cage is right," Heather muttered.

"I don't know all the rules though. *Am* I allowed to leave?"

"Of course you are. You're an adult."

"I know they assigned us, the Dogwood villagers, to specific towns," Margery offered in case she was missing something.

"That was to make you harder to find, especially at first." Heather put her feet up on the railing. "Right now, if too many of you congregated in one place, the Cosantirs might ask you to spread out, simply as a precaution. But there's no reason you can't leave this town and find one more to your liking. You're no different than the unmated males who sometimes wander for years before settling. Or the ones who think they should visit every Gathering in the country."

Oh Goddess, there is a Gathering tonight.

Margery's stomach tightened at the thought. Like all fertile female shifters, she'd go into heat with the rising of the full moon. Each territory held a monthly Gathering for unmated shifters where the males would vie for the females

—and the females chose those who interested her. With the Daonain population so low, the Gatherings mingled the genes and increased the birthrate. Multiple males increased the odds for twins or triplets, with each baby from a different sire. "I'd forgotten it's full moon."

"That's right." Heather tilted her head in a wolf-like movement. "A couple of my friends were raised by humans and found Gatherings uncomfortable at first. Since you spent the last decade with humans, how do *you* feel about full moons?"

"Uncomfortable is a good word." Margery drew her legs up and rested her chin on her knees.

The month after getting out of Seattle, she'd experienced her first full moon heat, and her body simply took over. "It was amazing to actually feel desire. The sex was fun." A little overwhelming, too. "It's just...the Gathering house gets so crowded, and the males are rather aggressive."

Too many of them reminded her of the brutal Scythe, although the shifters eventually backed off if they couldn't capture her interest. Some were rude about it—especially the pack betas, Brett and Caleb, who acted as if her lack of desire for them was an insult.

There was always a lot of shoving, yelling, and brawling too. "I don't want to sound pathetic, but in the Scythe compound, if a male raised his voice, it meant a female would get caned." Or beaten right into the ground.

"Oh, scat, I get it. The Gatherings here in Rainier Territory have turned rougher than they used to be. Too violent for someone with your history." Heather tapped a finger on her chin, thinking.

As the silence lengthened, Margery sipped her coffee and watched a pixie in a nearby tree. It'd found a patch of spring sun to enjoy while nibbling on a leaf bud.

"Okay." Heather pulled her feet off the railing. "First of all, not all Gatherings are as bad as here in Ailill Ridge. I don't like fighting, either, and since the Gatherings in the North Cascades are calmer, I time my visits to my mother in that Elder Village and *mo leanbh* in Cold Creek for the full moon."

Her baby? "I didn't know you had cubs."

"Sorcha isn't the baby of my blood; I was given the honor of serving as her *caomhnor*, her guardian-protector." Heather's smile showed the baby was very loved.

"Darcy, one of our Dogwood villagers, is in Cold Creek." Or she had been last fall.

Despite not being allowed to talk in the Scythe compound, the Dogwood captives had still grown close— and Margery missed them.

Having her brother nearby might have helped, but around the New Year, all the shifter-soldiers were sent to winter in the remote Elder Villages to amend their violent reactions and relearn shifter traditions and rules. She'd returned from her two weeks in the Elder Village a few days before Oliver was sent there. They'd barely had time to talk, share experiences, and show off their animal forms to each other.

It was spring now. Would Oliver ever come back to her?

Pushing the pitiful thought away, Margery asked, "Do you know how Darcy is doing?"

"Incredibly well, actually. She got lifemated to two wonderful males and has started a repair business."

Lifemated? Darcy? Margery blinked, remembering the two males who'd hovered over her friend when she was shot. Had that been them? "Good for her. There's no one who deserves happiness more."

"Want to go see her?"

"What?"

Heather grinned. "Let me rephrase. Would you like to attend the Gathering in Cold Creek tonight and stay there a couple of days?"

The air grew thin all of a sudden. "Really?"

"Why not? This evening, I'm driving to Cold Creek for their Gathering. After seeing Sorcha, I'll visit Mom's Elder Village for a couple of days. Meantime, you could stay in Cold Creek, see Darcy, and decide if you like the town." Heather lifted her eyebrows. "Yes?"

Margery hugged herself as excitement tingled in her blood. She could leave this place. And never come back.

Yes. Whether she liked Cold Creek or not, she wouldn't return to Ailill Ridge. In fact, she'd leave a note for Pete with the grocer, so he'd know she was gone for good.

"Yes," she told Heather. "Absolutely yes."

CHAPTER THREE

C old Creek, North Cascades Territory - full moon

The North Cascades Territory Gathering was *very* different from Rainier's. So much better, Margery decided. Quieter. Friendlier.

Despite her limp and scarred face, she'd been fairly popular with the males.

"Let me find you a table." The shifter who'd escorted her down from the mating rooms had his arm around her shoulders as if unwilling to let her go. They'd had a pleasant mating, and to her delight, he had a sense of humor. It was really fun to laugh during sex.

Spotting an empty table, he guided her across the tavern and pulled the chair out for her.

"Thank you." She sat and smiled up at him.

"Thank *you*." The werebear patted her shoulder and took himself off.

Margery leaned back, straightening the pretty top that Heather had given her.

Looking around, she tried to spot the redhead in the crowded room. No success, which wasn't a surprise. Since Gatherings were all about matings, females didn't stay together, especially at first.

But the moon was setting, and the Gathering was almost over. If she didn't find Heather, she'd head back to their bed and breakfast room by herself.

For the first time tonight, she wasn't surrounded by males and had a chance to examine her surroundings. Rather than in a house, the North Cascades Gathering was in a huge tavern, which was owned by the Cosantir. The shifters were well-behaved on the whole, although a male would occasionally burst out with a masculine challenge to all comers to gain a female's interest.

Fighting, however, was taken outside. Unlike Pete, this Cosantir supervised the Gathering and didn't tolerate brawling inside. In fact, the werebear said the Cosantir himself was tending the bar.

She turned to look.

Dear Goddess...

Leaning on the bar, the dark-haired Cosantir surveyed the crowd. A terrifying amount of power shimmered around him. His gaze landed on her, pinning her in place, stealing her breath, and then he nodded politely before turning his attention elsewhere.

She carefully turned her chair so she wasn't facing him before letting out a soft, "Whew." *Don't stare at the scary Cosantir.* No wonder there were no fights when he was around.

Still...scary Cosantir or not, she far preferred this Gathering to Rainier's.

"Who are you looking at, Donal?" A well-endowed brunette sat down beside the single male at a nearby table. "Seriously? That stumpy one? She looks like something a werecat wouldn't bother to drag in, even if the cat was starving."

Margery hoped she wasn't the stumpy one in question.

But the female was staring right at Margery. *Ouch.* Well, all right. The rude statement wasn't a falsehood. Margery *was* short, not particularly pretty, and the scar didn't help.

She glanced at the male and blinked. Tall and lean with cheekbones sharper than knives—the mesmerizing healer from the Scythe garage, the one who'd taken their trackers out. *Donal.* No wonder his name was familiar.

The way his thick black hair spilled over his pure white shirt made her fingers curl with a desire to comb through the strands.

When the brunette wrapped her hands around his biceps, clinging like a burr on a wolf pelt, the oddest pain sliced deep into Margery's heart. Talk about stupid.

Margery Lavelle, why would you think you could ever attract a male like him?

His silvery gaze met Margery's for an infinite, stomach-tightening second before he responded to the female tugging on his arm and turned away.

Without saying anything to Margery.

No recognition had shown in those eyes she would never forget. The way he'd tended to her and the other captives left an impression on her, but to him, she must have been just another face among many. No one memorable...which shouldn't bother her as much as it did.

Margery noticed the female was scowling at her.

As the animosity sent a chill down her spine, she rose. No need to stay where she was uncomfortable.

On the far side of the tavern, a cheerfully crackling fire drew her. Ignoring the shifters seated near the stone fireplace, Margery remained standing, holding her hands toward the flames.

Two salamanders danced in the fire, their sinuous red bodies twining and spinning in a celebration of their element.

"You guys are gorgeous," she whispered.

Hearing her, they blinked black eyes like cold coals and leapt higher in a fountain of flickering sparks.

"Aye, I'm going to have to look for work soon." A male's compelling baritone came from the shifters behind her. "It's resting I've been, but the itch is on me to do something."

The Irish accent was familiar. He sounded like the male

who'd bossed the shifters in the Scythe garage. The one named Tynan.

Warily, she checked over her shoulder.

It was him.

Standing, Tynan had one foot resting on the coffee table, his forearms crossed on his raised thigh as he spoke to his friends on the couch. A big-boned Gaelic male with fair skin and blunt features, he seemed even taller and more broad-shouldered than last fall. His square jaw looked purely stubborn—and somehow sent a low hum, accompanied by a wave of heat, through her body.

No. Absolutely not. He might be wearing jeans and a T-shirt here, but the memory of him in a uniform shirt and weapons belt chilled her.

As if he felt her attention, his head lifted. When his intent gaze met hers, his head tilted slightly. If he'd been in wolf form, his ears would have turned forward. After saying something to his friends, he straightened and walked toward her.

No, no, no, no. He even moved like a guard, shoulders military straight, head high.

She tensed, anticipating a blow from his cane.

But he wouldn't—of course he wouldn't. What in the world was *wrong* with her? Nevertheless, even though she knew—*knew*—he wasn't a Scythe guard, she fled.

Safely out of reach, she glanced over her shoulder.

His gaze trapped hers. He wasn't following, merely

watching her intently, his eyes a clear, clear blue that filled her world, leaving no room for fear or anger.

Then his gaze released her, and he turned to rejoin the others.

He wouldn't come after her, not here, because, unlike in the human world, here, the females chose. Whatever had attracted his interest in her was over.

Good. This is good.

So why did she feel the oddest sense of disappointment?

Frowning, Tynan returned to the sitting area where he'd been talking with Nia, a giggly little female he'd mated earlier, and Kevin, one of the Murphy brothers.

Kevin grinned. "The female didn't like your scent? That's a first."

"Not a first, no." But rare enough he'd been surprised, especially since her scent had initially indicated interest. "I have a feeling her head and her hormones weren't in agreement."

"Yeah, I get that sometimes." Kevin slapped his hefty chest, then tugged on his shirt. "The females, they like the muscles, but they see my old clothes and decide richer is better."

Nia frowned. "I don't know her. She doesn't live in Cold Creek."

Watching the female cross the room toward the door,

Tynan shook his head. "Her scent was familiar." And appealing.

Where had he seen her before? Short and curvy, with breasts and an ass that would overflow his hands. She had a long pale oval face with a pointed chin that said stubborn, and a full lower lip he wanted to nibble on. He wouldn't have forgotten if he had touched her in the past, held her close, and looked into those eyes as her wariness turned into passion.

A scar marred one side of her face.

His eyes narrowed. She was limping.

Ah, aye, that was it. He'd seen her the night they rescued the Scythe hostages. When he almost lost his brother. Poor Donal had almost no memory of that night—or perhaps his brother was lucky. Tynan still had nightmares, especially of the humans he'd killed. "She's one of the Dogwood villagers."

In fact, she was the one who'd stayed to tend the injured males.

She looked better now. No bruising on her face. No longer emaciated.

"I thought Darcy was the only Dogwood villager in Cold Creek," Nia said.

"She is." Tynan considered. "The captives had all winter to adjust to being free and living as shifters again."

"Eh. Betcha a bunch will want to wander after being trapped for years," Kevin said. The Murphy brothers were more known for brawn than brains, but they had tender hearts for the females.

"Sure they will. It couldn't have been an easy winter for them." Tynan dropped into a chair, feeling a tug of sympathy for the little female. "Merely *living* in the city for so long affected me. I can't imagine being kept captive and raised by humans."

Nia's gaze was sad. "Darcy had a hard time. Still does sometimes."

"Aye, I've talked with her about the differences between human and Daonain culture."

In Tynan's veins, the low mating hum faded away. It was morning. The full moon had set, and the Gathering was over. Time to go home.

As the little Dogwood villager headed toward the tavern door, Tynan had the oddest desire to go after her.

Which was obviously the last thing she wanted.

Still at the table near the door, Donal watched the petite, curvy female returning from across the room. Unfortunately, not to join him. Shoulders tense, movements stiff, she was headed for the door.

Limping. By the Gods, no shifter should be handicapped in that way. When her injury occurred, there must have been no healer to make it right. Now, it was too late to fix.

When she moved around his table, their gazes met

again. Her big hazel-brown eyes held a greenish tint reminiscent of deep summer forests. Lovely eyes. And haunted.

She seemed familiar, but from where? A Gathering, maybe? No. Although he pushed himself to mate with many females, he'd never been so uncouth as to forget someone he'd been with.

They'd never mated. More's the pity. Perhaps—

Beside him, Sarah deliberately rubbed her breasts over his arm and growled at the little female. A canine warning off another.

"Sarah," Donal warned and moved far enough to create space between them. Territorial behavior wasn't permitted at Gatherings, and Sarah had no reason whatsoever to act possessively. As a healer, he would never attach himself to one mate, even if he could find someone who appealed to him and Tynan.

The lovely stranger pulled open the door. For a second, the light from the wall sconce gleamed off the sun-lightened streaks in her rich brown hair, and then she was gone.

Sarah crossed her arms over her breasts and scowled. "Where did that female come from? I never saw her before."

"She's from Ailill Ridge, as it happens." Followed by a big, over-muscled male, Sarah's sister, Gretchen, sat down at the table. Tall, fair, and blonde, Gretchen was nothing like her sister...except in personality. The Daonain usually birthed males, and more than one female in a litter was exceedingly rare. As a result, the sisters had been thoroughly spoiled.

"Good morning," Donal said politely. He didn't know the male. Or Gretchen either, despite her flirting at Gatherings. He saved his time and efforts for local females—the ones who would be available to donate power if an emergency arose.

"Healer, this is Caleb, one of the beta wolves from Rainier's pack," Gretchen said. "Caleb, this is Donal, the healer in North Cascades Territory."

"Good to meet you," Donal said, getting a nod from the male who was built like a beefy bull.

"So, Gretch"—Sarah pointed toward the door—"who was the female?"

"Margery Lavelle," Gretchen said. "She's one of those Dogwood captives."

Ah, perhaps that was why she seemed familiar. A shame that night was such a haze in his memory.

"She's the female assigned to Ailill Ridge," Gretchen said. "More's the pity."

Donal frowned. "Why a pity?"

Having treated Darcy, Donal knew something of the horrors the hostages had suffered. If the little stranger was having problems, maybe he could intervene.

"She's as nasty as a weasel," Gretchen said. "Like how she pretends she's a banfasa, only we all think she's lying."

A banfasa? Donal stiffened. Although healers and banfasas worked well together in some territories, sometimes, one or the other grew territorial. Although his birth town had lacked a banfasa, he'd run into them later. Like during his apprenticeship. There, the local banfasa, Gil, had not only been incompetent, but he'd hated Healer Quany—all healers, actually. Donal winced, thinking of the damage the banfasa's lack of skill had caused.

"Gretch, what else?" Sarah leaned forward. "Go on."

"This week, Caleb almost bled to death because Margery insisted on caring for her friends first." Gretchen scowled.

Caleb nodded. "Even though Gretchen asked her to see to me first."

"That's not good." Playing favorites was unethical. Wrong.

Gretchen's mouth twisted, turning her platinum beauty into something hard. "You'd think she'd be good for the town, but she's always disappearing—like today."

"Doesn't she tell Pete or someone when she's going to be unavailable?" As Cold Creek's healer, Donal had taught the sheriff's dispatcher—another Daonain—where to send the injured for first aid when he wasn't around. Leaving town without warning, especially during a Gathering night, was deplorable. With tempers and testosterone high, a full moon was the worst day of the month for injuries.

"She didn't talk to Pete," Caleb said. "Fuck, he's going to start shredding things."

Rainier's Cosantir had the temperament of an annoyed badger.

Gretchen shook her head. "Really, although she knows one end of a bandage from another, she's not very good at the job. I don't think she had any real training at all."

"Of course not." Sarah shrugged indifferently. "She was in that Scythe place during the years she should have been an apprentice."

True enough. The poor female. Sympathy softened Donal's tone. "Tell Pete he can send her up here, and I'll train her."

Donal wasn't about to go to Ailill Ridge. Years ago, looking for a home, he'd paused there, but the town had an unhappy atmosphere. Pete had never forgiven him for walking away.

"You're so wonderful, Donal. But it wouldn't work." Gretchen gave him a sweet smile. "Margery resents the God-called—and says healers are stupid and lazy. She'd never be willing to work with you."

Donal's mouth tightened. She sounded more and more like old Gil. How many times had he and Healer Quany needed to fix the incompetent banfasa's mistakes? Or worse, see scarring that wouldn't have happened if the banfasa had sent the shifter to a healer. "In that case, I hope Pete can find a different way to train her."

While help would be nice, it was just as well that no banfasa had decided to live in Cold Creek.

CHAPTER FOUR

C old Creek, North Cascades Territory - day after full moon

Cold Creek was a charming town, Margery decided as she stopped on Main Street's center island.

With a relieved sigh, she sat on one of the wood-and-iron benches to give her aching ankle a rest. Touring a town on foot was hard work.

Earlier, in the B&B, the owner, Rebecca, had served a great breakfast and lingered to gossip with Heather. The dining room had been filled with shifters who'd come to Cold Creek for the Gathering. Heather knew most of them and had introduced Margery before leaving for her mother's Elder Village. They'd all been so welcoming.

As Margery walked around downtown, the people she

passed greeted her with nods and smiles. It was so different from Ailill Ridge.

Looking around, she smiled. Rather than being all concrete and buildings, the downtown had tall shade trees, antique streetlights, and benches everywhere. Flower beds on the island and sidewalk planters were bright with yellow daffodils and pink hyacinths.

The town was...pretty.

"I want to stay here," Margery murmured.

Could she? Pete would be angry, but in the note she left, she hadn't said where she was going. Just that she wouldn't be back. Even if he knew she was here, what could he do? Surely Cosantirs didn't chase down shifters who left their territory.

Okay, then.

Step one: Find a job. *Not* as a banfasa, even if that was where her experience and talents lay. She wouldn't venture into that trap again—not until she found out if Rainier Territory's treatment of her was normal or not. No, she'd do something else for a job. She was good with people, and really, anything that let her work with others would make her happy.

Anticipation filled her until her blood felt as if it was zinging in her veins. Rising, she headed for the first place Rebecca had mentioned.

Yes, the sign was there. Pushing open the door to Angie's Diner, she walked in. Gleaming wooden floors and chairs, blue checked tablecloths, and wooden ceiling fans created a welcoming atmosphere. A couple of customers were drinking coffee and eating pastries.

A middle-aged blonde woman stood behind a glass-fronted display and counter on the left. "Hi there. Take a seat anywhere."

"Um..." Catching the scent of the wild, Margery realized the female was a shifter. She straightened her shoulders. "Actually, I'm not here to eat. I saw the *Part-time Help Wanted* sign in your window."

"You're Daonain." The female gave Margery a slow scrutiny, before smiling. "I heard a Dogwood villager was at the Gathering last night—one of the captives."

Margery tried not to tense. Was being an ex-captive good or bad? "That would be me."

"Do you drink coffee?"

Margery blinked at the way the conversation had veered. "Uh, yes?"

"Well, then, let's talk. I'm Angie O'Neal, by the way."

"Margery Lavelle."

Picking up two cups and a pot, Angie led the way to a table in the corner. As Margery sat, the female poured the coffee and handed over a cup. "Where have you been living this winter?"

"In Ailill Ridge."

Lifted blonde brows asked for more. For why she was leaving.

Anxiety set up a twisting ache in Margery's gut. She didn't want to present herself as a pitiful survivor of abuse who'd been taken advantage of by a town. That wasn't how she wanted to see herself either. Her tone needed to be relaxed when speaking about the past months.

"Yes. In Rainier Territory." She sat back in her chair. "I learned a lot from living there, but I'm ready for a change. Heather recommended Cold Creek."

"Heather Sutharlan? She brought you to the Gathering last night?"

Margery nodded, hearing the pleasant change in the diner owner's voice. Heather was known here—and liked.

"In that case, have you ever waited tables before?"

"No, ma'am. But I learn quickly, and I get on well with people." Usually. Except for some of the Ailill Ridge shifters who turned every interaction into predator versus prey. By the Goddess, no matter what the mangy wolves thought, she wasn't prey.

"That's a good start."

Margery offered her best smile. "I have an excellent memory, and I'm good with numbers. I work hard, and"—the Ailill Ridge grocer had complained about his late-arriving help—"I know how to show up on time."

Angie laughed. "Sold."

The rush of victory made Margery want to leap and dance.

"The job is five days a week. You'll work split shifts to cover the lunch and supper crowds. Part-time at first, possibly full-time, eventually."

As Angie spoke about waitressing, Margery's smile

widened. She could do this job. The amount of time on her feet would hurt her ankle, but there was nothing new about that.

"Where will you be staying?" Angie asked.

"I-I'm not sure. I was hoping Heather would have suggestions."

"Do you like communal living or—"

Margery shook her head. Yet how fussy could a pauper be? "I...don't really like living with others. Maybe with being so isolated from each other in the compound, I got used to being alone. My goal—eventually—is to rent a really inexpensive house or apartment."

"Huh. Here I'd pegged you as a wolf."

Wolves were supposed to be sociable, but the last thing she wanted was to be dumped in with unfriendly strangers again. If she admitted to being a wolf, that would happen. Roger had insisted wolves didn't live alone—especially not female wolves.

But Daonain customs said a shifter didn't have to divulge her animal and asking directly was considered rude.

"Do you know of any non-communal places?" Margery asked, ignoring Angie's hint.

Rather than taking offense, the female huffed in amusement. "The territory provides temporary housing for shifters moving here—ones who've obtained a job—but the houses are shared."

Margery's hopes dropped.

"However, a shifter recently returned to the Mother."

Angie's eyes showed her grief at the death. "Leo was old and ill and left his little house a mess. It's too dirty to sell as is. However, it still has all his furnishings, dishes and linens and everything. Would you want to clean the house and yard in exchange for free rent for a couple of months? It would give you time to figure things out."

"As it happens, I'm an expert cleaner." The Scythe, her nurse mentor, and her communal house duties had seen to that. "I'll take it, no matter how much of a mess it is."

"You jump right in, don't you?" Angie grinned. "But good enough. I'll tell Calum you'll take the house. You can start work here tomorrow at six a.m. sharp."

Yes, yes, yes.

Angie held out her hand. "Welcome to Cold Creek."

Margery grinned and shook firmly. She would be the best worker ever.

Tynan stepped back to survey their kitchen—all rearranged. Plates, bowls, glasses in this cupboard. Food items in that one. Logical enough. Well, logical to *him*, anyway. His littermate apparently thought canned soup should be kept beside the bowls—or maybe he'd simply been bored and shoved everything up there last time he'd shopped.

When Tynan moved in a few months ago, he learned that Donal hadn't changed a bit since they were cubs. The healer kept everything neat in his clinic, but the house? By the Gods, he was still messier than a garbage gnome.

Smiling, Tynan shut the cupboard door. He didn't really care about the disorder. It was too fecking great to be back where he belonged—with the Daonain and with his brother again.

After helping rescue the Scythe hostages last fall, Tynan resigned from the Seattle police force. In the mountains, he'd lived in wolf form until the wildness crept back into his soul. Gradually, he'd spent more time in Cold Creek and with Donal, getting to know his littermate again.

As cubs, he and Donal had always known they'd live together. Even with Tynan stuck in the city, their plans hadn't changed. So they'd bought this house together, one big enough for them both, a mate and cubs, and Donal's healing clinic—even though it'd taken years for Tynan to finally leave Seattle.

He was here now.

He smiled, remembering when he'd fostered with relatives in Ireland. As police officers, his uncles were an essential part of the village—saving lives, protecting, making things better. And they were heartily loved by their mate, cubs, and grandcubs.

Living with a littermate, sharing their mate, having cubs, enjoying fulfilling work. His uncles had shown him what truly mattered in life. What he wanted for himself.

A noise caught his attention.

Donal was escorting a male shifter from the clinic to

the front door. He handed the limping shifter over to a female waiting on the porch, turned, and saw Tynan in the kitchen.

"Finished for the day?" Tynan asked.

"For the moment, at least." Donal rolled down his shirt-sleeves and pulled the leather band out of his black hair. "It's spring. Surging hormones mean stupid shifters having fights, or falling off mountains, or running into trees, or leaping into ice-filled creeks."

Tynan snorted. "You mean like that time you tried to out-jump another panther and landed in a ravine?"

"For Herne's sake, I was thirteen."

"And clumsier than a drunken dwarf on ice."

Donal thumped an elbow against Tynan's ribs as he walked past. "Is there anything in this place to eat?"

"I made you a sandwich when I made mine." Tynan pointed to the fridge. "Why don't you have a female around to cook for you?"

Even as he said it, he grinned. In the human world, his female officers would have walloped him for such a question.

"More hindrance than help." Donal opened the fridge and got his sandwich. "Cooking isn't what I'm after in a female."

Tynan leaned against the counter and studied his brother.

Healers were called by the Goddess to channel Her energy and heal the Daonain—and females chased the God-called like coyotes after a hare. It really was odd that Donal hadn't found anyone.

All the years Tynan lived in Seattle, he'd feared Donal would find a mate just for himself. Normally, littermates lived together and shared their female—but *normally*, one of them wasn't sent to live in a human city for a decade.

"All right, I'll bite," Tynan said. "What are you after in a mate?"

"Wrong question. I don't want a *mate*." Donal sat down at the table with his sandwich and a glass of water. "I simply need females who have an ample amount of power."

Energy for healing came from the injured and the healer —and a healer could easily drain himself and die. However, shifters who had a mating bond with the healer could offer their energy.

Tynan stared, unsure whether to admire or be appalled by Donal's reasoning. "Is that why you exhaust yourself mating with so many females during the full moon? To use them as *batteries*?"

"Judgmental much?" Donal scowled. "Yes, that's why I mate with multiple females at Gatherings, even when I'm not particularly interested."

If the female gave off an aroused scent, a male could usually perform. The thought was unappealing. "You're stronger than most healers. Do you come up short on power a lot?"

"No, but more often in the past year or so." Donal pushed his plate away. The lines around his silver-gray eyes, the same color as their mother's who'd also been a healer, deepened.

"What changed?" Tynan opened the window over the sink to let the spring breeze in.

"Human towns are moving closer, and hellhounds come with them. I used to heal mostly clumsy shifters who jumped the wrong ravines or ones who fought over a female. Now, every month or so, I get cahirs savaged by a hellhound. And fucking car accidents. Multiple patients with life-threatening wounds."

A healer's energy was finite. "I see the problem."

"Aye." Donal's shoulders sagged. "It's not only the hellhounds and human technology, brawd. The Scythe are after us. At that compound last fall, I emptied myself healing—and still almost lost people."

Tynan's mouth tightened. After passing out, Donal had roused and tried to keep healing. If Tynan hadn't yanked him away, he would've died. "You're catching a scent of the future in the wind?"

"The world is changing. We have humans in our towns. The Scythe are searching for us. There will be more battles, and I have to be ready."

When it came to dedication, they were much alike. Tynan's worst fear was that he'd fail in protecting others.

His littermate dreaded losing someone to death. His healing skills and power were unsurpassed among the Daonain, but he was still only mortal.

"I can follow the logic, Donal, but I question your taste in females. Did you really mate with Sarah last night?"

"She has an adequate pool of energy—and she tends to be around when shifters get hurt, although it sure isn't because she's there to help." Donal looked slightly sour.

Tynan snorted. "The female's a lookie-loo."

"A what?"

"Human term for the snoopy onlookers at accident and crime scenes." The idiots would mess up a crime scene or jam traffic by slowing down to gawk. He frowned at Donal. "Didn't you mate with Sarah in December. Why again?"

Donal shrugged. "I can pull energy through a mating bond—like drawing water from a well—but the bond thins as time passes. Usually after three or four months it's gone."

"So, you rotate through females each Gathering. That must take a lot of the joy out of mating."

"Aye." Donal took a bite of the sandwich. After swallowing, he added, "I had a female move in once—not for life-mating. Just a relationship."

"And?"

"Didn't work. She wanted more."

Tynan studied his littermate's disgruntled expression. "More what?"

"More time, more attention. An injured shifter who'd been gutted by a boar was brought into the clinic. She yelled at me because we were supposed to meet people at the diner for supper." Donal's jaw went tight. "Did she think I'd let him die while I ate pizza?"

"She did realize you're a healer, right?"

"By Herne's holy prick, yes. She kept telling me how sexy healers were." Donal rubbed his jaw. "It seems we're not so sexy when covered in blood and guts."

Tynan snorted. For someone so perceptive about his patients, Donal could be stupid-blind sometimes. "Someone whose priority is status probably isn't a good fit for someone whose priority is saving lives."

"I figured that out. Eventually. I'll stick to mating the females at the Gatherings."

Tynan started to speak and stopped. He'd assumed they'd find a mate at some point. Together.

But Donal wasn't thinking that way.

On the other hand, Donal changed his mind faster than the wind changed on a mountaintop. He didn't like pizza until Tynan talked him into trying it. Thought flannel shirts were unprofessional—and look at what he wore now.

If they found the right female...

Glancing at the clock, Tynan grabbed his jacket off the chair. "I need to head out."

Donal rose. "Where to?"

"Calum sent a message he wanted to speak to me." A small worm of worry crawled into his gut. A Cosantir held the power of life and death over all the shifters in his territory.

Tynan didn't know the Cosantir here all that well. When a cop in Seattle, he'd had contact with Calum only when shifters visiting the city got lost, arrested, or died.

Donal's black brows drew together. "What's he want with you?"

"No clue."

Donal scowled. "No more separations. I couldn't follow you to the city"—The God-called were damaged if they lived outside the God's influence—"but you're not leaving again. You tell Calum if he thinks to send you off somewhere, he'll be looking for a healer, too. This time, where you go, I go too."

Defying a Cosantir was a quick way to the grave, but a Daonain did have the right to decide where he lived, and healers were valued everywhere.

Tynan clapped his brother on the shoulder. "If it comes to that, I'll let him know. It's probably nothing."

"I'm not an optimist."

"Really? I had no idea." Tynan dodged the punch and headed out the door. Behind him, Donal was muttering about mangy, flea-ridden brothers who were wolves.

Tynan grinned. Could two littermates be more different? His brother was a werecat, an introvert, and as volatile as a pixie.

Their mother had called Donal her air elemental whereas Tynan was pure earth—stubborn and unyielding as the mountains. As a healer, she hadn't been the most loving of mothers, but she'd been pretty damn observant.

Once through downtown, Tynan strolled up the hill toward the Wild Hunt Tavern. The air held no stink of concrete and metal; it was crisp and fragrant with the moist scent of new growth. Although the mountains still clung to their snowy blankets like wizened old men, here in Cold Creek, the white was receding to expose brown earth and green sprouts. Up in the trees, pixies chittered while nibbling on the tender leaf buds.

At the tavern, he pulled open the heavy oak door and stepped in. Warmth surrounded him along with the aromas of beer and popcorn.

Behind the long bar at the back, Calum motioned toward a corner table where his sandy-haired littermate sat. Alec was not only a cahir—protector of the clan—but also the sheriff of their small county, serving as law and order on the human side.

Cosantir and sheriff. The brothers made a powerful team.

"Good to see you, Tynan." Alec rose and held out a hand to shake. The blade-shaped blue scar on his cheek marked him as a cahir as did the extra height and heavy musculature. Herne's gifts to better enable his cahirs to fight for the Daonain.

After shaking hands, Tynan took a chair across from the sheriff.

Alec studied him with a smile. "You're looking healthier these days, not so much like a rubber band that's been stretched too tight."

"The city isn't a beneficial place for shifters. It's good to be back in the mountains."

"Does that mean you're planning to stay in Cold Creek?"

Alec asked with his slow southern drawl. Odd how Daonain clung to habits absorbed after coming into their natures. Alec had been fostered in the south; Calum spent his teen years in England, Tynan in Ireland. Their acquired accents lingered on.

"I, too, would like to hear the answer to that." Calum placed a cup of coffee—black—in front of Tynan before sitting. A couple of inches shorter than his littermate, the Cosantir had an olive complexion, dark gray eyes, and black hair pulled back in a leather tie. As reserved as his litter-mate was sociable.

"I'd like to stay." Tynan took a sip of coffee. The fragrant dark roast was prepared exactly as he liked it.

The Cosantir had a reputation for discovering everything about the shifters in his territory. He was also known for being fair, although not easygoing in the least. He'd banished quite a few shifters, including a male who'd caused permanent damage to another during a Gathering fight.

Calum's smile was worrisome. The Cosantir was a werecat—and panthers played with their prey. "In that case, I'd like to hear how you came to be in Seattle. Unless it's a secret?"

Tynan's gut tightened. The reason he'd been in Seattle was an ugly part of his past. Calum might not want a shifter like him in his territory—which would be hard on Donal.

Damn. He stared down at his coffee. Words had come easily to him at one time as had sharing his emotions. No longer. Not after hiding his very nature from the humans in the city. After guarding each word that came out of his mouth.

"It's not a secret as such." But he'd buried the painful past deep in his soul. He looked at the Cosantir and knew he had no choice. "After I returned to the States from fostering, Donal and I traveled. Settled here and there. Traveled more. The way single shifters do. One night, we attended a Gathering where—"

A fist seemed to squeeze his chest, locking the explanation within him.

Alec frowned and pushed Tynan's coffee closer. "Take a sip of that and try again." The sympathy in his voice sang beneath the order.

Tynan took a drink. "It was a rough Gathering. Unsupervised. A male attacked me when I was taking a pretty female to a mating room. I struck him back. Hit him hard. No question about that."

He could still feel the impact of his fist on the male's jaw, and the familiar self-reproach swept through him. Admittedly, the male had been an asshole. Tynan hadn't wanted to fight; it wasn't his way—yet backing down wasn't in his nature either. "He tipped backward over a table, landed wrong, and broke his neck."

Tynan had stood there. Waiting to continue the fight. *Why didn't the male rise? Walking around the table. Seeing...a body. The face turning a bluish-gray. The chest so still, not rising.*

How long had he stood there in disbelief with horror

growing within him? He'd looked for his littermate. But Donal had been called away for a healing.

Brawls happened at Gatherings. The air was filled with testosterone and the scents of aroused, willing females. Males showed off their prowess for the favor of a female. But the Daonain Law stated a male must cause no permanent harm to his opponent.

Death was very permanent. "I was banished."

Alec tilted his head. "The Cosantir accused you of breaking the Law of the Fight?"

The Cosantir of that territory had slashed his claws across Tynan's face. *"Outcast you are, to be shunned by shifters and OtherFolk until the marks of banishment are gone."* Eventually, if a shifter repented, the Goddess might forgive the transgressor and turn the black scars to white.

"For an accidental death?" Calum frowned.

"The male was dead." Tynan's throat was tight. "And I was from out of territory. Not one of the Cosantir's clan."

"How long were you outcast?" Alec's expression made Tynan stiffen. He didn't need or deserve pity.

Although the banishment had been hard. To be shunned by the clan, family, and even OtherFolk like dwarves and pixies... It lacerated a shifter's soul. Often, the banished simply gave up and died. Tynan had approached that point. He'd caught himself stalking a grizzly, thinking suicide by bear was an honorable enough ending. But, thinking of Donal, he'd pulled himself back. And survived.

"How long?" He took another drink of coffee to erase

the taste of those days. "A month—maybe less. It's not like I was looking in a mirror to see when the marks disappeared."

"A month?" Calum shook his head. "Banishment for breaking the Law will last years, Tynan. I don't think the Mother agreed with your sentence."

Tynan sighed. "I caused a death, Cosantir, however it happened. Forgiveness wouldn't be right. Truly, I was surprised when I saw my reflection in a lake and realized the black scars were gone." All the scars had been gone, in fact, as if they'd never been.

Yet he'd remained in the wilderness for months after that. He'd killed someone.

The Cosantir's eyes met his in understanding. "The Mother forgave you, but you couldn't forgive yourself."

"I felt as if I owed more." Tynan rubbed his jaw where the scars had been. "I underwent the ritual to speak to the God. To Herne."

The God was not to be called upon lightly. In wolf form, he'd run for days, no food, no water, no rest, leaving everything behind him except the need in his soul. Finally, legs shaking, he'd scrambled up to an overlook and had stood there, wavering with every gust of wind. Too stubborn, too stupid to leave.

Herne had heard him.

Alec's eyes narrowed. "Herne sent you to Seattle?"

Tynan nodded. The God didn't exactly speak words, at least not to anyone who wasn't a Cosantir. "The Hunter gave me the knowledge there was a wrongness in the city. Something to do with the Daonain. I was to wait there until he needed me to act."

For a fecking decade he'd waited.

"You were there a long time," Calum murmured as if he'd heard the thought, "but to the immortals, time is an ocean, not an hourglass where each grain of sand is a moment of life."

Tynan sighed. "So I came to realize."

"No matter how long, you were there as needed when needed." The Cosantir's gray eyes darkened. "Without you, the Dogwood females would still be imprisoned—and dying —and the male shifters would be weapons in the hands of the humans."

Payment for a death couldn't be measured out like so much flour, yet Tynan's presence in Seattle had helped save dozens of young Daonain. The knowledge had released him. "I wish I could have found them sooner."

"Hard to do when you didn't have any information to act upon." Alec's voice held a snap. A cahir and a sheriff would know all about not clinging to guilt.

Tynan nodded an acknowledgement.

"I'm surprised you managed to survive in the city as long as you did," Calum said. "A wolf without a pack tends to have problems."

"Human police form a kind of pack. It's not the same, but...it helped." The longing to run with other wolves had grown greater with every year that passed. For security, he'd kept his visits to Cold Creek few and far between.

"Shay's pleased to have you in the pack," Alec said.

Shay was the alpha of the local pack—a damn fine alpha —and his littermate Zeb was as tough a beta as anyone could hope to find. "It's a solid pack." Despite a few problems remaining from the previous alpha's mismanagement.

He had to admit, he still didn't feel completely part of the pack. Unlike when he'd been a young male, he stayed on the outskirts. Maybe he'd lived with humans too long.

The air in the tavern stirred slightly—someone had opened the portal to the underground caves in the back— and Tynan caught a whiff of minerals, then saw three stout dwarves walk into the room. "Dwarves. In a bar?"

Calum's quick grin was white in his tanned face. "They've learned they like beer fresh from the tap. I keep a table reserved in the back corner."

Welcoming OtherFolk? This was a quite different Cosantir from the ones he'd known growing up.

"Excuse me." Calum rose, paused, and looked back at Alec. "I approve." He headed for the dwarves, moving with the prowling gait of a mountain lion.

Assuming the Cosantir meant he could stay, Tynan started to rise. "Right then. Can I assume we're done here?"

Leaning back, Alec stretched out his legs. "That would be a nope." The sheriff's dark green eyes were sharper than his slow drawl and easy manner suggested. "Would you happen to be getting bored with your day-to-day life here?"

Sharp, indeed. "Aye. As it happens, I am."

"Good." Alec smiled. "Azure is an exceedingly small county, and during the winter, the demand on law enforcement isn't strenuous. Trouble is, as the weather warms, the human traffic increases. We have more shifters traveling through the territory and more hellhounds."

"Makes sense." *Where is he going with this?*

"I have two deputies. A still inexperienced male and my mate. Our cubs were born last fall, so neither Vicki nor I want to work full-time." Alec paused and met Tynan's gaze. "I could use another deputy, if you're interested."

Law enforcement suited Tynan from snout to tail.

And Cold Creek was Donal's choice for a home. "I'm interested." He glanced toward the back where the Cosantir was serving the dwarves. "That was what he approved? For you to offer me a job?"

"Very good. Yes." Alec smiled. "I checked you out with the Seattle PD; your captain and fellow officers think very highly of you. But Calum wanted to know what drove a wolf to the city."

Tynan blew out a breath.

Alec's eyebrows rose.

"Sorry. To you, he's just your littermate. For the rest of us Daonain, being summoned by the Cosantir has a shifter wondering what he fucked up. Then you offer me a job. It's like falling off a steep cliff, expecting to be splattered on the rocks, and landing in a lake instead."

"Well, hell, sorry about that." Alec grinned and rose. "If

you're not too badly drenched, let's go start on the paperwork to make you official."

Tynan grinned back, even the thought of paperwork not a deterrent. "Let's do that."

Oh, gopher-guts. Angie hadn't lied, had she? Unable to move from the doorway, Margery stared into the house that she was supposed to live in. And clean.

Angie had planned to be here, too, but her daughter, who lived in a nearby town, had called for her help.

Hoping not to wait until she returned, Margery had asked for the key. She could manage.

Or so she'd thought.

The small house on Cumberland Street was *filthy*. An offense to her sensitive wolf nose.

Still...

Margery gave a happy hip-wiggle—the human equivalent of a tail-wag—and walked into the house. *Mine, all mine.* No one would yell her name with demands that she clean up their messes or their pups. No pushy males. No one expecting her to tend their injuries even as they called her gimpy and ugly.

She rubbed her face and dragged herself out of the paw-sucking swamp of pity. Part of her unhappiness there had been her own fault. Her cubling memories had turned

Dogwood into a glowing haven of peace and belonging. The other captives had done the same.

The reality was that all villages had good *and* bad people, whether shifter or human.

Nonetheless, Cold Creek would be better for her than Ailill Ridge. Here, she'd be a waitress, not a banfasa. Here, she had her own house.

In her heart, she lifted a paean of gratitude to the Mother for the chance to start again. For being alive. For spring.

Smiling, she looked around the open living room. Brown carpet, off-white walls, dark blue couch, two comfortable-looking armchairs, and lamps on the end tables. A bookcase covering one wall indicated the previous owner had been a reader.

Story-hunger squeezed her heart. *There were books to explore.*

Later. Cleaning first.

An island with three tall stools separated the kitchen from the living room. The kitchen was a celebration of wood, from maple farm-style cupboards to butcher block counters. Off to the right, an oval table with ladder-backed chairs formed the dining area.

The fridge had been emptied—thank the Mother—but the cupboards held canned goods, rice, and beans. Angie said the food was all hers.

She wouldn't starve.

However, the rancid smell and debris everywhere indicated she'd be spending a lot of time cleaning the kitchen.

She kept wandering.

The master bedroom was dominated by a king-sized bed with a blue and brown quilt. The tall dresser and heavy nightstands were dark wood. It was a very masculine room.

The closet was full of clothing.

The second bedroom was small, barely big enough to fit the queen bed. No need to deal with that today.

First things first. She needed a place to sleep tonight. After stripping the bed in the master bedroom, she found the laundry room behind the kitchen. The washer was like the one in Ailill Ridge. She sent up another grateful thought. Even if communal housing had been difficult, she'd obtained the skills to live on her own.

She located cleaning supplies so she could clean the stinky bathroom—*ew*—before starting on the kitchen.

Outside, a door slammed, making her jump, and she realized the sound came from the house next door.

Scolding herself for curiosity more suited to a cat than a wolf, she stepped to the window and looked out. Unlike her tiny house, her neighbor had a large two-story with a wide wrap-around covered porch.

"Demon choke you"—a skinny male on the porch shook his fist at the house—"you're a piss-poor excuse for a healer!"

The healer named Donal stepped out. "I'm an excellent

healer, as a matter of fact. What I lack is tolerance for rudeness and stupidity."

"You fucking—"

"Since you can't be polite, tend your wound yourself. Being healed isn't a Goddess-given right, you mangy mutt." Donal shoved the male right off the porch.

The male landed on his ass, lurched to his feet, and stopped. After eyeing the healer—who admittedly looked a lot more deadly than any healer should—he snarled and strode away. A blood-stained shirtsleeve indicated he was wounded.

And the healer had refused to care for him.

Margery stared. *Is that allowed?*

After an audible snort of disgust, Donal stalked back into his house, totally a werecat whose fur had been ruffled the wrong way.

Margery let out a sigh. He sure was compelling. His shirt couldn't hide the lean musculature, and his jeans were tight enough to let a female appreciate the lean strength of his ass and legs. Add in the stunning self-confidence of a panther, and he was simply fascinating. Intimidating.

And way, way out of her comfort zone.

On top of all that, he was a healer. And...the realization made her spirits soar like a hawk catching a thermal. Since Cold Creek had a healer, the town had no need for a banfasa.

Here, she really was free.

Laughing, she spun in a circle, arms over her head, sending the Mother the gratitude in her heart.

After a couple of spins, a movement caught her attention, and she halted.

On the sunlit sidewalk, a male stood, looking into her window. With the kitchen light behind her, he could undoubtedly see her quite clearly.

She could see him as well. His black leather jacket was open, revealing a thick black, weapons belt and a uniform shirt with a shiny badge.

Like a Scythe guard. Memories of vicious beatings set off a firestorm of fear and anger inside her, and she stumbled away from the window.

Who is in old Leo's house?

From the sidewalk, Tynan stared into the house next to his. The movement from inside had caught his eye, but it was the female's exuberant, whirling dance that had captivated him. Joy simply fountained from her.

Until she saw him.

Now, she backed away, expression frozen with rage...and fear. Of him.

He recognized that expression. And her. The Dogwood female from the Gathering. By the Gods, what'd he ever done to her—aside from help rescue her and the rest of the captives?

Blowing out an exasperated breath, he walked up his sidewalk and into his house. "It's me," he called.

"'Bout time." Donal emerged from the laundry room, accompanied by the faint citrusy scent of soap. "What did the Cosantir want?"

After pulling off his old black jacket, Tynan patted the shiny badge on the new khaki uniform shirt, then rested a hand on his duty belt. "He approved of the sheriff giving me a job."

"By Herne's horny hooves, I'm pleased." Grinning widely, Donal smacked Tynan's shoulder.

"Yeah, me, too."

His littermate scowled. "As long as you're not planning to arrest me or anything."

Tynan snorted. "Like Alec would let me. Law or not, Daonain don't mess with healers."

"This is as it should be." With a smirk, Donal dropped down on the couch and set his feet on the coffee table.

Oh, scat. Tynan recognized that smirk. No matter how much time they spent apart, he'd always be able to read his brother. And that was Donal's *I-did-something-I-shouldn't-and-I'm-okay-with-it* expression.

Stalling by detouring to the kitchen for a glass of apple juice, Tynan settled into his favorite armchair. Fuck, it was good to be home...even if it meant dealing with a werecat littermate. "All right, I'm ready. What'd you do this time?"

Donal gave him an innocent look. "Nothing."

At Tynan's disbelieving stare—the one every cop

mastered—his brother sighed. "Relax, brawd. I just kicked a mouthy mutt out of the clinic without fixing his lacerated arm. Nothing to arrest me for."

"Will the mutt be all right?" He knew the answer. Donal wouldn't refuse to tend anything truly serious.

"Aye. Eventually." Scowling, Donal waved his hand in the air. "Some mangy-tailed mongrels think they can be fucking rude, and a healer is still obligated to care for them."

"You know, I kind of thought that was how it worked, too." Their mother had never refused to heal anyone.

"'Fraid not. Admittedly, the Goddess wouldn't gift someone who lacked a strong moral code. But the Mother doesn't direct our actions. Doesn't say we have to do anything at all. Healing is a calling, not an obligation."

"Huh."

"Exactly!" Donal pointed a finger at Tynan as if his grunt had been agreement. "If the flea-brained idiots are allowed to be rude, healers will soon be putting up with all kinds of scat. If we don't demand respect, we won't get it."

"Bet the mutt will be more polite next time."

"One can only hope."

Tynan frowned. It'd take someone with a brain smaller than a pixie's to be rude to a healer. Then again, Donal could set off even the most placid of shifters. He wasn't exactly tactful.

Their neighbor Leo had openly enjoyed the drama of living next to a healer...but someone else might not feel that way. Like the intriguing female in Leo's house who'd looked at Tynan with fear in her big eyes.

"Cat." Tynan eyed his littermate. "Did you do your shouting inside, or did you upset our new neighbor?"

"What new neighbor?" Donal sat up, glanced to the right as if he could see the adjacent house that held three males, their mate and cublings. His gaze turned left. "Old Leo's house? Someone's living in that stench-filled cave?"

"I don't know if she's actually living there."

"A female?"

"Aye. One of the Dogwood villagers." A female who didn't seem to like him—and worse, might even be afraid of him. The knowledge hurt somewhere deep inside him. His job was to defend the pack, not frighten little females. "She looks interesting."

"Interesting, eh?" Donal grinned. "I'm feeling the need for a cold draft, oh, my brother, along with the latest rumors."

"Fecking feline." Cats reveled in gossip. "Right then, let's go get a beer. I'm sure the Cosantir will know what's going on. If he doesn't, Angie will."

An hour later, they'd learned that Angie was out of town...and that Calum hadn't heard about the new shifter moving into the vacant house.

Or into his territory.

CHAPTER FIVE

old Creek, North Cascades Territory - waning gibbous moon

"Margery, don't leave yet," Angie called.

On her way out of the diner, Margery stopped in the doorway. Her first shift as a waitress had gone well. She wasn't fast—yet—but she hadn't messed up any orders. It'd been a good morning. "Sure, boss. What's up?"

A line appeared between Angie's blonde eyebrows. "We need to visit the Wild Hunt."

"The tavern?" Like tiny ants, anxiety prickled over Margery's nerves. "Why?"

"The Cosantir called to ask about you." Angie motioned Margery out the door and headed down Main Street, slowing her pace to accommodate Margery's limping gait. "I can't believe you didn't speak with Calum about moving here."

Dread tightened Margery's stomach as they walked. Was she supposed to have gotten permission? Silently, she considered her conversations with Heather about moving to the North Cascades. No, Heather hadn't said anything about getting permission from the Cosantir.

"Angie." Up the hill, they turned off the road into the parking lot. The big log tavern seemed darker than normal. Ominous. "Am I in trouble?"

Hand on the tavern door, Angie glanced back. "No, no, girl, don't look like that. The Cosantir's not going to claw you. You didn't break the law. It's simply tradition to introduce yourself to a Cosantir *before* moving to his territory."

"Oh." Margery let out a relieved sigh. "Is he angry that you're letting me use the house?"

"No, not at all. He gave me charge of that problem." Angie pulled open the door and waved her through.

Into chaos.

Screaming cublings. Bleeding cublings. A lushly curved female was trying to calm things. A younger slender female dashed from the back, carrying a first aid box. Skidding on a patch of blood, she fell. The box rolled across the floor.

"By the Mother's breasts." Angie pushed Margery farther inside so she could enter.

After a second of shock, Margery pulled in a slow calming breath.

"No matter what, dear child, keep it together. If the nurse

panics, so will the patient." Phyllis, the Scythe nurse, had repeated that advice over and over until the understanding was buried deep.

Moving forward, Margery grabbed the dropped first-aid kit while doing a quick visual survey. The injured were all children. Two had deep parallel slashes on the torsos and were bleeding heavily. Looked like werecat damage. There was a slashed thigh. Another had a scraped arm. A cut over a boy's eye was trickling blood—as head wounds would do. All cubs were conscious and breathing with no obvious broken bones.

"Well, then." She used a volume loud enough to get attention without scaring the cubs more. She turned to the big-boned female with honey-colored hair who stood in the center of the children. "Can you put pressure on the one with a scraped forehead?"

"Can do." The blonde took the gauze packages from Margery and turned to the little dark-haired child.

"Angie, can you check on that cub?" Margery pointed to a youngling with a cut thigh.

"Got it."

Dropping down between the boy and girl with torso slashes, Margery smiled at them. "Hi there. Let's get you fixed up, shall we?" As she pulled more gauze from the box, she stroked the quieter cub's back in a comforting movement.

He stopped crying, big blue eyes full of tears.

Unbuttoning his ripped-up shirt, she smiled. "I have a

job for you. Take a big breath and say *fart* really loud."

As he giggled and yelled, "Fart," she quickly pulled the fragments of his shirt from the wounds.

She stared at the torn flesh and long ugly gashes.

What kind of a werecat would hurt a cubling? With an effort, she pushed her anger aside.

"That was nice and loud. Good job." She laid the gauze over the wounds and applied pressure.

Behind her, the girl started to scream.

A quick look showed the pup hysterically shoving away the hands of the young adult who pleaded, "Robena, *please.*"

Tiny Robena wasn't hearing any of it.

"Hey there." Margery put a reassuring hand on the dismayed adult's shoulder. "I'm Margery. How about we trade places?"

"Nia." Nia's gaze swept over Margery's calm patient, and she gave a shaky laugh. "Please, yes. I'll take Kinnon."

They switched, and Nia settled beside the sweet little boy who was asking if he should yell *fart* again.

Young males, old males—they were all alike.

Robena couldn't be more than four, reminding Margery of when the captives were that age.

"Come here, sweetling." Ignoring the ear-piercing screams, Margery gently drew the flailing little girl into her arms. So light, so young. *Oh, childling.*

First calm her, then deal with the blood.

"Shhh, I have you, lambkin. Shhh." In her mind, she settled at her still mountain lake, breathing in cool, moist air, feeling the peace grow deep—deep enough to share with the tiny soul in her lap.

After a second of struggling, the cubling quieted and nestled closer. "Hurts," she whispered, her cheek against Margery's breasts.

"I know. I'm going to fix it." Margery reached for more gauze, covered the ugly cuts on the girl's belly, and pressed firmly enough to slow the bleeding.

Before she could do anything else, a big warm hand covered hers.

"Let's see what we've got here." At the sound of a male's smooth, deep voice, Margery looked up into silver-blue eyes.

Black hair, lean face. The healer.

Donal gave her an unreadable look, before his gaze shifted to the pup in her arms. His smile lightened his eyes, and his voice changed to a smoky croon. "I'm going to fix you all up, Robena. As the scratches go away, it'll feel all sparkly inside. Like stardust."

Margery blinked. *Really? That sounds so cool.*

Robena pushed at Donal's hands, starting to panic. "No, no, no, I don't—"

"I like stardust," Margery murmured. "Maybe Donal should do the other cub first, and I'll go watch Kinnon getting stardust." She rocked as if to move.

The girl latched onto Margery tighter than a baby possum. "No, me first. Stardust," she demanded of the healer.

His lips twitched before he lifted the gauze to expose sluggishly bleeding cuts. "Ah, not very deep at all." He pushed the edges of one laceration together, as if gluing them shut, but as he held the wound, his other hand traced over the pinched line—and the skin melded together. The wound closed.

Tears prickled the backs of Margery's eyes at the wondrous sight. No hurting for days, no scars for this little one. Thanks to the Goddess—and the healer.

"It sparkses in me," the girl whispered...although her grip on Margery didn't relax.

The healer's deep chuckle was like dark velvet. "Excellent. Let's do another scratch."

Slowly, he healed the long ugly gashes until nothing was left. "There we go." After giving the cub a smile, he turned to the boy. "Kinnon, your turn."

The boy cub scrambled away from Nia to dive at Margery. She barely had time to free an arm to grab him.

Now she had two cubs in her arms. Big blue eyes, freckles dotting flushed faces, red-brown hair. She was holding littermates.

At the silence in the room, she looked up.

All the adults in the room stared at her.

As her face heated, she murmured, "Cublings like me," and turned her attention to the little boy. With some repositioning, both younglings were settled and comfortable on her lap.

Thumb in his mouth, Kinnon stared up at her, big eyes

heartbreakingly worried. With his other hand, he took one of her fingers and rubbed it against his cheek.

The curvy blonde had a melodious laugh. "That's what Minette does with my hair. I bet he'll be a cat when he grows up."

"Any comfort I can give is good." Margery bent to whisper to the boy, "The healer gave your sister tummy-sparkles. Do you want some too?"

Leaning against Margery's left side, the girl cub was half-asleep, her tiny fingers still gripping Margery's shirt.

Oh, she'd missed having little ones in her lap.

After eyeing his sister, Kinnon nodded.

Margery looked up. "We're—" The healer was frowning at her, the warmth gone, his gaze assessing, and her words stuck in her throat. If she'd been unencumbered, she'd have moved back.

He turned his attention to the cub, and his tanned face gentled. "One helping of stardust coming up."

As he repeated what he'd done before, Margery watched. It was fascinating how the flesh, then the skin, grew back together. When he was done, the only remnants of the slashes were blood streaks and pale pink lines.

"That is so wonderful," she whispered.

He made an acknowledging grunt and ran his hand down the cubling's soft red hair.

Yesterday, he'd eviscerated the arrogant male patient with his words. Today, he was so tender with the pups that her heart ached. And the way he could heal...

She thought of the wounds she'd stitched at the Scythe compound, leaving the inevitable scarring behind. The broken bones that she'd not had the equipment to ensure would heal right. Sorrow over what could have been fixed was a river, pulling her down into its depths.

Eyes stinging, she looked up.

A line had appeared between his dark brows as he studied her. After an intimidatingly long second, he went to sit beside the blonde adult. "What happened here, Emma?"

He examined the redheaded cub's wound. Red hair, freckles—another of Robena's littermates, Margery guessed.

Emma hugged the boy. "I was teaching scales on the piano, and a teen shifter ran in. Naked."

"It was Athol," Nia said.

"They crowded around him to say hi," Emma continued, "but a car peeled out in the parking lot, and Athol panicked and trawsfurred and—"

"Slashed the cubs," the healer finished for her. "Where is he now? He must be terrified."

"The Cosantir caught him"—Emma huffed a laugh—"by the scruff of the neck and gave him a shake."

Recalling the power around the Cosantir, Margery almost cringed.

"Poor Athol went limp as a terrified kitten," Emma said.

Donal snorted. "Calum has that effect."

"Indeed." The clipped voice came from behind Margery.

She jumped, bouncing the cubs in her lap, looked around—and really did cringe.

The gray-eyed, dark-haired male who'd been behind the bar at the Gathering stood right behind her. The Cosantir of North Cascades Territory.

Her breathing almost stopped.

"Calum, is Athol all right?" Emma asked him. "It wasn't his fault, he was just—"

"Panicking. I realize that. Since the Murphy brothers were returning from a run, they took him out for a lesson on being a panther. They can tell him he isn't the only shifter to panic and lash out—Kevin Murphy's first trawsfur was quite the mess." The Cosantir had a deep voice with a faint English accent. After assessing the room, he took a chair, looking quite accustomed to having shifters laid out all around him.

Then again, since he supervised Gatherings, he was undoubtedly used to casualties, even if adults rather than pups.

His gaze landed on her boss. "Angie, might I have an introduction to your new waitress?"

"Of course." Angie was repacking the first-aid kit and listing which supplies had been used. She closed the lid. "Cosantir, I bring you Margery Lavelle, a Dogwood villager who lived in Ailill Ridge over the winter. I hired her as a waitress at the diner and to clean Leo's house in exchange for permission to live there rent-free for two months. Margery, meet Calum McGregor, Cosantir of the North Cascades."

Margery held her breath as the Cosantir looked at her.

The power simmered around him like heat waves from a fire. And the others had called him Calum.

Uh-uh. She'd never thought twice about calling the Rainier Cosantir *Pete*, but this one... She bowed her head properly. "Cosantir."

"Margery Lavelle," he acknowledged and leisurely studied the drowsy littermates on her lap. "It appears you have a way with cublings."

"And a way with first aid," Emma said. "No panic. Knew precisely what to do. Where did you get so skillful?"

"At the Scythe compound." Margery didn't explain further. No way. She wouldn't fall into that trap again. She added hastily, "I only know the basics. It's good you have a healer here. Really."

"There are times Donal needs help," Calum mused.

Donal had knelt beside the cub with a slashed arm. At Calum's suggestion, the healer's head snapped up. "No, I don't," he said sharply even as her own refusal escaped her lips, "*No.*"

Everyone stared at her. Again.

Her face heated. "I...I have a job. I work for Angie, and that's what I want to do." Her mouth tightened. She wouldn't be forced back into being a banfasa. Maybe being a banfasa had been her life's goal, but look how that dream had turned into a nightmare.

Donal's expression held all the flexibility of a granite cliff as he told the Cosantir in a curt tone, "I'm not in need of help, thank you."

The way the Cosantir lifted an eyebrow indicated that the healer wasn't being particularly truthful. And she knew what that meant. Donal might need help—just not her help. The hurt of being disliked, being unwanted, was like lemon juice rubbed into a gash.

At one time, she'd thought working with an actual healer would be amazing, but not here. Not with this healer.

As the cublings on her lap stirred, she realized they'd caught her emotions. She pulled in a deep breath, asked the Mother for tranquility, and with her next breath, pushed away the pain.

Two breaths and the waters of her soul were calm again.

"Now, there's control like I've never seen," the Cosantir murmured.

She looked away from him to fall into the healer's silvery gaze. Once again, he was studying her. Like the Scythe had studied the shifters.

Her jaw jutted out. *Take your opinions, healer, and knot them into your tail.*

He blinked.

And the Cosantir grinned. "Margery, if you're pleased with your employment with Angie, then it shall be as you wish." Even as she relaxed, the Cosantir rose and added, "Choices are not written in stone if you should change your mind in the future."

Be a banfasa? Work with the healer? *Never, ever happening.* "Thank you, Cosantir."

"Be welcome in the North Cascades Territory, Margery Lavelle. I'm pleased you've joined the clan."

Warmth swept through her at the genuine acceptance in the Cosantir's words.

As Calum walked away, the healer resumed tending the last few scratches.

Settling down beside Margery, Angie let out a laugh. "Most people meet the Cosantir more formally. Not sitting on the floor, covered in blood and younglings."

"Oh, well." Margery blew out a breath. "Lucky me."

A snort drew her attention, and she saw the healer's lips twitch in a second of amusement.

A sense of humor, gentle with younglings, blessed by the Mother with the talent for healing. The kind of person she'd always wanted to work with.

Instead, somehow, she'd earned his dislike. Or maybe he was just extremely territorial? If so, no problem.

You can go ahead and piss all over your boundary lines, healer. I'd already planned to stay far, far away.

After Donal healed the younglings, he escaped down the tavern stairs into the caves below. Bonnie was on dispatch at the sheriff's station, and he called to warn her he was taking some time for himself.

"Have a good time, Donal. Sounds like you need a break after that mess."

"At least no one was seriously injured." By the Gods, it broke his heart when cubs were hurting. He hung up, tossed his phone on top of his clothing in the hollowed-out cubby, and shifted.

The wave of love from the Mother swept through him like a sun-warmed breeze, and he chirruped his pleasure. Stopping to rub against the cave opening, he left his scent and scratched off the last itch of trawsfurring. The scent of the forest drew him outside, and he bounded along the first trail, letting the movement stretch out pinched muscles.

Patches of the trail were slushy with melting snow—an annoyance to panther paws—but who could resist the call of springtime? Up he went, veering off to one of his favorite noon spots. The trail disappeared, but a quick squirming through underbrush let him exit into a sunny clearing with rock outcroppings.

After taking a moment to flex his claws on an available tree, he leapt to a smooth-topped boulder. Nice and dry. Perfect for a nap in the sun.

It had been a long winter.

But a satisfying one. His littermate was home where he belonged. His absence had been an ache in Donal's heart for over ten years. He'd wondered if they could even live together again, but it felt as if they'd never been apart.

Mostly. Donal turned on his side so he could lick the annoying mush from between his paw pads.

Tynan had changed. Well, that was normal enough. Living among humans. In a human city. Alone. Aye, that would have been the worst part. His littermate was quieter now, thought before speaking, his emotions more difficult to read.

The humans had changed him.

Humans had that effect on shifters. Donal switched to the other paw, extending his claws to get the irritating dirt out.

What about the pretty hazel-eyed female—the banfasa? What had she been like before the Scythe? Margery looked to be about Darcy's age, mid-twenties maybe. Had been captured before her first shift. The thought of Daonain cubs being imprisoned hurt his soul.

He tried to imagine her as a bouncy twelve-year-old cub. As an adult, she had incredible control over her emotions. Even Calum had commented on it. What had the Scythe done to her that she had to learn such restraint?

But she'd survived. Perhaps even grown stronger for the ghastly experience.

The scene in the tavern had been exactly what Bonnie had called it—a mess—but could have been worse. Apparently, Margery had straightened things out with concise directions. She hadn't done anything wrong medically speaking...not that cat scratches called for much knowledge.

The kits trusted her. Had clung to her. Because of that, although banfasas made him wary, he might've chanced working with her...if he hadn't been warned.

Uneasiness made him change position on the boulder. It wasn't often that his instincts about a person were wrong.

Nonetheless, considering that the banfasa had worked in Ailill Ridge all winter, the residents must know her well. He wouldn't put it past Gretchen to deal in rumors, but what she and Caleb had said was far past rumor and quite simply damning.

He wouldn't—couldn't—work with an incompetent banfasa or an irresponsible one. Admittedly, he might be fussier than some healers. After all, he'd been at this a long time. The Goddess had woken his healing abilities when he was young, and he was yanked right into the clinic to help. Mother had been a dedicated—almost fanatical—healer with extremely high standards.

By the Gods, he'd envied Tynan for getting to play rather than suffer through anatomy lessons.

As for Margery, well, she obviously knew her skills weren't up to par. She'd refused Calum's suggestion, choosing waitressing over being a banfasa. So that was that.

He frowned, remembering the word Tynan had used about her: "*Interesting.*" His littermate rarely pursued the shifter beauties. No, Tynan was drawn to intelligence, courage, warmth. Surely, he wasn't seeing that in this incompetent banfasa.

The memory of the two cubs nestled in her lap made Donal pause. She'd shown an abundance of warmth then. In fact, her concern for the kits had almost radiated from her. So very, very appealing.

Cat-scat. It would be extremely awkward if Tynan pursued her.

Really, they both needed to avoid her, so she didn't get any ideas about working with him.

He snorted. As if that would happen. She'd been very vocal about not wanting to help him out.

Be honest, gnome-brain. He needed to avoid her so *he* didn't get ideas.

Because she was as tempting as his favorite patch of catnip.

CHAPTER SIX

C old Creek, North Cascades Territory - third quarter moon

Cold Creek was a wonderful place to be.

Margery stepped into her backyard and reached for the sky in a long, painful stretch. And groaned. Her arm and shoulder muscles ached from carrying heavy trays of food at the diner. Her feet were swollen and sore from the hard floors. Her left ankle felt like a bear was chomping on it for lunch. And after a week of cleaning everything in the entire house, her joints throbbed like she was a hundred-year-old granny.

Ow.

None of it mattered...because her heart was happy. The

soreness was simply from exertion, not from being hit by a guard.

Besides, working at the diner was *fun*. People were in great moods when they went out to eat.

Everyone had been kind—and she'd received generous tips. Real money.

Tilting her head back, she smiled up at the faint hint of a moon in the daytime sky. "Thank you, Lady, for the town. For the job. For the house. And for the bicycle, too."

She'd found a bicycle in the garden shed. With a bit of oil and pumping up the tires, she had transportation. 'Twas a good thing since, whenever her limping grew too pronounced, her boss got worried.

Getting fired for her own good would be infuriating.

Yes, she'd exhausted herself. Been on her feet too much. She'd been a bit frenzied about getting the house cleaned.

She glanced back inside with a sense of satisfaction. The windows and back door were open to waft away the last of the cleanser smell. She'd washed the floors, walls, even the ceiling, scoured the oven and fridge, cupboards and counters. The bathroom was spotless. The steam vacuum she'd borrowed from Angie had turned the dark, dingy carpet to a light brown.

Almost everything from the closets had gone to the Cosantir's stock for shifters in need. Angie had made her keep a couple of coats and raingear—all a bit too big—and then dug through the Cosantir's hoard to find jeans, sweaters, and shirts in Margery's size.

It was amazing how nice it felt to have unripped, unstained clothing that actually fit.

Life was going well.

Several days ago, Heather had returned from visiting her mother. Delighted Margery was staying, she'd offered to bring Margery's belongings here.

But...her offer hadn't been needed.

"You didn't leave anything in Ailill Ridge? Girl, you only brought a daypack."

"Mmmhmm. It held everything I owned."

"That little thing couldn't have held more than a couple of changes of clothing and a few toiletries."

"I have clothes now—and I'm earning money."

When Heather's face turned an angry dark red, Margery patted her arm. "I'm here. And I'm happy. Thank you for bringing me, Heather. I really, really appreciate it."

"The God needs to wake his furry ass up and appoint a new Cosantir in Rainier." Heather muttered the blasphemy before giving Margery a hard hug. *"You call me if you need something—anything. I'll see you at the next Gathering."*

Margery smiled. Having a friend like Heather was amazing.

Inhaling the spring-scented air, she looked at the back-yard—her next task in the house renovation process.

It was quite the mess. A five-foot-tall board fence surrounded the backyard with a small garden shed in the back corner. Old leaves, winter-killed tall grass, and dead weeds lay in ugly piles over the barely sprouting lawn. The forest came right to the other side of the fence, and she could hear the gurgling creek that paralleled the line of houses. The dark line of bare deciduous trees forked several times, running up into the mountain wilderness. Angie said her Daonain neighbors used the creek side trails to visit the mountains.

Maybe she could go for a wolfy jaunt soon.

A quiver ran through her. She hadn't shifted since coming to Cold Creek, mostly because she didn't know the area or rules or anything. Rainier's pack alpha, Roger, hadn't been forgiving of mistakes. What if the alpha here in North Cascades Territory was even nastier?

Her jaw tightened. Well, she didn't give a sniff. She'd be careful—and would keep to herself. Not every wolf needed a pack.

Turning away from the forest, she set her hands on her hips and surveyed her messy domain.

Time to pick up some groceries and a pair of gardening gloves.

The green scent of produce mingled with the faint odors of meat products and cleansers in the grocery store. Margery waited patiently as Albert Baty rang up her groceries. Short with stringy gray hair and drooping jowls, the grocer had tried to hide his kind nature under bluster, but she'd figured him out.

"There you go, Margery." He handed her two small shopping bags. "I think you'll like the meatloaf recipe. It was my mum's favorite."

"I'll try it tonight." The inexpensive meat dish should keep her in leftovers all week. She grinned. "I'll invite you over after I've made it a few times. I'm good at messing up even basic dishes—it's embarrassing."

"You're still learning." He snorted. "When I was a pup, I destroyed quite a few *impossible-to-ruin* meals."

"Really?" In the Ailill Ridge communal house, most of the dinners were slow-cooker style—the easiest way to deal with charity-meat like venison and rabbit. Meat with beans or rice or potatoes. Difficult to ruin.

Cooking on her own without a slow cooker was much trickier. "I was starting to think I lack a cooking gene."

"No, child." He patted her hand. "Cooking simply requires a decent recipe, paying attention—and practice. Go forth and practice."

"I will. Thank you!" She headed outside to her bike, her feet lighter than when she'd come in.

After setting the bags into the rear rattan baskets, she unlocked the chain securing her bike to the streetlight and started to wrap it around her waist.

"Margery." A gratingly hateful voice made her spine go rigid.

She tossed the chain over the handlebars and turned.

Roger, the alpha of Rainier Territory's pack, stood way too close with Brett, his beta, behind him.

Cat-scat. If she had more room to escape, she could tuck tail and flee on her bike.

Keeping her expression cool and unreadable, she folded her hands at her waist. "Hello, Roger. What are you doing in Cold Creek?"

Big-bodied and thickly muscled, he invaded her personal space to loom over her. With scraggly yellow hair, winter-pale skin, and almost colorless eyes, he looked like the brutal Viking in a movie she'd once watched. "The question is: What are *you* doing in Cold Creek?"

"I live here now," she said coldly.

"No fucking way," he growled. "Every village got a Dogwood female—you're ours."

"Yours?" Anger rose inside her. She wasn't a meaty bone for a pack of coyotes; she was a person. "The Dogwood females were scattered for the winter for orientation and less chance of detection. My orientation is complete, and there's only one other villager here. It's my choice where to live."

"No, it's not. You might not be a healer, but you're better than nothing." His fingers closed around her upper arm. "You're coming back with us."

As she tried to jerk away, her ankle wobbled, and his grip tightened painfully.

Brett grabbed her other arm. "You can't run fast enough to escape us, gimpy bitch."

Her anger boiled over. "Leave me alone!" Grateful for her hard boots, she kicked Bret's shin with all her strength.

As he staggered back with a shout, she twisted. Her foot connected with Roger's knee. Not hard enough.

"Fucking *shrew*." His fingers ground against her bone as he jerked her closer and his right hand lifted.

Before he could slap her, a baton struck his forearm. He yelped and jumped back. His grip loosened.

She yanked free.

Her rescuer stepped in front of her, facing the Rainier wolves. He glanced over his shoulder. "Are you all right, lass?"

The frozen steel of the male's voice held a hint of Ireland. She knew that voice. It was the male from the Scythe garage. *Tynan*.

Her mouth went dry.

"Who the fuck do you think you are?" Teeth bared, Roger rubbed his arm. "Do you know who I am?"

"I don't care who you are." Tynan's grip tightened on the baton. "I'm Deputy O'Connor with the Azure County Sheriff's Department, and right now, you're looking at an assault charge."

Taking a hurried step back, Roger lifted his nose, his nostrils flaring as he checked the air. Undoubtedly, he caught the scent that Tynan was a shifter. A mean smile grew on his face. As an alpha, Roger had power almost equal to a Cosantir's. "I'm alpha of the Rainier Territory and she"—he pointed to her—"is one of my pack."

"Is she now?" Tynan moved sideways to look at her and

still keep the two Rainier males in his field of vision. "*Are you in his pack?*"

Could Roger force her to return? Heather hadn't mentioned pack rights. "I was." Margery smoothed damp hands down her jeans. She took care with her words, "I live here now. I won't return to Rainier Territory or be in his pack."

"Right. That's clear enough." Tynan narrowed his eyes at the males. "You heard her. Be off with you."

"I'm not leaving without her." Roger's voice rose. "She's *our* banfasa."

No. I'm. Not. She was done with being anyone's banfasa. Her jaw set tightly. If Roger managed to take her back, she'd escape again, and go much, much farther next time.

Shaking his head, Tynan said mildly, "Apparently not any longer."

Roger's face darkened, and his fists came up. Brett, who was almost as big as the alpha, moved forward.

Tynan's muscles tightened with a rippling motion beneath his shirt.

Oh Goddess, two to one—he'd get hurt.

Should I give up and go with Roger? No, she couldn't. Wouldn't. But she could fight beside this male. Her rescuer.

She lifted the bike's heavy security chain from the handlebars. The thick, rough metal links were icy cold in her hands. If she swung the chain hard enough, it would slow—maybe stop—one of them.

Fear made her heart pound painfully in her chest, but

her grip was solid. She'd do what she needed to do to protect Tynan.

He glanced at her, saw how she held the chain, and his eyes crinkled slightly before he told Roger, "Just so you know, if she damages a person, she won't bandage them up afterward—and neither will our healer."

"Well said, brawd."

At the deep resonant voice, Margery jumped. Turned slightly.

Donal stood in the doorway of BOOKS. His perfect lips curved in a cold smile. "Want some help? Been a while since I performed abdominal surgery using my claws."

An older shifter stood behind him—the one named Joe Thorson from the Scythe garage. He looked like he'd had more fights than all the younger males combined. "Shifters who bother females don't live long. Not in *our* territory."

Outnumbered, Roger backed a step and bumped into Brett. "Fine. We're leaving. But"—he pointed at Margery —"she's Rainier Territory's banfasa. Pete isn't going to let her walk away."

As the two retreated with the stiff-legged gait of pissed-off wolves, Margery realized she wasn't breathing. Her knees threatened to buckle. Dropping the chain on the bike, she grabbed the streetlight pole for support.

How could this happen? Once free of the Scythe, she'd been sure she'd be safe and happy. But...then there had been Rainier Territory. Pete. Roger.

I got away.

Out of Rainier Territory, she'd thought she'd be safe and happy in Cold Creek.

Wrong again.

Nowhere was safe.

Don't I get to be happy?

Black spots danced in front of her eyes.

Tynan shoved his baton into his belt. "Don't pass out on me, little female." He wrapped a muscular arm around her waist and tugged her away from the streetlight.

Too dizzy to protest, she let him lead her to the center island where he sat her on an iron bench. "Donal." He motioned toward the healer. "Maybe a quick check?"

Joining them, Donal took her hand for a second. His fingers were warm. She could almost feel the simmering healer energy as he assessed her.

Straightening, he spoke to Tynan—not to her, "No damage, just the shaky aftermath of an altercation."

"An altercation that shouldn't have happened." Tynan's hard voice made her flinch. "Some gobshite, he was."

Rule number two of captivity: *Avoid annoying the ones in charge.*

She sat quiet and still, braced for whatever actions his anger would take. When nothing happened, she checked him from the corner of her eyes, keeping in mind Rule Number Four: *Don't look an irritated male straight in the face.*

"She'll be fine." Donal turned his silvery gaze to her and smiled slightly. Coolly.

How pitiful was she to crave a warm smile like he'd

given the cublings at the tavern?

Tynan was watching her as well, and his gaze held...a very male look.

The healer looked at her, then Tynan, then her, and without another word, he walked away. Back to the bookstore.

Leaving her with the deputy who turned to scowl after the healer.

Uh-oh. He was definitely angry. She edged away from him on the bench.

His anger disappeared as if it had never been, and he went down onto his haunches in front of her. "Lass, I have never hit a female in all my life. I'm not going to start now."

Oh. She'd...hurt his feelings? That was the last thing she wanted. He'd been willing to fight for her.

She swallowed. "I'm sorry. I was...I learned to be...careful...when I lived in Seattle. In the compound. I've mostly gotten past it."

Tynan was as motionless as a cat stalking a field mouse. "Your head knows you escaped the bad guys, but you were imprisoned long enough for your body to get set in its ways. It'll take time."

His clear blue eyes were like the Seattle sky when the wind from the Sound swept away any trace of clouds. Eyes a person could fall into.

Looking down, she saw his police badge, and her chest went tight, squeezing the air from her lungs. Quickly, she averted her gaze. "Thank you, Deputy O'Connor."

"It's Tynan, and you're quite welcome." His gaze went past her, looking at something across the street. "Are you ready for the next challenge of the day?"

What does he have planned for me now?

She'd thought he was a good person, a rescuer, but Gods, what if she was wrong? How had she let her guard down even a whisker? Her muscles tightened. "Like...what?"

He started to put his hand over hers. And stopped. "Nothing scary, merely something to take care of before there are problems."

"Take care of?"

Rising, he motioned for her to stand. "You need to be seen and accepted by the pack alpha here so Roger has no claim on you." He shook his head before she could protest. "There is gender inequality in the Daonain; I'm the first to admit it. But with so few females, our instincts demand that you be protected."

"Protected would be nice. Imprisoned is what I..." Her voice trailed off as she realized she was going to irritate a male. Not just *any* male, but one with weapons hanging all over his belt. She took a careful step away.

His mouth tightened slightly, but he simply waved for her to walk with him across the island. "Our alpha, Shay, and his mate are having lunch in the diner. Let me introduce you."

The diner. Very public. Relief ran through her. "Okay."

"See? Nothing to worry about. Angie's there, and she'll protect her new waitress, even against the alpha."

Margery stopped dead before she stepped down into the street. "No. She mustn't. Never. She'd end up getting hurt and—"

"By the Gods." He impatiently ran his hand through his short brown hair. "Margery, no one will get hurt. No one will yell, either, for that matter. Admittedly, the previous alpha here was a bad egg, but this one—Shay—is one of the finest I've ever met, and I've run with some of the best."

She stared at him. He was so blunt—which probably caused him problems—but it was nice. Somehow, she couldn't imagine him lying.

Aaand... It seemed as if she'd be joining a pack after all. So much for well laid plans.

As they reached the sidewalk, a uniformed male approached, one even bigger than Tynan.

Margery stepped back and slightly behind Tynan.

Ignoring her wariness, the male smiled at her before shifting his focus to Tynan. "Problems?"

"Problems are handled, but we need to talk later," Tynan said. "Margery... *Margery.*"

Realizing Tynan was speaking to her, she yanked her gaze from the new male and looked up.

Brows drawn, Tynan studied her. His voice turned even softer, the Irish accent deeper. "Sweetheart, Alec McGregor is the county sheriff—and a cahir. Alec, this is Margery Lavelle, a Dogwood villager, who was living in Rainier Territory."

Alec. She blinked and looked up, past the uniform, to

his face. Shaggy, golden-brown hair. Dark green eyes. The blue blade-shaped cahir scar over his left cheekbone.

She knew him—he was the cahir who'd been at the Scythe compound. One of the two who'd led the female captives into the garage. How could she not have recognized him right away?

"Ah, Calum mentioned we have a new shifter. Welcome, Margery." The sheriff had a nice smile, a faint Southern accent...and his hand rested on his weapons belt.

How she hated those belts that screamed of cruelty.

No, that was then.

I'm here now.

She reached deep for peace. "Thank you, sir."

"Just Alec." When the radio on his belt chirped, he nodded and moved away.

"Come, lass. Let's find Shay." Tynan guided her down the sidewalk toward the diner, nodding in response to greetings from two shifter females.

"Good afternoon, Margery. It's a fine day, isn't it?" The white-haired, rotund woman nodded her thanks to Tynan as he held the door open for her and her pudgy poodle.

"It really is." Margery smiled at Mrs. Neilson—and her pet. Two of her favorite customers.

As Tynan kept holding the door, Margery stepped into the diner.

Joining her, he stopped just inside and waved his hand toward a table at the front window. Two big males sat on each side of a curvy female with long hair the colors of sunlight.

"Which one is the alpha?" she whispered.

Tynan raised an eyebrow. "Use your instincts, little wolf."

Instincts. Something she was still learning about. The Daonain usually experienced their first trawsfur at puberty. However, being on birth control and held in a human city, she and the other Dogwood females hadn't shifted until a month after they'd been freed.

Her animal's primal senses still needed honing. Here in Cold Creek—away from Roger—she might be able to spend more time as a wolf. Which she craved more than anything.

The shifters at the table took note of Tynan, then her.

Dear Goddess, but those males are huge.

After another calming breath, she could focus and take in the blade-shaped blue scar on each male's cheekbone. They were both cahirs like Alec. The warriors of the God; the enforcers of the Cosantir. Scary, but scary in the defense of the Daonain.

Unlike Tynan, they had no uniforms to send her into a silly rabbit-freeze.

So, which one is the alpha?

She lifted her chin and met the dark, mean-looking one's eyes. Then she considered the one with disheveled brown hair.

Like Tynan, he had the appearance of a Celtic warrior with thick, heavy muscles and a strong face. As she met his gaze, the power of pack hit her. Her eyes lowered in an instinctive—almost comforting—surrender to the alpha.

"Him," she told Tynan.

"There you go. Good instincts." He motioned her forward.

Both males stood, the female remaining seated.

Tynan kept his voice quiet so only those at the table could hear. "Shay, I'd like to introduce a new wolf to the territory. Margery is one of the Dogwood villagers."

"Margery." Shay held out his big hand, and she reluctantly set her fingers in his. "Are you planning to live here?"

"Yes. If it's possible that I can?" Her answer came out sounding almost like a question.

"She works for me, Shay." Angie walked up and put an arm around her shoulders for an affectionate squeeze. "Margery is amazing. Meant for better things, but I'll keep her as long as she's willing to stay."

Margery's throat clogged. "Thank you."

"S'truth." Angie squeezed again before bustling away.

Shay motioned to the other two at the table. "Margery, meet Brianne, our mate and the alpha female of the pack. Zeb, my beta and brother."

Zeb nodded.

Brianne held out her hand to shake. "I'm so glad to meet you. Don't be worried—I'm a *nice* alpha fem."

Shay smiled. "You two will probably understand each other better than most. Bree was raised from birth among humans."

Margery's mouth dropped open. "Oh Gods, and I thought *I* had a learning curve."

"I know, right?" Bree grinned.

Margery studied the pack males. Over the years, she'd gotten better at picking out which males were cruel in nature. These two seemed extremely dangerous yet without seeming vicious. And they weren't in uniform or carrying badges or weapons.

She returned her focus to the alpha female. "Is there anything I need to know?"

"You bet. How about you come up to the Wildwood Lodge tomorrow after your breakfast shift?" Bree said. "I can give you the deets on meetings and pack runs and all that."

She could totally do that. Bree seemed really nice. "Sure."

"In addition, I'll assign you a mentor," Shay said.

Margery went stiff. Her mentor in the Rainier pack had been...not so nice. "The wolves in the Rainier pack said I was doing okay and didn't need a teacher any—"

Zeb snorted. "Like they'd know anything."

"Really?" Tynan cut in. "Have you had some run-ins with the Rainier pack?"

Shay smiled slightly. "We fought hellhounds in Rainier for several years. The pack's cohesiveness and morale were already sliding then. Older, skilled wolves were withdrawing. If that trend hasn't changed, the wolves overseeing the new members would be—"

"Worthless. The alpha and betas are as energetic as slugs in winter." Zeb eyed Margery. "You don't look lazy."

"The opposite if what Angie said is true." Bree leaned forward. "I'd love to mentor you, but I'm still learning myself. I do know that the North Cascades—and different seasons—might have dangers you haven't encountered yet."

"Oh. I hadn't thought about that." Different seasons. Different location. And having a weak leg already put her at a disadvantage—although that was part of why the last mentor had disliked her. Ridiculed her. She sighed.

Shay eyed her. He had a jaw as stubborn as Tynan's. "I'll find you a good mentor."

No choice. What the alpha said was what would happen. She bowed her head slightly to Shay and tried not to sound as if she was lying. "I'm pleased for your care, Alpha."

A minute later, the little female left to take her groceries home—and Tynan stayed. As Shay and Zeb resumed their seats, he looked at Shay. "Alpha, a minute of your time?"

"Of course. Get comfortable, Deputy." Shay pointed to a chair.

Tynan hesitated. "I can't stay; I have duties."

"Duties to the pack, as well," Shay said evenly. "I'd like to talk about that now."

Fuck. Good thing the sheriff was also a shifter. Alec knew about multiple obligations.

As Tynan took a chair, Angie dropped off a full cup of coffee without even slowing down.

Tynan took a sip and frowned at Shay. "Were you after needing me for something?"

"Aye, but first, what can I help you with?"

That question right there was one of the reasons Tynan respected the alpha so highly. He took his responsibilities very seriously.

"Right." It helped that Shay and Zeb knew—and disliked—the Rainier alpha, Roger. "You know the Dogwood females had it rough."

As Zeb's face darkened, Shay said in a tight voice, "We know."

"I get the impression the little wolf didn't have an easy time in Ailill Ridge either." Tynan shook his head. "Roger, the alpha, was just here. He was about to drag her back there when I intervened."

"He what?" When Zeb growled and started to stand, every customer in the diner tensed.

"I sent him and his beta home," Tynan said quickly. "Still, today might not be the end of it. Roger seemed to think that since Rainier doesn't have a healer, they could keep Margery."

Shay frowned. "Why would they consider a waitress as a substitute for a healer?"

"He said she was their banfasa," Tynan answered.

"What's a banfasa?" Bree asked.

"One of the wise women." Shay stopped at her look of confusion "That's not a human occupation, is it?"

"For humans," Tynan told her, "a banfasa would fit somewhere between a medic and a nurse practitioner. Not God-called like a healer, but with the talent and training to care for the wounded and sick. And with an emphasis on health."

Shay half smiled at his mate. "Daonain don't get as many diseases as humans, but we excel at being injured and getting old."

"I've noticed that." Bree grinned then tapped her fingers on the table. "Ailill Ridge was going to keep Margery as if she was a slave or something?"

"That's the impression I got. If I hadn't stepped in, she'd be on her way there now. Against her wishes." Tynan jerked his chin toward Shay and Zeb. "I brought her to you since Roger appears to think he *owns* his pack members."

"What the fuck is going on in Rainier?" Zeb growled, low and dark.

"They're getting worse," Shay agreed. "I'm glad you were there, Tynan. What did Margery have to say about her treatment there?"

"That is my other concern. She didn't."

When the three gave him a blank look, he sighed and tried to elaborate. Feck him, but he'd gotten out of the habit of talking about anything other than police work.

But the little wolf needed help.

"I thought at first she didn't like males, but the problem

is deeper." Tynan tapped the badge on his chest. "When she met Alec, I saw—I think—our uniforms are what the humans call a trigger. She acts like she expects me or Alec to pull our batons and pound her into the ground."

Zeb ran his gaze over Tynan's clothes and shook his head. "Your uniform?"

"I saw it too." Bree nodded. "Whenever she looked at you, her gaze snagged on your weapons or your badge."

"Those Scythe guards." Shay's mouth twisted into a scowl. "They all wore uniforms and carried weapons. On a belt."

Tynan thought back to the nightmare of the battle. *Ear-splitting gunfire and shouting and screams. Thorson's snarling when a bullet hit his foreleg. The human sniper aiming for the old werecat again. Leaping through the window, glass gashing his sides. Hot metallic blood filling his mouth as he slaughtered the human.*

Shaking his head roughly, Tynan tried to dispel the images...and the taste of flesh.

How many times had that ugliness in his past come back to haunt him?

Margery had lived with violence for years—and had never been able to fight back. By the Gods, what night-mares did *she* suffer through?

He flattened his hands on the table. "The uniforms—or weapons—probably make her think of her Scythe abusers. Can you work with her on getting past it? Any town with humans, any traveling she does—uniforms are everywhere. If she stays in Cold Creek, Alec and I will scare her."

He scowled at the unpalatable realization.

Because he definitely didn't want to frighten that little wolf.

A corner of Zeb's mouth turned up in a bitter smile. "It bites when a female takes one look and flees."

Zeb would know. The scarred-up beta had terrified more than just females. Yet, despite his lethal appearance, Zeb made as fine a friend as anyone could wish for.

"At least I know now why she reacts so badly," Tynan said. "Trouble is, a law enforcement officer might well consider her behavior as an indication of guilt."

"Well, that's sure the last thing she needs right now." Bree lifted her chin and gave him a firm nod. "I'll talk with her."

"Talking won't remove what has become instinctual after so many years." Shay took a sip of his coffee and contemplated Tynan. "It might help for her to get to know someone who wears a uniform at times...and fur the other times."

Wary of what Shay had in mind, Tynan shook his head. "No, that's—"

Bree clapped her hands together. "Yes. That's a great idea."

"She needs a mentor." Zeb tilted his head at Tynan. "It's time you took on some pack duties."

Oh, fuck.

The alpha and beta must've seen he tended to stay on

the sidelines. "Margery is terrified of me; I'd be a poor choice for a mentor."

"If she'd never shifted, I'd agree with you. For a first trawsfur, there must be trust between a mentor and a child," Shay said quietly. "However, she's not a child and is months past her first shift. She simply needs additional lessons. You've been here long enough to know our mountains—and you're highly skilled."

"You stepped in when Roger would have dragged her away. She won't forget who the good guy is, no matter what you wear." Bree's smile faded. "But if you don't like Margery, we should rethink this."

Trouble was...he did like her. More than was probably wise. "I like her." He let out a soft laugh, recalling the moment he knew she had his back.

Shay's eyebrows rose.

Leaning his elbow on the table, Tynan motioned to the street. "Out there...when I faced-off against Roger and his beta, she was terrified—and she'd already started to swing her bike chain to smack one of them."

"Another tough female?" Zeb actually smiled as he glanced at his brother. "We're keeping her in the pack."

"Aye." Shay grinned. "Train her well, Tynan. And we'll all keep her safe."

"We will." Tynan's vow came out as a deep growling rumble. Because he'd rip the throat out of anyone who tried to harm her.

And wouldn't think twice about it after.

CHAPTER SEVEN

C old Creek, North Cascades Territory - third quarter moon

Yesterday's altercation had been...exciting...if that would be the right word. *Terrifying* would work, too. But, hadn't it been amazing when Tynan told Roger he couldn't take her away?

Uphill past the tavern, Margery spotted the sign for the Wildwood Lodge and turned her bike down the muddy dirt road.

During the almost-fight, the cop had radiated anger, and afterward had been so...nice. Really concerned for her. There'd also been that very odd moment when he and the healer had both been watching her. Looking at her as males look at a female.

She pressed her hand to her stomach, feeling little quivers of heat. Last night, her dreams held the sound of Tynan's Irish-accented voice, the strength and gentleness of his grip.

One time, she dreamed of keen silvery-gray eyes framed by black lashes.

She was as addlepated as a drunken dwarf.

With a huff of exasperation, she braked in front of the big lodge building.

The leaden gray sky was spitting an icy rain down with the same vindictiveness as a newly wakened pixie would throw acorns and twigs. Bikes and rain were a bad mix, but she didn't have any other transportation. And hey, she'd wasn't out of breath. Okay, her ankle hurt, but otherwise, she was in good shape. Last fall, she'd been dying. Her blood had felt like sludge in her veins. Now, she felt as if she could dance.

So this was the Wildwood Lodge. Margery glanced around. The massive two-story log building had a wide covered porch and log railings. Continuing past the lodge, the dirt road narrowed and branched off to small cabins nestled in the forest.

Heather occasionally rented one of the little fishing cabins if she had a craving for something more rustic and quieter than the Victorian B&B downtown.

Margery carried her bike up onto the porch and tapped on the thick wooden door.

Bree's voice came from inside. "Door's open. Come on in."

Margery entered and stood on the wide mat. "I'm pretty wet. Do you have—"

"Just hang everything on the coat rack beside the reception desk." Bree hurried out from the back of the house and laughed. "You look like a drowned rat."

Margery grinned. "It's mostly my hair. I'm actually dry underneath all this." She pulled off her bulky rain jacket, boots, and finally the rain pants.

"I think you lost three sizes just now." Bree took the boots and set them out on the covered porch.

"Those were Leo's clothes. Too big for me, but I love being dry." After smoothing out her jeans, dark green sweater, and brown-and-green flannel shirt, Margery decided she'd worn exactly the right clothes to the rustic lodge. Thanks to Angie digging through the Cosantir's stock of clothing, she'd been able to dither over what to wear. It'd made her feel so...female. So normal.

Bree led the way to the fireplace sitting area. "Come and sit by the fire. I have hot chocolate and the cookies are just out of the oven."

"I never turn down cookies." In fact, no Dogwood villager would turn down a dessert—not after eleven years of oatmeal, vegetable soup, and thin stew. Sweets had been nonexistent.

Following Bree, Margery looked around. The downstairs

was huge with a reception desk and office in the front left, a book-filled room to the right. In the center, stairs separated the sitting areas on each side. A long dining room had windows overlooking a stream—and probably the kitchen to one side.

The masculinity of oversized leather couches and chairs was softened by colorful throw quilts and pillows. In the glass-fronted fireplace, a fire snapped cheerfully. Margery took a seat on a chair and held out her chilled hands. "Oh, that's lovely."

Bree grinned. "Isn't it though? During the winter, I live on the hearth." She filled two mugs of hot chocolate from a massive insulated pitcher.

How much liquid did Bree think they would drink? But it was great stuff. Dark chocolate, rich and creamy, and there was a bowl of mini marshmallows just for fun. "You are an amazing hostess."

"Hostessing is my thing." Bree plopped some marshmallows in her mug. "I used to be a Seattle chef. Now, I bake pastries for Angie's diner, make the breakfasts here—as well as provide food for the lodge's patio parties."

"That seems like..."

"Coming down in the world?" Bree stretched her feet out toward the fire. "In a way. In the city, I had status, but what I really wanted was to belong. To have a family. Here, I have Zeb and Shay, a wolf pack for family, and a community of shifters. I've never been so happy." Contentment radiated from her like warmth from the fireplace.

"I'm glad for you." A bit of envy was to be expected...

because Margery would never have all that. At least not the mates. Males liked beauty, not scarred cripples. She'd settle for somewhere to belong and acceptance. "So, tell me, what does a new pack female need to know?"

Bree lifted a clipboard and waggled her eyebrows. "I have a list."

She actually did.

There were pack runs before the full moon and occasionally in-between. Mandatory service hours, but she could choose whether to help with the injured, the elders, or the cubs.

Margery stomped on her first response—the injured. "Cubs. Absolutely." Hey, it wasn't a lie. She adored pups.

After covering who to call for help and for transportation, Bree warned about hellhounds, especially during the dark of the moon.

Hellhounds. In Ailill Ridge, there had been a hellhound attack in December. The cahirs had managed to kill it, but not before five shifters had been torn apart. She'd never seen anything as savage as their deaths. At least the two other victims and the cahirs had lived. She'd done her best to sew them up, but there would still be some scarring.

"I think that's everything." Bree ran her finger down the checklist on the clipboard and shook her head. "I'm still learning alpha female duties."

"The one before you didn't help?"

"Hardly." Bree scowled. "The pack was a mess when Shay took it over. The alpha had let his crazy-vicious beta prey on females. His—*their*—behavior warped the pack culture, and we've been trying to fix things ever since."

Maybe this pack had problems, but...

"At least you're trying." Roger and his betas weren't. "Um. Shay said something about a mentor?"

"Your mentor, mmmhmm. He should be here soon to take you for a run."

Soon? Wait...*he*?

They'd assigned her a *male*? "But—"

A knock interrupted her protest, the door opened, and Darcy walked in.

"Darcy!" Margery almost flew across the room—and realized her friend was carrying a baby.

A baby?

Bree barely had time to take the cubling before Darcy grabbed Margery for a hug. "Gods, I've missed you."

At the hard, encompassing hug, tears filled Margery's eyes, blurring the room. Eventually, she pulled back and wiped her eyes, then realized someone else had entered. "Sorry. I hardly saw Darcy after our escape."

"Everyone got scattered," Darcy grumbled. "And the Cosantir told me I couldn't visit anyone until spring."

"Well, it's spring. I heard you have mates now, but...a cub already?" Margery tried to count out the months in her head and came up short.

Darcy laughed

So did a petite, dark-haired female who held two more babies. "The cub isn't Darcy's. All three of these are mine."

Margery did a double take. "I know you, don't I?"

"From that night at the compound." The female looked down at the cubs in her arms and at the one Bree had taken. "I'm Vicki, and two of these cubs are alive because you kept them safe from the Scythe. Thank you."

Uneasy with praise for what she hadn't thought twice about, Margery moved her shoulders in a small shrug. "No thanks needed. Anyone would have done the same. Cubs are what it's all about."

Vicki's slow smile made her beautiful. "If everyone realized that, the world would be a better place."

"Hey, if greetings are done, I have cookies." Carrying the cub, Bree shooed everyone to the sitting area.

Ah-hah, that's why there's an entire pitcher of hot chocolate and extra mugs.

When one of the kitlings in Vicki's arms squeaked and kicked little feet, cub-craving overwhelmed Margery. "Can I hold one? Please?"

"Absolutely. This is Sorcha."

Sorcha? Heather's Sorcha? The kitling had fluffy golden hair not much longer than fur, and eyes edging toward green. When Margery cuddled her close, the little girl gave a sigh and fell asleep.

As everyone took the couches and chair, Margery settled onto a mound of soft pillows and blankets by the fireplace. From the human-sized indentations, the blanket-pile was a favorite napping spot.

The females talked about the babies, then all the babies

in Cold Creek, before letting the conversation range: the Scythe proving difficult to locate, problems with the wolf pack, a hellhound possibly in the territory, new-shifter antics.

Vicki talked about her fifteen-year-old stepdaughter, Jamie. "The girl's insane. She and a couple of her werecat friends are leaping around in the tops of trees. Jumping from branch to branch. Making what they call *treeways*."

Darcy had escaped the Scythe compound using a path high in the trees. Margery pointed at her. "I bet the younglings are trying to imitate you."

"Not me, uh-uh." Darcy's long black hair rippled with the vehement shake of her head.

"Yes, *you*." Vicki snorted. "You're the kiddies' new role model, woman."

Darcy frowned. "Tree trails aren't safe, especially for clumsy new shifters."

"No kidding. Last night, I was at the grocery when a mama hunted down Donal. Her pup had missed a branch and broken his arm." Bree snickered. "You should have heard Donal fuming about suicidal cubs starting on new fads."

"His language is even more inventive than my old drill sergeant's." Vicki grinned. "But he's fucking good at healing."

"You're so lucky to have him. Even a skilled banfasa can't do—" Recalling herself, Margery shut her mouth.

"Banfasa?" Vicki asked.

"Tynan said a banfasa is like a nurse practitioner and medic," Bree explained.

"I only met the Dogwood banfasa once," Darcy said. "She was Margery's grandmother. People said Margery had been helping in the clinic since the day she learned to walk."

Margery looked away. Grandmama had died in her clinic, fighting the Scythe.

"That's why the human nurse practitioner in the Scythe compound grabbed Margery to be her assistant. And why the Scythe let her tend everyone after Phyllis was gone." Darcy smiled at Margery. "Caring for people is in your blood."

No, she wasn't going to get caught in that trap again. "I'm even better at waitressing," Margery said lightly. "It's where I belong."

Vicki eyed her.

Margery looked down at Sorcha. "Hmm. Smells like someone needs her diaper changed."

"All of them, undoubtedly." Vicki rose. "Bree, do you have a spot I can use?"

"Sure. C'mon."

"I'll help," Darcy said. "If I get more cookies."

Margery considered joining them, but if she was going to be running with this mentor person, she'd better rest her ankle. "Have fun. I'm going to take a nap right here, me and the salamanders."

"You rest, then we'll dump the pups on you when we

come back." Darcy picked up Sorcha and told the other two females, "Margery is a cubling tranquilizer."

As their voices drifted away, Margery gave a sigh. The fire was warm, the blanket-mound unbelievably soft, and she had really worked hard at the diner.

She roused somewhat when little bodies were tucked in around her and cuddled them close before clouds of sleep engulfed her again.

Following his littermate into the Wildwood Lodge, Donal saw the females socializing around the fireplace. Not surprising. Breanne loved company and took any excuse to feed someone. In fact, the aroma of something sweet hung in the air.

Cookies? The day's looking up.

Until he saw the black-haired, troublemaker named Darcy. He snarled. "You."

She blinked, all innocence, although her lips quirked. "Me?"

"You're a menace, you are. Trees are for perching and sunning, not for leaping around as if the Gods had made a freeway system in the canopy."

"Sorry, Donal." Her innocent look wouldn't fool a pup, let alone a healer.

He growled under his breath.

Tynan had the temerity to chuckle. "Be warned, Darcy. He's grumpier than a badger today."

Even the Cosantir's mate was grinning. Catching his glare, Vicki held up a hand. "We're not heartless, Donal, really. But Tynan wouldn't be laughing if someone had died."

Bree, the sweetest of females, looked worried. "Did someone else get hurt?"

Donal sat beside *her*—the only nice one of the bunch. "I was the one who wanted to die." He leaned back, letting the peace of the lodge ease his irritation. "The cub with a broken bone wasn't a problem. Brave lad. But the next one... Idiot wolf pup. Lacking real claws, he *slid* all the way down the trunk and got scraped from chin to crotch. And he didn't stop yelling, even after I'd healed every scratch. By Herne's hairy balls, my ears are still ringing."

The heartless females in the room gave him no sympathy. Even Breanne had her hand over her mouth and was chortling like a drunken pixie.

"Poor Donal." Darcy grinned before asking, "Doesn't Margery live next door to you? Next time you have a screamer, get her."

Donal had no intention of opening that can of worms, but Tynan tilted his head. "Why's that, Darcy?"

"She can calm nearly anyone down, especially cubs." Darcy gestured toward a mass of blankets and pillows by the hearth.

After a second, Donal realized Margery was nestled deep in the pile, curled around Vicki's cubs, all of them sound asleep. Artair had his tiny hand wrapped around one of her fingers; Toren had gripped a strand of her wavy brown hair.

"There's a pretty sight," Tynan said softly.

Aye, it is.

Donal frowned. The slashed-up younglings at the tavern had clung to her in the same way. *Interesting.* If she was as heartless and self-centered as Gretchen and Caleb had said, why were the young so drawn to her?

"She'd try to calm the Scythe guards that way. Sometimes, it worked." Darcy's expression turned bleak. "If they were hitting one of the younger children, she'd always try."

Tynan's voice had an edge. "And if she didn't succeed?"

"Then she got bruises and welts right along with the original victim."

Yet she hadn't stopped intervening after the first time she failed?

Intrigued, Donal studied the banfasa. Hair the brown of warm pecan, light golden skin. Sturdy bones. Scars on the backs of her hands and arms.

So many scars. He frowned. The long scar on her face bothered him every time he saw it. If he'd been there, he could have prevented that.

She was sleeping as soundly as the cubs. "She looks exhausted."

"She had an evening shift at the diner last night, then worked the morning and lunch hours for a waitress who had a problem." Breanne pointed at Donal. "The waitress's child broke an arm climbing a tree, and some bossy healer told her to stay home to keep the child quiet."

Everyone broke into laughter.

"Margery is cuddling all three babies." Tynan turned a dark gaze on Vicki. "I had to charm you for *weeks* before you let me hold even one of your cubs."

"Margery can have them anytime she wants. They're alive because of her."

"What?" Donal frowned.

The hardened ex-military female's voice was shaky. "At the Scythe compound, we tried to sneak to the garage. I was in panther form, so the other females carried the babies. Margery had Artair, but Sorcha started crying. Margery took her to quiet—"

Darcy grinned and raised her eyebrows. "See?"

"You're right. Sorcha calmed down the second Margery had her."

Donal's gut was tight. There was more to the story. "But there was trouble?"

"A guard heard." Vicki's hands fisted. "He grabbed for Sorcha, and Margery kicked him away. The fucking asshole swung a cane at Artair, but Margery twisted. Took the blows instead."

"Damn." Tynan's soft curse echoed what Donal felt.

Damn, indeed. That night still troubled Donal's dreams. How could anyone, human or shifter, harm a cubling?

Bree eyed Vicki. "How long did that guard live?"

Vicki smiled, but her eyes were cold. She'd been in the

human military and was now a werecat. Undoubtedly, the guard had died messily under her claws.

Well fucking done.

The door of the lodge swung open with a thud, and Shay walked in. "You're having a party without me?"

The noise roused Margery, and she sat up, yawning. Blinked sleepily at Shay and Donal. Saw Tynan and froze. Face pale, she moved to put her body between him and the pups.

By the Gods, what is she doing?

Tynan noticed—of course he did. The cop never missed anything. His jaw went tight.

And his eyes soft.

Too soft. Donal stiffened. Sure, it was obvious that Margery was brave. Good with cubs. That didn't make her trustworthy. The Rainier Territory shifters had painted a picture of an irresponsible, incompetent banfasa.

If Tynan was interested, the situation could get ugly. *Bloody hell.*

Even worse, Donal couldn't blame his brother. The female was incredibly appealing.

Jostled by Margery's movement, a cub roused and squeaked. Unable to resist, Donal went over, planning to scoop up a baby.

Margery blocked him with an outstretched arm. Pale, smelling of anxiety and fear, she didn't move her hand until she had a nod from Vicki.

He liked the way she protected the cubs and would have

said so, but she looked away. Dismissing him from her notice. Well, fair was fair. After all, he'd told Calum that he didn't want her help.

He picked up Sorcha—his favorite. Moving away, he rubbed his cheek over her golden hair and grinned as she gurgled at him. Without a mate, he'd never have the joy of raising cubs, of sharing in the thrill of the first word, first step, first trawsfur.

The knowledge hurt a little more each year.

At least as a healer, he got to hold as many kitlings as he wanted. Inhaling Sorcha's milky scent, Donal shook his hair to make it dance. She chortled and waved her tiny hands in delight. This one was much like Alec—she loved to laugh.

Tynan had a soft spot for babies and had already nabbed Artair. Donal watched him with eyes and healer senses. Being back in the Gods' domain had restored Tynan's health, and the deeply carved lines had almost disappeared from his face.

Daonain didn't do well in human cities. Wolves didn't do well alone.

And brothers were meant to be together. The return of his littermate was like receiving rain after a long ugly drought.

Donal touched Sorcha's fuzzy hair. Like Vicki, he'd bring out his claws if anything or anyone tried to separate him from his family.

His mood lightened as Shay coaxed Toren away from Margery.

When Breanne saw her mate cuddling the tiny boy, her face turned soft.

Donal eyed her with professional interest. Lifemating upped the odds of a pregnancy, and Breanne would make a fine mother.

Now unencumbered, Margery pushed her hair out of her face and gave Bree an apologetic look. "I'm sorry, Bree. I didn't intend to fall asleep."

"You needed the rest." Bree pushed the platter of cookies toward her. "Here, sugar-up before Tynan takes you on your run."

Margery's hand stopped halfway to the plate. "Tynan?"

"Yes, he's your mentor." Shay reached over Bree's shoulder to snag himself a couple of cookies.

"No," Margery snapped. "Absolutely not."

Donal frowned. Why in the Hunter's forest would the female not want his littermate? There could be no better wolf, no better mentor for her. For anyone.

Curious, he leaned forward. "What do you have against Tynan?"

Margery ignored the healer. Why should she speak to someone who openly disliked her? Even if he *was* God-called. Even if he made her hormones pick up each time she saw him.

He could still go take a long leap into an icy pond.

Instead, she told Shay, "Pick a different mentor. Please."

"'Fraid not. Tynan is well experienced." The alpha's gaze held more amusement than sympathy. "Try not to kill him. The Cosantir frowns on that sort of behavior."

Her anger and fear rose until her hands were starting to shake...and the alpha was making *jokes?*

When she turned to Tynan, she couldn't see anything except his uniform shirt. His badge.

She tried to talk reason to the cold terror flooding her veins. The male had been nice. Polite. He'd rescued her from Roger. He wasn't a Scythe.

Maybe he'd protest and tell the alpha that it was impossible to teach a cripple? That's what her mentor in Rainier had done.

One more try. She forced a smile. "Tynan, I'm sure I'll be fine with a less experienced mentor. I know you're busy and—"

"Not that busy." He brushed his fingertips over Artair's round cheek. How could such big hands be so gentle? His clear blue gaze turned to her. "Training is something I enjoy, whether it's inexperienced police officers or newly shifted cubs. And I haven't had the joy of teaching cubs in a long time."

"I'm not a cub," she huffed.

"No, you're not," he murmured. The masculine appreciation in his eyes made her blink.

After handing Artair to Vicki, he turned back to Margery. "Let's be off, lass. I'll show you the portal here at the lodge. Donal, if you'd take our clothing to the Wild

Hunt when you leave, I'll show her *that* portal on our return. Take her bike, too."

Donal hissed under his breath. "Sssst, do I look like a dwarf to be hauling your loads around?"

"Aye, now, and you have the right of it." Tynan tilted his head. "I never noticed the resemblance before. Perhaps it's a beard you should grow."

The healer scowled...yet his lips quirked up. "Go on then. I'll be here eating cookies while you're out getting your fur soaked."

"Then, my dear brother, don't be whining to me when your arse grows fat." As everyone burst into laughter, Tynan motioned for Margery to rise.

Damn, there was no way out. An alpha's orders had to be obeyed.

As she rose to her feet, anger rose inside her as well. Toward the obstinate alpha.

Toward herself because her ankle was so tired she couldn't conceal the hitch in her gait.

Toward stubborn mentors who wore a uniform—and made jokes that forced her to remember he wasn't a Scythe guard.

Tynan led the way to the back of the lodge, turned left down a short hallway, past a laundry room, and finally to a small room at the end. "This is where you'll strip, trawsfur, and take to the forest during pack runs."

"Oh, joy. Pack runs," she said under her breath. In the far corner, she started to remove her clothing.

He chuckled. "Yes, little wolf, pack runs."

Oh Gods, how had she forgotten the keenness of shifter hearing? Holding her shirt and bra in one hand, she couldn't seem to move. "I-I'm sorry."

"Lass, you're allowed to have feelings." Tynan waited until she sat to pull off her socks before continuing, "Wolves usually look forward to the pack runs. The sense of being part of something is fulfilling. It's rough when we don't have our brothers and sisters nearby."

His voice held a note that spoke of loneliness.

Surprised, she looked up. And kept looking. *Dear Goddess...*

He'd removed his uniform shirt. One foot on the bench, he was unlacing his boot. His body was made for strength and power, from his corded neck to thick pectoral muscles to a ridged abdomen. His chest held a light brown scattering of hair, and his fair skin was lightly tanned—all over.

She... How could she possibly want to touch someone so much even when he scared her?

When he stripped off his jeans, his shaft lay, long and thick, in front of heavy testicles. And it was impossible not to look.

Ignoring her gaze, he pointed to the wall shelves. "Normally, you'd leave your clothing there, but today, we'll pile everything on the bench so Donal knows what to take."

Shifters weren't body-conscious, she told herself, even as she felt her breasts jiggle as if to draw attention to how big they were. Too big.

Did males like big breasts? He had big hands. What would they— Why was she even thinking like this? Her cheeks blazed with heat. Hurriedly, she finished stripping. Moving to the bench to stack her clothing tidily, she felt his gaze on her bare bottom.

How could a female walk normally when a male—a commanding male like this one—was looking at her?

"Come over here and memorize this." Standing to one side of the door so she could see, he slowly punched in a lock code and waited for her nod. The door unlocked, and he opened it, waiting for her to walk through.

She stepped outside, the ground cold beneath her bare feet. The rain clouds had moved on, leaving patchy blue sky above. The setting sun slanted redly through the trees.

Turning in a circle, she saw only tall, thick underbrush and conifers. No one would be able to glimpse a shifter changing forms. "This is nice."

"Aye. Thick brush." His blue eyes lit with laughter. "Any curious human would have to go on hands and knees to get through."

A snort of amusement escaped her as she imagined Scythe guards crawling head-to-butt in a long line along the tiny animal track. "What now?"

"We'll go catch some dinner and stay out long enough to let you get a feel for the landmarks."

He'd undoubtedly watch to see how badly she did. Well, if he was like her first mentor, the lesson wouldn't last long.

His gaze held hers as if he could see her doubts. "Shift, please."

As Margery trawsfurred into her wolf, the Mother's love swept from her paws straight to her heart in the welcoming every Daonain received when changing to animal form. Skin tingling, she gave her fur a shake.

Oh, she did love being a wolf. She pranced a few steps on her paws, reminding herself she had four legs, before looking around.

Still in human form, Tynan was watching. Going down on his haunches, he reached for her hind leg. The bad one.

When she started to sidle away, he simply looked at her. "Let me look, lass."

And she stilled.

He picked up her leg. His hands were warm and careful as he palpated the injured joint, undoubtedly feeling the scar tissue, the misalignment, the swelling.

With a grunt, he set her paw down carefully. "You have some heat and swelling there."

Waitressing wasn't the best career for messed-up ankles.

She looked away.

Firmly, he cupped her muzzle and forced her to meet his eyes. "We'll take it easy, and you let me know if it starts to hurt. You can hide your limp if you wish, but as your mentor, I need to know when an injury becomes more than a bother. Or when you get tired. Is this understood?"

His stern eyes were direct. Level.

And her gaze dropped immediately. He was an alpha even without having a pack.

Realizing he waited for her answer, she looked up and flickered her ears forward in agreement.

"Good." His lips curved slightly, then he ruffled the fur on her nape, making every bone in her body go limp with unexpected pleasure. Strong fingers scratched behind her ears, along her spine. "Having been injured a time or two, I know a few tricks on how to manage with a hurt leg. I'll tell you if I see something that'll help."

Rising, he shifted into a heavily muscled wolf. Fur the silvery gray of exposed mountain granite shimmered in the setting sun. He was even bigger than Roger. *Wow.*

He circled her, sniffing. His shoulder brushed down her side, sharing his scent in the wolf manner of getting acquainted. Unlike Roger and his betas, Tynan didn't "stalk"; his wolf simply exuded strength. He had an alpha personality without the need to assert his power.

She'd never met anyone quite like him.

He nuzzled her ear, sending tingles from her ruff to her tail, and then trotted off down an almost concealed trail. Expecting her to follow.

And she did.

She used her nose to read the trail news. The scent of other shifters gave information about their general health, gender, and age.

A rodent cowered in the underbrush.

A non-Daonain bear had crossed the path to reach a

nearby stream. The bear had caught a fish and dined on the riverbank, leaving the wet stink behind.

Slowly, Tynan increased their pace to an easy trot, one she could maintain for a long time. Eventually, they hit rougher terrain—downed trees, pools of water—that slowed her. He watched her navigate the obstacles with calm yellow-brown eyes that spurred her on to do her best.

In an area of loose rocks, he shifted to human to instruct on moving her weight forward to provide better balance. He didn't insult her even once.

Over the course of the evening, she relaxed. She caught two rodents for her supper, and he gave her some hints on tracking and pouncing. He had her practice a neck-snap technique to kill small prey. It was more efficient—and cleaner—than the crunch method she'd used.

She'd never met anyone so patient.

At a small mountain lake, Tynan shifted to human...and took her breath away again. When he went down on one knee at the lake, she couldn't keep from staring. From his broad back to flat butt to heavy thighs, he was *all* muscle.

Bending, he washed off the blood from his own kills and drank some water. He caught her watching, and his quick grin transformed his stern face. Changed everything about him. "Deep in wolf-brain, I don't notice the blood, but if I think about being human, then I feel like I rubbed my face in blood."

She ran her tongue over her bloody muzzle. *Ick.* Trawsfurring, she joined him on the bank. When she knelt beside him, she noticed—again—how very big he was. Yet he'd been nothing but nice to her. Kind.

A vigorous face scrub was wonderful. Honestly, even her teeth felt icky, and she drank a ton of the snow-cold lake water before sitting back with a sigh. "Thank you for teaching me the neck-snap thing."

"You're very welcome." Rising, he leaned a shoulder against a young sapling. "The basics of hunting are usually taught in the first few outings." His voice was gentle, very carefully nonjudgmental.

She bit her lip. Exposing how the others felt about her problems was embarrassing. "My previous mentor felt that teaching me hunting skills—or most skills—was a waste of her time. Since I'm handicapped."

Tynan's face hardened to resemble the rocky cliffs towering over the lake. "Skills come in different levels and are never a waste of time. You can quite obviously hunt."

"I learned from watching, although thanks to you, I'll be better at it after tonight." Which was so awesome. With a happy sigh, she sat back on the damp grass. Her butt would be freezing soon, but she was still toasty warm from trotting up the steep trail.

"Margery." He stopped and shook his head. "I swear you look more like a Meggie to me."

Meggie. The name brought grief sweeping through before it passed into nostalgic warmth. "That's what my grandmother called me."

He waited, patient as the hunter she'd seen him to be.

"I like Meggie."

"Right, then. Meggie." He stood with his back against the tree, gaze on the lake, obviously enjoying the night.

The beautiful night. The waning moon hadn't risen yet. The stars were bright in the black sky with a hazy Milky Way along one side. As a breeze rustled the alder leaves, the lake lapped softly at the bank.

She smiled and let the peace of the night engulf her.

Not yet feeling the cold, Tynan stood quietly, breathing in the moist night air. Nothing was pushing or pulling at him. His mind hadn't shut off, but he didn't feel the need to be doing anything.

Peace. That's what he felt. Simple...peace.

Resting against the tree trunk, he savored the feeling.

It couldn't last forever, and after a few minutes, the chill broke into Tynan's quiet. The air was too brisk to stay human for long.

He looked down at the little female at the center of the pool of calm. Sitting on the grassy bank.

So pretty. Dark hair, big eyes, and a determined jawline. Compellingly full breasts. Curves that he'd love to enjoy under a full moon. Or any time at all.

With a sigh, he turned his thoughts away from that line of thought.

Mentor, remember?

Right. Okay, then. She had healthy, sturdy legs...with scars.

Despite the dark night, wolf eyes could discern the appalling number of white lines on her skin. "Can you tell me how your ankle was injured?"

She froze like a rabbit spotting an eagle overhead, making his protective instincts roar to life.

Fecking git, why had he let his mouth ask that question? "I'm sorry, that was out of line."

After a second, she gave him a wry smile. "Was it out of line? I haven't quite figured out where the boundaries lie. In the compound, we weren't allowed to speak to each other, so my knowledge of even basic manners, let alone traditions, can come up short."

Ah, he hadn't considered that handicap of imprisonment. Something else a good mentor should probably tackle. He rubbed his shoulder against the tree as he considered how to answer. "My question wasn't completely out of line for a mentor. At the same time, it was...because you're not yet comfortable with me."

She nodded.

"As for the Daonain culture... Shifters, especially cats, are curious. Wolves stick their noses into anything having to do with pack members. In comparison, humans hide their bodies and emotions. Perhaps because of our animals, Daonain show more and worry about it less."

"That's...the most coherent explanation I've heard."

He grinned. "When I went to live in Seattle, human

behavior surprised me every day. After being there for a decade, now I can find it bumpy to be among shifters. So I do understand some of what you and the other hostages are experiencing."

Her eyes narrowed. "Did the alpha figure that into his calculations when he assigned me to you?"

Smart females were so fucking appealing. "Shay weighs things out before he acts."

"I bet you two are a lot alike." Her shoulders straightened—and, aye, being a healthy male, he enjoyed the wobble of her full breasts. He could almost feel the weight of them in his palms.

No, mentor.

Pulling in a determined breath, she touched her ankle. "To answer your question, my ankle was broken soon after they let us out of the basement laboratories. We were weeding one of the vegetable gardens. Barbara—my friend —had never gardened. After a guard backhanded her for pulling a broccoli seedling, she was too scared to move. I got caught whispering to her, and the guard started hitting me with his cane. When I begged for him to stop, another guard joined in."

A decade ago. Meggie couldn't have been much older than thirteen. Tynan's lingering guilt over killing Scythe guards disappeared. "The second guard broke your ankle?"

"I'm not sure which of them did." Her hand tightened on her leg. "Darcy yelled at them. Shoved them away. They beat her—horribly—and came back to me. I guess I was an example to the others. By the time they finished, I had a lot of broken bones."

Unable to speak past the growl in his throat, he watched as she unconsciously touched the long scar on her face, her arms, her ribs, her legs.

"The uniforms locked me and Darcy up for days. Left us. I'm still surprised we survived."

"I'm glad you did." *Uniforms?* A sick taste fouled Tynan's mouth. Was that what she thought when she looked at him when he was dressed as a deputy? That he could be the type to brutalize children and females?

Fuck him, but he wasn't going to let her continue to think that way. Not about uniforms. Not about him.

"Come, Meggie. It's getting late. Time to head back to town."

A while later, Tynan watched the little female as she followed him through an unmelted patch of snow. Her gait had slowed. She held her left hind leg off the ground—obviously because it hurt.

Despite his order earlier, she hadn't said anything about growing tired or hurting. Next time, he'd watch her more closely...and choose a shorter route.

At the clearing outside the Wild Hunt caves, he paused so she could get a good sniff and orient herself. She understood, and her tail wagged as she looked around. Next time, he'd make her prove she could find the lodge and the tavern portals again.

Once in the cave, he sniffed out their clothing. Donal had stuffed the bundles into one of the carved-out cubbies in the rock walls. Good brother.

Tynan trawsfurred and winced. Bare feet on an ice-cold cave floor.

After shifting to human, Meggie stood, keeping her weight on her good leg. Her smile was so bright she could have brought an early spring to the mountains. "That was wonderful. I learned so much. Thank you!"

He leaned against the cave wall as interest heated his blood. Not because she was a naked female—although, she really was lovely—but the way she took joy in the simplest things was incredibly appealing.

"I'm glad you enjoyed the run." Smiling, he pointed out her clothing and started dressing. "Are you off tomorrow?"

"In the afternoon. Will that work for you?" She sat on a bench to pull on her jeans. Because her left leg probably wouldn't hold her weight by itself.

Pity made his heart ache.

"Late afternoon will work well." He set the rest of her clothing beside her so she wouldn't have to stand again, then pulled on his jeans.

"Meggie, I can see you're in pain." He kept his voice soft. "Next time, tell me when your ankle begins to hurt. We should have stopped earlier."

As he waited for her answer, he donned and buttoned his shirt.

"It's not that bad. It's that—" After looking up, she jumped to her feet and backed away. Her hands were in fists.

He turned and saw no predator in the cave. A sniff confirmed his visual check.

No, she was staring...at him. At his uniform shirt and badge. By Herne's hooves and antlers. He'd hoped their time together would remove her fear of him.

But once again—because of his uniform—she acted like he was a Scythe guard. Perhaps he should be grateful he'd left his firearm and weapons belt locked in his vehicle.

"Meggie," he said gently. "I wear this shirt and badge because I've sworn to protect people. The opposite of what the Scythe did."

"Sure, sure. I know that." She took another step away from him.

But her hands were fisted, her muscles tensed. She was as likely to punch him as to run.

He doubted she realized that. How much rage did she have stored inside? Oftentimes, a victim would blindly lash out, not at their abuser, but at another who'd triggered the response. If Meggie attacked someone in law enforcement, she'd get locked up—and being a shifter, might well die in a jail cell.

Even more terrifying, if she lost control and trawsfurred

in front of humans, the Cosantir would have her killed for endangering the Daonain.

The world was filled with uniforms. She needed to get past this reaction and quickly.

He pointed to the bench. "Finish getting dressed, please, so we can leave." Giving her space, he walked to the cave opening and waited with his back to her.

"I'm done." She was standing by the bench. Still pale. "I'm...sorry."

"We'll talk about it another time. Let me show you how to access the doors in and out of the cave." He climbed the stairs. The heavy door at the top opened into a closet. After showing her how to operate the locking mechanism from the other side, he took her through the sitting room. "The door from the hallway is always locked unless there's a Gathering here."

He demonstrated how to work the combination-lock and made sure she had the code memorized.

"Good." Past the tiny kitchen, restrooms, and the stairs to the second floor Gathering rooms, the hallway opened into the main tavern.

It was late with only a few people remaining. Probably expecting Tynan's report on the new pack member, Shay and Zeb were talking to Donal by the fireplace. Calum was behind the bar. Ryder was playing chess with Thorson. No humans were in the room.

Perfect. If needed, the alpha could help calm Meggie.

If Tynan pushed her too far.

His gut tensed a protest at what he was about to do.

"Donal's here so we'll give you a ride home." Tynan stepped closer to Meggie.

"No." As he'd expected, she jerked back. She stumbled on her sore ankle. "I'll bike."

Even knowing the origins of her antipathy, it burned after the comradery of the last few hours.

"No, ye will *not* bike home." He raised his voice to ensure the tavern occupants were listening.

When Calum's eyes narrowed, Tynan shot him a look. *Stay out of this.* The Cosantir didn't speak—but his stillness was that of a cat ready to engage.

"You need to give your ankle a rest." Tynan crossed his arms over his chest—drawing Meggie's gaze back to his uniform. He tapped a finger on his badge. "I'm in charge here."

Her body stiffened. The furious, fearful look in her eyes said she saw only his uniform, not him.

Come, little wolf. Lose your temper. He added a taunting edge to his voice. "You're getting a ride, like it or not."

"You don't have any say over me." Even as she snapped out the words, her body tensed against a blow.

"I'm your mentor. I have all the say over you."

Buzzing filled Margery's brain until she wasn't sure what she was hearing. Could only see the badge on the guard's chest.

She wanted to hit him, to kick him, and to run and run and escape the beating he'd give her.

"*Margery*." The sharp authoritative tone made her take a step back.

Her fisted hands rose.

"You don't like me." The badge kept getting bigger.

She tried to find the calm that had worked on the guards before. "I'm sure you're—"

"Don't bullshit me, female. By the Gods, you don't even see my face, only the uniform. You hate it, don't you?"

"Yes." The word hissed out.

"Yes, what?" He stepped forward and pushed her shoulder.

She punched his arm away. "Don't touch me."

No, what was she *doing?* Her pulse hammered, hurting her chest. She knew better, knew what he'd—

He shoved her again. Harder. "What's the matter, little female? You going to let a *uniform* take over your world?"

"Stop it." Her brain roared with anger as her vision filled with the glittering badge. Nothing else existed...just the evilness of it.

He pushed her again, making her stumble, as if to drive home she was a cripple. "What are you going to do about it?"

The taunting voice wrapped around her, drowning out everything else except the red of fury. *Badge. Uniform. The guards. Hurting her. Killing her friends.*

Screaming, she hit him. Hit him over and over, slamming her fists into his chest, the horrible uniform a target for every blow.

Someone was yelling, "No, no, no," punctuating every slam of her fists—

And the person yelling was her.

Her.

She'd lost all control. Lost...everything.

Tears filled her eyes as she stared at the wide chest, not seeing the uniform, but...a chest. *Tynan.* A sob stuck in her throat as dismay and guilt—and loss—filled her. She'd hit the mentor who'd been nothing but kind to her.

"What's my name, little wolf?" His voice was calm as a summer lake, the lilt of his Irish accent like white froth on the water. Where was his anger?

"Meggie. What's my name?"

"T-Tynan."

"Good. Say it again."

"Tynan." Realization swept through her, and she choked. "You did that on purpose. Wanted me to hit you."

"Aye."

"Bu-but why?"

"Ye need to realize a uniform is merely a piece of cloth. To look past it and see the person wearing it. *Then* decide if they're evil or not."

A sob escaped her, and his expression turned gentle. "Ah, lass." His arms came around her, pulling her against the chest she'd been beating on.

And he held her as her world fell apart, while she could only cry.

Tynan scooped up the soft female he'd started to think might be the one to break him...because her crying was dredging aching hollows into his heart.

Fuck, he hated what he'd done, but when she'd finally looked at him and seen past the uniform, he knew he'd been right.

Even if she hated him after this.

He'd do anything to keep her safe, even from herself.

When he carried her to the fireplace sitting area, Donal moved from the couch to a chair so Meggie could be closer to the fire's warmth.

On the other couch, Shay was still in place, although Zeb had retreated to the bar. The dark, taciturn cahir didn't handle a female's tears well.

In law enforcement, Tynan had dealt with more than his fair share of crying women. He envied the way they could release their emotions like springtime thunderstorms cleared away a winter's debris.

But Meggie had more than a season's emotions built up. Settling her more comfortably on his lap, he cuddled her close and stroked her back. There wasn't much else a male could do than provide a safe shelter.

And there wasn't anything more rewarding than to *be* that safe shelter.

The silence from the room drew his attention.

At the bar, Calum gave Tynan a measured nod. Apparently, the Cosantir had decided not to kill him and return him to the Mother.

Shay eyed him, coldly. The alpha's nature was akin to Tynan's—protect the vulnerable. "Those were drastic measures."

"Drastic is the correct word." Tynan rubbed his cheek against Meggie's silky soft hair. The tears had stopped, and she was in the half-drowsy aftermath of violent emotions and exhaustion. "I'd hoped you were right that spending time with me in fur would help. But the minute I dressed, my badge and uniform triggered her. And I realized she was as volatile and angry as she was fearful. If she attacked a uniformed human, well..."

Shay's mouth tightened. "I see your point."

"So you set her off?" Donal's scowl was directed at Meggie. "If she'd had a knife, I'd be trying to heal you—or bring you back from the dead."

Fuck. Donal had focused on her attack, rather than the reason behind it. That wasn't like his soft-hearted littermate. Then again, after their time apart, Donal tended to act like a cougar defending its cub.

"I checked her for weapons. It's not her fault, Donal." Tynan kissed the top of her head. "It's time to call it a night and head home."

"Yes, it really is." Donal's words didn't conceal the

underlying snarl. He rose to his feet, movements stiff. One cat who wouldn't be letting down his guard.

Shay nodded. "Can you drop by the Wildwood tomorrow?" The alpha wanted his update.

"Aye. In the morning." Tynan rose and half-smiled when Meggie startled awake.

"Tynan?" She looked up at him. Seeing *him*.

"I think I won the argument that you'll accept a ride home." He smiled down at her, keeping her in his arms. By the Gods, she fit right there...perfectly, so soft and female. "It's not like you're out of the way, aye?"

"Gods, you're stubborn," she muttered. Sighed. And whispered, "Thank you."

CHAPTER EIGHT

C old Creek, North Cascades Territory - Beltane - waning crescent moon

Following the posted signs and the sounds of people, Margery walked around the side of the Wildwood Lodge to the back patio.

Bree had said that every other Sunday during the warm season, the lodge held barbecues, open to their guests and the town. Today was special since it was Beltane—or what the humans called May Day. If the fire festival day had arrived closer to full moon, the Cosantir would've celebrated during the Gathering, but this year, Beltane fell near the new moon.

She smiled at the bright red tulips in a bed by the side of the lodge. Farther out in a sunny patch, apple trees bloomed, casting a heady scent. Beneath them, wild straw-berries showed off their white blossoms.

Under a vine-covered arch, a middle-aged female served as the lodge's gatekeeper. Spotting Margery, she motioned her forward and said in a rough voice, "You're the new one in town. Angie's waitress, right?"

Small towns were so fun. Introductions were almost unneeded. "That's right. I'm Margery."

"Rosie. I work at the Wild Hunt. Next time you're in there, I'll buy you a beer. Us waitresses have to stick together."

Margery grinned. "We do."

"Go on in—and be warned, Breanne's drafting people to help."

"I'm up for that." A quick sniff said Rosie was a shifter. "It's an honor to serve an alpha like her."

"That's the spirit." Rosie gave an approving nod. "Bright Beltane to you."

"And you." Feeling thoroughly welcomed—and betting that Rosie and Angie were good friends—Margery walked past and stopped to get her bearings. Because...people.

Whew. She hadn't been expecting such a large party.

Along the back wall of the lodge, long tables held a wealth of food, from appetizers to desserts. Nearer at hand, Shay was turning steaks and burgers on a huge grill. A closed grill gave off the fragrance of smoked barbecue.

Across the wide patio, people at tables were eating, playing board games, and socializing. On the grassy area between the patio and the stream, cubs were playing soccer.

A darling small playground had a batch of kits swinging and bouncing and climbing. *So cute.*

"Margery, I'm glad you came." Blonde hair pulled back in a long braid, Bree hurried up and gave her a one-armed hug before stepping back to study her face. "Shay told me about the trick Tynan pulled on you at the tavern last week. Zeb said you cried. Are you all right?"

The alpha female's concern warmed Margery's heart. "I'm fine. Really."

Bree's eyes narrowed. "Tynan can be damn intimidating when he goes all authoritarian. But you're *fine.*"

"Really, I am." Although Bree had a point. The commanding cop *was* daunting. Scary.

And disconcertingly captivating. How could someone make her anxious, yet melt her insides at the same time? Every night since then, she'd dreamed of being in the circle of his hard arms, her cheek pressed against his muscular chest. What if he hadn't been trying to comfort her, but to do something else? Something...intimate?

Oh, wow.

Shaking off the unexpected carnal thoughts, she tucked her hair behind her ear. "On Friday, Tynan took me for another run and explained why he pushed me. He said if I panicked at seeing a uniform—and shifted in front of humans—it could be deadly."

Breanne's expression went tight. "He's right. Revealing

our existence is a death sentence. I almost broke that Law when I was a new shifter, and Zeb, Shay, and I came close to being terminated."

Gods, that sounded bad.

Margery puffed out a breath. "So, Tynan was right, and honestly, his intervention and explanation helped. Yesterday, I walked past the sheriff's office a bunch of times and worked on my reaction to seeing Alec and his deputy in uniforms."

There was nothing like half-panicking, over and over. However, after a few trips, she'd started to relax.

"Good for you." Responding to a greeting from across the patio, Bree smiled, started to wave, and winced.

"You're hurt."

"No. Well, maybe a little." Bree scowled at her left arm. "I chased a wood rat and caught my foreleg between a couple of rocks. I think my wrist is a bit sprained, nothing worse."

Margery held her hand out. "Let's see."

The joint was swollen, slightly warm, no obvious break. "The healer would be able to mend it right up."

The ever-so-gorgeous healer who didn't like her.

Bree grinned. "You sound like Zeb. Donal's helping at a birth, but he'll be here later."

No, Margery's pulse did *not* just pick up. She didn't want to see that grumpy, bull-headed male. "Until then, how about if I wrap it and put your arm in a sling to remind you not to use it."

"That'd be great. I keep trying to pick up pans and embarrass myself when I yelp."

After raiding the lodge's medical supplies, Margery settled Bree in a quiet corner of the kitchen and tended the injury. After the sling was on, she finished by settling an ice pack on top of the ace-wrapped wrist.

"That feels a lot better." Bree smiled as she rose. "It'd really started to ache."

"Because you kept using it." Margery glanced around the busy kitchen. "What's my assignment? Angie said the pack was helping out."

"We had no idea quite so many people would show up today. Thank the Goddess for the pack's help." Bree gave the kitchen an assessing look. "Can you take a pitcher of iced tea and refill drinks?"

"Absolutely." Margery grinned. "Waitressing has turned into one of my favorite things. It's such a great way to meet everyone."

"Thank you. And thank you, banfasa, for the tending." Bree patted the sling.

At Bree's gratitude, Margery felt as if the sun had grown brighter.

She pulled in a breath as the realization shook her. Being a banfasa was who she was. What she loved. Nothing, not even waitressing, fulfilled her quite the same way, and... face it, she missed it.

Two hours later, Margery joined three other pack females to eat.

Although *eat* was perhaps not the right word—she almost inhaled the food. "This barbecued pork is...I've never had anything so good."

Bonnie, who was a dispatcher in the sheriff's office, laughed. "You can thank Alec for that. He fostered in the south and talked one of his uncles out of the recipe."

"Did I hear my name?" The relaxed masculine voice had them all turning.

Huge male—wearing a badge, firearm, baton, uniform.

Margery froze, her hands closing on her fork, ready to...

He wasn't moving. In fact, he was holding perfectly still. Her gaze lifted to his face, to the sympathy in the dark green eyes.

Oops. She breathed out and set the weapon down. "Hi, Sheriff."

She'd seen him at the station and strolling the streets off and on yesterday. One more breath, and she could lean back. Her muscles relaxed. Thank the Goddess for Tynan and his shock therapy. "Bonnie says we have you to thank for this amazing barbecue."

"I merely persuaded the recipe out of my uncle. Shay did the actual cooking." Alec grinned. "I far prefer talking to cooking."

The sheriff was a charmer. No wonder he caught Vicki.

Margery studied the golden-brown hair, green eyes, and

easygoing smile. So familiar. "You're Sorcha's daddy, aren't you?"

A dimple appeared. "Calum and I are the sires for all of Vicki's litter, but, aye, Sorcha might have caught a few genes from me."

For few minutes, he chatted with them all before sauntering away.

And Margery realized she would no longer have trouble seeing past the uniform to the good male who wore it.

Just as she now saw Tynan rather than his badge. Even when he'd come into the diner for breakfast on Friday and Saturday mornings, she hadn't been afraid.

Okay, Margery Lavelle, admit it. There's more.

All right, yes. She'd been disconcertingly happy to see him. To hear his Irish-accented voice and to tease him and watch the way his austere face changed when he smiled.

Glancing around, she checked the party for him...again.

There he was, standing next to Zeb. Looking right at her.

His eyes were warm, and his approving nod indicated he'd seen her overcome her fears when the sheriff caught her by surprise.

Seen her victory.

Wanting nothing more than to be closer, she smiled at the other females. "I'd better get back to work before Bree tries to do it all herself."

Grinning at the groans as they agreed and rose, she headed for the kitchen. Pitcher filled with iced tea, she made the rounds...working her way over to Tynan. Laughing at herself all the way.

Obvious much, Margery?

As she filled his glass, he grinned at her. "Nice job with overcoming the panic. With Alec—and with me." He motioned to his uniform.

"Actually, I hardly notice your uniform now," she admitted. Her gaze lingered on where his shirtsleeves fit over the hard curve of his biceps.

"Good to hear, since I like being a law officer, and I'd rather not have you fleeing—or punching me—because of my badge."

When she snorted, his smile widened.

"It's pretty obvious you like what you do."

"I love it. Law enforcement—for some of us—is a calling." His eyes held a determination, a purpose that she recognized in herself. That was how she felt about being a banfasa. Or it had been.

Her grandmama would be so disappointed in how she'd turned tail and fled. Because it was also her heritage, in a way.

She winced away from the uncomfortable thought. "Is your mother or father a cop?"

"No, our mother was a healer. Since Donal and I were Gather-bred, we don't know our sires. But I fostered in Ireland with Mother's old clan, and my uncles were in the *gardaí*."

Seeing her confused look, he added, "The Irish police force."

"Oh. The law is in your family, in a way. You wanted to be like your uncles?"

His smile was crooked, the right slightly higher than the left, adding a rakish charm. "Absolutely. I was a pup with an advanced case of hero-worship."

How could she not love how humble he was? "But isn't what you do dangerous?"

"Aye, it can be." He ran his big hand up and down her arm as if to dispel the goosebumps that had appeared.

And more goosebumps appeared at his touch. His palm was warm. Callused.

"But someone must stand between danger and the cubs, aye? That's my job." He chuckled. "Or maybe it's to provide good stories for the clan. Like when Uncle Turlough saw a flock of sheep on the road and tried to herd them back to their field. A pushy ram knocked him head over heels."

"You were there?"

"Aye, on a ride-along. He bribed Uncle Odhran not to tell that he'd landed in a mud puddle." Tynan grinned. "He forgot to bribe me."

Margery laughed. "You told on your uncle?"

"For months afterward, the villagers were telling sheep-versus-man jokes." Tynan's lips quirked up. "And when I rewired the doorbell to sound like *baaaa*, Uncle Turlough busted out laughing every time he heard it."

Tynan's uncle was a police officer, but he could laugh at

himself. That was totally opposite to how a Scythe guard would react.

From the fond tone in Tynan's voice, he loved his uncles.

Why did the knowledge make her feel all happy inside? She dropped her gaze.

Then, after a second, she realized she was staring at his chest...at the way the shirt fit over his formidable musculature. How the open top button revealed his corded neck. Her lips could press under his jaw—there—and nibble...

She gave herself a shake and looked up, trying to recall what he'd been talking about.

Bending down toward her, he breathed in. "Well, this is more than I'd hoped for," he murmured and tucked a lock of hair behind her ear. Turning his hand over, he rubbed his knuckles so gently over her cheek.

It felt as if her bones were melting.

"Margery," Albert Baty called from a nearby table. "Did you try the recipe?"

She jumped and laughed because the old gruff grocer was grinning at her. "I did. It's great." Okay, maybe she'd scorched the bottom a little, but the rest had been really tasty.

Besides, the gnome that lived under the street grate had enjoyed the burned part.

"Told you." He turned back to his chess game against Joe Thorson, the owner of BOOKS.

"Collecting recipes?" Tynan asked.

"I lost out on the usual housekeeping training, so I'm trying to make up for lost time."

"Good for you. Perhaps I could help to get you up to speed." The flickering smile softened his stern jaw. "I have a recipe for rosemary chicken and potatoes. It's one of my favorite meals."

"Oh, that sounds good. Can I have a—"

"No, little wolf. You can come over, and we'll make it together."

Her mouth dropped open.

He ran a finger over her lower lip, and his eyes warmed. "Come for supper, Meggie. I have next Thursday evening off."

Her breathing lost its rhythm, but under his clear blue gaze, she could find only one answer. "Okay. Yes. I'd like that."

It wasn't until later that she remembered Tynan lived with the healer.

CHAPTER NINE

C old Creek, North Cascades Territory - day before dark of
the moon

On Thursday evening, Margery leaned against the kitchen
counter as she watched Tynan toss potatoes into the
roasting pan. Although she'd had second thoughts about
coming to his house—to his and the healer's house—to
learn to cook, Tynan hadn't let her weasel out. He'd said her
kitchen was simply too small.

Well, it was true. And Tynan's big kitchen was wonderful. The dark gray countertops set off the white cupboards.
The teal tile backsplash and matching teal ladderback
chairs around the breakfast table added a cheerful pop of
color.

But as they prepared the meal and Donal hadn't yet

made an appearance, she'd grown increasingly nervous. As Tynan put the chicken and potatoes into the oven to roast, she asked, "Are you sure this is all right? I mean with your littermate?"

Turning, Tynan met her gaze in the straightforward fashion she'd come to love. "Admittedly, he's less people oriented than I am, but we both live here. If I can put up with shifters coming to get healed, he can welcome an appealing female into the kitchen."

Margery felt her cheeks heat. "I'm not appealing. I'm scarred and—"

"Sweetling." Tynan moved forward, forcing her to retreat until she was trapped at the corner of the counters. With one hand on each side of her face, he tangled his fingers in her loose hair. "You have scars...as do I. Most male shifters do. Are you saying I can't attract the females because I have white lines here and there?"

Her mouth dropped open. He did have scars, and she'd insulted him, albeit unknowingly. "No, no, that's not what I meant. You're really..." Her face felt as if it was on fire.

The satisfaction in his smile didn't help. "Ah, progress. Does that mean you find me appealing?"

Appealing was such a small word for how much he attracted her.

She could feel the warmth of his body, so very close to hers, and...and unable to help herself, she leaned into him. He was all hardness.

His breath brushed her face, and oh, she wanted more. If she moved, just a little, she could...

She tipped her head, rose on tiptoes, and brushed her lips over his.

Like wildfire, heat lit his blue eyes.

With a rumbling growl, he slid an arm behind her, pulling her fully against him. His other hand was in her hair, holding her head as his mouth came down on hers.

Slowly, devastatingly thorough, he kissed her, plundering her mouth before withdrawing to nibble her lips, her jaw, her neck.

Desire opened like a summertime flower within her.

He gently bit the curve between her neck and shoulder, then returned to take her lips, deepening the kiss in a way that had her knees sagging.

"Tynan, could I get you to help with—" Donal's voice stopped abruptly.

Margery froze, then tried to push Tynan back.

Chuckling, the cop captured her hands in his, taking the time to kiss her fingers before he turned. "Sure, I can help. What do you need?"

Donal stared at her, his gaze dark, then turned to his brother. "Can you hold a wound open so I can irrigate it? Get it cleaned out?"

"All right." Tynan frowned. "Unless Meggie would work better. As a banfasa, she'd know—"

"No." Donal scowled, not looking at her. "Your help is all I need."

What in the world had she done to make the healer so dismissive of her? Or maybe that's how he felt about all banfasas? Even as she thought that, the happy warm lust she'd been feeling disappeared. Anger turned into an icy flame directed at Donal.

"Donal." Tynan's brows drew together.

It was time she stood on her own. Margery stepped away and faced Donal. He was a superb healer, she knew. Someone she admired for his work. A male who drew her as powerfully as his brother did.

That he disliked her so openly... It hurt. A lot.

But, over the past few days, she'd thought of how much she'd loved caring for Breanne's injured wrist. How much she missed tending the ill and injured. Being a waitress wasn't going to be enough for long.

It was time she told this...this badger-butt exactly that. She lifted her chin, stared him straight in the face, and ignored the quiver of anxiety in her gut. "Your clinic is your own, healer, and you choose who helps you."

Donal gave her a very human look. Like, *well, duh*.

She flushed. Of course, it was his clinic; he sure didn't need her permission to keep it the way he wanted.

When he started to turn away, she sharpened her voice. "However, *elsewhere?* I'll tend wounded shifters and sick shifters if they need and want my help."

Donal's face darkened. "You aren't—"

"I'm a banfasa, and it appears that you don't like my

profession much. I don't care. In fact, you can take your opinion and shove it in a gnome-hole."

The healer stiffened like she'd stomped on his tail. "You..." After a glare at Tynan, he turned and stalked out of the clinic.

Oh Goddess, what had she done? Clutching the counter edge, she kept her knees from buckling and dared to look up at Tynan. Did he hate her for angering his brother?

"He sure got his fur ruffled." Tynan stared after his brother, then met her gaze, and his eyes softened. "Meggie, relax. You were right to set out your limits."

"Maybe." Her stomach jittered. It hurt to have the healer act like she was pond-scum. Because Tynan loved him. Because he was someone she would have loved to work with.

Setting limits was one thing. Her harsh words hadn't made her feel good at all. "You'd better go help."

He stroked her hair, the touch soothing. "Are you—"

"I'm fine." She started to push his hand away and couldn't help but kiss his palm and breathe in his scent before stepping away. "Go, Tynan. The injured shifter needs help, and they come first. Always."

"Sounds familiar." He touched her cheek tenderly, hesitated, then motioned toward the spinach and vegetables. "If you could start on the salad, I'll be back in a few minutes."

As he walked out, she narrowed her eyes. Sneaky mentor to assign her a task so she wouldn't follow her inclination to slip out while he was gone.

Her unsettled feelings eased as she ripped spinach into small pieces and cut up carrots. Tynan hadn't been upset by her behavior or Donal's. No, he'd been as undisturbed as a mountain in a spring thunderstorm. Solid. Unmoving.

And simply wonderful.

Ten minutes later, still unsettled by what had happened in the kitchen, Donal finished with his patient and dismissed the young male. "Be more careful, aye?"

"Aye." Pulling on his bloodstained shirt, Warren headed out of the clinic, calling back, "Thanks, healer."

With Tynan standing near the door, Donal shook his head, washing his hands. "Who knew hardware stores could be so dangerous?"

A worrisome silence was his only response. Tynan wasn't easy to rile up. Didn't spit out his emotions like Donal did. But when he did get angry, the wolf could rip and tear with the best of them.

In fact, if Tynan had been a werecat, his claws would be embedded in Donal's ass about now.

Donal sighed. "Since you're not heading back to the female in the kitchen, I'm guessing you have something to say."

"Aye. That I do."

Donal turned. "Let's hear it then."

Rather than furious, his brother looked perturbed.

"Even a wolverine guarding our den would have behaved better than you did. Why, Donal? Has she been rude to you in some way?"

Donal rubbed his jaw. He could hardly admit he'd never said more than a few words to her. "When I was apprenticing, the master and I had constant problems with a banfasa. I've had altercations with others since then."

"But not with Margery."

"No." Donal shrugged. "It's not as if she's working as one. It's that I'm not of a mind to encourage her."

"Which is why you refused to let her help, even though she'd have been a better choice than me."

"True. I simply have no interest in working with a banfasa, brawd."

Tynan gave him an assessing gaze. "And no interest in being with any female outside of full moon Gatherings."

Donal sighed. "That, too." Although it wasn't...exactly... the truth. He'd been attracted to Margery from the moment he saw her.

Even worse, when he saw Tynan kissing her, his first reaction had been an almost uncontrollable urge to join his brother. To share her with his littermate.

"All right." Tynan's expression darkened. "However, I don't feel the same. As it happens, I like females. Especially this one."

"Your choice, brawd." The distance between them seemed to be growing. "Not a problem."

Tynan crossed his arms over his chest, a cop behavior

that Donal disliked. "The problem arises when you make the little wolf feel as if she isn't welcome."

Donal opened his mouth—and Tynan didn't wait.

"No, let me be clearer. You were rude to a female who grew up under verbal and physical abuse. A female who is trying to find her place in the Daonain world—and doesn't need someone destroying the trail in front of her."

Guilt swept over Donal. Fuck, he had done exactly that. "You're right." He pulled in a breath. Perhaps it was time he looked at her more carefully. "You're right, and I was wrong. I'll be polite. And welcoming when she's in our home."

Tynan nodded. "Thank you."

As Donal watched his brother walk out of the clinic, the distance between them seemed to stretch into infinity.

CHAPTER TEN

C*old Creek, North Cascades Territory - first quarter moon*

Over a week later, on a sunny Saturday, Tynan strolled down Cumberland Street toward Main Street, planning to visit the Wild Hunt for a brew.

Near the intersection of Main Street, a pup ran past, screaming happily, followed by an exasperated mother who trailed him into the city park.

More shouting came from the depths of the long rectangular park that ran along the slope behind the north side of the stores on Main Street.

Curious, Tynan wandered a few feet in, past the screen of brush and trees.

Ah. The playground held a batch of wolfpack cubs. And

one non-pack child. Minette was a daughter of werecat Ryder, the cahir grizzly Ben, and Emma the bard. Over the winter, Tynan had come to know them well. Since the bard taught the Daonain preschoolers, the pack often gave her a break by watching over Minette.

In the pack, single wolves often cub-sat. Mothers got a break; pups were socialized. Wolves learned what was important in life.

Today, Nia, Lacey, and Bonnie were sitting near the climbing web. At the top of the dome structure, little Tyler shrieked his victory. His littermate headed up the thick spider web ropes toward him. Minette happily dangled from one of the bars. Two more cubs were on the swings.

Bonnie, the weekday dispatcher for the sheriff's office, spotted Tynan and waved. Hard to believe the soft-voice petite blonde had birthed such noisy, mischievous cubs as Tyler and Luke.

Tynan waved back and continued, smiling. Cold Creek reminded him of the village in Ireland where he'd fostered as a teen.

So different from Seattle. Here, he recognized almost everyone, knew which cubs belonged with which adults.

Even the gossip was entertaining.

When he'd stopped in the bookstore for a coffee, Thorson had shared that last night, a drunken Peterson had treated the tavern to his infamous top-of-the-bar dancing.

That'd teach Calum to let Rosie handle the place for a night.

Tynan snorted. By the Gods, he loved living here. And living with his littermate.

And seeing Meggie. She was coming to be...more...than he'd expected.

Mornings, he'd have breakfast at the diner so he could enjoy watching her work. The sociable female already knew the names and favorite foods of the regulars.

It'd been two weeks since her first mentoring run with him, and he'd continued teaching her. Her delight in being a wolf reminded him of the wonders of having fur and paws.

Unfortunately, the cooking lesson nine days past hadn't led to more. Despite her brave words, Donal's disapproval had shaken her.

Tynan rubbed his neck. There was nothing he wanted so much as to share Meggie with his littermate, but that was going to be fecking difficult.

Donal had been as good as his word and was polite to Meggie, but he was spending more time in his clinic and dodging Tynan. It was time to corner the elusive cat and have another talk.

Discussions about emotions? Not a prey Tynan wanted to chase, but it needed to be done.

He was partway down Main Street when a scream cut through the air.

He spun. That was a woman, not a cub. The screams that followed—from both women and children—were laden with terror.

Get backup. Yanking his phone out and calling, Tynan sprinted toward the park.

Alec answered. "Tynan?"

"Problem at the park. Children, women screaming."

"On my way."

Running at full speed, Tynan entered the park.

Red-haired Nia lay on the ground. The red splatters around her were blood. A cub lay beside her.

By the Gods, what had happened?

Farther in, screaming in fear and anger, Lacey swung a dead branch at a black bear. Blood covered her arm.

What the fuck? Black bears didn't attack groups of people.

When Tynan caught its sick sour scent, his gut went tight. That was a shifter who'd gone *feral*—deep into insanity, driven to kill and kill.

A snarl came from a wolf. Clothing strewn behind her, Bonnie darted in to tear at the bear from behind.

Yes, wolf form would be better to defend the cubs. Yanking off his clothes, Tynan trawsfurred and sprang across the park.

Roaring, the bear rose on hind legs, swinging its claw-tipped arms at Bonnie.

Tynan attacked from the rear. He sank his fangs into the bear's right hind leg and darted away before those massive claws could reach him and rip his flesh right off the bone.

Dropping down, the bear charged after him, then broke

off to return to the helpless children and unconscious female.

Tynan yipped to get Bonnie's attention and flicked his ears toward the bear's rear legs. Killing it was unlikely. But they could divert it from the children.

She charged in and bit the bear. When it tore after her, she leaped away, and Tynan dove in. He bit down hard, cursing its thick fur that prevented serious damage.

The constant turns and charges began to erode the bear's energy.

Then the feral caught Bonnie with a swipe and knocked her into a tree. Her fur turned red, and she didn't rise.

With a triumphant growl, the bear charged Lacey, who was guarding the injured child, and Nia.

Not happening.

With a howl of fury, Tynan attacked from the side, springing up to savage its neck. There was too much fur and loose skin to kill it.

Roaring, the bear turned. Claws slashed Tynan's side and knocked him loose.

He landed hard, rolling, and felt something crack. As he scrambled to stand, one leg gave out. *Fuck.*

Shaking his head to clear it, he saw the bear coming for him.

Okay, okay then. He'd lure it from the children. From the park. Tynan turned—tried to turn—one leg dragged.

This wasn't going to end well.

With a scream of outrage, a panther sprang in front of the bear and slashed it across the eyes and muzzle. *Alec.*

As the bear roared and turned—a grizzly—the cahir, Ben, landed on it, driving it into the ground. One bite crushed the feral's throat.

Back legs crumbling, Tynan fell into blackness.

In the bookstore, Margery had been chatting with Alec and Joe Thorson when the sheriff received a call. She'd heard Tynan's voice—and more distantly, high-pitched screaming.

Even as Alec dashed out the front, she turned to Joe. "Do you have an emergency pack?"

"Yeah. But you stay here, female." Thorson grabbed a pack from under the counter and disappeared through the stockroom door that led to the back.

It sounded bad. Screaming. Margery's heart was already hammering, her mind shouting, "Stay back."

Her heart overruled everything. *That was Tynan. And cubs. Go.*

She followed Joe out the back.

The park ran in a long line behind the stores, and she saw frantic activity near the playground. *Oh, Mother of All.*

Ignoring the stabbing pains in her ankle, she sprinted, caught up to Joe, and ran past.

She saw the sheriff trawsfurring from panther. He picked up his pants.

A huge grizzly stood over a dead bear.

Terrified, crying cubs clung to the climbing dome.

Pushing away her own fears, Margery concentrated on the job. *Who is hurt?*

A pup and female lay side-by-side, bleeding heavily, both awake and breathing and moving.

Another female had a ripped-up arm but was standing.

A wolf—Tynan. He had an obviously broken leg. His side was laid bare, exposing ribs. Unconscious. His chest rose and fell—breathing intact.

Another female in wolf form had blood spurting from a leg wound. And she was moving, which was bad. She might rip the artery open further.

Tynan first.

Can't.

Margery's heart felt torn in two as she snatched the medical pack from Joe, turned away from Tynan, and dropped down beside the wolf female.

"Don't move. Let me get the bleeding stopped first," she said, pushing her own fear away, breathing in calm. *Gauze. Pressure. Bear down.*

The wolf snapped at the sudden pain, but...*thank you, Goddess*...the teeth met air. She didn't rip Margery's arm off.

"Tynan!" Donal yelled. He headed straight for his brother.

"Healer. Here first, I have an arterial bleed," Margery shouted.

Donal glared but ran to her. He frowned at the wolf. "Who is—"

"I have no idea. Fix this artery, then Tynan. If you start on her, I'll get help for the others."

He looked shocked, but he knelt and closed his hands around the wolf's leg. "I've got this. Tend the rest."

She rose and intercepted Joe. Slapping dressing packets into his hands, she pointed to the woman and child lying on the ground. "Help them until Donal can."

The old werecat growled his agreement.

"Sheriff."

Alec turned at her call.

She handed him supplies and motioned to the woman with a ripped-up arm who still stood but seemed in shock. "Help her and corral the cubs before they run away."

"That's smart." Alec patted her arm and headed toward the climbing web.

Finally, *finally*, she could run to where her heart had been pulling her from the first moment. Her ankle burned like fire as she dropped onto her knees. "Oh, Tynan, what did you do?"

"Done went and saved a bunch of lives." The bass voice held a Texas drawl. A huge male knelt down beside Tynan. "The bear mucked him up good."

"Yeah." She winced at the sight of the broken leg but left it alone. Instead, she worked on the area where the bear's claws had torn away muscle and skin, exposing Tynan's ribs. *Slow the bleeding.*

She took the big man's hand and set it on the dressings. "Press here while I check his head."

Pupils normal, breathing slow and even, pulse fast but steady. As she ran her fingers over the soft fur of his head and found a nasty lump, the wolf whined.

"Easy, easy," she whispered.

Whining again, he tried to roll. Bending her head, she shared her breath and her calm. "It's over. All okay. Everyone's alive and safe. They're all safe, Tynan. Shhh."

Yes, that was what the big protector was concerned about. Gaze starting to focus, he looked at her, then past her at the giant male who'd been the grizzly.

"She got it right, Ty. The feral's dead. Donal's here and fixin' people. You might want to trawsfur before we get curious humans." The male glanced at her and said, "I'm Ben, by the way."

"Margery. It's—"

A little girl slammed into Ben's side. "Da, you came."

"Darlin'." Freeing one hand, he wrapped a huge arm around her. His brows drew together. "How did I not see you here, Minette?"

"I took Lucas to hide in the bushes." She motioned to a cubling about her age standing behind her. Looking terrified.

Margery silently held out one arm. Offering.

A second later, the pup was burrowing into her side as if to find a cave to hide in. After giving him a quick squeeze, she settled him beside her so her hands were free. She hummed a calming note, pleased when both cubs and both males relaxed.

Before she could resume her work on Tynan's injuries, he trawsfurred to human, growling in pain.

Blinking at the naked male under her hand, Margery remembered Ben's advice. *Humans. Right.* She pulled off her jacket and draped it over Tynan's groin.

His lips curled into a slight smile. "Not the usual reaction I have from females."

Even as she turned her attention to the ripped-up flesh over his ribs, a startled laugh escaped her.

Donal knelt and scowled at her. "What's funny about injuries like these?"

"What the fuck, Donal." The big male shot Donal a displeased look. "If you don't want laughter, then tell your littermate not to make jokes."

Tynan's frown at his brother was equally displeased.

To her surprise, Donal gave her an apologetic look. "Sorry, Margery. I have trouble seeing him hurt."

"Me, too," she whispered. Tears prickled her eyes at the rush of relief. The healer was here, and her wolf would be all right.

Tynan's hand closed around hers. Bending her head, she kissed his fingers. Wonderful warm fingers—he was alive.

When he lifted his hand to touch her cheek, she realized he was wiping the tears from her face.

His lips curved. "You were worried about me?"

More tears fell.

. . .

Donal stared at the little female who was silently crying. Not wailing to attract attention, but turning her face away, trying to hide her tears. To hide her emotions.

She really did care for Tynan; it was obvious. Even so, she'd ignored those feelings and done what was best for everyone. Had sent him to tend to Bonnie who would have died otherwise. Who had taken long enough to arrange for the others to be cared for.

And who was upset enough about Tynan that she was visibly trembling.

By Herne's horny hooves, these weren't the actions of a banfasa who tended her friends first. Or of one who didn't take her duties seriously as Gretchen and Caleb had stated.

An ugly feeling grew in Donal's gut. Had the Rainier Territory shifters lied to him?

As he took a bottle of saline from Margery and cleansed the debris from Tynan's side, he considered. Over the last week, he'd asked about her around town.

Everyone had a Margery story. How she'd taken a meatloaf meal to an elderly neighbor. How she'd stayed with a sick child so his mother could go grocery shopping. Injured shifters showed up at his clinic with gashes expertly dressed, broken bones splinted. She'd done first aid and sent them on to him for healing.

He'd been wrong about her.

But this wasn't the time to address that.

Bowing his head, he set his hands on each side of the torn muscles along Tynan's ribs. Gently, ignoring his litter-mate's involuntary growl, he pushed the flesh together as best he could and let the power flow through him. Tissues knitted together. Veins, arteries, muscles, fascia, subcutaneous tissue, and all the layers of skin.

As he finished, he could feel the emptiness inside where his pool of power had lain, depleted by the number of healings he'd done.

His hands shook as he straightened up. The sweat on his face turned cold in the bitter wind.

With little Lucas still cuddled against her side, Margery gave him a concerned look. "Healer, maybe—"

"You're turning pale, Donal." Tynan's brows drew together. "Stop, *mo deartháir*."

Donal scowled. *Mo deartháir, my tail.* Tynan only used the Irish "my brother" when drunk—or when one of them came too close to death. "I'm fine."

"Dammit, I can wait." Tynan moved as if he'd try to get away and groaned when the movement jarred his broken leg.

Donal snapped, "Don't move, idiot," even as the banfasa growled, "You lie still."

Her hazel eyes flashed with anger as she glared at Tynan.

Someone who could stand up against the cop. *Hmm.* Donal tilted his head. "I think...perhaps...I might decide to like you."

Her astonished expression almost made him laugh.

Donal turned his attention to Tynan's leg and considered his own energy. "You're right, brawd. I need more power to finish."

"So, I assumed." Calum's voice came from behind him. "I sent for some of your females."

"We need to get out of here," Tynan said. "It's a park. There'll be humans."

"Not for long." The corners of the Cosantir's lips tipped up. "Victoria is here. Seeing the cubs injured put her in a vile mood."

Ben snorted. "I'm fixin' to be sorry for any humans who run afoul of her."

Donal noticed Margery's confusion. "Having served in the human military, she gives orders and expects them to be obeyed. Or else."

Chuckling, Ben elaborated. "Alec will move them along politely. Vicki will knock them off the mountain."

"Indeed. Thus, no need to move the injured until you're ready, Donal." Calum's gaze turned toward the street. "It appears your help is here."

With relief, Donal saw Farrah running across the park.

"Healer." Kneeling behind him, she wrapped her arms around his waist. The bond from the last Gathering was still strong, and as he opened himself, power flowed from her, replenishing his empty stores. His cells revived like dry plants under a soft rain.

"Thank you, sweetheart," he murmured, patting her hand.

"Anytime, Donal." She rubbed her cheek against the side of his face and disappeared as quickly as she'd come.

Margery stared after the female, then frowned at him.

"Now, let's get this fixed." Donal moved to where he could work on Tynan's broken leg. It was a fucking mess.

"You look confused, Meggie." Tynan winced as Donal covered the break with his hand.

"I didn't know healers took time out for hugs." The disapproval in her voice was oddly amusing.

Donal smothered a smile.

Tynan huffed a laugh. "Healers store only so much of the Mother's power. Once it's gone, they can get power from shifters with whom they have a bond."

"Like their littermate?" she asked.

"No." Tynan stiffened as Donal probed the wound. He added, "A bond from mating. From sex."

"Oh."

Donal looked up to see that the little banfasa had flushed.

Sex was a normal function to every animal on the planet —except humans. Apparently, she'd absorbed their inhibitions.

Being a werecat, he couldn't resist. "The pink is a good color on her, don't you think, brawd."

Tynan winked at him. They both knew that if the word made her flush, the act itself would have her face turning a bright red.

Damned if Donal didn't want to see if that was true.

After a second, he blinked. If...if she was as fine a banfasa as he was starting to think, and *if* she was as sweet a female as she appeared...perhaps he'd find her during a Gathering. He might well see her turn that color during mating.

He and Tynan might even share the little female. It'd been a long time since they'd enjoyed a female together.

"Where is Lucas? I need my cub."

Donal recognized Bonnie's frantic voice and glanced at the cub huddled next to the banfasa. "Margery, you have her pup."

"Oh, right." Margery released Tynan's hand and kissed the top of the cub's head. "Lucas, let's get you to your mama."

The boy had a firm hold on Margery's shirt, but he whispered, "Mama."

"Come on, sweetling." She tried to stand and winced.

Before Donal could move, she released the cub to push herself up with both hands. After getting her balance, she smiled and took Lucas's hand.

And the pup clung. Because Lucas recognized a caring heart.

I've been blind.

He wasn't blind any longer. Donal glanced around the park at the wounded shifters. "Margery, could you check the injured for me, please? See if they need anything else or need me urgently?"

Her startled expression told him he really had been a boggart before.

Far more polite than he would've been, she didn't give him any grief. "Of course, healer. I'd be happy to check on them." She led Lucas toward Bonnie.

"She's limping," Ben commented.

Tynan frowned. "Her leg wasn't that bad yesterday."

"You didn't see her running like a charging bull to get here." Thorson joined them. "Made my bones hurt just to see it."

"She did good to get here when she did. Bonnie was losing blood fast." Donal motioned to Ben. "Griz, can you pull on Tynan's leg so I can set it?"

"Aye." Ben gave Minette over to Thorson, and Donal grinned. The old werecat terrified most adults, especially young males, but the cubs saw through the gruffness and adored the bookstore owner.

As Minette snuggled up to Joe, she watched Donal with an intriguing intensity. Was he going to have a healer apprentice in a few years? Although the God didn't call females of bearing age to be cahirs, the healers and blademage professions had no such restriction.

Ben gripped Tynan's leg, one hand above the break, the other on the ankle, and pulled slowly.

Tynan's back arched, his jaw tight as he muffled what would have been a howl of pain.

Herne's heart, but it was gut-wrenching to see his litter-mate hurting.

Donal swallowed and forced a smile. "Perfect, Griz.

You're my favorite bone setting assistant." The grizzly cahir was outrageously strong.

Tynan growled under his breath as his muscles spasmed.

Setting his palms over the injury, Donal eased the congestion, loosened the tight muscles.

Good. Time to work. Closing his eyes, Donal finished aligning the bones by feel—forcing himself to ignore the whine of pain from his littermate. A burst of power, fast, then slow, fixed the break, then the damaged tissue around it.

Slowly, he worked his way out, then sat back and pulled in a shaky breath. Tried for a light tone. "Not a bad break, really."

"Oh. Well. Glad I didn't put you to too much effort." Tynan unfisted his hands. "By the Gods, I'd forgotten how much a busted bone can hurt when you fix it."

How fucking much pain would it take to make his littermate say that? Donal felt as if a rope was wrapped around his chest. "Sorry, brawd."

"Hey, no, feck, I didn't mean it that way. It's healed." Tynan's face was still pale, but he grinned. "Thank you."

The words let Donal breathe again. And realize how much of a pain in the tail Tynan would be until he was back to normal.

"You're healed, but weak." Donal pointed a finger at his idiot littermate. "Sleep today and tomorrow. Take it easy for a week after. Lots of fluids."

"Yeah, got it." Tynan brightened when Margery carefully knelt beside him.

After taking his hand, she ventured a small smile at Donal. "I took care of the superficial wounds on Bonnie. But if you have more...power left, could you check Nia? She has a few scratches that will heal all right on their own. I went ahead and cleaned and dressed those. But the one down her neck will leave a scar. If you could..."

Her tentative look almost broke his heart. A shifter should never worry about asking for help from a healer. Especially for someone else.

"Of course, I will." He smiled. "If I don't have enough power right now, I'll ask another female to give me some. There is no need for any shifter in our territory to have scars if I can get to them in time."

Despite the scar on her own face, she smiled in relief. She half-extended her free hand. "Could I offer you..."

Could she give him power? A totally selfless, generous offer.

His misjudgment of her made him feel lower than a dwarf's ass. "I'm afraid not, Margery. Not without a bond—not unless we'd mated recently."

She turned pink again, and how appealing was that?

He couldn't resist running a finger down her cheek and stilled in surprise at the lake of power he sensed. She wasn't a healer, but...

The Mother loved this shifter.

That evening, Margery was spending more time grumbling than reading her book. Reclined on her couch, she had her leg elevated on a pillow and ice on the swollen joint...but the damage had been done. Her ankle was totally, completely in revolt.

Tomorrow, she'd be lucky to walk across the room. How was she ever going to handle the breakfast and lunch shifts at the diner?

With a sigh, she drank her willow bark-and-peppermint tea. She'd manage. Somehow.

Because that was what she did.

Hey, look on the bright side. Everyone survived. The cubs, the mothers,

Tynan had too, despite how badly...

As her hand started to shake, she hastily set the cup down. He'd been so damaged, so bloody.

A rap on the door made her jump.

"Yes?" Through the front window, she could see Donal on her porch. "Hold on. I'm coming." She swung her leg down, dislodging the ice pack.

His dark brows drew together. "Stay put, female. I'll let myself in."

The lock rattled; the door opened, and he sauntered across her living room with a werecat's predatory grace.

"How did you get the door open?" *Does healing include the power to unlock doors?*

He smirked slightly and held up a ring of keys. "Leo gave me a key years ago. Just in case."

"Oh." Well, this probably wasn't the time to demand he give the key back. But why was he here? In her house?

And why in the world did she feel a tremor of excitement at having him here? "Can I help you with something?"

"Bonnie's mates brought over a big basket of fried chicken as a thank you for the rescue. Tynan figured you'd be hungry and wanted you to join us for supper and a movie."

"Really?" Be with them both? *Oh Goddess.*

No, Margery. She wasn't about to intrude in their evening even if she could get there. "Please, tell him thank you, but I, uh, I'm not hungry."

"You, sweetling, are a lousy liar." Donal eyed her before raking his hand through his long dark hair. "My fault. Let me try this again. Both Tynan and I want you to join us."

When she shook her head, he went down on his haunches beside the couch. Close enough she could touch him. "I know I've been ruder than a starving badger, and I'm sorry for it." His rich voice was smoother than warm honey. "Can you give me a chance to make things right?"

Mother of All, when he sounds like that, what female would say no?

She frowned, pulling her senses together before she blurted out an acceptance.

Still...he did look sorry, and she'd never been able to

hold a grudge. "Of course." Then she shook her head. "But I'm giving my ankle a chance to rest, so I can't..."

"I can." He scooped her off the couch and walked right out the door, turning long enough to catch the knob with a finger and close it behind them.

Howling hobgoblins, but he was strong. Her head spun at how easily he'd picked her up, at how very closely he held her. She was close enough to breathe in his fresh-washed scent. Clean and crisp, like after a spring rain.

She couldn't let him just...carry...her. As he strode down the steps, she gripped his shirt. "Healer. Donal, this isn't a good idea. I should—"

"Please, Margery, my littermate isn't feeling well at all. Won't you sacrifice an evening to help him out?"

Oh, no. Poor Tynan. He'd hate feeling weak. "Of course I can. It isn't a problem at all."

"Good. Lie still then." The amused glint in the healer's eyes said she'd been played by a master of manipulation.

Her eyes narrowed. "You are a total werecat."

"Was that supposed to be an insult?" Chuckling, he thumped a boot on his front door. "Brawd, get the door for me."

Margery squirmed. "Let me down. I can—"

The door opened...and there he was. All power and strength, and more masculine than any male she'd ever met. A day's shadowing of beard covered the angular lines of his jaw making his smile even whiter.

Her heart sped up.

His eyebrows rose as he looked at her in Donal's arms, then he grinned at his brother. "Donal, no. I wanted you to *ask* her to dinner—not drag her home like prey."

"If my brother asks for a female, I'll do whatever it takes to see he gets one." Donal sighed most pitifully. "I'll be fine, really. She didn't claw me...much."

Margery's mouth dropped open. "I didn't claw you at all!"

"You should see my chest and arms, brawd. All bloody."

"Lying cat." Tynan chuckled. "She doesn't scratch. She's a wolf."

"Ah. Oops." Donal walked in and set her in the center of the couch. He lifted her legs onto the rectangular leather ottoman before smirking at his brother. "I had to carry her. She messed up her ankle, remember?"

"How did I forget that?" Tynan sat beside her and took her hand in his big warm one. "How bad?" he asked Donal.

"I intend to find out." Donal took a seat on the ottoman beside her legs. Pushing up her jeans, he laid his hands over her ankle and visibly winced. "For fuck's sake, there's a mess."

She gave him a good frown. "That was not even close to an appropriate comment from a healer."

Tynan chuckled. "He's never been into a healer's traditional conduct or attire. Made our dam furious."

That's right. Tynan had mentioned their mother was a healer.

Donal scowled at her ankle, then her. "The bones were

shattered and weren't set correctly. You can feel the bumps of misalignment. A couple pieces haven't stabilized. The cartilage isn't happy either. It's a wonder you can walk at all."

"Mother's breasts, do you talk to all your patients like this?"

Intent on her ankle, he didn't even notice her shock. She had a feeling he wouldn't have cared even if he had noticed.

Tynan squeezed her hand. "He believes in honesty, although, admittedly, his manner could use some work."

"No kidding." Her laugh died when Donal looked up, his frown dark. "What?"

"It's not going to get better."

"Since it's been this way for years, I rather figured that."

He blinked as if surprised at her answer, then rubbed his jaw. "Sorry. A lot of shifters refuse to see a problem. I should have known you wouldn't be one of them."

"Can you help her at all?" Tynan asked the question she hadn't been able to speak.

"Right now, I can improve the circulation and reduce some of the swelling and pain. But that's only a temporary fix." Without waiting for a response, the healer bent his head and did just that.

Tingling and warmth radiated from a point deep in her ankle. It wasn't quite pain, but an uncomfortable gnawing she couldn't scratch.

At her disgruntled frown, Donal blinked. "What?"

"Why didn't I get stardust?"

With one smile, his severe austerity transformed into a very masculine charm.

And took her breath away.

"Sorry, sweetling. I should have warned you. It only feels like stardust with superficial injuries. Bone-deep healing isn't pleasant."

Didn't that just figure? She pouted. "I was looking forward to stardust."

Tynan laughed. "We're of the same mind."

Oh, ow. He'd had a big nasty healing today. "Now that I know what it feels like, I can't believe you didn't bite his hand off when he fixed your leg."

"I've been tempted a time or two."

Donal muttered something rude under his breath, but a smile curved his lips.

Rotating her ankle, Margery beamed. "It almost doesn't hurt at all. I'd forgotten what that felt like."

The healer's smile disappeared completely.

When Tynan made a rumbling sound, she stared at him. "Are you growling?"

"You're in constant pain because of those scum-sucking weasels. I'd like to go back and kill them again."

He'd killed during the rescue. This male who was a protector to his bone. One who believed in the laws. She leaned her head against his shoulder, letting her body speak her gratitude in the way of wolves.

And, oh, she wouldn't mind showing her gratitude in other ways, too. Would he want that? He...he liked her.

"What about a permanent fix?" Tynan asked his brother.

"So." Donal kept his palm on her ankle, the warmth reassuring. "There's only one way to fix this permanently—but it's not pleasant."

Tynan's wince indicated the healer's idea of "not pleasant" was probably torture from a patient's point of view. "Let's hear it."

"The bones would have to be rebroken—basically shattered. At that point, I could cut the ankle open, reassemble the jigsaw puzzle, encourage extra bone tissue to fill in the gaps, and fuse it all back together the way it should be."

A shudder ran through her. Shifters didn't get sedatives. The pain would be horrendous.

Tynan tensed. "She'd not have to be awake for that, would she?"

"That's the catch." Donal's gaze met hers. "You'd have to be asleep for the breaking and reassembling. No one could hold still with that much pain."

However, there was a reason that shifters weren't sedated. "I'd trawsfur to wolf the minute I started to rouse."

"Exactly. You'd panic, attack anyone in the room, and mess up all my work." He sounded more displeased about getting his work ruined than the thought of being attacked.

"Then there's no way it'll happen." Her momentary hope burst like a pin-pricked balloon.

"Just one—and only because you're a wolf. Because your

animal will submit to your leaders. If someday, you come to trust your pack alpha and betas enough that they can keep you calm, then it can be done."

Trust the alpha and beta? She didn't really know Shay and Zeb, and the wolf inside her didn't trust them—not enough. After what she'd been through, well, the level of trust needed might never happen. She blew out a breath. "Got it. If I get to that point, I'll let you know."

Acceptance—and respect—was in his nod.

Tynan frowned. "Shay is a good—"

"Trust comes or it doesn't," Donal said.

"By the Gods, I wanted an easy fix." With a disgusted sigh, Tynan tucked an arm around her and pulled her closer. "Guess easy isn't in the works."

Her smile came easier than she thought it would. "Easy is over-rated. I'm alive to feel my ankle hurting. That's a win in my mind."

"So it is." Donal rose and picked up a stack of DVDs. "After much argument, Tynan and I agreed we would enjoy seeing any of these."

Tynan's low chuckle was a relief. He'd moved on. "Donal prefers fantasy and science fiction or animated. I like horror, action, or mystery. We both like historicals."

"It's a wonder you two don't kill each other." After a moment's consideration, she lifted one—Heather had said something about eye-candy. "How about this one? *300?*"

"You got it." Donal went to start the movie.

"I'll get the chicken." Tynan gave her a squeeze.

Margery leaned forward. "What can I—"

"*You* can stay put."

She sat back at the snap in the healer's words.

He turned a dark look on his brother. "As can *you*. For tonight, I'll be the house brownie. *Do not get used to it.*"

"Um. Right." She added an extremely polite and subdued, "Thank you, Donal," and got an approving smirk back.

"Aye, thank you, Donal." Tynan winked at her and pulled her closer, nuzzling her hair. "We'll let him take all the time he needs to get things together."

And he took her mouth in a slow deep kiss that swept away every thought in her head.

CHAPTER ELEVEN

C old Creek, North Cascades Territory - waxing gibbous
moon

The shrieks coming from his waiting area were appallingly
high-pitched. Although Donal's heart ached for the
cublings' pain, his sensitive ears protested.

"Easy, little one," he murmured to the nine-year-old girl
on his table as he squirted saline over the long scrape on her
shin. Birghitta bore it silently although her fair face was
whiter than her platinum-colored hair. A courageous one,
she was. "Almost done."

Unfortunately, the two young males in the other room
were yet to come. Hissing under his breath, he turned to
the open door and addressed one of the mothers who'd

been unable to quiet her offspring. "Go next door and see if Margery is willing to help out."

Maybe the banfasa would have more luck. Even if she couldn't do anything about the wailing children, she'd improve his mood. Aye, she really would.

Tynan had been right when he asked Donal to give her a chance. She was gentle, peaceful, kind—and had forgiven him with a generosity of spirit that he knew he lacked.

Two nights ago, as he and Tynan watched the *300* movie with her tucked between them, he'd felt as if he'd found a sunny rock in a snowstorm.

Had he ever felt such contentment?

And if he'd read her correctly—after being blind as a drunken dwarf at dawn—she'd not refuse a request for her help.

A couple of minutes passed, and Margery's soft voice came from the waiting area.

The screeching stopped.

After finishing healing the girl-cub, he took her hand and walked her to the hallway. In the doorway, he breathed in the quiet.

Margery had a boy cuddled up against her on her left. To her right, a lad sprawled over her lap as she cleaned the scrape on his arm. Towels under his arm caught the water.

Donal almost purred. Cleaning wounds was often the most painful part of treatment.

"Birghitta, are you all right?" The girl's mother rushed

over. She dropped to her knees and held her child by the arms. "Urbain said the tree you were in fell down." She was patting her child, looking for the damage, finding the bloodstains.

"All healed. She only had a bunch of scrapes." Donal didn't mention he'd had to repair her eyelid and the scrape on her cornea. No need to give a mother nightmares. The child could share if she wanted.

From Birghitta's grateful glance, they'd both agreed on silence.

"Who's next?" Donal asked.

When both boys' mothers started to talk, Margery spoke up. "Take Urbain. They're both equally gashed, but I don't like the way he's guarding his stomach. He says he hit a branch—belly-first—on the way down."

Shifters were sturdy creatures, but spleens damaged easily.

"Come, Urbain." He motioned to the cubling.

"What in the world? Jonty's bleeding!" Lottie, the other child's mother scowled, standing over Margery in a threatening posture. "Why are you taking her word for anything? She's no healer. She doesn't know—"

"She's a banfasa, a very skilled one." He looked at Jonty who was cuddled against Margery. The banfasa hadn't moved, but her shoulders hunched. "If she wasn't here, your cub would still be screaming—and bleeding from dirty wounds."

Lottie flinched. "I—"

Turning his back on her before he spoke too harshly—

something he really did try to avoid—Donal led Urbain into his healing room.

With a sigh, Margery tried to wiggle out from under Jonty. *Time to go home.* Apparently, Cold Creek didn't respect a banfasa much better than Ailill Ridge.

The cub gripped her shirt looking up with pleading brown eyes.

"Oh, someone should rip my tail off and use it to gag my stupid mouth." The mother dropped down beside Margery on the bench. "I'm sorry."

"No problem." Margery tried to ease her shirt out of the child's grip.

"Donal sent me to get you, but he didn't say you were a banfasa. Just *get Margery.*" Lottie touched her son's cheek. "I panic easily."

There was more to the story. Margery waited.

"Jonty had two littermates, but one went on a trip with his sire, who was visiting. They were in a car crash and...." The mother shook her head.

Oh Goddess, to lose a cub? Margery reached out and took her hand. "I'm so sorry."

"Thank you." Lottie pulled in a shuddering breath. "My cubs are my heart, but when they get hurt now, I overreact. I know it. Please forgive me for being so rude."

"Of course. Forgiven and forgotten."

No, the Cold Creek shifters aren't like Ailill Ridge's at all.

When it was Jonty's turn, at Lottie's pleading, Margery went in to help Donal tend to the child.

An hour later, the clinic room was empty—and she had to laugh because little Jonty had bounced out of the place as if he'd never been hurt. Cubs were so cute.

"I'll get these to the laundry room." Donal motioned to the dirty towels, then obviously noticed his flannel shirt and T-shirt were bloody as well. Shaking his head, he pulled off the shirts and dropped them on the pile.

"Do you need me to wash anything for you?" He turned —and caught her with her mouth open.

Because...well...all that tanned skin over rippling muscles. He was sleek as a feline—and a tensile work of art.

Staring, Margery. Oops.

His lips curved in a very masculine smile.

"My clothes stayed clean, thanks," she said, embarrassed at the breathless sound of her voice. Oh, she hated the awkwardness of male-female stuff. "I should get going."

"Stay for a while. We both deserve lemonade and some time in the sun."

It would be easier to talk if she didn't keep noticing how his dark lashes and brows made his silvery-gray eyes even more potent. "Thanks, but—"

"Don't flee, banfasa. I need to talk to you." His eyes glinted with amusement. "About healing stuff." He was using that... that *voice* on her, the one that sounded as dark and rich as molasses. The one that could make a female's knees weaken.

Not fair. But she was better than this. *Medicine. Right.* And if her insides quivered a bit at the thought of talking to him, he'd never need to know.

Although it'd almost been easier to deal with him when he'd been rude to her. This was a total case of *be careful what you wish for*, wasn't it? "Of course. All right."

"Good. Go sit." He pointed her toward the front door while he turned toward the kitchen.

As she settled onto a chair, he returned with glasses of lemonade. And—good for her peace of mind—he'd donned a shirt.

Before he could speak, a young boy trotted up onto the porch with a basket in each hand. "Healer, Mama sent cookies."

"Enzo." Donal grinned and accepted a basket. "I love cookies. Tell her thank you."

The boy turned to Margery, and his brow crinkled with worry. He whispered to Donal, "Is she the banfasa?"

"She is."

With an adorable grin—and familiar big brown eyes— Enzo deposited the other basket in her lap. "Mama says thank you."

Before she could respond, the boy jumped off the porch, not bothering to use the steps, and headed down the street at a speedy run.

She stared after him. "Is he, perhaps, a littermate to Jonty, cub of Lottie?"

"Very good." Donal took the other chair and investigated his gift. "Oatmeal cookies. My favorite."

Cookies. Mouth watering, Margery pulled away the pretty cloth napkin covering her basket and stared. "I have *lots* of cookies."

Picking up the note, she read the careful writing.

"By the Law of Reciprocity, you were owed for my poor behavior. The cookies are sent in balance—and with gratitude for the way you eased a cubling's pain and a mother's worry. Thank you, banfasa."

As Margery's eyes stung with tears, Donal plucked the note from her hand.

"Ah, good. Lottie is a fine female. We all mourned her cub." He handed the note back and leaned over to check her basket. "A variety, eh? Once she knows what you like, you'll get those instead."

Margery nibbled on a peanut butter cookie. *Yum.* "You, healer, are a tad spoiled."

He chuckled. "I'm very spoiled, aye."

She studied him as he leaned back and rested his long, lean legs on the railing. During the healing, he'd worn his hair tied severely back in a leather band. Now the black waves covered his blue flannel shirt to mid-chest. He looked younger, closer to her age.

Although his head was back as he soaked up the late afternoon sun, the sharp edge to him hadn't disappeared. He seemed very much the feline who could purr...and then slash a person to shreds.

But he'd wanted to talk. This was her chance to ask questions. "As a child, I heard stories of healers. But you don't match my mental image of them."

Without opening his eyes, he smiled slightly. "Mother was a very conservative healer. And my attire and attitude began as typical adolescent defiance. But I discovered I'm far more comfortable in flannel shirts and jeans than in a suit."

Huh. "My grandmother wore calf-length denim dresses, partly because the material was strong enough to let her keep supplies in her pockets. But I hate skirts."

"It's good to examine what we unthinkingly absorb from our teachers and to decide what we wish to retain." He lifted an eyebrow. "Your grandmother was a banfasa?"

"Yes. Dogwood didn't have a healer. Everyone went to her, and from the time I could walk, I helped her every day." Margery set her basket down and sipped her lemonade.

"I know how that goes. My mother yanked me into her clinic the minute I showed power. There's nothing like starting early." Donal pinned her with a keen look. "Did you tend to your villagers in the Scythe compound?"

"As much as I was allowed." *The Scythe.* Appetite gone, she set her cookie back in the basket. "Their nurse practitioner got permission from the Director to use me as her assistant. We cared for shifters and humans."

"You picked up human techniques then. Did you use any when you were the banfasa in Ailill Ridge?"

The muscles tightened in Margery's jaw. The conversation had certainly taken a downward turn. The Scythe, then Ailill Ridge. But the healer was right to ask the questions. "Humans do have useful equipment and supplies, but the Cosantir wouldn't purchase them."

Donal gave her a quizzical stare. "That's why we're given a general fund in addition to the stipend. Budgeting for the larger items can be—"

She growled.

"I'm missing something, aren't I?"

"There was no general fund, *healer*." Because she wasn't one of the God-touched. "There was *no* money at all. Someone else stocked the medical bag and with only the very basics. Nothing else. I did not get paid; I got room and board, for which I also had to do all the cleaning in the communal house as well as being a banfasa. Apparently, banfasas aren't worth much."

"Penny-pinching Pete." Donal's lips formed a straight line of disgust. "Your grandmother probably didn't tell you, but banfasas receive a stipend—like healers. The amount is negotiated depending on the time the clan requires and the kinds of injuries and treatments routinely needed."

"I should have gotten money?" She *knew* it.

"Aye. Each clan maintains a fund to pay for healers and banfasas, bards, soulweavers, blademages—all those—and for things like communal houses, Gathering supplies. Whatever is needed for the well-being of the Daonain in the territory." He grinned. "Calum is considering subsidizing a hacker and document forger."

"I should have gotten real money," she repeated, refusing to be sidetracked.

"Aye, banfasa, you should have." Donal shook his head. "At one time, Pete wasn't a bad Cosantir, but he's grown short-sighted and penurious. I don't think he spends money on himself—just piles it into the bank."

"Older folk do that sometimes when they start losing control of their lives and fear for the future." Margery eyed the tidy, well-maintained houses on the block. Like a house, a clan required constant upkeep. Fixing things. Investing in preventative care. "Pete's territory isn't doing well. Can't Calum do something about that?"

"No. Cosantirs are limited to their own territory. If the Rainier clan wants change—or for the God to call a different Cosantir—they'll have to bestir themselves. The shifters in that territory could fix things if they got their paws moving."

They weren't moving. They just did what Pete wanted. She looked down at her hands. "They made me feel like I wasn't worth paying. But it was a trick. I heard Roger and his beta say the lack of money would keep me from leaving."

"That's a vile thing to do to anyone, especially someone putting her life back together after being a captive."

His anger at how she'd been treated was...heartening. Wonderful. She found a smile. "Thanks to Heather, I did manage to leave."

"She's a feisty wolf." Donal took Margery's hand.

Touching. He was touching her. His fingers were lean, the warmth seeping into her skin, making her aware of the rest of his body, of—

She shook her head. *Focus, female.*

"Speaking of your leaving Rainier Territory..." He gave her fingers a squeeze. "I wasn't going to tell you this, but if 'twere me, I'd want to know."

This what? The way his mouth turned down in a sour grimace was a warning, and she braced herself. "You'd better tell me, then."

"At the Gathering last moon, I talked with two shifters from Ailill Ridge and was told you were..." He paused, considered, then said simply, "Basically that you weren't a good banfasa."

"*What?*" Although Pete and others had whined that she wasn't a healer, only a banfasa, they'd never complained about her skill.

Anger roused like a wakening bear, and her words came out clipped. "I worked with my Grandmama from the time I could walk—and in those years, I met a lot of banfasas who visited her. Not to sound conceited, but I *am* a good banfasa. A very good one. The years picking up human techniques only made me better."

"I'd agree, just from the little I've seen." He leaned back.

"So why would they come here and lie about me?" The ugliness that was Rainier Territory swept over her like dirty floodwaters. "Why?"

"I'm guessing it was to prevent your finding work elsewhere. To force you to return to Ailill Ridge."

By the Gods' forests and hills.

Unable to sit with the rage inside her, she rose and paced up and down the porch, stomping hard enough the wood reverberated like a drum under her feet.

"Wait..." Stopping, she pointed at the healer. "That's why you were rude to me. Why you told Calum you didn't need help."

He rubbed the back of his neck, his expression rueful. "I was wrong to believe what they said without checking for myself. I'm sorry, lass."

The sincerity in his tone dispelled much of her anger. Although she'd like to slap the shifters—no, *Pete*—because he would have been the one to come up with the idea.

She stood still, letting her fury recede.

Watching her quietly, Donal patted the chair beside him.

With a sigh, she resumed her seat. "I guess there's nothing I can do. Protesting isn't highly effective against something like slander."

"If you don't mind, I'd like to deal with this myself." His eyes, more gray than silver, held the cold wrath of an approaching blizzard. "Since I was the one lied to and heard exactly what they said."

"That doesn't seem fair to—"

"I'm a werecat." The curve of his lips was almost cruel. "And I do so enjoy playing with my prey."

"Ah, uh-huh. Sure." Lesson one in survival: annoying this healer would be bad for a person's health. "Um, thank you?"

"That's the right answer," he almost purred.

Okay, okay, she would simply try to put that stuff out of her mind. She'd moved on. Donal had learned the truth about her and wanted to work with her. No need to wallow in the past. "So, what's next?"

"Advice." He smiled. "Earlier, I saw how you reacted to Lottie's rudeness."

If she hadn't been pinned down by the cub, she'd have retreated to her own house. She sighed...and waited.

This was a male who didn't need any encouragement to tell her what he thought.

"Having seen you work, I know you're very skilled. Unfortunately, you've had years of being undermined, first as a captive and later by Pete. It makes you insecure, even when you know you're skilled."

She nodded at the truth.

"Lass, don't let your patients or their families be rude to you. Either they treat you with respect or you walk away."

Her eyes widened. "I can't do that."

"No, not if the lack of care would truly hurt someone. But, for example, last month, I told an overly aggressive cat not to come to me unless he's dying. For one year, he'll have to get broken bones and gashes treated by human medicine —or his friends if he has any."

She'd seen the healer kick a shifter out of his clinic and thought he was awfully harsh. But maybe he was right.

Grandmama had been much like him. Actually, she'd have walked out of Rainier Territory the first week.

Don't I deserve to be treated with equal respect?

She did.

Donal waited quietly, his expression caring. Once he'd changed his mind about her, his true personality came forward. And he was...kind.

Shay had assigned Tynan to be her pack mentor, but it appeared Donal had appointed himself to be her medical mentor.

"Okay. Now that you've pointed out this vulnerability, I'll patch it up." She had a feeling her smile was a bit crooked. "Thank you."

"Exactly what I hoped you'd say." He rubbed his hands together as if starting a new task. "So, banfasa, we have older shifters in the area who need better monitoring. In addition, I can't keep up with visiting everyone after healing broken bones or extensive healing, and some need extra care. Let's talk about therapy and how we can work together to handle..."

His words disappeared under a sparkling wave of happiness.

This was what she'd hoped for all her life.

CHAPTER TWELVE

*C*old Creek. North Cascades Territory - one day before full moon

The night before the monthly Gathering, only the barest sliver was missing from the golden ball in the sky. The air held a hint of cold, and moonglow lit the paths on the mountain.

Tynan had never seen such a beautiful night for a pack run.

He could taste the hint of rain though. Tonight, the wolves would run the moonlit trails. Tomorrow, during the storm, the Daonain would gather in the Wild Hunt Tavern to mate all night.

Perfectly timed. All too often, contrary weather left the pack running and singing in the rain. Although his fur's outer layer shed water, a prolonged rain would eventually penetrate even his thick undercoat.

There was nothing more disgusting than a cold, heavy coat of fur and mud-caked paws.

As the trail opened into a high mountain meadow, Tynan's pace quickened. He loped over the soft spring grass and through the clear water in the glacier-fed stream. He heard a rustle, pounced, and snapped his jaws closed on a field mouse.

After a quick look, he tossed the treat to an aged female who could obviously use some extra nutrition.

Ears forward, she investigated the fresh meat in the grass, then gave him a tail wag of thanks as she devoured it in a bite.

Hmm. Tomorrow, he'd ask Shay and Bree who she was and where she lived. During patrol, he'd stop by to ensure she was doing all right and getting enough to eat.

Now, if he hadn't seen the elderly female, he'd have offered the mouse to Meggie...although that was courting behavior when not at a Gathering.

Fine with him.

It'd been four days since the feral's attack in the park, and he'd managed to spend time with Margery each day, although his thrice-cursed littermate had optioned much of her time, sending her off to the clan's ill and elderly. Tynan couldn't begrudge her time, not when she was this happy. She loved being a banfasa.

Her life before Cold Creek *had* been a rough one, so

perhaps it was good their relationship was moving at a snail's pace.

Although it was difficult to pull in his instincts. She was soft and curvy and her laugh so infectious he ended up laughing, too. Then she'd turn around and do something so caring that his chest ached. And he'd kiss her and end up with aching balls the remainder of the night because she made him so hard that even a cat's claws wouldn't scratch his dick.

He watched her crossing the meadow, her fur almost golden in the moonlight. Her ankle slowed her pace, so she'd run with Angie among the less competitive mid-aged wolves.

He'd seen that the pack was beginning to accept the newcomer. Wolf instincts said to drive away a physically challenged stranger, but shifters were more than their animals.

This pack had a good heart.

Which was good because his own heart was speaking to him.

Tongue lolling, he trotted across the meadow toward the little wolf. Her stillness made him slow.

Her attention was focused on two wolves facing off near the tree line.

The male wolf deliberately knocked into the female hard enough to throw her sideways.

The female—was that Lacey?—scrambled for her footing.

Tynan growled, expecting the alpha or beta to intervene. Ah, no, Shay and Zeb were on the other side of the meadow, dealing with a couple of males who wanted to fight. Young males turned stupid as the moon neared full.

Up to him, then. He loped that direction.

As the aggressive male bit Lacey's shoulder and drove her into a tree, Meggie reached the two.

She shifted to human, set her hands on her hips, and yelled, "What in the Mother's name are you doing? Do males here think it's fun to hurt their female packmates?"

Tynan opened his jaws in a wolfy smile. The last time he'd heard such a set down, a human elder had scolded two young shoplifting males so thoroughly they'd slunk out of the corner market with heads hanging.

But this shameless male snarled at Meggie, fangs bared.

Tynan growled. Pack enforcement wasn't his job, but too bad. He sprang, hit the male hard enough to knock him off his paws, and closed his jaws over the insolent boggart's throat.

The male froze, then went limp in submission.

Now what? In his mind, if an adult saw scat like this happening, he should act, authority or not. But, would the alpha see it that way?

"Thank you, Tynan." From behind, Shay answered the question.

Zeb, still in wolf form, stalked over.

Releasing the male, Tynan stationed himself beside

Meggie who'd knelt to put her arms around the shaking young female wolf.

Meggie whispered, "Thanks, Tynan."

It seemed he wasn't in trouble with the alpha or Meggie. Life was good. Crouching beside her, he placed himself between whatever happened and the two females.

The aggressive wolf shifted to human form. He was probably in his twenties. "I didn't do anything, Shay. That asshole from Seattle attacked me without any reason. He's probably been around humans too long and—"

"You're lying, Chad. You hurt Lacey, got scolded, and snarled at Margery. Showed your fangs, no less." With the moon behind him, Shay cast a long shadow.

"But..."

"Just because the pack's former beta was crazy and gave you young males a fucked-up example to follow is no longer an excuse. We've given you numerous warnings—and over a year to change your ways." Shay's infuriated growl, even coming from a human chest, made every wolf in the pack lower slightly.

Chad took a step back.

"Daonain females are protected—not hurt—by males. This is our Law. And your time is up, Chad."

The young male turned a pasty white.

"By the Law of the Pack, I cast you out. You have until tomorrow at midnight to leave. After that, if we find you anywhere in our lands, you will be driven away with fangs and pain and blood."

"You can't..." the male gasped.

Shay crossed his arms over his chest. "Leave."

When the male took a step forward, Zeb's subterranean-sounding growl changed his mind.

Shifting to wolf, Chad fled.

When the whispers started up, Tynan tilted his ears to hear.

"Good thing."

"...been damned patient. Stupid Chad."

"Had to make an example..."

"Couple of others better learn from this."

Not one voice spoke in dissent.

Meggie had one arm around Lacey and gripped Tynan's ruff with her other hand. Her fingers tightened in his fur as Shay approached.

The alpha stopped. "Are you all right, Lacey?"

The young female wolf nodded and edged closer to Meggie.

Amusement tickled Tynan's throat. The pretty banfasa was a comfort to all ages, wasn't she?

"Margery, Darcy told us you were always trying to protect the Scythe captives. I'm sorry you had to intervene here." Shay smiled at her. "But I'm glad you're in my pack."

Tears gleamed in her eyes, and Tynan felt her fingers tremble. He gave her cheek a comforting lick. She leaned harder against him.

"Tynan." Zeb had shifted to human. His voice sounded like coarse gravel. "Our pack needs another beta."

Unsure whether to run for the hills or volunteer, Tynan pricked up his ears.

Shay grinned. "We need another strong protector. A teacher. A good example for our cubs. Someone stable, since as cahirs, Zeb and I often get sent away on the Cosantir's tasks."

Ah. They wanted a beta who wasn't a cahir, one who could stay with the pack.

But...there were wolves who'd been with the pack for years. Decades. Ones who really belonged. Tynan shook his head hard enough to make his ears flap.

Zeb almost grinned. "You really think you can refuse?"

Meggie gave his fur a tug in an unspoken order. *Say yes.*

Shay's gaze met his. "We really do need you, Tynan."

By the Gods, what was he thinking? A wolf didn't refuse his alpha's request...let alone a pretty female's. Shifting to human, Tynan rose to his feet. "Aye. I'll serve."

Shay grinned and spoke to the wolves who'd congregated around them. "And that answer is why we wanted him. A real beta doesn't terrorize the pack—he serves. Protects."

Nods and smiles showed the pack agreed.

Expecting disapproval and rejection, instead, Tynan found only acceptance. As the bonds connecting him to the pack strengthened with their welcome, he swallowed against the tightness in his throat.

Shay slapped Tynan's shoulder. "Come to the lodge tomorrow. We'll treat you to Bree's chocolate cake and talk."

"You caved too soon." A corner of Zeb's mouth tilted up. "I looked forward to walloping you until you gave in."

Tynan snorted...and felt the hum of the moon rising in his blood. Zeb was a worthy, canny fighter. "We can still indulge. For fun."

Zeb grinned. "Wear comfortable clothes when you show up tomorrow."

"You're on." Reaching down, Tynan helped Meggie gain her feet and, without thinking, put an arm around her waist.

Shay grinned. "Good."

Although Meggie looked confused, Tynan knew exactly what the alpha meant.

Even better, she didn't step away. They were both naked, and her warm, smooth skin against his incited all sorts of interesting sensations.

Rather than carry her off into the forest—his first choice—Tynan smiled at the young wolf who stayed beside Meggie. "Lacey, I've heard Jody likes teaching wolf fighting. Shall we see if that's true?"

Lacey shifted to human. "Oh, wow, for real? She didn't say anything about that. *Yes.*"

In the circle of his arm, Meggie gave a bounce. "Tynan, would she teach me, too?

Fuck, what have I started?

Shay nodded. "Jody enjoys teaching fang and claw."

"Then let's make it so," Tynan said. It would be good for both females to have the skills and confidence that the ability to fight would give them.

Smiling, he brushed his chin over the top of Meggie's head. She'd learn that this pack would support her, help her grow stronger.

As would he.

The moon was high in the night sky. It must be around midnight, and the wolf pack was still in the meadow. Margery realized she wasn't the only shifter shaken by Chad's expulsion.

Rather than continuing the run, Shay had told everyone to shift to skin for a while. The clever alpha was letting them all vent.

Margery had heard tales about the previous alpha and how his insane beta hurt females. Discovering Klaus had assaulted Bree at a Gathering, the Cosantir delivered the God's judgment. Margery shivered. Everyone said Calum had merely touched him, and the beta dropped dead.

Unfortunately for the pack, Klaus's influence still lingered with the younger males. Bullying of cubs and females still occurred. Chad had been the worst offender.

After roaming the meadow for a while, she joined the group that held Bonnie, Bree, and Angie.

"I agree with driving Chad out," Bonnie said. "But my heart hurts at the loss of what he could have been. He was a good pup at one time."

"I've seen that happen before with young males," Margery murmured.

"What do you mean?" Bree asked.

Now the center of attention, Margery tensed. In Ailill Ridge, attracting attention never ended well for her.

But this was a different pack—and she wasn't going to flee from the past.

Bree gave her an encouraging smile.

All right then. "In the Scythe compound, the older guards caned us for the slightest mistake. Although the newer guards hated the brutality, they didn't protest." Her hands fisted. Would the bitter lessons give her more compassion, more strength going forward? Surely something good should come of such pain. "Maybe if the decent guards had spoken out in the beginning, cruelty wouldn't have become a habit for them all."

"By the Hunter's horns, that's exactly what happened here," Albert Baty said. "We didn't speak up, so our younglings absorbed Klaus's beliefs. We bear much of the responsibility for what Chad has become."

"Aye, we neglected our responsibility to pack and clan." Angie crossed her arms over her chest. "Shay shouldn't have to do everything. Pack pressure is a force to be reckoned with. We mustn't be silent in the face of cruelty or bullying or lack of respect."

The group around them had grown, and growls showed Angie's words had hit home.

Even as people started to move away, they nodded at Margery, patted her shoulder in gratitude. Their approval warmed her more than if she'd stood in a pool of sunlight.

She'd helped.

This pack was so different than the one in Rainier where she'd decided that her dreams of belonging were only that—dreams. Here, she was accepted and welcomed. Needed, even.

She drew the feelings of belonging around her, as close as her own fur. Deep inside, the pack bonds were forming, tying her to them all.

A yip drew her attention.

On the other side of the meadow, Shay trawsfurred to wolf, and the moonlight gleamed on his fluffy silver-gray fur. With a sharp bark, he ordered his pack to shift.

Responding with yips and barks, his wolves complied.

Surrounded by the others, Margery trawsfurred, soaking in the wave of the Mother's love even as fur enfolded her. Tail waving slightly, she gave a little shake to settle her fur. Her nose sharpened, bringing her the scents of the other wolves, the fragrance of a stream.

Would she ever get past the wonder of becoming a wolf?

A heavy-boned wolf with a coat the color of mountain granite stalked over to her. *Tynan*.

Her paws danced in happiness when he joined her.

He rubbed his side against her in a possessive blending of their scents. Tail waving, she licked his muzzle and got a teasing nip on her nape in return.

Wolf-flirting was...*fun*.

Margery took a slow breath. Overhead, the round moon hung so low it seemed a leap would lift her to its heart.

Facing the pack, Shay lifted his muzzle and howled—a song of love to the Goddess. Bree joined him a second later.

Zeb joined the alpha pair's song with his lower rougher howl.

When Tynan came in, his smooth, deep tone sank deep into Margery's soul.

For a long lovely minute, the four leaders' voices twined together, and then the rest of the wolves joined in.

Her own howl lifted high, and deep inside her, she felt the pack bonds strengthening.

As the moon filled the dark sky with her glow, their compelling paean of joy swept past mountains and forests and rose to the Mother of All.

"That was a wonderful run," Margery said as Tynan pulled into the driveway between their two houses. Then she remembered what else had happened. *Chad.*

She shook her head and sighed.

Tynan unbuckled his seatbelt and studied her for a moment. "You're thinking of Chad?"

"He's all alone now. Probably not sure what to do or where to go."

Tynan ran his hand over her hair. "It's a hard lesson. I was like him once, you know, only maybe worse, since it was banished, I was."

Oh, dear Goddess. "Banished?"

"Aye, after a young male attacked me during a full moon, and I hit him. He fell wrong, broke his neck, and I was cast out."

Margery stared at him, hearing, almost feeling the sadness pouring off of him. "But if he simply fell wrong, your punishment was awfully brutal."

"I'm not sure if the God agreed with the Cosantir, but I did. I felt so fucking guilty then—and later, as well. I asked the God what I could do to restore the balance." He was looking through the window at the moonlight on the lawn.

Asked the God? She blinked, realizing he'd undertaken the arduous ritual to speak to the Gods. What had Herne told him to do? Oh, no, she knew already... "The God sent you to Seattle."

"He did. That's why I was there."

Sympathy—and admiration—filled her. Had she ever met anyone so honorable? He'd made a mistake and tried to make things right. Really, that he'd tell her about the death and his banishment—what he saw as a black mark on his past—was amazing.

His gaze was on her, patient. Waiting for her to condemn him or question him.

She wouldn't, didn't need to. Instead, she took his hand and pressed a kiss to his palm. "Do you think Chad will learn from this?"

Relief at her acceptance softened his expression. Then Tynan caressed her cheek. "Chad might change. It must have shocked him that his behavior wasn't condoned by the pack like he thought. Young males can misjudge and think others admire their actions. More often, the others are wary —and don't like them at all. Tonight, Chad learned the truth."

Perhaps the truth would give him a chance to turn his behavior around. Margery leaned her head into Tynan's touch. The cop was more than a shield between the good and bad. He understood people. "I hope so."

"It's a good pack." He dropped a kiss on her head and got out.

By the time she'd opened her door and was sliding out, he was there.

"How's the ankle?" Shutting the car door, he curved an arm around her waist. A support...and more. An embrace.

Oh, yes.

Firmly, he moved her a step back until her butt and back were against the car door. He tangled his fingers in her hair, brushing it back in long tugging strokes.

Each breath brought her his scent, a werewolf's wild forest tang and his warm, dry woodsy fragrance. Leaning into him, she rubbed her cheek against his chest. She'd dreamed of his kiss. Of his hands. "Mmm."

"All right then," he murmured. He set two fingers under her chin and lifted her head. His mouth tilted up at the corner before his lips touched hers.

Warmth spread through her in a slowly kindling fire.

His firm lips were like velvet. Beard stubble was a slight rasp when he nibbled along her jaw and back to her lips. He deepened the kiss, teasing her mouth open, possessing her with his tongue, even as his hand against her ass drew her closer.

His hard, thick erection pressed against her abdomen, delighting her because...even though it wasn't a Gathering, he wanted her.

Wrapping her arms around his neck, she simply enjoyed.

The sound of a car coming down the street broke the moment.

With a low groan, Tynan moved back slightly. "Invite me in, lass."

She laughed. "Please come into my home, Beta."

He kept her next to him, hip to hip, as they walked up the sidewalk to her house and inside. After glancing at her bedroom door, he shook his head, took the couch, and pulled her down. On top of him.

She would have gone to the bedroom with him. Of course, he probably knew that from the scent of her interest. But he'd said he intended to go slow.

Apparently, he really did mean that.

When he was finished getting settled, his head was on the soft armrest, and she lay with her breasts crushed against his chest.

"Nice," he rumbled before cupping her ass with one big hand. His other hand closed over her nape, pulling her mouth back to his.

Oh, he could kiss, using teeth and tongue and lips until her entire body was one big pool of desire.

He slid his hand under her shirt to caress her back. The same touch that had comforted her when she'd had a meltdown sent tingles rampaging through her with every slow stroke.

Lifting up, she squirmed on top of him, needing...more.

The heat in his blue eyes lightened with laughter. But he pushed on her shoulders until she was sitting upright on top of him.

He didn't want her? "But..."

"We're not stopping, little wolf." His voice was as heady a caress as his touch. Smiling, he ran his hands up her sides until they rested on the outsides of her breasts. "I simply want access to these. I've wanted to touch you...everywhere...since I saw you at the last Gathering."

When she walked away from him that night, it had been the right thing to do—for her—at the time.

Now, he'd won her trust.

His touch had grown more intimate every time they were together. Tonight...

He waited for her to decide.

She pulled her baggy shirt up and over her head. She hadn't worn a bra—she never did on pack run nights.

His appreciative grin was a flash of white in the dimly lit room. His warm hands cupped her breasts, moving over the sensitive flesh, molding, lifting. The calluses on his palms added an edge to his careful touch.

Heat streaked through her, and she could smell the way her own scent changed with arousal.

"Mmmmmm." His deep rumble of approval was like a heady caress, making her shiver.

Putting an iron-hard arm around her, he drew her down so he could take her lips again. Even as his mouth closed over hers, his thumb circled one tightly bunched nipple.

Pleasure exploded through her, and she moaned.

A screech of brakes brought her out of the fog of desire. A car door slammed, followed by pounding from next door. At Tynan and Donal's house.

"Donal, need help! Got banged-up shifters here. Two-car accident," a man yelled.

"By Herne's hooves." Tynan pulled in an exasperated breath.

He set her up, gliding his fingertips over her cheek. "I should go help. There might be more injured or a mess on the highway."

Or bodies. "Of course." With a grunt of effort, she swung off him, feeling the ache of unresolved need deep in her pelvis.

As he rose, she bit her lip. "Do you think Donal would like my help, too?"

Tynan bent to kiss her again. "Banfasa, you have his approval, which means he'll always appreciate assistance. The cat loves help."

Oh. That was perfect because she loved giving help.

Smiling, Tynan handed over her shirt. "I'll walk over with you, and we'll take care of things."

Delight sparkled like stars inside her chest.

Hearing a male's raised voice in the waiting area, Donal tuned it out. He didn't have time for peacemaking, not with the way Kepler's lacerated liver was bleeding.

"Am I dyin', healer?" Kepler lay supine on the exam table.

"No, bear, you're not." With the abundance of alcohol in the idiot's system, he probably wasn't in too much pain, either. "Now, shut up while I try to put your liver back together."

And next time wear your seatbelt.

No point in saying that now. Not when the shifter's brain had sopped up that much alcohol. Bending his head, Donal extended his sight, sent forth power, and slowly, carefully, mended the tears on the liver, then healed the rest of the mess.

Finished, he straightened and saw Kepler had passed out. Didn't that just figure.

After washing his hands, Donal walked out into the waiting area. If anything, the noise had gotten worse. To his surprise, little Margery was there, standing in front of Emma and Darcy, defending the injured females from Kepler's littermate, Norman.

"I don't care whose fault it is," she was saying calmly. "This isn't the place or the time. Leave them alone."

Norman started to advance on her—*lovely, he, too, was*

intoxicated—and Donal stepped in front of him. "Norman, you—"

"What's going on in here? I could hear you from the street." Tynan walked inside. His frown at Norman had the werebear taking a step back.

Excellent timing, brawd.

Hearing the unspoken words, Tynan nodded to Donal. "Vehicles are secured off the road—and you have no more injured, other than this bunch."

Now that was the kind of report Donal liked.

"Deputy." Donal gave his littermate a quick grin for the use of his official law enforcement title. "Can you collect Kepler from the healing room and see that he and Norman here get home safely."

"Sure and I can do that." Tynan shot a look at Norman. "Norman, you're going to want to back away from our banfasa and healer. Right this fecking minute."

The growl that ended the order made Norman backpedal clumsily. "Sorry, sorry," he said to Donal and Margery, before turning to Tynan. "Deputy, hey, those females, they caused that fucking accident. It wasn't Kepler's fault, not at all. They—"

Ignoring Norman, Tynan disappeared into the healing room and returned with Kepler in his arms. "You can tell me all about the accident on the way to your house. Your littermate needs to be in his bed, don't you think?"

Not waiting for an answer, Tynan winked at Donal and Margery and simply walked out the door.

After a moment to get his brain into gear, Norman followed.

"Whew, wasn't that fun," Margery muttered and pulled in a breath. "Healer, Darcy has a fractured wrist. The side window broke and gashed Emma's head and shoulder. She might have a bit of a concussion, too—she thinks it was her head that broke the window."

She'd stepped back to stand between the two women who were seated on the bench. Both women leaned against her, like she was their pillar of strength.

But their pillar was shaking, too.

Donal stepped close and touched Margery's cheek with his fingertips. Evaluating. Pale face, skin too cold, heart racing. "He scared you."

"Some." She drew herself up and nodded at the two females. "He scared them worse."

Aye, and Norman's yelling would certainly frighten the already shaken females. Especially these two who, like Margery, had experienced violence in their pasts.

"Darcy, let's get that wrist taken care of." He could see Margery had done quick patch jobs on both female's wounds and splinted the fractured wrist. He gave her a nod of gratitude. "Nice work. Thank you, banfasa."

With Donal's help, Darcy rose. One step into the healing room, and she was trying to back away. "I can't. Just can't—it's too much..."

Gnome-guts, he should have expected this. She'd had a similar reaction before. Another Dogwood female. Her friends and family had died on the laboratory tables that apparently looked too much like his.

"Shhh, it's all right." Margery put an arm around Darcy's waist. "I'll be with you."

Stilling, Darcy leaned on her, breathing hard.

Emma made a tiny whining sound.

Donal realized she didn't want to be left alone out here. She'd had her own trauma in the past—and males yelling would trigger those memories. "Emma—"

Before he could say more, the banfasa, who had set aside her fears to protect these females, arranged matters for him.

"We'll all go in so Donal can get you healed. I'll sit with you both." Margery gave him a look that said he'd better go along with her plan, then grinned at the other females. "I kind of like outnumbering the lonely male, don't you?"

With a weak laugh at the joke, Emma rose, staggered one step, and then Margery tucked her arm around the bard.

Donal waved them all into his healing room. He had quiet, cooperative patients and an extra set of hands. There was no way he'd complain.

On the contrary, he planned to thank the Gods later for the gift of this banfasa.

CHAPTER THIRTEEN

Cold Creek, North Cascades Territory - full moon

The next night, Margery smiled at herself in the mirror, filled with the joy of wearing the first new clothing she'd ever bought on her own. With her very own wages.

The top's jade color brought out the green in her hazel eyes and set off her light tan. Best of all, the shirt had breast support built in. No messing around with a bra during the Gathering.

She'd left her hair loose, and wasn't it awesome that it now reached past her shoulders. She batted her eyelashes and tossed her hair back in the flirty way other females used. Maybe she'd missed learning how to be a female during her teen years, but she was catching up now.

Tonight, Tynan would be at the Gathering.

So would Donal.

The female parts between her legs tingled in anticipation even before the rising of the moon. Because she was pretty sure she'd be with Tynan tonight—no, she *knew* that would happen. She couldn't wait. Finally, she'd be able to kiss and touch all of him. Feel his weight on her. Have him kiss her and take her and...

The room had certainly gotten warmer.

And maybe...Donal. Would he want her? There were times he looked at her like he saw her as more than a banfasa. As a female. Like his concern for her last night. How he'd touched her cheek. And when she'd said goodbye to return home, he'd thanked her, given her a wicked, very masculine smile, and said he'd see her tonight.

But maybe that was simply hopeful thinking on her part. He was probably mobbed by females at the Gatherings.

Just like that, her stomach tightened because...females probably mobbed both Donal *and* Tynan, and really, she wasn't what males looked for in a female. She wasn't muscular or particularly fit. Not beautiful.

But that didn't seem to bother Tynan. When he looked at her, she felt beautiful. And Donal made her feel the same way. Her hopes rose again. And jumped higher because sometimes littermates shared a female. She'd never done that before, had never even thought it would be something she'd like, but...Donal and Tynan together?

Yes, please.

The knocking on the front door startled her, and she ran to answer it.

"Heather!" She drew the redhead into a hug.

Heather hugged back. "Don't look so surprised. I told you I'd be back for this Gathering."

"It's great to see you. Come on in."

Stopping in the living room, Heather pursed her lips. "Small but really cozy. Angie said you've done a ton of work. Are you going to stay here?"

Margery half-laughed. "A waitress's salary doesn't go far enough for a house. I only have the place rent free for two months in exchange for making it sellable." In fact, she needed to start thinking about her next step. "Did you want to hang out here before the Gathering? I have iced tea."

"Hang out, yes. Here, no." Heather ran her fingers through her thick hair. "Angie realized you might not know there's usually a clan meeting before moonrise. Vicki is commandeering the fireplace seats for a bunch of us—and said one of the seats is yours."

Vicki was so nice. But would she be intruding? "Well..."

Heather nudged her shoulder. "C'mon, you. I need another unmated female there."

Heather needed her. "Sure, I'd love to join you."

"Perfect. If we leave now, we'll be right on time."

A few minutes later, they hurried up to the tavern's front door where the Murphy brothers stood guard to shoo away any humans.

"Heather." Kevin waggled his eyebrows at her. "Save me 'n' Cody some time if you can."

"We'll see." Heather patted his arm. "Have you two met Margery?"

"Our favorite waitress," Cody said with a smile. "We're at the diner a lot."

Heather arched an eyebrow at Margery. "I hadn't thought of that. You picked a fine way to meet everyone in town."

"I did." Margery smiled at the brothers as Kevin held the door open.

Inside, shifters filled the tavern, sitting at tables and the bar, standing against the walls. And this time, the experience was so different from the Gathering last month. This time, Heather—*and* Margery received cheerful greetings. From packmates, diner customers, the shifters she'd tended as a banfasa.

The glow of belonging had her smiling as they crossed the room to the fireplace.

On one couch, Vicki sat with Sorcha and Toren in her lap. On the other couch, Darcy had the third cub. Bree was in the chair.

A new fire in the fireplace was beginning to catch. Smoke swirled around the biggest log where a salamander perched, impatiently waiting for the heat to build.

"Yay!" Bree made a happy sound. "My wolves are here. I don't like being outnumbered by felines."

Baby in one arm, Darcy reached up to hug Margery. "Thanks for last night."

"I'm glad I was there. You look all better."

"You and Donal do good work." Darcy smiled. "I stopped by your place earlier to round you up, but you weren't home. Heather said she'd fetch you no matter what it took."

"There was no problem in talking her into joining us." Heather blew on her fingernails, rubbed them on her shirt, in a human mannerism that Margery had never quite understood. "I'm just that convincing."

"Manipulative, you mean." Vicki handed the blonde cubling to Heather. "I was hoping you'd come up from Rainier this month."

"Ah well, I have to make sure you're treating my Sorcha like the princess she is." Heather settled into a chair and started telling Sorcha about her horrible week. Apparently being CEO of a software company was akin to being in a war zone.

The kit waved her hands every time Heather laughed.

"I need a snuggle, too." Margery gave in to her own cub-craving and picked up Toren. As she nuzzled his downy-soft black hair, he gurgled his enjoyment.

Vicki shook her head. "You know, I've noticed the first thing any female wolf does is cuddle a baby. Angie doesn't even say hi before she snatches one up."

"Us wolves are all about the pack—and the pack is all

about cubs." Heather blew a raspberry on Sorcha's tummy, getting a squeal.

Sitting down beside Vicki, Margery looked at the females around her. "Did you just come for the meeting? Cuz...aren't most of you lifemated? I thought Gatherings were only for single shifters."

"We're not here to have sex." Darcy nibbled on Artair's fingertips to make him laugh. "We're here to keep Vicki company until our males drag us home for fun times."

"Okay, then why is Vicki here?" Margery put Toren on her knees to let him practice sitting. His wide smile said he liked the position.

"For Calum. Having the Cosantir here keeps the males in line, so he stays for most of the night." Vicki took a sip of her drink. "He likes lifemated males here for the same reason. Discouraging a brawl is easier than breaking one up."

Brawling. What she'd hated most about the Ailill Ridge Gatherings. "Bless him."

Bree nodded. "What with the abusive examples of the previous alpha and betas, Shay and Zeb try to keep an eye on our wolves. Me, too, because a couple of our female wolves sometimes need a good bite on the butt. So, I'm here to keep them in line."

Heather smirked. "Until your two cahirs give in to the full moon's effect on their testosterone levels and haul you away."

"Well, yes." Bree flushed a colorful pink. "Last month,

we didn't even make it back to the lodge. I got ravaged right there on the path—bare-ass naked in freezing weather."

Snickers broke out.

Margery sighed because, admit it, she could imagine herself there with Donal and Tynan. But thinking there could be anything permanent with them? Those were autumn leaf thoughts, doomed to be swept away by a brisk wind.

Because, realistically speaking, all she had to do was look at Heather—so pretty and lean and smart and nice, yet still unmated.

Before the conversation continued, the Cosantir's deep voice rose over the noise. "Daonain. It's good to see you here tonight before the rising of the moon."

As the room quieted, Calum started the meeting. He talked about humans encroaching farther into the territory. About hellhound sightings. He reminded them to stay inside and safe on the dark of the moon.

Finishing up, he told of births and deaths and ended with, "We welcome a new shifter to the North Cascades Territory. Margery, originally from Dogwood, is a server at Angie's Diner. She's also a banfasa and is working with Donal. The clan increases."

The crowd in the room echoed back, "The Clan increases," and Margery was the recipient of a myriad of smiles.

———

Donal was used to people not being *completely* honest.

To his littermate, everything was black or white, and lying was wrong. Period. Many law enforcement people had that mindset.

But, truly, dishonesty came in many shades. Lying to a healer was common, and his patients misled themselves as much as they did him—and for the same reason. Fear. They wanted to deny anything was wrong with their bodies, their minds, their loved ones. Understandable enough, although not something he would allow.

However, malicious lies about another person fell into a whole different category.

If he'd been in cat form, his claws would be unsheathed right now.

After talking with Margery last Monday, he'd dropped in at the B&B and the Wildwood Lodge. On Gathering day, there were always a few Rainier Territory shifters in town. Donal had sniffed out any Ailill Ridge shifters who'd been tended by Margery—like the two cats after a wolf-cat brawl —or had relatives or friends who'd been her patients. They all said she was excellent. Were appalled she'd left. Wanted her back.

Self-reproach nipped Donal's conscience. He should have asked Gretchen and Caleb more questions. They'd out-and-out lied to him about the little banfasa, and he now had proof.

Now he could play with them.

His gaze turned toward the bar and the two lying weasels.

The meeting was over. Seniors, lifemated adults, and children were heading home, leaving the tavern to females of child-bearing age and single males.

Donal strolled up to the bar and halted behind his prey who sat on barstools. "Gretchen, Caleb. Just who I wanted to speak with." His voice was loud enough to attract attention, and curious gazes turned his way.

"Donal, how nice to see you." Gretchen leaned forward to give him a view of her breasts.

Pretty breasts. Not interested.

Gretchen's outer appearance might be perfection, but inside she was pure ugliness.

Beside Gretchen, Caleb growled at what he saw as competition. "What d'you want?"

"Last Gathering, you told me about a banfasa named Margery." He moved within sniffing distance. The moon hadn't yet risen so the air was mostly free of the scents of testosterone and heated females. If he made Gretchen or Caleb nervous, everyone around would be able to sniff out their lies.

Gretchen sneered. "What about Margery?"

Behind the bar, the Cosantir silently moved closer.

"You said Caleb almost bled to death because the banfasa insisted on caring for her friends first." Donal tilted his head in consideration. "Yes, that's exactly what you said."

Gretchen frowned. "So?"

"Where were you injured that night, Caleb?"

Caleb scowled. "None of your fucking business. I'm not—"

"I'd like to hear the answer, as well." Tynan joined Donal.

Brows drawing together, Caleb looked around...and tensed.

Scars like white tattoos running up his forearms, Thorson stood on Caleb's other side. The old werecat had a deadly look in his eyes.

Alec took the stool next to Gretchen. Owen, his fellow cahir, stood beside him.

"Caleb? I'd like an answer, please." Donal kept his tone polite, his claws sheathed. Mustn't kill the prey too quickly. "Where were you injured?"

"My arm. A cat clawed my arm."

"Ah. Show me where. Exactly."

Scowling, Caleb curved his fingers and motioned down the outside of his left arm.

"There are no arteries there." Donal put a snap in his voice. "Were you really in danger of bleeding to death?"

A long growl preceded the answer. "No."

"So, Gretchen lied to me, and you backed up her lie."

Another growl, that of a trapped dog. "Aye."

When Tynan growled back, Donal shot his brother a *shut-it* glare, before turning his attention to Gretchen. "You told me the banfasa was terrible at her job. Is that a lie, too?"

"Of course not. I wouldn't—" Gretchen faltered when Donal and the others lifted their noses and sniffed. The air held the foul stench of a lie. "Fine, yes, I, maybe, stretched the truth a little bit."

"You lied," Donal said flatly. "Aside from her move to Cold Creek, was there any time someone needed the banfasa where she wasn't available?"

"I have no idea. I don't keep track of her movements."

"That you know of—was there any time?"

"No," Gretchen muttered.

"Why did they lie about our banfasa?" Alec's soft voice was louder than normal.

Clever Alec. It would be good to let people know how Rainier Territory tried to manipulate the people in Cold Creek. "You tried to destroy her reputation as a banfasa with us—so she wouldn't be able to work here. Is that right?"

Gasps sounded around the room.

Neither Gretchen nor Caleb spoke.

Their fucking lies could have destroyed Margery. The anger grew inside him until he was ready to shift and start ripping guts out. He hissed a warning.

Caleb flinched back, then gave a jerky nod.

"You wanted to make sure she'd have no choice except to return to Ailill Ridge and be your banfasa there?" Donal looked at Gretchen.

The silence lengthened.

"*Answer* me."

"Yes, okay. Yes." Gretchen scowled at him. "That was why."

A lust-filled howl sounded from near the door. The moon was rising.

"You fecking, lying weasels." Tynan's voice went guttural with his rage, and his hands were in fists. He took a step forward.

Donal did, too. "Let's rip them to pieces."

"Sorry, lads." Alec gripped Donal's arm, then Tynan's. "You two would destroy them—and the Cosantir gets irritated about blood on his pretty hardwood floors."

Tynan's response was a threatening growl.

"Now, Deputy." Alec half-smiled. "Don't do this, because...I'll help. And if I jump in, Calum will lecture me... again...on decorum and other annoying subjects."

Tynan's hands slowly unfisted. "Fecking liars."

"Dammit, Alec," Donal muttered, exchanging a frustrated glance with Tynan.

"Yeah, I'm sorry." Alec rested his hand on his weapons belt. "However, I daresay Calum will express his displeasure."

As if to confirm his littermate's opinion, Calum leaned on the bar. "Gretchen. Caleb. If I could have your attention, please."

The two stiffened and turned slowly.

They should be worried. The Cosantir's expression was

colder than the glacier on Mt. Baker. "Dishonesty is repugnant, in and of itself. But your lie wasn't to escape trouble. You deliberately lied about another Daonain to force her to do what you wanted. To destroy her life if she didn't."

Both shifters stared at the Cosantir, too terrified to even move.

"You aren't in my clan and not mine to punish, but I can and will keep you out of my territory. In the morning, leave —and do not return."

Donal heard Gretchen heave a relieved breath...until Calum looked over her head at Alec. "Sheriff, I have no interest in monitoring these two during a Gathering. Remove them to your station and lock them in separate cells until moonset."

The sheriff covered his mouth, trying to smother a laugh.

And Donal had to do the same. Talk about torture... When the moon rose, Gretchen would grow desperate for males and matings. Being penned up in a cell would be acutely painful.

Jailed next to her, every breath bringing him the scent of a female in heat, Caleb wouldn't be much better off.

Tynan grinned as Alec snagged the two and escorted them out of the Wild Hunt. "Good punishment, but how'd Calum know?"

Donal bumped his shoulder against his littermate's. "The Cosantir has exceptional hearing. It's why I ambushed them at the bar."

"You're a credit to your feline genes." Tynan narrowed his eyes. "Their lies... That's why you were so rude to Meggie? Why didn't you tell me?"

"Since she said—at first—she didn't want to be a banfasa, her incompetence wasn't important." Donal shook his head. "Only she's not incompetent. Quite the reverse."

"Couldn't you tell she was extremely skilled from seeing her with our wounded in Seattle?"

"In Seattle? You mean at the compound?" Donal frowned, trying to remember through the fog of that night. "Was she...? Of course, she must have been there."

"Oh, gnome-nuts," Tynan said. "You don't remember, do you?"

"I vaguely recall removing the females' trackers...I think."

Tynan snorted. "You took the trackers out while Meggie dressed the incisions. Then you dropped like a rock, and even though all the other females left, she insisted on staying behind to care for the injured."

A captive in the middle of a battle. She must have been terrified. Yes, she stayed. Because it was who she was. Yes, she belonged here in the North Cascades Territory where they would treat her right. "I know the truth now. Even better, she forgave me for being a boggart-brain."

Tynan barked a laugh. "You're lucky she's not a werecat, or you'd have lost some blood."

"Ah, but she's a wolf. A sweet little wolf...who likes us

both." As Donal felt the slow rise of desire in his blood, he smiled at his littermate. "It's Gathering night."

A corner of Tynan's mouth tilted upward. "Shall we see if she's interested in two unworthy males this night?"

It had been too long since he'd shared a female with his brother. "Aye, we—"

"Healer!" Rebecca hurried up to him. "Three yowling idiots were showing off for a female and jumped off their balcony at the B&B. Can you come?"

Cat-scat. With a resigned sigh, Donal asked, "How bad is it?" Would he need additional power?

"One broke his ankle. Couple sprains. I think the third dislocated his shoulder."

"All right then." There were days that life simply wasn't fair. The air was scented with the potent fragrance of fertile females. Shifters were already heading to the mating rooms upstairs. And he had to *leave*. "The mangy, sprite-brains are going to get a healer grumpier than a burrowless gnome."

Rebecca burst out laughing. "They'll deserve anything you say."

With a sigh, Donal nudged Tynan's shoulder. "Don't wait for me, brawd. Go let the little banfasa know she's desired."

"All right." Tynan nudged back, sympathy in his gaze. "Perhaps this is better—for her. She's still new to Gatherings. Two-on-one might be best saved for later. There will be other nights."

Trust Tynan to find the good in a situation.

Donal followed Rebecca out.

Really, shouldn't I claw the stupid fairy-farts just a little? For their own good?

Under the power of the full moon, Margery had dutifully mated with one shifter, then another. Mother's breasts, but it was embarrassing to realize she didn't even remember their names.

Back downstairs, she found herself at the bar, standing like a fool as sensations swirled around her. The forest scent of shifters was intensified by the masculine musk of so many males. The rumble of their deep voices created a captivating song.

However, her body was satisfied enough...at the moment...that she could tell she was thirsty. And look, she stood at the bar. How convenient was that?

The Cosantir was working, serving drinks as needed, and watching the interactions of his clan. Occasionally, amusement would flash over his face.

Although he must feel the moon's effect as much as anyone else, he never looked uncomfortable or impatient. The territory's guardian had amazing control.

Turning, he spotted her and walked over. "Banfasa, might I get you something to drink?"

Being given the respectful title by the Cosantir sent pride rushing through her. "Yes, please." However, she'd never learned to like the alcoholic stuff. "Do you have any fruit juice?"

"Apple, cranberry, and orange."

"Oh, apple would be wonderful." Her favorite.

When he set the glass in front of her, she drank it down within seconds. "Thank you."

Plucking the glass from her, he refilled it and leaned against the bar top. "I was hoping to speak with you tonight."

Alarmed, she took a step back. What had she done wrong?

No, she'd done nothing wrong. *Don't scurry off the trail at a few crackles of the brush.* She swallowed. "Of course, Cosantir. Your will."

"Donal is pleased you agreed to work with him tending our people's health."

Oh, by the Mother, Donal had said that to the Cosantir? Sweet happiness rushed through her. "I'm pleased, as well. To be of value to the clan would be..." The most wonderful thing she could imagine, but she couldn't say something so emotional.

His severe expression lightened with his smile. "He said you want to continue serving meals at the diner, but also work as a banfasa."

"The diner is a wonderful way to meet people." And she couldn't afford to quit. Sometime soon, she'd have to talk with Donal about money. "And it pays the bills."

"Aye, Donal mentioned your treatment in Rainier Territory. It's not how things are done here."

The Cosantir looked pissed, and his eyes darkened.

Shifters standing at the bar were edging away.

As Calum pulled in a slow breath, his eyes returned to gray—and he continued. "In most territories, a shifter who provides essential services to the clan receives a stipend, the amount dependent on the time they put in. Most, like cahirs, work other—regular—jobs."

She nodded. Alec was the county sheriff. Shay and Zeb ran the Wildwood Lodge.

"Donal has no other job—he already puts in too many hours as a healer. I'm pleased you'll give him a chance to cut back."

The thought of making Donal happier was simply lovely. She'd seen how hard he worked. Seen the lines in his face that disappeared when he laughed.

Calum said, "Until we know how much time your banfasa work requires, I'll start you at the minimum amount. If you provide me your bank account number, I'll get automatic deposits set up."

"Automatic deposits?"

"Aye. Vicki is slowly dragging us into the current century." He glanced toward the fireplace where his mate sat, then smiled at Margery. "Donal also said he likes having you next door. Something about his sensitive ears?"

"Oh, that. He hates when pups cry or scream—and he's started sending someone over to fetch me."

Calum snorted. "The cat is the most skilled healer I've ever met and has the least amount of patience."

Margery slapped her hands over her mouth to smother her laugh. *Fail.*

Totally not upset, Calum grinned. "Would you like to continue to live in Leo's house? Rent-free?"

She squeaked like a pup smelling milk. "Yes! That would be wonderful."

He inclined his head. "Then we are in balance for now and will reevaluate in a few moons." After another quick smile, he moved down the bar to deal with a rowdy group of thirsty males.

Margery wrapped her arms around herself. She'd get money, maybe not much, but real money for being a banfasa, and a house to herself.

This was the best week ever. *Donal saying he needed her help. Tynan kissing her. Cookies for doing what she loved to do. Friends who saved her a place at a Gathering. A house.*

She shivered in delight, wishing only that she had someone to share her good news with.

And then...

"Meggie." Tynan stood beside her. He wore jeans and a blue shirt that matched the stunning color of his eyes. Eyes that were now alight with interest and amusement. "You look like the wolf that caught the breakfast bunny."

"I totally caught the bunny." She bounced on her toes. "The Cosantir is going to give me a stipend and let me stay in Leo's house."

"There's good news." He ran his fingers through her hair, and just like that, her body melted, simply melted.

Whatever look was in her face drew him closer until she could feel the heat of his muscular body. Breathe in his woodsy scent.

How could parts of her tighten in need while other parts felt like a molten lake?

She set her hand on his chest and felt the rock-hard muscles tense under her palm.

"Meggie." He put his hand over hers, holding her to him. "And I have to ask now, lass, if you'd like to go upstairs and celebrate your good news?" The lilting Irish of his rich voice was a siren call of wicked desire.

The blue in his eyes captured her, like falling into a warm sunlit lake.

She tried to regain her footing. "Celebrate? Is that what we're calling it now?"

His quick smile lit his face, and he rubbed his cheek against hers. "With you? Aye, and it will be a celebration."

When he swept her into his arms, she squeaked and grabbed his shirt.

Chuckling, he carried her up the stairs and pushed open the door to one of the tiny mating rooms. This one had no fireplace, and the cool air brushed against her heated skin.

Candles in the wall sconces sent soft light across the brown velvet cushions covering the floor. Toeing off his shoes, he left them outside the door, crossed the uneven footing, and laid her on a pile of fat golden pillows.

She pulled off her slippers and tossed them toward the door. Suddenly desperate to have him, she yanked off her shirt—and got caught up in simply staring.

Tynan had closed the door and stripped. As the light rippled over his broad shoulders, he looked like an ancient Gaelic warrior with more than enough muscles to wield a claymore.

Her fingers turned all fumbly as she tried to undo her jeans buttons.

"Why don't you let me do that, lass?" On one knee beside her, he brushed her hands aside and slowly undid each button. "I've been looking forward to this. I wanted to be with you earlier but got called outside to break up a brawl."

Sitting back, he ran his finger over the soft skin of her lower stomach, then up and over her breasts. "You are very beautiful." His gaze said he wasn't lying. That he actually thought that.

The knowledge caught in her throat and squeezed her heart.

Cupping the back of her head, he kissed her. Gently. Reassuringly.

She didn't need reassurance. In her veins, her blood was surging like the ocean tide, her need growing to unbearable heights. This was Tynan who'd run with her through the forests, who'd held her when she was frightened. Who she trusted.

And he smelled like wolf and dark desire.

Lying back, she pulled him down on top of her and ran her hands over his back. His skin felt like satin stretched over steely muscles. She hummed a song of need. "I want..."

"Aye, of course you do," he murmured. He took her lips, demanding her response, and everything in her lower half began to burn.

"I will take you, lass, and it will be as hard as you want—but will last as long as *I* want." His resonant voice held an edge of iron as he cupped her bare breasts.

His palms were warm, the calluses slightly abrasive, sending wonderful warring sensations rippling through her. Her back arched, pushing her breasts into his palms.

He responded by rolling one nipple between his thumb and forefinger and licking around the other.

The sensations tangled in an overwhelming blast of heat, and she moaned, digging her fingernails into his shoulders, trying to pull him down on her.

"Demanding wolflet." He nipped a sensitive spot on the underside of her breast and continued in a heady circle around her nipple. When she began to whine, he closed his mouth over the nipple.

The exquisite pulling on the sensitive nub almost sent her over.

His tongue lashed a quick circle around the areola. Even as he sucked again, he molded her other breast with a powerful hand. And then he switched breasts.

Back and forth, licking and sucking, nibbling and teasing.

By the time he moved down her body, her swollen breasts throbbed around jutting, burning nipples.

A brushed kiss against her belly button made her laugh. "*Tynan.*"

With a quick yank, he divested her of her jeans. Breathing in, he smiled, then licked over the crease between her thigh and groin.

"Oh Goddess." She reached up and grabbed his shoulders, trying to pull him upward. On top of her. "I want... need you inside me."

"And do you now?" He leaned forward and captured her face between his hands. "*A leannán*, you've only been a shifter for a few months. How much experience have you?"

"Lots." There, with that answer, he couldn't stall any longer.

Her gaze slid down his chest, his ridged abdomen to his groin and the trimmed brown hair. His cock was erect, long and thick and so unbelievably beautiful, and she had to have it inside her.

"Any experience outside of mating rooms on a full moon?"

She blinked, met his intent blue eyes. "Um, no."

"I know most shifters give in to a female's demands, let her grab them, and yank them down. Aye?"

"Yes. Do that." Her entire lower half ached with need. She gripped his shoulders and tried to do exactly what he'd said.

He grinned. "As your mentor, it's my duty to broaden

your education." To her complete shock, he rolled her over and set her on her hands and knees.

"What are you *doing?*" She tried to turn back over so he could take her, but he covered her with his body, limiting her movement.

Then his cock pressed against her entrance, and she went still.

There. Yes. She was going to get what she wanted...just different. Her ass tilted up.

Slowly, he pushed inside, thicker than the others before, stretching her around his girth.

Shivers coursed through her as her body welcomed him despite his size. "Yes. Yes. More."

He kept going, so big, filling her to a point where she wasn't sure she could take him, but everything inside her demanded he continue.

And then he was in, his groin hot against her buttocks, his thighs against the back of hers.

She wiggled her demand that he move.

With his chest tight against her back, she could feel as well as hear his rumbling laugh. He nipped her shoulder, sending goosebumps coursing over her arms. "Now, let me show you the advantages of this position."

He was thick inside her, but unmoving. She growled a complaint.

"Mmmhmm." Leaning his weight on one arm, he moved his free hand to her dangling breasts. Teasing and pulling. Pinching her nipples.

Zings of overwhelming pleasure shook her whole body as, somehow, her insides clenched harder around him. She squirmed, needing, needing.

His hand moved downward, over her stomach and...

When his fingers slid through her wetness and over her clit, everything inside her exploded in pleasure as she spasmed around his shaft and shook with the incredible sensations. Coming so hard, she couldn't breathe through the all-consuming waves.

As the sensations slowed and the tingles of pleasure continued to run over her skin, she sucked in air. And realized...his shaft had never moved.

"Mmm, that did feel nice," he murmured in her ear.

Nice was an understatement, Tynan decided. The last few rhythmic clenches around his dick was damned fantastic— and required a tight grip on his control to keep from taking her forcefully.

Instead, he sat back onto his feet and pulled her with him so her back remained against his chest. Now, not having to support himself, he could use both hands on her.

Cupping her left breast with one hand, he felt how her heart still pounded. Her knees were widely parted, outside of his, and his cock impaled her nicely, further anchoring her in place.

When she looked over her shoulder at him, he curled

his other hand around her throat—enforcing the vulnerable wolf position—and kissed her.

Her soft mouth opened to his tongue. Fuck, he loved kissing her.

When he lifted his head, she squirmed on his dick and frowned. "You're...you're still hard. You didn't come. Don't you want to?"

She was delightful.

"Oh, we're not finished. After you come for me again, I'll indulge myself."

"B-but it takes a while before my need will rise again."

What in Herne's hairy balls was wrong with her previous mates? He rubbed his cheek against hers. "It won't take long this time, little wolf."

Rather than explaining, he started to caress her. Her lovely responsive breasts were already swollen and sensitive from his teasing before.

Her gasp told him precisely how sensitive.

Smiling as she began to wiggle, he bit down on the big muscle between her shoulder and neck. Another way to pin her in place while he learned her body. He rolled her nipples between his fingers. He pinched. He tugged. And he watched how her muscles tensed. How her breathing changed with each action.

When her cunt tightened around him, he slid his hand down to cup her pussy.

The way she jumped—and widened her legs farther apart—made him grin.

Gently, he traced circles around the sensitive ball of nerves, took a moment to rub the tightly stretched flesh around his cock, and returned.

Almost too quickly, her breathing sped up, and he could feel her temperature rise, her skin heat.

He pressed against her clit more firmly as he tilted his cock to hit a new area, and suddenly he was holding a very squirmy female.

"Tynan," she demanded, wiggling more, setting off all sorts of sensations.

"Now we will play again," he whispered in her ear and leaned forward, dropping her back onto her hands. Staying inside her the entire time, going nicely deep.

A tremor ran through her, and her fingers curled into the cushions.

He braced himself with an arm on the floor, ran his free hand over her tightly peaked nipples, and down to her clit.

"Now, this is wolf fun," he growled in her ear, pulled almost out, then drove deep.

Her head came up, and she gasped.

Slowly, he pulled back and slammed in again. Opening his hand, he kept one finger rubbing her clit while using his palm on her pelvis to yank her back on his dick.

Feck, she feels good.

She dropped to her elbows, moaning in counterpoint to his thrusts.

Her core tightened around him, her muscles tensing, her breathing almost coming to a halt.

He rolled his hips to give her a change of pace and continued with hard, driving thrusts.

With high-pitched yips, she came, the rolling, clenching of her cunt pulling at him.

Now. With a groan, he let go of his own control, pounding in, long and hard. The tingling ache moved past the base of his spine as the pressure and pleasure grew. Heat rushed through his cock in surge after irresistible surge as he released his seed.

She was still spasming around him as he recovered his senses and kissed her nape. With one hand around her waist, the other on her breast, he toppled them both over onto the cushions.

Soft, giving female. No, more than that—his Meggie. *Meggie mine.*

On his side, he was still intimately deep within her. And with a sigh of pleasure, she wrapped her arms over his, holding him tightly, keeping him wrapped around her.

There was nowhere in the entire universe he'd rather be.

Some time later, Margery pulled in a slow, contented breath. For a long, wonderful while, Tynan had held her against him, then turned her and pulled her on top of him and cuddled her some more.

She could happily stay here forever.

Sure, she'd never come so hard in all her life. But...it was more than that. After mating, her emotions usually felt storm-tossed, and the males always wanted to be done and move on.

Tynan hadn't. He'd pulled her to him, kept her in his arms, nuzzled her hair, stroked her back, held her hand. There had been a different timbre to his rumbling voice as he told her how beautiful she was, how pleased he was to be with her, and how wonderful she'd made him feel. A sound that left her feeling warm. Happy.

The way she'd felt when her mother had told stories to her and her littermates, or when Grandmama had hugged her. Like she was special and appreciated.

Even loved.

"I suppose we have to get moving, don't we?" she murmured unhappily.

"Aye, lass. Unfortunately, I'm not allowed to keep you up here all night." Tynan gave her another slow kiss before rising and pulling her to her feet.

"I wish I could spend the entire night with you, *a lean-nán*." He touched her cheek. "But…"

"It's against the rules. I know." She'd attended enough full moons to know the rules. After mating, a shifter had to return to the Gathering room. She didn't have to choose a male unless she was interested in mating with him, but she still had to be there.

After they showered, he walked her back down to the tavern.

"Where would you like to sit now?" He glanced around the room. "I can stay with you until—"

"You know that's not a good idea." Although she'd love it. Her over-protective warrior. She smiled up at him, surprised at his tender expression. "Emma and Heather are over by the fireplace. How about there? Or does that break some rule of no females together?"

"It's more of a tradition, but simply because when your heat rises, you're interested in seeking out a male and don't want to compete for one."

"Huh. That makes sense." She grinned at him. "However, thanks to your...thoroughness...I'm good for a while. I'll sit with them."

His laugh was like a slow stroke of pleasure deep inside her.

At the fireplace, he saw her seated and kissed her, not the quick peck males usually extended after mating, but a long, slow, deep, almost possessive kiss. "I'll see you tomorrow, Meggie mine."

As he walked away, she couldn't help but watch. Those long, lean legs, the way his jeans fit over his male ass. His... She realized the other two women were awfully quiet and jerked her gaze back. "Um. Hi. How's your night going?"

Heather burst out laughing. "Usually a female looks that lustful *before* a male takes her, not afterward."

Margery felt herself flush—and could only grin.

"He's well worth watching," Emma said in her melodic

contralto. "And is a good male according to my Ben and Ryder. It's nice Donal has his brother home."

"It is." Margery smiled. "Although they sure argue like littermates."

Emma leaned forward. "Really? Tynan looks as if he'd be difficult to rile up."

"Donal's talented that way." Margery grinned. "Like yesterday, Tynan had given him grief for not cleaning up after himself, so the poor cop came back and all the wall paintings were tilted, the chairs and end tables way out of alignment, and the throw rugs crumpled up."

Heather and Emma broke into giggles.

"Tynan said he spent the next half hour straightening things before he could even relax." Margery snickered. "Donal's one sneaky cat."

"A female they shared would be in for interesting times." Heather's comment made Margery's heart give an odd leap.

Share a female? Some littermates did that, not only as lifemates, but in mating rooms.

Donal and Tynan. Together. Heat spread through her in a whole different way than the full moon heat. This was softer, more...glowy. More wistful, because she'd seen how popular both males were with the most beautiful of females.

Margery didn't even reach averagely attractive.

Nodding at the lifemating bracelets on Emma's wrist, she changed the subject. "Are your mates helping to super-vise the Gathering like Vicki, Bree, and Darcy's mates were?"

"Ryder's home with our cub, Minette, but Ben's here. This late at night, Calum takes a break to join Vicki and Alec, so Joe Thorson supervises. Since there've been a couple of fights recently, Ben said he'd back Joe up." Emma smiled. "No one messes with my grizzly cahir."

"Not anyone who wants a long life," Heather said in a dry voice.

"And after last night, they're both keeping an eye on me —even though Donal fixed me up just fine." Emma wrinkled her nose. "Margery, I'm so glad you were there."

"What happened?" Heather asked.

"Darcy was giving me a ride home, but she swerved to avoid a fox. Well, she's still a new driver, you know?"

Heather lifted an eyebrow. "Lost control, mmm?"

"Exactly. We skidded sideways, and it would've been okay, but Kepler and Norman had"—Emma rolled her eyes —"perhaps a bit to drink and roared up, hit us from the side. They slid into a tree. Kepler wasn't wearing a seatbelt, I guess, and he got thrown out, so he was a mess."

Heather stared. "That sounds like a horrible mess. You and Darcy are all right?"

"Donal has magic hands." Emma smiled at Margery. "And Margery was there to defend us when Norman started shouting."

"Gods, Vicki would call that a sheepfuck...no, it's a *goatfuck*, although I don't get why one animal is better than the other." Heather gave Emma a sympathetic look, then smiled at Margery. "I'm glad you were there, too."

"Hey, there's my favorite redhead." A male sauntered up and leaned over the back of Heather's chair. "Can I entice you to spend some time with me?"

He wasn't a bad-looking male, and his confidence was appealing. Margery gave a mental nod of approval if Heather wanted him.

She did. Offering her hand, Heather let him pull her to her feet and toward the stairway.

Margery eyed her friend. As far as she could tell, Heather wasn't overwhelmed with lust, just pleasantly interested.

"I'm so happy I found Ben and Ryder," Emma muttered, then turned red. "Sorry. I have ugly memories from my first Gathering."

Ugly enough that the bard's eyes were haunted. Margery moved to sit beside Emma and squeezed her hand. "You didn't say anything wrong. I'm really glad you found life-mates—and I'm sorry you had a rough Gathering."

"It's years in the past, but now and then, something brings it back...like all the shouting last night, actually." With a sigh, Emma leaned against her. "I see why the cubs didn't want to leave your lap. You simply exude peace."

Margery laughed. "It's a talent. My grandmama had it, too."

"Useful for a banfasa." After a couple of minutes, Emma straightened. "I'm all right. You probably want to check out the males."

"I'm good." Margery looked around, listened, breathed

in the scents. "No one is setting off my *want-to-have-him* bell."

Laughing, Emma got up and added another log to the fire. As fresh flames ignited, a salamander spiraled around the highest one, adding a shimmering glow to the reds and oranges of the flames.

"So, what's it like living with a bear and a...what animal is Ryder?"

"He's a cat." Emma considered. "I think it's easier than living with a wolf and panther combination, like Tynan and Donal. Ben's huge, but bears are mellow. Ryder has a hard time riling him up—and being a cat, he really does try."

Margery busted out laughing. "Cats. All snark and claws."

Benighted, sprite-brained, testosterone-poisoned males. After dealing with the second brawl of the night, Donal walked up the cave steps ready to claw someone just to ease his temper. And it'd help him warm up.

He was shaking with the cold.

Only he didn't start fights for stupid reasons, not since his twenties. Well...maybe thirties.

Shredding someone might help his mood tonight. So far, it'd been a completely crappy night.

Because his interest in sex was completely gone for some reason. By the Gods, with the two matings earlier, he'd been so bored his cock had barely risen to the task. And a *task* was what the sex had felt like. Neither Nia nor Francesca were to blame. Both were lovely, pleasant females, thrilled at being taken upstairs by the healer.

Although being classified as the *healer* rather than Donal grew more tiresome every year, it'd never wiped out his desire to mate. Nothing did.

Until tonight.

At the top of the stairs, he yanked open the door and stumbled inside. Through the closet, out of the portal room into the hall, then into the main room of the tavern.

At least, the number of aroused shifters meant the place wasn't cold. Not that he could tell. He wasn't sure he'd ever get warm again.

"Whoa, Donal, you look half-frozen." Rather than the Cosantir, Ben was tending bar along with Thorson. "Want a hot coffee?"

"Bless you, yes." Donal slid onto a bar stool, set his hands on the bar, and watched them shake.

The grizzly cahir set the coffee in front of him. "Emma's over by the fire. Get on over there and warm yourself up."

"That's the best plan I've heard all night." Forget mating. He wanted a different kind of heat right now.

He tried the coffee and was shaking hard enough he burned his lips. Grumbling under his breath, he crossed the room, trying to avoid collisions with heedless younger males who saw only females. Clumsy pups.

Around the fireplace, the temperature increased and

Donal's legs went weak. With an oath, he hastily sat down at the end of the couch. *Don't spill the coffee.*

"Donal!"

"Healer!"

"What's wrong with him?"

Someone touched him.

"He's freezing. Build up the fire some more, Emma." Now there was a lovely voice.

Someone sat and wrapped her arms around him. As the soft body pressed closer, warmth seeped into him. The scent of flowers drifted to his nose.

"Margery?"

"Well, your brains haven't frozen, at least." The humor in her voice lightened his mood. "Here, drink your coffee." She set her hand under his shaking one and helped him raise the cup to his lips.

The hot liquid burned all the way down but started to warm him from inside. Ben must have laced it with bourbon from Calum's private stash under the bar. *Good grizzly.*

Another set of shivers hit, and Margery moved the cup away. "How did you get so chilled?"

"Fight outside—bear versus panther. Bloody mess."

"I bet you forgot your coat and got so involved in healing you didn't notice the cold."

"You'd be right. At least it wasn't raining."

Emma tsked at him. "You need a keeper."

"This from the female who gets in car accidents?" But

then the next set of shivers hit, and his laugh strangled. "Aye. I'll take a keeper."

As the spasms eased off, Margery helped him drink more coffee.

The heat from the fireplace and the warmth of her body on the other side finally penetrated. With a sigh, he leaned back. "Thank you."

She giggled. "Caring for the healer wasn't in the list of things we discussed for a banfasa, but I can take that on, too."

Caring for him. He looked down at her, aware of the curves of her body. Imagining her hands on him. Those soft lips under his.

A different kind of heat started to burn away the chills.

"There, now, you're feeling better, aren't you?" She was stroking his shoulder and arm.

Soothing was no longer what he had in mind. He took the cup from her, pleased his hand was steady again, took a sip, and set it on the coffee table. "I'm definitely feeling better."

"Margery, it's Margery, right?" A male walked over, face flushed with lust. One of the wolves. Hopeful and focused on Margery. "Want to come and talk with me or..."

Or go upstairs? Donal's lips curled up in a snarl, and a sound escaped that he'd never heard himself make. The sound of a panther ready to defend its territory.

"Uh, got it, sorry." The male jumped back and hurried toward the other side of the room.

Donal didn't feel repentant in the least.

His gaze met Emma's. She winked at him and rose. "Since you're doing better, I'll go help Ben hand out drinks. See you later, Margery."

"Um, right." Margery watched her friend stroll away. "Was she—"

Donal interrupted by raising her hand to his lips. He kissed her fingertips, then more intimately, her palm. Her personal scent was fresh, not sultry, more like a flower garden at dawn. He breathed it in with another slow kiss before looking down at her.

Her eyes were wide and surprised. Lovely hazel eyes, the firelight bringing out the green. Apparently realizing how she was pressed against him, she started to edge away.

"Please stay, Meggie. I'm still half-frozen," he lied.

She immediately leaned against him. "Of course. I—"

His pleasure must have given him away. Her eyes narrowed. "Sneaky cat."

She moved away.

"Worth a try. Lust is an excellent medicine for hypothermia, it appears."

Giggles came from the little banfasa, so he took his chance, slinging an arm around her and pulling her back against him. "Stay where you're put, female."

Those wide eyes again. Could she not feel the attraction between them? He needed to be more obvious. Bending, he brushed a swift kiss over her mouth.

Yes, her lips were as soft as they'd looked. And her cheeks turned a delicate pink.

Normally, a male would discreetly check a female's interest by sniffing her wrist, but since she was right there in the curve of his arm, he nuzzled her cheek, her ear, her neck, breathing in. The scent of her desire had his shaft growing until it strained against his jeans.

How strange. Margery hadn't been at all interested in mating again...not until Donal sat down beside her. Then every cell in her body had jumped up and started bouncing around like a shifter at her first trawsfur.

He smelled like springtime in the foothills, so enticing she wanted to rub her face on his skin and nibble on his sharp jaw.

After finishing off his coffee, he set the cup on the table and leaned back, pulling her against him again. His arm was an iron band around her shoulders. In fact, all of him was lean muscle.

What would he feel like on top of her?

"Are the panther and bear going to be all right?" she asked, feeling as if her brain had gone into hibernation. Normally, she didn't have trouble talking with people, but Donal and Tynan often left her stumbling over her tongue.

"They'll be fine." A crease appeared in Donal's cheek. "Although sometimes I think I shouldn't completely heal idiot fighters. I could leave some scars as a stupidity penalty."

She giggled. "Can you get the Cosantir to agree?"

"Calum? In a heartbeat. He..."

As Donal's fingertips made circles on her bare arm, she lost track of what he was saying. "Uhhh, say that again?"

His lips curved up, turning his severe features more compelling than she could handle. "He thinks the best way to teach young males to control themselves is a hard paw swipe over vulnerable skin."

Ouch. "I'm glad I'm female," she muttered.

Donal's resonant laughter was so very masculine that quivers started deep inside her.

"I'm glad, too, as it happens." He lifted her, set her right onto his lap with her legs dangling to the left of his, then drew her arm around his shoulders.

"Are...are you still cold?"

He chuckled, curving his arms around her, molding her to his hard torso. Her hip rubbed against a hard erection. "I can pretend I'm still cold, but we both know that's no longer true."

In fact, his body positively radiated heat. Or maybe that was her.

He stroked his hand up and down her back, sensitizing every inch.

She swallowed.

"So, Margery, would you care to go upstairs with me?" His gray eyes were the shade of dawn through a morning fog, holding her gaze until the room disappeared. Until she saw only sunlight.

She could think of nothing better—because this was Donal. Not just a stunning male, but someone as dedicated as she was to healing, to helping. Brilliant and grumpy and funny and heart-wrenchingly kind.

"Yes. Oh, yes." Her voice emerged husky, almost too soft, but he heard.

"Then that's what we'll do." Leaning forward, he lifted her in his arms and rose to his feet. Holding her, he rubbed his cheek against her hair, marking her and claiming her with his scent as a panther would.

And then his lips took hers again in a long, drugging kiss, teasing her with his tongue, demanding a response as she sank into a whirlpool of passion.

At the top of the stairs, Donal considered the open rooms and picked his favorite—the purple room. Inside, he toed off his shoes and laid Margery down in the center of the cushioned floor.

The tiny fireplace held a nice blaze, sending heat through the room.

Margery propped herself up on her elbows. "Purple? Seriously?"

"My sweet, purple is the color of royalty. Only cats use this room."

Her expression indicated she wasn't sure if he was serious or not.

He was totally lying and grinned as he stripped off his shirt and jeans, then dropped down beside her. "Actually, I like the fabric." Taking her hand, he ran her palm over the silk pillows and floor cushions.

She stroked the material. "So smooth. I see why you like it."

"Exactly." He lay on his side, playing with her hair, confusing himself. Normally, he'd be reacting to the female's need.

With Margery, despite the growing urge in his dick, he wanted to take his time. Lots and lots of time.

Running his hand over her cheek, down her torso, he flattened his palm over her pelvis. Healthy female, healthy lust. He could swear her hormones were calling to his.

"Donal," she whispered. But rather than dragging her down to him, she framed his face with her hands. Looking him right in the eyes, much like she had when she told him he was rude to a patient, when she tsked at the mess he left in the kitchen, or when she scolded him for teasing Tynan.

Because she saw not a healer, but *him*.

It had taken him far too long, but he saw her in return.

And liked everything he saw.

Smiling, he leaned down to kiss her and almost laughed at her enthusiastic response. At the way she wiggled closer.

He enjoyed her mouth—*oh Gods, yes*—then her neck, inhaling the subtle scent there. He pressed his lips to the pounding carotid artery and felt the way her heart rate increased.

She reached down to unbutton her jeans, and he caught her hands. "My job, sweetling."

"You're too slow at doing your job." Her face was flushed and her pout absolutely endearing.

"I'm working my way there. But we can start here." He helped her sit and pulled her shirt off.

No bra. Beautiful full breasts with large pink-brown nipples already hard and pointed. His cock went from hard to painful with one look. Mother's blessing, but she was going to test his control.

He'd die happy, now, wouldn't he?

To prove that, he tipped her back and took possession of her breasts with both hands, before burying his face between his presents. Soft, so fucking soft, and fragrant. He licked between each soft globe, over and around. As she started to moan, he reached her nipples. With healer hands, he could feel her response to his lips and teeth on the sensitive areolas, and the zinging of nerves through her body gave him more of a rush than alcohol.

Pleasing her satisfied everything inside of him—and in return, she pulled him into opening himself more than any other female ever had. Why? What was it about her?

Eventually, when his dick and her squirming impelled him to move, he unbuttoned her jeans, punctuating each new exposed inch with kisses. Just as well he'd lost his hair tie since it would've been gone by now. She had a good grip on his hair.

How high could he drive her before the wolflet bit him?

He wouldn't mind being left with a few fang marks from this night, to remind him of someone very, very special.

At last, at damned long last, Donal pulled Margery's jeans off. She felt as if her skin was on fire, stoked by the too-knowledgeable healer's hands. Nothing she did had made him move faster; instead, he'd lingered and teased each sensitive inch until she was nigh to combusting.

But her jeans were off. Nothing was stopping him from taking her and—

He put her legs over his shoulders, and his mouth...his *mouth*...right there on her. His hands were under her ass, holding her up to his face as his tongue swirled over her, circling and teasing and sliding inside.

"Mmm, you taste like the finest of desserts."

"*Donal.*" Oh Goddess, was that her voice? So whiny and desperate.

"Mmmhmm, I have to see if you're ready, sweetling." He lifted slightly, so he could use his fingers on her, between her wet folds, before ever so slowly penetrating her with one, then two fingers.

"Oh, oh, oh." The rush of sensation almost sent her over, and her hips lifted uncontrollably.

He chuckled and pinned her down with his other hand

as he bent to lick over her. His fingers kept moving in and out. Everything inside her tightened, and every teasing lick added to the conflagration of desire until... She burst into flames as pleasure swept through her in blast after blast of overwhelming sensations.

Panting, moaning, she stared up at him, at the slight smile on his perfect lips, on the satisfaction in his eyes. "This isn't the way it works. You're supposed to use your..." How could she blush hotter when she knew her face was already red from a climax?

He ran a finger down her cheek, and his low smoky chuckle was smoother than the cushions beneath her. "You don't think you should come until my cock and seed are inside you?"

Well, Tynan had shown her that it could happen, but still...

"Don't worry, sweetheart." He was kneeling between her legs, his black hair loose over his bare shoulders. A male shouldn't be allowed to be so gorgeous. "You'll have my seed before we leave this room."

She felt like she was going to melt right into the floor beneath her.

Until he ran his finger over her, around her clit, and things inside her started to waken again. "Donal..."

"It's near the end of the night, so I can take my time." His grin was dark and wicked. "Let's see how many times you can come before my control gives out."

"Wait, no—"

When his skilled fingers teased over her, her protest turned into a moan.

And more and more moans.

Sometime later, after she'd turned into a limp heap on the cushions, he lay on top of her, all lean, hard muscle. When he kissed her, she could taste her own essence before he plundered her mouth. His lips moved over her cheek teasingly, and she felt his smile.

"Open your eyes, *cariad*."

He'd called her darling? Her eyes popped open, and she stared up into his silvery gaze. His lips quirked. "I think you're ready for me now, don't you?"

She was far too weak to hit him as he deserved. "You...cat."

His resonant chuckle made his chest shake as he lay on her.

Reaching down, he positioned his cock between her legs and slid in, ever so slowly. Her pussy was swollen from the night's endeavors—from his endeavors—and she inhaled sharply as he penetrated her. The feeling of stretching, of being taken was amazing, and her eyes closed.

"Look at me, wolflet."

Holding her gaze, he pressed in farther, deeper, his voice lowering to a purr. "By the Gods, you feel magnificent."

He filled her, sheathed as completely as possible, and held right there in the most primitive of claiming. Looking into her eyes.

The world seemed to fade around her as he encompassed her, inside, outside.

His lips curved. "Put your arms around me and hold on."

He began to move, all hot iron, sliding in, filling her completely, then pulling out. Harder and faster. He claimed her lips again, even as the heat rose inside her despite all the times she'd come.

Her hips lifted, pushing against his, taking him deeper and deeper, until all she could feel was him, his cock, and the glory sweeping through her.

As everything inside her burst into overwhelming pleasure, and he came inside her in hot spurts, her cries of satisfaction filled the room.

CHAPTER FOURTEEN

C*old Creek, North Cascades Territory - morning after full moon*

Her legs were so weak that Donal had to help her walk as they went down the stairs. The moon had set—and the evil healer had played with her right up to the last moment. She lost count of how many times she'd come.

She felt floaty, almost adrift. Tynan, then Donal. The most amazing males she'd ever known had mated with her. Cherished her. It was like the stars in the sky had come down to touch her world.

"Sweetling?" Donal pulled her to a stop.

"Uh." They'd reached the main room of the tavern. The raised blinds showed that dawn had arrived. "Sorry. My thoughts wandered off the trail."

"I understand." He cupped her cheek in one lean hand and bent down to kiss her lightly. "The night's over. I'll take you home."

She put her hand over his...and got lost in his eyes, the gray of a sunlit fog. Gathering night was over; the moon had set, so why did she want to lead him off to bed again. "That would be—"

"Margery!" The shout came from near the door, the voice so familiar.

"Oliver?" She spun.

It was her *littermate*. He stood just inside the door, his grin wide as the sky outside.

They met in the center of the room.

She hugged him hard enough to make his ribs creak. "You're here, you're finally here."

"Well, yeah."

For a long moment, she held him as the littermate bond warmed with his presence. His face had filled out, no longer gaunt. His stomach wasn't sunken any longer. He'd gained weight and lost the sour unhappy scent he'd had when first freed from the Scythe. The winter months in the Elder Village had been good for him.

Finally, she stepped back. "When did you get here?"

"Me?" He frowned. "What about you? You're supposed to be in Ailill Ridge."

"I left a moon ago. But I asked the Cosantir here to send you word at the Elder Village."

"It probably passed me when I was on the trail. I didn't hurry on the way down."

Even as a cub, Oliver had preferred forests to people. He'd loved sharing the wonders he'd found—the incredible intricacy of moss and lichens, how a fallen tree would become a nurse log and raise tree babies, how owls used abandoned woodpecker holes for nesting.

"But you found me, and you're here now." She spotted Donal at the bar with the Cosantir. They were both watching.

She pulled her brother forward. "Calum, Donal, this is my littermate, Oliver. Oliver, the Cosantir of the North Cascades Territory"—she motioned to Calum, then Donal —"and the healer."

"It's a pleasure to meet you, Oliver," Calum said.

"Cosantir." Oliver bowed his head before turning to Donal. "Healer. Good to meet you."

"Welcome to Cold Creek. Margery's been eager to have you here." Donal smiled at Oliver. "Since we're neighbors, let me give you two a ride home."

Oliver didn't speak, letting her make the decision as had been his way when they were cubs.

Margery hesitated, but her ankle was protesting a long walk. "A ride would be wonderful."

Donal set his glass down. "Get some sleep, Cosantir. Healer's orders."

"A shame you probably won't be able to do the same,"

Calum responded. "There will probably be more brawls before the young males settle down."

Donal shot him a scowl, then headed out, muttering, "Belligerent, pixie-brained, cox-combs."

The Cosantir was laughing as he waved Margery and Oliver after Donal.

Outside the tavern door, Oliver grabbed a backpack.

It looked heavy. "Did you carry that all the way from the Elder Village?"

"No, I traveled as a bear."

"Ah." She remembered his form—a medium-sized black bear, more cute than scary.

"The Elder Village sent the bag to Ailill Ridge for me. I picked it up there and begged a ride here."

She tensed slightly. What had the people in Ailill Ridge said about her?

"Here we go." Donal opened the passenger door for her. He ran his hand down her upper arm...and sent tingles chasing after his touch.

No, behave, Margery. Gathering night was over.

Oliver took the back seat. "When the grocery clerk at Ailill Ridge told me you were here, there were a couple of shifters listening and getting all pissed-off. Growling, even. What's with that?"

Oh Gods, how could she explain?

Settling into the driver's seat, Donal gave Margery a glance, then said smoothly, "No banfasa or healer will remain in a town where they're not treated well. Margery is just the last one to walk away from that territory. Being idiots, they probably feel as if she abandoned them."

"Got it." Oliver snorted. "Sounds like it's good you left, but, knowing you, you stayed until it was unbearable."

"Pretty much, yes." Margery still felt as if she'd abandoned people who needed her.

"If the town had disrespected Grandmama," Oliver said, "she'd have left them with tattered ears and shortened tails."

"Oh. You know, you're right." The ugly feeling of guilt lifted.

"I think I'd have liked your granddam," Donal murmured.

Margery grinned. "I daresay. She was a cat, too, and like you, she was..." *cantankerous, irritable, bristly.* "Um, well, you're a lot alike."

Donal gave her an amused look.

After he parked the car in his driveway, Margery paused with her hand on the door. "Thank you for the ride, Donal."

"You're welcome, sweetling. I'll tell you what I told Calum—get some sleep today." Still in the driver's seat, he tucked a strand of hair behind her ear. His touch made her shiver with longing. "Come over tomorrow, though. I have a couple more shifters to add to your schedule."

"I can come over now."

"How did I know you'd say that?" he murmured. His gaze lingered on her lips, then with a sigh, he shook his head. "Tomorrow, banfasa."

She slipped out of his car and reminded herself that a Gathering mating wasn't a prelude to a romance; it was merely a sexy time under a full moon.

The full moon had set.

She and Donal would work together. And that was all.

The lack of sleep was catching up to Tynan. He yawned as he left the diner after downing a cup of coffee. He was on duty, patrolling Main Street, until Alec relieved him at noon.

He'd already broken up three brawls.

After a Gathering, there were always fights between those who'd succeeded in mating and the ones who'd lost out. Having five times more males than females meant some males weren't chosen. Although females usually mated more than once, some males were chosen several times a night, some never.

And there were always those who were bad losers.

A shout and growls caught his attention, and he snorted. Looked like his brawl-count was rising to four.

He rounded the corner, and there they were, in front of BOOKS. Two males going at it with fists and kicks, battering at each other for all they were worth.

"Break it up," he ordered loudly. When they ignored him, he yanked out his baton, expanded it, and whacked one idiot in the meaty part of his thigh hard enough to paralyze the muscle.

As that male staggered back, the other dumbass swung at Tynan.

Tynan whipped the baton around and caught the male's upper arm. A baton was quite useful, really.

Separating, the combatants rubbed their injuries and cursed him in foul terms.

Seriously? "You're standing on Main Street. Your mamas would have their paws over their ears if they heard you."

One flushed.

The other had no shame—or sense. "You dickless dog." He charged at Tynan. "I'm gonna—"

Tynan palmed the male's face and shoved him back, then swung the baton. It thudded against ribs hard enough that the male dropped to his knees. The bones hadn't broken, but would be sore for days.

"Nice job, Deputy." Joe Thorson stood in the doorway of his bookstore. "Want help?"

"Got it handled, Joe, but thanks." Tynan leveled a stern look at the two whimpering pups. He'd not seen them before. "In this territory, both the Cosantir and the law forbid fighting in town. Cubs shouldn't see this kind of violence...or hear language like you used."

The two flushed, gazes on the ground.

"Sorry," one muttered.

"Yeah. Won't happen again," the other said.

"Then, go." Tynan motioned with the baton.

After a disgruntled exchange of glances, the males rose, heading for opposite sides of the street.

"Young and stupid." Thorson growled, although amusement lurked in his eyes. "Can't say I was much better at that age."

"I've seen the scars on your arms, Joe. You were far worse."

With a hissing laugh, Thorson disappeared into his store.

Tynan continued his foot patrol.

At the diner, Angie had mentioned Meggie wasn't on today and was probably catching up on her sleep.

More's the pity. He'd hoped to see her, to assess how she felt about him. Emotions during a Gathering could be as capricious as a leaf blown in the wind. What a shifter thought was undying love under a full moon was often dead and buried by noon the next day.

Today would be the test as to whether the little wolf's emotions were ones that would last longer than the waning of the moon.

Because his feelings were more solid than the mountains behind him.

He nodded at Bonnie who was trying to get her two cubs moving in the same direction. Unsuccessfully.

Typical enough. Littermates were bound to head in different directions—unless and until they lifemated a female. Then...their world had a center.

The thought slowed his pace.

Although they hadn't been able to share Meggie last night, Donal must've returned to the Gathering at some point. With luck, he'd taken Meggie upstairs.

Perhaps next time, they could be with her together, as littermates should

---

Despite her need for sleep, Margery couldn't stop smiling. Oliver was back.

In the guest room, she started to make the bed. "You look healthy."

"The upside of living in an Elder village. Those older shifters really enjoy cooking." He grinned. His shaggy hair was brown and his eyes hazel, the coloring they shared from their mother. Although a few inches short of six feet, he was a bear shifter with big bones and bulk.

"What did you do all winter?" She fitted the sheet over the mattress corner as he did the same on his side. "Were you the only shifter-soldier in the village?"

"Nah, Patrin and Fell were there. Two elders worked with us—a shepherd who did a lot of listening and a teacher of the traditions. We talked. Spent time in animal form."

Patrin and Fell were Darcy's littermates, and like Oliver, they undoubtedly needed both teaching and counseling. It was a shame there wasn't a soulweaver in the area, but like bards, the God-called menders of souls had grown exceedingly rare.

She added the top sheet and soft blankets. "I bet it was a long winter in such a small place."

He shrugged. "It was okay. We did handyman stuff. The elders appreciated the repairs, since after they get snowed in, they don't get much help. Played board games. Learned Daonain history, traditions, and laws."

That had been the Cosantirs' plan—that the shifter-soldiers would have a chance to merge back into the Daonain culture. Would have counseling from a shepherd and basically a lot of socialization. "Did it help?"

His smile looked so much like their mother's that her heart ached. "I guess. I'm more settled. Not on edge all the time. Patrin and Fell are doing better, some, but...yeah, like me, they're still having trouble."

"Darcy said they trained as assassins."

He tugged a wrinkle out of the dark green quilt. "Yeah. And they led us. Protected us when they could. Patrin was the one who told the Scythe I'd make a lousy killer, but that I was good at blending in and getting information."

Bless Patrin. Being a killer would've damaged Oliver irreparably.

Blinking back tears, she smiled. "You blend in, hmm? Considering we look alike, that's not what a female wants to hear."

He led the way out of the room. "Sis, you're not gorgeous, sorry. But you *are* pretty. And, you know—nice."

"Nice, huh." How bland was that? Is that how Donal and Tynan thought of her?

"Smart, kind, brave. That stuff." He flushed. "The Elders sent us to the closest villages for Gatherings. After a few times, we'd learned that beauty can hide an empty heart."

Oh. She had no words. Not only because he was being super sweet, but...this was her brother talking. Her *brother* had attended Gatherings. Had mated with females.

In the kitchen, he started opening and closing cupboards. Evaluating the food situation. Such a bear.

An *adult* bear. She gave herself a shake. "I forgot that time passed for you, too. Part of me still thinks of you as the kid you were when the Scythe took us. Then you talk about attending *Gatherings*."

"We're from the same litter," he pointed out.

"I know, I know." She shook her head. "Sometimes I feel a lot older than I really am."

He nodded, his eyes holding a sadness that would probably never go away. "Violence, being treated like animals, killing. That shit changes things. Patrin says other shifters our age seem like younglings."

Opening the fridge, Margery pulled out the leftover roast beef and a loaf of bread. When Oliver's eyes lit, she started making sandwiches. "Most of the time, I feel old—and then I trip over a tradition everyone else knows and feel like I'm five."

The haunted look disappeared from his eyes as he snickered. "Oh, yeah. Like I didn't remember shit about life-mating stuff. It's not as if Mom or Grandmama had lifemates. So...I was trying to flirt with a pretty female. And two big werecats saw me trying to get her interest. Turned out they were her new lifemates."

"Uh-oh. Nice ones?"

"Not. Hardly. They bashed me into the wall, ready to tear my throat out. Thank fuck an elder stepped in and explained I was still learning the traditions."

Margery felt her breath shudder. The males could have hurt Oliver badly. "I heard new lifemates were unstable, but wow."

"Yeah." He drank some lemonade, then grinned. "Do you remember when we were seven, and you asked the Howatt littermates to wait for you so you could be their lifemate?"

"They were so nice. They didn't even laugh." Her mood darkened. The Howatt brothers had died on the street the day the Scythe attacked.

Oliver saw her face and looked away. Picking up the sandwich, he moved out of the kitchen. "So, you're going to work as a banfasa like Grandmama?"

"Maybe. Probably. I have a job as a waitress, but the healer has work for me to do, too. With older shifters and pregnant ones as well as the ones with injuries that take a while to heal."

"Sounds boring," Oliver said.

"Not to me." She settled into a chair in the living room. "I don't like all the bloody stuff the healers are so good at. I'd rather do therapy to help someone recover their strength, make sure a pregnant shifter is eating right for the unborn cub. I'm good at that."

"You're good at all of it." Oliver sat on the couch. "Grandmama was really proud of you."

Tears prickled her eyes. "Thanks." Earning her grandmother's praise had been difficult—but very rewarding. They'd planned to be partners when Margery was an adult.

Many plans for the future had died the day of the Scythe attack.

"So...have you figured out what you want to do?" she asked.

"Not really." He scowled. "The human spymaster who helped get us out—his name is Wells—said something about us helping him kill off the rest of the Scythe. At least that's what he mentioned before we got sent to the Elder Villages."

His worried expression unsettled her. "I don't like that idea."

"Me, neither. Guess we'll hear soon enough now that it's spring."

"It doesn't seem right. The Scythe are human; Wells is human. *He* should have to deal with them, not our people."

"Wishful thinking never gets a person very far."

His bitter tone broke Margery's heart. "You're here now, though. And you'll have to let me pamper you."

If Wells wanted him to fight, he'd have to go through her first.

"You always did." Oliver's smile slowly changed until it

was almost as carefree as it had been when they were young. "I've looked forward to being back with you since the day they parted us."

Maybe she couldn't imagine what the shifter-soldiers' lives had been like or how horrible it would have been for a small unaggressive werebear like Oliver, but he was here now.

He'd have the time—and all her help—to finish healing.

A constant stream of wounded shifters kept Donal moving most of the day. By the Gods, full moons were a pain in the tail. But this was the last injured male today...he hoped. He set his hand over the deep abrasions on Devin's forearm. As his power flowed, he melded the flesh together and then the layers of skin.

When Donal straightened, the middle-aged male smiled. "Not even a scar. Thank you, healer."

"You're welcome." Donal rolled his aching shoulders. "I'm surprised you're here, though. Post-gathering, it's usually single males in here."

Devin and his two littermates had a mate, Jody, and they all ran a cleaning service.

"Ah, well, this wasn't from a fight." Devin rubbed his arm. "A pup got herself stuck in a tree out at the Wildwood Lodge, and I climbed up to get her. I was halfway down when she started panicking, and I didn't have enough hands to hold her and reach the ground without collecting a few good scrapes."

Donal groaned. "More of that tree-highway stupidity? I was hoping they'd stopped."

He heard his brother laugh and turned to see Tynan in the doorway.

"The cubs haven't stopped. They're just getting better at not falling." Tynan walked in and bumped the older male's arm in a greeting. "Good thing you were there, Devin. The cub's dam says thank you, and Breanne sent you carrot cake as a reward for the rescue."

"Carrot cake?" Devin jumped to his feet. "I'm all over that. None of us can make a dessert even a gnome would eat."

"In the kitchen," Tynan said.

"Thanks, Beta." Devin made a beeline out of the clinic to the kitchen.

"I deserve carrot cake, too," Donal grumbled. By the Gods, he was hungry.

Tynan laughed. "That's what I told Breanne you'd say. She sent enough for us—and for Meggie and her littermate, who we heard about."

"You're a very good brother." Donal washed his hands and headed straight for the kitchen.

Devin had already left.

Donal took a piece of the cake and bit in. Sweet perfection. "If it was anyone other than Margery, there would be no sharing."

"Knowing you, we'd better take her cake over now and get the temptation out of the house." Tynan stretched. "Maybe she and her brother would like to go for a run. I've got a craving to get out of the human skin."

Donal scowled. "You had to say that, didn't you?" Now his body itched with the need to be in fur, to leap and run and climb. He didn't get out nearly often enough and almost never with Tynan these days.

He picked up the second plate. "Let's go."

Next door, Margery answered their knock.

"Well...hi." Her lips curved up, a little shy and a lot sweet.

Donal smiled because her eyes brightened when she saw them. Not with cunning or ambition the way he often saw in the females who wanted a God-called male. No, Margery was simply pleased to see him and Tynan. As the younger shifters would say, the pretty wolf *liked* them.

By the Gods, the glow of the Mother simply radiated from her. How had he missed seeing that before?

Instead of purring, he handed her the plate.

"Carrot cake?" she asked.

"It's from Breanne as a welcome for your brother from the alphas of our pack," Tynan clarified.

"Cake?" Oliver joined them at the door. "Awesome. But I'm not a wolf."

Donal eyed the male, taking the time he hadn't earlier to look him over.

Oliver's gait was more lumbering than prowling. His

bones were big, but less bulky than a grizzly. He stood next to Margery, but with a few inches between them, not touching the way a wolf or cat would.

"You're a black bear?" Donal guessed.

"Uh-huh."

And hungry in the way young males always were.

"I'm Tynan, Donal's littermate." Tynan smiled. "Our alpha female, Breanne, likes to feed people, especially her pack and their families. Enjoy."

"Tell her thank you if you see her before I do," Margery told Tynan and handed the plate to her brother with an admonishment: "Leave me at least a quarter, greedy guts."

"Been a long time since I heard you say that." Oliver's voice came out husky.

"Yeah." Sadness filled Margery's expression, then slipped away. She gave Tynan a puzzled look. "I know Cold Creek has predators, but does it take two of you to ferry cake to next door?"

Tynan's laugh was as open and hearty as it had been before he'd buried himself in a human city. If the sweet banfasa could bring back that side of his brother, Donal would never let her escape.

"Actually," Tynan said, "we're going for a twilight run. Would you and your brother like to come?"

"Oh, yes." Margery bounced once on her toes. "I would. Oliver?"

Bears had excellent hearing, and he called from the kitchen. "I just spent weeks in fur. I'd rather find a book and lay on your big couch. You go have fun with the neighbors."

Neighbors? Donal's mouth twitched. He exchanged a glance with his littermate. They intended to be much more than simply neighbors.

———————

Tynan led his tiny pack—although his cat littermate would be insulted by the term. In Meggie's shed, they stripped and trawsfurred, then slipped out the wolf-sized door in the back.

The last of the sunlight filtered through the trees along the gurgling creek, and the soft grasses were cool and damp against his paws. He paused to lap clear cold water before jumping the narrow stream.

Trotting up the trail to the mountains, he picked up scents of other shifters, deer, and a wolverine. Behind him came the light patter of Meggie's paws and occasionally the sound of Donal in the brush.

If Donal wanted, he could be entirely silent. And deadly, too. There were reasons wolves needed a pack to take on a panther.

When young, Tynan had thought it unfair his littermate was more dangerous. But now, Tynan wouldn't trade. He loved having packmates for hunting, playing, and simply being together. Felines and bears missed out.

Tynan checked over his shoulder.

Meggie ran behind him, a beautiful, dainty wolf. Rather than common gray fur, her outer coat was a warm brown. Near the skin, the fur was almost black before lightening to milk chocolate at the tips.

Tynan caught a glimpse of Donal, a lean, tawny-gray panther, disappearing into the underbrush for a quick mouse-appetizer. Or to catch one for Meggie in the shifter method of pleasing a female.

With a soft woof, Tynan increased his speed, to get farther from town before they stopped. At one time, an inadvertent sighting would mean simply calling the Cosantir to erase the human's memory. Now, humans whipped out cell phones faster than a horny man would his dick. These new times called for discretion.

Once away from town, Tynan left the creekside trail and headed up a steeper slope. He kept an ear turned back, evaluating the sounds. Meggie had grown stronger. Her gait was even. Donal was behind her.

Tynan opened his jaws in a smile. It was rare he and Donal found time to enjoy a trail together.

The forest gave way to a pretty meadow with wildflowers blooming pink and white. Snatching up a hefty stick from a fallen tree, Tynan crouched with his butt in the air. Tail waving. *I got a stick, want to play?*

Stopping, Meggie stared at him as if she had no idea what to do. Then her instincts took over, and with a high yip, she lunged at the stick.

The game was on.

Tynan tore across the meadow, staying barely out of her reach, taunting her with high-paw prancing to show her just who owned the toy.

She was quicker than he'd expected, balancing the weakness of her leg with unexpected bursts of speed. Twice he evaded her, and the third time, she lunged...just as Donal leaped out of the brush. The cat batted the stick out of Tynan's jaws and skittered away.

Pouncing, Meggie darted off with *his* stick in her jaws.

Tynan gave chase, and damned if his sneaky littermate wasn't putting his paw on the female side of the scales. It was difficult to catch Meggie when two hundred pounds of feline kept jumping in the way.

When Tynan managed a successful feint and grabbed his stick back, he noticed her limp.

Time for a break.

He set the stick by a tiny trickling stream, trawsfurred, and dipped up water to scrub his drool-covered face.

Laughing, Meggie did the same, and he was pleased to see she'd grown more comfortable with being naked around males. Mostly.

She frowned. "Why couldn't the magic that lets us trawsfur let our clothing shift with us?"

Donal shifted to human. He settled on the meadow grass, propping himself up on his elbows. "Probably because our wild hunt ancestors were lusty fae and disinclined to have any barriers to getting it on."

At her wide-eyed look, Donal grinned, then tipped his head back to savor the last few rays of sunlight.

Unable to resist, Tynan shifted to wolf and pounced on Donal's stomach, yipping in gratification at the whoofed exhalation.

The sound changed...to a panther's snarl.

Uh-oh.

Tynan tore across the meadow.

The panther was right on his tail, then knocked him sprawling. Rolling to his paws, Tynan charged the feline, and almost...almost shouldered him over. Up on hind legs, they grappled, fake biting, growling and hissing. Donal's barely exposed claws were defeated by Tynan's thick, not-fully-shed undercoat...although a few painful pinpricks got through.

Meggie had jumped to her feet, obviously unsure if they were serious.

Ah, she'd never gotten to play as a teenaged shifter, had she? Tynan broke away and did a speeding zoomie circle around his littermate, voicing taunting, puppylike yips.

Donal chirruped a laugh, sprang, and the fight was joined again.

He had time to see Meggie's alarm change to a grin.

Shifting, the little wolf danced forward and nipped Donal's hind end.

Hissing, Donal spun—and Tynan bit his ass. Yeah, this was what he'd been missing—a partner to help fight the feline.

Back and forth, he and Meggie went, keeping the panther turning.

The game ended when Tynan achieved the win—Donal's tail.

"His face!" Margery was laughing so hard, her sides hurt. By the Mother, she could barely breathe, and if she giggled harder, she'd wet herself. She crossed her legs, almost fell, and giggled harder.

Whoever said cats didn't show emotions? When Tynan nipped Donal's tail, the panther's eyes had gone wide, then his ears went back, and his eyes slitted.

But before the cat could do anything, Tynan shifted to human and dropped down beside Margery, laughing his ass off.

Trawsfurring, Donal scowled, hands on hips. "Brawd, you're going to pay for that one."

Oh, no. Was Donal really angry? Remembering Ailill Ridge when minor altercations turned into bloody fang-fests, Margery jumped to her feet.

But Tynan was still snickering, obviously unworried.

Donal was grinning as he sat down. He patted the grass between them. "Relax, sweetling. It's a game."

Relieved, she did just that, the grass cold on her bare buttocks and legs.

"You've never played shifter games, have you?" Tynan guessed. The breeze brought her his scent, so very masculine and tempting. When she didn't answer, he cupped her cheek with his thumb under her chin. His blue eyes held hers. Patient. Determined.

"No." Her voice came out husky because his touch and scent brought back all the desire of the night. How his lips felt, his hands, the way he'd filled her.

"Mmm." Donal's resonant voice held a cat's purr as he picked up her hand, kissing her palm, then her wrist, sending goosebumps up her arm.

And she knew he'd caught the fragrance of her desire.

A smile flickered over Tynan's lips before his thumb lifted her chin so he could take her mouth. His mouth was firm, his kiss so thorough that warmth rushed through her.

A hand between her breasts pushed her backward, and an arm behind her shoulders eased her down onto the grass. "We wanted to do this last night, but I got called away," Donal murmured. "Unfortunately, we're too close to town here to do more than hands-on play."

"Hands-on is good, though," Tynan agreed. His grin flashed. "So is tongue."

Donal's mouth covered her breast—and Tynan moved down. His lips teased her other breast.

So many sensations. A mouth on each breast. When both males began sucking, her back arched at the exquisite pleasure.

Donal's hand slid down between her legs, and she gasped as his fingers slid over her clit, teasing her right into need.

Tynan lifted his head to study her expression for a second.

"More." She slid a hand behind his neck and pulled him back down. The low rumble of his laugh and Donal's deep chuckle were as heady as they had been the night before.

Donal's tongue circled one nipple, then she felt Tynan's teeth on the other with a gentle tugging, then sucking.

The sound of approaching people broke into the quiet. Both males lifted their heads.

"I was afraid of this. They're coming up the trail," Donal said. "Maybe a few minutes away."

Tynan paused. Sighed. "They're probably shifters, but we can't be sure."

And three naked people would cause comment.

"Donal, head out to the left." Tynan pointed. "Meggie and I will meet you on the trail farther down."

Margery rolled over and shifted. Even as Donal disappeared into the underbrush, she followed Tynan down an almost hidden deer trail.

Just a couple of wolves running about. Nothing to see here. No indeed.

She gave an annoyed growl. The hum of need still reverberated in her body. Everything inside her wanted to shift back and drag them into the bushes to finish what they'd started.

As if to complete her frustration, it started to rain halfway home.

Back at the garden shed, Donal shivered. Cat-scat, but the rain had been like ice. He gave a frustrated huff as he dragged his jeans up over his still-damp legs. "It's been a while since I experienced what happens to an erection in a cold shower. Did the trick quite effectively."

Margery made a choking sound.

Tynan grinned. "Apparently, she's shy about mating jokes."

"About anything to do with mating, I'd say." Taking advantage of the way she'd gotten stuck trying to pull her shirt over her head, he fondled her breasts. "You have the prettiest breasts, sweetling."

The shed let in little light, but he could smell the sudden bloom of interest.

She huffed at him. "My littermate is here. You stop that."

"Ah, true enough." Regretfully, Donal dropped his hands, already missing the feel of the soft flesh. After helping her adjust her shirt, he planted an apologetic kiss on her lips. "Forgive me."

She leaned forward and gave him a better kiss.

"Hold still, *a leannán*," Tynan tugged her jeans up and buttoned them. "There, all respectable for Oliver."

"Thank you." She reached up and pulled Tynan down for a kiss, too.

By the Gods, she was sweet.

As they walked her to her house, Donal tried not to think how pleasant it would be to start a fire and enjoy Margery in front of it. Savoring her without the urgency of the full moon matings. Sharing her with Tynan.

Although, in all reality, he'd been looking forward to simply spending time with her, mating or no mating.

But her littermate had arrived. She would need to be with her brother tonight.

A creak heralded the door opening and Oliver. "I expected you back sooner, sis. I heard the storm and was going to come and look for you."

"You were?" Margery looked stunned, then almost tearful.

Donal stilled. How long had it been since anyone worried about this little wolflet that she'd be shocked when it happened?

She was going to have to get used to the feeling. By Herne's hooves and horns, she was.

"Well, we're all fine, if a bit wet." Margery bumped her shoulder against Tynan's, then Donal's. "We were having fun."

Oliver tilted his head, his nostrils flaring. The scent of desire in the air couldn't be missed. His brows drew together. "Fun, huh." After a narrow-eyed stare at Tynan and Donal, he smiled at his sister. "I made supper for us."

Catching how the *us* meant for two and not four, Donal sighed.

His littermate gave him a wry look, then tugged a strand

of Margery's wet hair. "Right. We'll be off, then. Have a good meal, you two."

"Oh, but—" Margery turned an unhappy look at her brother.

"It's fine, sweetling. You and your littermate have catching up to do." Donal ran a hand down her arm. As a cat, he loathed being left out, but Margery needed time with her brother. Family was important. "Go shower and warm up. Come over to the clinic tomorrow, and you can start doing follow-up visits."

Her smile was like sunlight streaking through rain clouds. "Perfect. I've got the breakfast shift at the diner, then I'll see you."

"Goodnight, you two. C'mon, sis." Her brother leaned forward and took his sister's hand.

Before Oliver could pull her away, Tynan, who normally was more diplomatic, cupped her cheek and kissed her lightly. "I'll see you tomorrow, little wolf."

As they walked away, Donal rubbed his shoulder against Tynan's in approval. Because they both knew where they were going with this, no matter what Oliver might think.

CHAPTER FIFTEEN

C old Creek, North Cascades Territory - waning gibbous moon

Grumpy bear. A frown tugging at her lips, Margery strolled through the cool evening air, up the hill to the Wild Hunt tavern.

She'd tried to get Oliver to join her, but since last night, he'd been as irritable as a badger with a thorn in a paw.

Frustration and worry for him was a dull burn in her stomach as she crossed the parking lot. Dear Goddess, she was tired. It'd been a very full day.

Despite her exhaustion, she couldn't help but smile.

She'd worked as a banfasa.

Today, she'd taught Walter—and his mate Sandy—some

exercises to strengthen his muscles around a newly healed leg.

Then she'd visited three senior shifters to check nutrition and see how they were managing.

The elderly cat was doing all right since her daughter lived in a nearby village.

The senior wolf needed more help. With his permission, Margery discussed his needs with Bree who would get the pack involved.

Generys, an older bear shifter, had no one. Her only family lived in Canada.

When Margery reported the problem to Donal, he'd told her to talk with Calum. Scary thought, but the healer was right. Finding the needed resources for a patient was part of her job...and the Cosantir of a territory held *all* the resources.

She pulled open the tavern door and stepped inside.

Even though it was midweek, a Tuesday night, people filled the tables.

Then a woman raised her voice in song, and Margery stopped dead just inside the door.

To the left in the front corner that held the piano, Emma strummed a guitar as she sang *The Legend of the First*, telling of one of the first Daonain—the half-breed children of fae and humans. How the werewolf padded through the forest. All by himself. As the moon's glow called to him, he sang to her of his loneliness.

The melody changed and brightened as Emma and the two males behind her swung into the chorus. And then every wolf in the tavern joined in the howling, telling the shifter that he wasn't alone. That the pack was there—a shield, a family, a home.

As Margery lifted her own voice, her eyes burned with tears.

Finishing the song, the bard—because, oh, that's what Emma must be—paused and started a new tune, *Song to the Mother*. The males behind her added a baritone and bass, and then the entire tavern sang along.

Tears spilled down Margery's cheeks.

These, these were her people.

As the song ended, Emma rose. "Thank you all. May the Mother's love forever light your trail until you return safely home to her."

When Emma put her guitar into the case, Margery whined, "She's finished? *Nooo*."

At a table, a female chuckled. "I'm afraid so. But she sings twice a week. Get here earlier next time."

"Oh, I will." Margery made her way across the room to Emma and bent her head in respect. "Bard. Thank you. I'd forgotten..." She couldn't think of the words to express the feelings that welled inside her. "Thank you."

A rumble of laughter came from the huge male behind her. It was the grizzly cahir named Ben. "I get it. I felt the same way when I first heard her sing."

"That's why I play. Thank you." Emma gave Margery a happy hug. "Margery, I think you know Ben from when the feral attacked at the park. This is my other mate, Ryder."

Ryder was sleek, dark, and deadly, reminding her of Donal. Another cat shifter.

Emma smiled. "Since I'm finished, let's have a drink and catch up."

A fair number of people were leaving, now the singing was done, but at the bar, Calum looked busy. Margery could wait a while to talk with him. "That'd be great. Is your cub here tonight, too?"

"No, Minette is playing with Bonnie's litter—and instigating trouble, I'm sure."

"Margery, Emma—over *here*," Darcy called from a large table in the corner. She had a male on each side of her, and across the table, Vicki grinned and pushed out two chairs in invitation.

"We are summoned," Emma said. After kissing her mates and shooing them toward the bar, she grabbed Margery's hand, pulling her along.

"Margery, look who's here." Darcy was beaming. "My littermates, Patrin and Fell."

"Margery, good to meet you." Patrin looked like Darcy, lean and dark with black eyes and hair. He smiled at her.

Fell was brown-haired and more muscular. His icy-blue eyes looked as if they'd seen far too much death. He nodded at her. Apparently, that was his idea of a greeting.

"It's a pleasure to meet you both." She didn't remember

them very well from Dogwood. Darcy's family had only moved there a month or so before the Scythe destroyed the village. And during their captivity, the shifter-soldiers were permitted to speak only with their own sisters.

"Is Oliver here?" Patrin looked around.

"No." It was a shame. Surely, her littermate would have wanted to see his friends. "He was planning to go run in the forest."

Fell frowned.

The knot of worry in her gut tangled more. "I know he had a hard time of it, but he still seems awfully unhappy."

Patrin gave her a steady look. "All the Dogwood survivors changed, all in different ways. Being free is the first step to recovery—not the last."

It was a dismal truth. "And Oliver...?"

"He didn't adapt well to being a soldier," Fell said baldly.

"Some shifters have a predator's instincts. Being a soldier comes naturally. He isn't like that." Patrin rubbed his neck. "And he's a solitary beast. In the compound, we were stuffed into barracks, muzzle to tail, and even on a mission, never left alone."

Impossible conditions for her brother. When upset as a cub, Oliver would hide in the forest and return only after he'd calmed himself. "You're saying he never got his balance."

"No, he didn't," Patrin said. "Although Elder Village was good for him, his head is still in the past."

Fell confirmed this with a dark scowl.

"What can I do?" Margery asked.

"Don't know." Patrin moved his shoulders. "Give him time?"

Darcy gave her a sympathetic look and rubbed her head against each brother's shoulder.

Oliver wouldn't have permitted even that small amount of affection.

"If Oliver isn't here, does that mean you walked up the hill by yourself?" Vicki asked with a frown.

"Sure."

Now they all frowned at her.

Vicki glanced at the dark windows. "Cold Creek isn't a shifter-only village—there are humans as well as strangers passing through. Unless you're good with a blade and firearms—preferably both—you shouldn't wander through town at night."

Margery blinked. "Oh. I guess I never thought about it." No one had cared when she was out at night in Ailill Ridge.

No one there had cared about her at all.

"I used to think that once I escaped the Scythe, my world would be safe." Darcy's lips twisted. "Wrong."

"I know. I had so many dreams of how wonderful life would be if I was free. Talk about mistaken." Her entire time in Rainier Territory had crushed most of her dreams.

But what about being with Donal and Tynan on Gathering night? "Then again, some daydreams fell completely short of reality."

Although Patrin and Fell looked confused, all three females snickered.

Oh, she did love having friends. "Much as I'd like to visit, I didn't come to the tavern to socialize. I need to talk to the Cosantir."

"Banfasa business?" Emma asked.

Margery nodded.

"We need to get you a car." Vicki tapped her fingertips on the table. "Donal hates vehicles but knows he has to use one. You should have one, too, for urgent stuff and so you're not walking around at night."

A car? "I don't even know how to drive."

"Someone can teach you. Only don't pick Donal." Vicki grinned. "The first time you run over a curb, he'll have a hissy-kitty fit."

Emma burst out laughing. "He will."

Donal and his ranting. Margery snorted at the thought.

"I'll ask Tynan to teach you." Vicki nodded to herself. "Superb driver, patient teacher. And he'll be easier on your nerves."

"Not as much fun for the rest of us, though," Darcy said. "I've picked up some great insults from listening to Donal."

That set them off, comparing the best insults. Arguing over fecal matter versus sexual imagery in insults.

Margery noticed Vicki had turned to stare at the bar. At the Cosantir.

After a minute, the Cosantir looked directly at his mate and raised an eyebrow.

Vicki pointed to Calum, held her arm out, and moved her hand forward several times. Then she pointed to Margery.

He tilted his head in acknowledgment.

"There. He should join us in a minute."

As the recipient of puzzled stares, Vicki added, "Alec had me teach the cahirs some tactical hand signals from the military. Of course, Calum decided to learn them, too."

"I noticed he turned around without you doing anything," Patrin said slowly.

"Well, you know how you can feel someone watching you when you're making a covert approach?" Vicki asked.

Both males nodded.

"I think it's a Cosantir thing, but Calum can feel if someone stares at him, even in a crowded room."

Emma glanced at the bar. "Cosantirs are scary."

When Margery nodded soberly, Vicki grinned. "Or he's tended bar so long he can sense when someone needs a drink."

"Who's cubsitting for you while you're down here?" Emma asked.

"Alec and Jamie. Thorson planned to join them. He takes being a *caomhnor* very seriously." Vicki's smile faded. "So does Wells, although I haven't seen him for a while. Patrin, Fell, do you know what he's been up to?"

Fell shrugged. The male sure wasn't into speaking.

"He just got back from the Mideast. He said the new unrest over there was instigated by the Scythe," Patrin said.

Margery shivered. Although the Daonain had destroyed the Scythe compound in Seattle, the Director had escaped and their network of rich, influential humans was intact.

Whenever she thought about the Scythe, she wanted to hide.

From the shifter-soldiers' deadly expressions, hiding wasn't in their plans. Patrin leaned forward. "Don't worry, Margery. We won't let anyone hurt you."

A corner of Fell's mouth turned up as he looked at her, then Patrin. "*Anyone?*"

"Good point." Patrin grinned at him and turned to her, his dark gaze dancing. "*We're* the only ones who get to hurt you."

She blinked. Was that a threat or was he flirting with her? "Ahhh..."

"Did Shay tell you that he'd asked us to teach you how to fight?"

"You?" She stared. "But Jody is—"

"Her, too. I think we'll have the whole wolf pack there." Patrin's smile deepened. "We were hoping to have a smaller class. Of one."

They'd wanted to give her...personal...lessons?

"Banfasa." The Cosantir's deep voice interrupted. He set a drink in front of her and handed one to Emma.

Next to him was Tynan.

Everything inside her reacted, as if she was hearing bone-shaking thunder, feeling a storm approach through her whole body. She licked her lips, and her voice came out husky. "Tynan."

He smiled down at her and tugged a strand of her hair. "Meggie mine."

Oh, she knew that "mine" was merely part of the common phrase. She shouldn't want it to be true.

When she smiled up at him, he traced the backs of his fingers down her cheek. And her whole body blossomed with desire.

"Well, cat-scat," Patrin muttered for some reason.

Before she could look over, Calum said, "Did you need to speak with me, Margery?"

Work. She pulled her thoughts into banfasa business. "Yes, if you have a couple of minutes, Cosantir."

When he nodded, she pointed to an empty table. "There?"

"If you wish."

Tynan lifted his chin in inquiry.

"Um, you, too, please?" A person's medical needs shouldn't be common knowledge, but the town's law enforcement should know Generys had a problem. The elderly shifter had given Margery permission to share with whoever might be useful. Open hunting, she called it.

And Tynan was the kind who'd help anyone who needed him.

How could a female not lo...not care for a male like Tynan?

As Margery settled at the new table, Emma started a

new conversation with the ones left behind, tactfully, distracting them from Margery's group.

"I was visiting some of the senior shifters today. I've found help for two of them, but one needs more than I can find for her." Margery went on to tell them about the older shifter. How her balance was poor, her hygiene worse, and her diet inadequate. Her daughter was in Canada with younger cubs, and Generys didn't want to be a burden.

Calum tapped his fingers on the table as he considered. "I'll talk with the Jasper Territory Cosantir. We can find out if the daughter knows about her dam's problems and wants to be involved."

Perfect. That was exactly what Margery had hoped for.

Tynan frowned. "Our wolf pack has a support system for those who need it—our seniors, new mothers, cubs, invalids. Perhaps the town needs something similar, Cosantir?"

"Aye, I think it's time we took steps." Calum smiled at Margery. "Now that we have someone capable of evaluating needs, we should be able to establish a support network."

"That sounds like a great idea," Vicki chimed in from the other table.

Beside her, Emma coughed politely. "Sorry, but I couldn't keep the conversation going—not without help." She frowned at the others at the table.

Calum gave Margery a rueful smile. "My mate has an insatiable curiosity."

"Since we heard the end of your discussion," Emma said,

"Ben and Ryder are using some younger shifters in volunteer work and teaching them the construction trade. They can help out."

"Perfect." Margery felt her enthusiasm rising. "I've been researching ways to convert houses to be elder-friendly. I'd like to talk with both of them."

"They're still over at the bar. We'll talk to them and get it set up." Emma's eyes held equal enthusiasm. "Historically, bards were used to recruit for wars. It's time we drew people to something better—like charitable efforts. I'll see if I can't find you shifters, young and old, who have spare time on their hands."

"The younger ones will probably want to be paid," Patrin said.

"You're so cynical." Darcy thumped her littermate in the ribs. "Count me in for repair work. I bet Bree will cook if the clan's budget would buy the ingredients."

Margery's heart skipped a beat. A support system was being born as she watched.

Darcy nudged her littermates. "Are you two going to help?"

"*Chwaer,* we don't know where the shifter-soldiers will end up," Patrin told his sister. "Not until we talk with Wells."

The thought sent a chill up Margery's spine. The human spymaster apparently still planned on involving the shifter-soldiers in eliminating the Scythe.

What would her littermate do?

Later that night, Tynan parked his car in the driveway and got out. His SUV pinged quietly as a cold drizzling rain splatted against the heat of the hood. Grateful for their bright porch light, he walked around the vehicle as Meggie slid out of the passenger side.

When he'd told her he was driving her home, she hadn't argued at all. *Progress.*

He smiled. Everyone at the table—other than Meggie—had noticed the shifter-soldiers' interest in her. And that the only male she'd reacted to as a female was Tynan.

Mine.

He glanced across the side yard at Meggie's dark house. "Looks like Oliver hasn't come home yet. Or he went to bed early."

She shut the passenger door. "A rainy night in the forest doesn't bother him in the least. He says he finds a dry hollow and enjoys the quiet." Her voice was tight as she whispered, "I don't understand. Why doesn't he want to be here with me?"

Heedless of the rain, Tynan pulled her into his arms, the only way he knew how to comfort her. "After I left Seattle and came here, I spent days and weeks in the mountains. We shifters go into the forests when stressed—and even something as simple as change can be stressful."

"Oh. I hadn't thought of it that way."

When she relaxed and laid her cheek on his shoulder, he

felt as victorious as if he'd dragged home a moose for her supper.

"You needed the forests, and you actually like people. It must be worse for an introverted bear." She gave Tynan a squeeze. "Thank you. I'll try not to worry so much about him."

"At least you're not harassing him about what he might need or what he should do. Donal, as you can imagine..."

She had the cutest throaty giggle. "I'm sure he told you exactly what to do to get better and was offended when you didn't take his advice. Noisily offended."

Tynan laughed. "You know him well, banfasa."

Her head was tilted back, and raindrops glittered in her dark eyelashes. Her eyes danced with laughter, her soft lips curved, and she offered far more temptation than any male could resist.

He lowered his head slowly, giving her time to object, and then kissed her, savoring her mouth, pulling her closer. Her breasts flattened against his chest, and when he slid his hands under her shirt, her damp skin was warm and silken under his rough palms.

She kissed like a dream.

"Seriously? If you're going to do that, get your tails inside and out of the rain." Donal stood on the porch, hands on his hips.

"Worried about us catching cold?" Tynan asked, amused.

"Hardly. I simply want her between us on the couch. Or

better yet, the bed." With a cat's exasperated stalk, Donal disappeared into the house.

Meggie's eyes were wide.

"Little wolf."

"He didn't really mean that," she tried to tell him.

Donal didn't say things he didn't mean. As Tynan's cop friends would say, the healer lacked a filter between brain and mouth.

However, there were three of them, and one hadn't indicated her preference. "He meant exactly what he said. But, Meggie, if you're not interested in him that way—or aren't interested in two males at once, then simply tell us." He put a finger under her chin, tilting her head so he could see her expression in the glow of the porch light.

Had he ever thought she wasn't beautiful?

He couldn't remember. These days, it seemed as if the beauty of her spirit engulfed the merely physical. Is this what shifters saw when they looked into the face of the Goddess—a radiance that overwhelmed anything else?

Meggie leaned against him like a wolf pup seeking reassurance. "Saying I'm not interested would be lying. I just don't want the two of you to be...disappointed. I...I've never... Two at the same time."

He could scent her interest. She was still so very inexperienced, which meant they'd go slow...and thoroughly enjoy making sure her desire was at white-hot levels. "It's our job to make sure none of us are disappointed. Trust us, *a leannán.*"

After enjoying another kiss, he took her inside to his littermate.

To share.

In their living room, Donal heard the front door open. Anticipation rising within him, he added a log to the fire and tossed cushions, blankets, and pillows into a pile next to the hearth.

It was good that yesterday he and Tynan had readied the unused female bedroom upstairs. The largest bedroom—the heart of the house—was surrounded and protected by the smaller male bedrooms.

He'd never bothered to make up the room before, but for Margery... *Yes. Absolutely, yes.*

When she and Tynan walked into the living room, Donal stared at the drenched pair. "By the Gods, even pixies know to come in out of the rain."

Margery's hair was soaked, and she was shivering, yet she grinned. "I'm blaming your littermate."

"Humph." Donal raised his brows at his brother. "When *I* kiss a female, her shivers aren't because she's cold."

Tynan laughed...and kissed Margery again.

The mangy mutt was disgustingly difficult to provoke.

After grabbing towels from the downstairs bathroom, Donal handed one to Tynan. "You look like a drowned dog. Dry off before you catch your death."

His littermate gave him an amused glance. "You sound like Granny."

"But I'm so much better looking."

Margery's giggle was unexpected—and delightful.

When she fumbled unsuccessfully with the buttons of her sweater, he tossed the towel over his shoulder and brushed her chilled hands aside. "Let me, sweetling."

With years of experience, he efficiently stripped her sweater, shirt, and bra off.

Undid her jeans...

"Donal," she gasped, making a futile grab for the waistband.

...and tugged them down to her ankles.

"Too late." He left her feet tangled in the mess. "Such a shame, little banfasa, but it doesn't look like you're going to be able to escape."

"You're sneakier than a weasel," she muttered, then simply laughed in a way that told him she wasn't worried. She trusted him.

From the wary survivor, it was a compliment he'd cherish.

Smiling, he dried her legs, rubbing briskly until her skin flushed pink. Soft, smooth, pretty skin. Although the faint white scars still pissed him off. At least, he knew the ones who'd hurt her were dead.

He ran his hand over her calf and down to the wet jeans. "Brawd, lift her up?"

"I can do that." Tynan, already naked and dry, scooped her up into his arms.

She squeaked in surprise.

"You sound like a flower fairy that landed on a thorn." Laughing, Donal pulled the jeans over her feet and off.

Her eyes narrowed at Donal. "I'm going to bribe Ben to yank you into his arms and see what you sound like."

"Ben?" Tynan burst out laughing. "That'd do it."

The grizzly cahir could lift anyone without breaking a sweat. "You're certainly a mean one." In revenge, Donal scraped his fingernail down the sole of her foot and won himself another amusing squeak...before she kicked him.

"Aye, she has a vicious streak." Tynan grinned.

"I rather like the ones with dispositions like badgers," Donal noted.

Margery's appalled expression was what he'd been hoping for. By the Gods, she was fun to play with.

He waved toward the fire. "Go warm her up and see if her temper doesn't settle. I'm sure she's only like this because she's cold."

Her narrow-eyed frown promised an undoubtedly amusing retribution. Not that he'd worry. She was a wolf, not a cat.

Shifting her in his arms, Tynan kissed her into smiles, before laying her down on the big soft blanket pile.

"Oh, the blankets are warm." Her husky sigh pleased him...and roused his dick.

As Tynan lay down beside her, Donal stripped his own clothes off and settled on the blankets on her other side.

Her eyes were wide as she stared first at Tynan and then at him. "I...uh...noticed you didn't give me any clothing."

"Guess we're getting as forgetful as elders." Tynan ran his knuckles over her cheek and down her neck.

"We'll find you some clothing...eventually." Catching the scent of her growing interest, Donal cupped the breast closest to him—and ran his thumb around the bunched nipple, exploring the tiny nubs around the peak. Breasts were so fascinating.

Tynan grinned, then did the same.

Margery flushed an appealing pink. "I... This isn't right."

Felt right to him. Under his palm, he could feel the way her heart rate accelerated. "What isn't right, sweetheart?" He tugged at the nipple, smiling at her sharp inhalation.

"Where can I touch?" Brow creased, she lifted her hands in the air. "I...don't know what to do."

Why wouldn't she... His eyes narrowed. "That's right. You've only mated at Gatherings."

She nodded.

During full moon Gatherings, a female's heat drove the interactions—and didn't allow for mutual exploration. Unless very experienced and determined, males simply mounted and satisfied the female. "Hmm."

"I'd say it's time to widen your experience." Smiling, Tynan winked at Donal, returning to the patterns they'd worked out years before as young males. "Donal, lie on your back."

"I can do that." Donal rolled.

Hands around Margery's waist, Tynan lifted her and...

Set her on top of Donal. Her warmth came down right on his erection, and the need to be inside her roared through him. He ran his hands over her hips, seeing arousal light her eyes. "You feel good, Margery."

She smiled down at him and grasped his forearms as if needing the connection.

"All right, little wolf, it's lesson time," Tynan murmured. "Explore his body with your hands, with your lips and tongue."

"Ohhh." The breathy word sounded as if she'd been given the best present.

"Donal, keep your hands behind your head. No touching."

"Well, fuck."

Margery sputtered a laugh at Donal's curse.

Grumbling under his breath—because he wanted to run his hands over all that soft skin—he put his hands behind his head.

A second later, she leaned forward, kissed him slowly, and started nibbling, kissing, and licking her way down his body.

Little sharp teeth, soft lips. Hot, wet tongue. Over his neck, down his chest. Around his nipples. And down...

By the Gods, he might not survive her first lesson.

This didn't make sense, Margery thought, as she stroked Donal's ridged abdominal muscles, then over his rigid shaft. Although neither male was touching her, she was wet and increasingly excited. Her skin felt as heated as if she'd been sitting in the sun.

By the Mother, she wanted them. Both of them.

She wiggled downward on Donal's body.

"Here you go, sweetheart." He obligingly spread his legs so she could kneel between his thighs.

During the Gatherings, she'd rarely looked at a male—not when he was erect.

The firelight glowed over Donal's beautiful cock. He was intimidatingly long. How in the world had he fit inside her at the last Gathering?

She ran her fingertips over the head and down, mesmerized at the changing textures. The soft, spongier top, the tightness of the silky skin over the incredibly hard shaft. Elastic-feeling veins wound around the length.

When his erection bobbed under her fingers, she snatched her hand away. "I'm sorry."

"Sweetheart, your touch feels amazing." Smiling, Donal took her hand and put it back on his shaft.

Maybe he was just being nice. Then again, Donal wasn't the sort to say what he didn't mean.

Biting her lip, she glanced at Tynan.

His rumbling laugh was reassuring. "Look, *a leannán*." Tynan curled his big hand around his own erection—and she'd never seen anything sexier in her life.

"Like this." He tightened his grip.

Her eyes widened. That didn't look comfortable. But at Donal's nod, she did the same.

Donal's low groan was the most wonderful reassurance —and so arousing. Her insides felt like a molten pool of desire.

Tynan moved his hand up and down his shaft. "This is what a male does if he doesn't have a female—because he can pretend it feels like when he's inside you."

Up and down. She could do that. Stroking Donal's erection was...fun. Amazing. Carnal. Because she could imagine he was inside her. And she could see the way his stomach muscles tightened, feel the way his cock hardened even further in her grip, see the flush heating his face.

He really *liked* this.

The sunlines beside Tynan's eyes crinkled. "You won't hurt Donal by touching. Or licking or sucking."

At the memory of Donal's mouth on her clit and how he'd teased her there... Her own cheeks heated, and her clit tingled. Could she give that amazing sensation to them?

Yes. Bending, she licked over his cock.

"Herne's hairy balls, that feels good." Donal's face flushed a darker red. His hands were behind his head, and his biceps turned to rocks as if he was trying not to move.

Knowing if she did anything wrong, Tynan would stop her made it so much easier. She smiled at him.

He grinned back. "Avoid biting or scraping the healer with your teeth, and it's all good."

Donal huffed. "Aye. No biting, female."

Laughing, she gave a bounce that made her breasts bobble, then bent and experimented. *Enjoyed.* Licking was fun, especially since every breath brought her Donal's clean masculine scent. She took him in her mouth, growling as a rush of heat ran through her.

Tonguing him or sucking him made his hips lift. It was such an amazing feeling to gift him with the sensations she'd loved. Then she got the hang of it and started using her hands and bobbing her head.

It wasn't nearly long enough when he sat up and caught her shoulders in a firm grip. "Enough, sweetling, or this will be over far sooner than I'd like."

Dismayed, she sat back, wiping her lips and chin. His heady taste still lingered on her tongue. "Did I do something wrong?"

"Fuck, no—you did it all too *right*." He cupped her cheek. "If a female is good, she can make a male lose control and climax. The problem is that males don't recover as quickly as females. I'm not ready to come yet."

"Oh. Okay." She'd done it right. Done it well enough that she might have made him come. She looked down at his straining shaft, tempted to continue so she could—

Tynan laughed. "Bad puppy. No, you may not continue."

"Actually, it's your turn, brawd," Donal said. "Let's try some multi-tasking."

Play with Tynan? Smiling, Margery turned.

But what did multi-tasking mean?

A few minutes later, she knew.

Kneeling between Tynan's legs, she'd started off licking and sucking on his thick cock. He'd shown her how to grip the base and then how to cup his testicles.

The male loved to teach—and nothing embarrassed him, did it?

But, hey, she was a good student. She learned that sucking hard made his breathing catch. His grip tightened in her hair when she pumped the base of his cock with one hand while licking the top. She took him fully in her mouth...and bobbed.

"Meggie." The controlled power of his voice stroked over her, adding to the sense of restraint from his fingers in her hair.

Dark hunger created a burning pulse between her thighs.

Tynan spread his legs wider, then looked at his brother and nodded.

Kneeling behind her, Donal ran his hands up over her back and down her sides. "You have the softest skin," he murmured.

When he teased her breasts, so wickedly knowledgeable, every skill she'd mastered disappeared under a fog of need. She whimpered a plea, even knowing they would take her only when they decided.

"Patience, sweetling." Donal ran his hand over her buttocks and down between her legs. To her pussy. His fingers traced a line between her folds, through her wetness, and he made a purring sound of approval. "Our wolflet is enjoying your cock, brawd."

The teasing touches up and over and around her clit made her suck in air as every nerve down there roused to fever pitch.

She lifted her head from Tynan's shaft, unable to think as Donal's fingers circled, rubbed.

"Ready, Margery?" Donal's resonant voice stroked over her in the same way his fingers had.

Ready? Oh, past ready.

She managed to nod, and then his cock pressed at her entrance. Penetrated. He sheathed himself to the hilt with a smooth, determined thrust.

Such a full, hot sensation. "Ooooh." Her head tilted up at the overwhelming rush of pleasure.

Steadying her with his hands on her shoulders, Tynan smiled slowly. "I think the multi-tasking portion of the evening is done."

Donal had a firm grip on her hips and was sliding in and out slowly. "I see that."

She flushed, realizing she'd abandoned Tynan's cock. "Oh...oh, I'm sor—"

"*Mo thaisce*, I've never enjoyed anything as much as sharing you with my brother." Tynan caressed her cheek. "You are so very beautiful."

She stared at him in disbelief, then joy.

He pulled her down to kiss her slowly, lingeringly, then tucked her head against his shoulder. "Now, take her hard, Donal. After, I'll enjoy more slowly while you start preparing her for future fun."

"Good plan." Donal's chest was hot against her bare back. His voice was a sonorous velvet as he said, "Brace yourself, pretty wolf."

Brace, right. She'd barely gripped Tynan's shoulders when Donal pulled back and started thrusting, hard and fast.

And then Tynan's fingers were teasing her nipples, tugging, rolling them between his fingers, and somehow, the feeling tangled with the hammering.

Waves of need rolled over her, tightening her insides, the sensation unstoppable, impossible.

Every muscle in her body drew taut with the exquisite torment.

"Let go, little wolf." Tynan's dark blue eyes held hers. He pinched her nipples hard, even as Donal mercilessly hammered into her.

The orgasm rolled through her in a crashing wave of stunning pleasure. The blood sang in her veins, locking out everything as the release tore through her. She could hear the keening cry she gave as the pleasure went on and on.

Gasping for breath, she shuddered, feeling her muscles going limp. Her arms gave out, and she dropped down onto Tynan's chest

With a growling, purring sound, Donal pressed deeper, pulsing inside her.

Even as she clenched around him in another spasm of sensation, she felt something different, the budding warmth of...connection. Of a bond forming.

Tynan pulled Meggie up so he could kiss her damp cheek, then wrapped his arms around her. She'd gone as limp as a pup in the sun, and he could feel her heart pounding.

But she trusted him to hold her. To care for her after.

Truly, he'd never seen anyone so lovely when she came. Never enjoyed sharing anyone with his brother as much as this little wolf who had such a soft heart and gentle spirit. Had he ever met anyone who gave so generously?

As he breathed in the fragrance of warm female and sex, his cock hardened, hoping for its turn.

Not yet.

Could there be any finer contentment than to cuddle Meggie? Stroke her back and kiss her?

Donal kissed his way down her back, pulling out so he could lie beside them and play with her hair. His expression held a stunned pleasure.

Soon enough, Meggie stirred, then sat up, kneeling between his legs. He was pleased to see her eyes held the same languorous satisfaction as Donal's. So beautiful.

She met his gaze and smiled. "It's your turn, right?"

Thinking of him, even though her need had already been met. Generous and giving.

"Aye and so it is." He smiled back. "Since you're enjoying being the active one tonight, why don't you climb on?"

By the Gods, he loved when her eyes widened like that.

"Climb on...how?"

He'd thought it was fun mentoring her in the wolf pack. This was...there were no words to describe the pleasure of initiating her into the joys of making love. Because...aye, this was far more than a simple mating. Yet, indeed, it was still *fun*. "Straddle me, first. Hands on my shoulders."

Donal sat up and helped her get in position so her knees were outside of his hips. She eyed the cock that was straining toward her, and her lips twitched. "I think I'm getting an idea of how this will work."

Tynan said without breaking a smile, "I thought you might."

Donal snorted.

And Meggie laughed.

Fisting his cock, Tynan held it up. "Lower yourself onto me. Slowly, *a leannán*."

Biting her lip, she went down slowly, engulfing the head of his cock. Eyes widening, she halted.

Halted.

His shaft throbbed with such urgency he had to force himself to stay still. "You feel amazing." Like the warmest of silk. "More, please, Meggie mine."

Her hands gripped his shoulders as she dropped, inch by intense inch until he was completely sheathed in her tight, wet heat. *By the Gods.* He let out a low groan.

Donal had moved away, and now he returned, settling down beside her hips, one hand gloved and glistening with lube. The healer had all the fun equipment.

Meggie didn't even notice as she squirmed on Tynan's cock, adjusting to his size. She stared at him, her lips parted and pink. "Now what?"

"Now, you go up and down." Smiling, Tynan reached down—because this position left his hands free—and ran a finger over her clit.

Her cunt clenched down on his cock so tightly he almost came right then.

He pulled in a breath, regained control. After a second, he continued, rubbing one side, then the other. Wasn't it handy that the little nub got pressed outward by the girth of his cock?

She started to wiggle, and he watched the flush of heat climbing from her breasts to her face.

By the Gods, he loved mating with her. "Up and down," he reminded her, winking at Donal.

Making little huffing sounds, she started to move. Up, almost off his dick. Then down. Slowly.

But as he teased her clit, her movements grew faster and faster.

Oh Gods, she felt so ignorant about all this sex stuff. But Margery decided she didn't care, not in the least, because all she could really think about was the way Tynan felt inside her and how his fingers were moving on her clit. The combination was too much.

His heated gaze was on her face, those blue eyes watching her. His lips quirked up in a slight smile of enjoyment and satisfaction and...and caring.

When he lifted his gaze, trapping hers, she froze. He reached up with his other hand and touched her cheek. "Meggie."

Her heart seemed as if it was falling, tumbling out of her chest into his keeping.

No, no, that wasn't right. She mustn't think that way.

Worried, she bit her lip.

His expression turned tender, but then he smiled. "Move, little wolf. It's time for you to move." He started rubbing her clit again.

Her body reawakened in a flash. Each stroke, each touch made her more sensitive, drew her closer and closer to—

A hand gripped her hip. Donal had moved behind her. He parted her buttocks and ran his finger over...over her anus.

"What?" She started to sit up.

Tynan wrapped his fingers around her wrists, holding her hands against his chest. "No, don't move, Meggie." His gaze was intent on her face.

She looked back at Donal, then him.

His slow smile eased her worry. "It seems this might be something else you didn't know. When males share a female, that area is sometimes used as well."

Donal circled his finger around the rim, creating an intoxicating kaleidoscope of sensation.

As sizzles zinged through her, she shivered. "*There?*"

"There," Donal answered, his voice gentle. "If you don't like it, I'll stop, sweetheart."

Tynan nodded. "But try it once first, aye?"

"O-okay." Another shiver ran through her as Donal's finger pressed in slightly. The slick intrusive sensation felt totally wrong as he opened that part of her, yet the nerves felt electrified, and everything inside her clenched.

Tynan groaned. "By the Gods, that feels good."

Happiness swept through her that she'd pleased him.

But then Donal moved his finger in and out of her, sending all sorts of strange sensations through her. He added another finger, stretching her almost uncomfortably, yet the disconcerting pleasure overwhelmed everything else.

"Ready for you, brawd." Donal's hand tightened on one buttock with his fingers deep inside her.

She shivered at the consuming sensations—Tynan's cock so thick in her pussy, Donal's fingers...elsewhere.

"Time to move, little wolf." Tynan said.

Move? Was he crazy?

Gripping her hips, he didn't wait, but lifted her up and almost off his cock—and then he drew her down, hard enough to make her gasp—and the two fingers in her ass went along. When Tynan's cock was completely inside her, Donal moved his fingers in and out, sending a seething tension through her.

The need started to grow.

Tynan lifted her up...

Up and down, in and out, and everything increased the delirious hunger until each cell in her body burned with urgency. Vibrated with the need to come.

More.

Hands moved over her, Tynan's cock penetrated her, Donal's fingers possessed her. Both males were focused on her, only on her, and the knowledge of their careful nurturing and concern filled her heart to overflowing.

And sent her over.

Her head went back as her entire core exploded with pleasure, as waves of heat rippled through her, outward along her nerves and blood vessels and muscles until her whole body shimmered with ecstasy. Until the whole room turned blurry.

Through the haze, she heard Tynan laugh, rock her up and down twice more and then anchor her against him as he came with hard spasms.

She sagged down on top of him, hearing Donal's

chuckle, and as he pulled his fingers out, she jolted at the flash of pleasure.

Every muscle in her body went limp.

When Donal returned, Tynan tucked her down between them. Hard bodies on each side, deep voices.

Their callused hands stroked her gently as she fell asleep.

CHAPTER SIXTEEN

C old Creek, North Cascades Territory - waning gibbous moon

Not even a pouring rain could diminish her spirits the next morning. Margery let herself back into her house, closing the front door quietly in case her littermate had come home.

"No need to pussyfoot around." At the dining room table, Oliver scowled. "Or act like you've been out killing pixies."

She laughed. "No pixies have been slaughtered today. I didn't want to wake you if you were asleep."

"Where in the Hunter's green forest have you been?" His voice came out a growl. "I was worried."

"Oh, cat-scat. I'm sorry. I should have left you a note."
She hung up her wet coat. "I was next door."

"Oh." He looked happier. "I didn't realize the healer
started work so early."

She exhaled. Letting him assume she was only working
with Donal would be a form of lying. The Scythe had taught
her to hate lies. "Donal doesn't open his clinic this early. I
spent the night over there."

Oliver's brown brows drew together as he sniffed the air.

She flushed, all too conscious of the scent of sex clinging
to her, of her beard-reddened cheeks, chin, and neck. Of
her swollen lips. Of the bite-mark on her neck. Of her
tousled hair.

Worry crossed his face, before he scowled. "Isn't it
considered poor form to fuck your boss?"

What? She jerked back, then her eyes narrowed. "That
was rude. And uncalled for."

His expression blanked. "I just... Yeah, sorry."

Her eyes narrowed as she looked him over. Hair tousled,
a day's beard scruff, eyes bloodshot. His T-shirt showed a
bear watching a human on a bicycle with the text beneath:
Meals on wheels.

Same T-shirt he'd worn yesterday. And he smelled like
alcohol.

"Is this the fairy calling the bird, flighty?" She put her
hands on her hips. "Were you even home to notice I was
gone?"

He turned a dull red. His hands had a fine tremor. His skin looked sallow.

"Bro, you said you didn't like crowded taverns," she said softly. "Were you having drinks with Patrin and Fell or something?"

"Nah." He looked away. "I was drinking—got a bottle of whisky at the store—but it was in the woods."

A niggle of anxiety came to life. Drinking alone. That wasn't healthy, and it appeared Oliver had imbibed the entire bottle. "That doesn't seem... Is everything...?"

Mother's breasts, why was it easier to discuss health issues with patients than with her own brother?

"I'm fine." He shoved his chair back and rose. "And I'm not a cub, sis. What I do, what I drink is my business. Not yours."

As he disappeared into his bedroom, she stared after him. Honestly, he gave her that line after asking *her* where she'd spent the night?

Huffing out a breath, she headed into her own bedroom to take a shower—and managed not to slam her door.

She'd forgotten how Oliver could act like a dwarf whose gold had been stolen when he got in a mood.

Well, really, couldn't they all?

Guilt reared up. Perhaps she should have come home last night. He was having a rough time.

But alcohol was never the right answer. She stripped off her clothing and stepped into the shower. What if he—

She shook her head. No, she was being a worrywart. He

was back in civilization from the tiny Elder Village with no stores. Over-indulging in drink just once wasn't the sign of a problem.

He was fine.

She'd make sure he was fine. Because she was all he had left now.

Orson was gone. If the mere thought of their brother sent an echo of sorrow through her, how much worse must it be for Oliver? Male littermates were closer to each other, probably because they stayed together through life. If Orson had been alive, he and Oliver would have their own place or—like many other young males—would have been wandering through the territories before settling down. She'd have been looking for her own place. For her own males to love.

To *love*.

The thought sent tremors of hope and anxiety through her.

Last night had been something she'd never experienced before. Being with Donal and Tynan together was so special. Would they want to...to be together like that again?

She scrubbed her skin hard, needing to wash away her silly hopes.

Paws on the trail, Margery. She mustn't get enticed into chasing butterflies that would flit away into the sky, leaving her in a tangle of brambles.

CHAPTER SEVENTEEN

C old Creek, North Cascades Territory - third quarter moon

Two days later, Margery looked around at the group of wolves. On a slight rise, Patrin was lecturing. It was his second day of teaching them how to fight in animal form against those in human form...like the Scythe.

Margery shivered, despite the warmth of the day.

I'm a banfasa, I don't hurt people.

Yet... If the Dogwood villagers had been better fighters, some of them might have escaped. Might have found help before so many had died.

I'll kill anyone who tries to capture me or my people again.

Patrin reviewed the techniques he'd taught them yesterday. The circling, the leap. Where to bite to disable and what bites would kill.

The Daonain had all hunted deer and rabbits. Humans weren't much different. Just bigger.

Too big, she'd thought at first. In yesterday's class, Margery had been a total failure. Too slow, wrong angle, too weak.

Last night, Tynan had hauled her into the forest and made her practice "killing" him, saying if she could take him down, she could take anyone down. Over and over, she'd leaped at him. Until suddenly it all clicked. *Spring from here. At this angle. Lock onto the throat here.*

Afterward, Tynan and Donal had "rewarded" her with so many orgasms that she'd slept like a hibernating pixie.

Today, though, all that practicing had left her with legs that ached like she'd been pounded on. Leaping on someone wasn't for wussies.

Margery watched Patrin for another minute, then... inevitably, her gaze was drawn to the side where Tynan stood beside Fell.

A male shouldn't have eyes the color of the sky.

His gaze met hers, pulling her in, drowning her in blue heat.

A cleared throat pulled her attention away.

Kori, a middle-aged shifter who taught in the small school edged closer and whispered, "I know this isn't the place to ask, but, banfasa, could you visit my neighbor,

Zaneta? She's well over a hundred now and having trouble getting around."

Because of Ailill Ridge, Margery's first reaction was to tell Kori to talk to the healer. But, no, dealing with daily living activities was more a banfasa's skill than a healer's.

Stop huddling in caves, Margery.

First, she should establish the problem wasn't from a new illness. "Has Donal seen her to discover why she's having trouble getting around?"

"Aye. He said there's no cure for old age." Kori sighed. "We all want the miracle cures, don't we? My sire told me healers are for instant fixes, and banfasas are for everything else."

The knot in Margery's stomach disappeared. "That's pretty much how it works."

"Will you go see her?"

"Certainly. I'll go over tomorrow and see what can be done." Delight sparkled inside her like sunlight on a burbling creek. She loved that her clan had started to come to her for help. "Thank you for letting me know."

Kori grinned. "Thank you for—"

A growl interrupted her.

"Oh, spit," Kori said under her breath and inched away from Margery.

Margery looked toward the front and shrank slightly. Because Patrin's scowl could send a grizzly into hiding—and he was staring right at her and Kori.

Oops.

Standing beside Patrin, Tynan ran his palm over his mouth, all too obviously trying to conceal a grin. Oh, she was going to get teased tonight, wasn't she?

After another menacing stare, Patrin continued. "To warm up, I want to see your one-on-one attacks. Row one—human form—against row two as wolves."

The row in front turned. Margery faced Van, one of Bonnie's mates, who'd arrived a few minutes ago. He nodded at her. "You can do this."

Though his smile was encouraging, his gaze and stance showed he didn't think she had a chance.

She shifted to wolf and assessed him. He was almost as big as Tynan—and not nearly as muscular. She circled him once, then again, her haunches tightening. Compensating for her weak ankle, she sprang upward, paws landing on his chest, jaws angled exactly right for her teeth to close on his throat. She bit down hard enough to let him know he was dead and leaped away.

"Gods blast it." Staggering back, he stared at her and then grinned. "Perfect kill, banfasa."

"Agreed. Good job, Margery," Patrin called. From the front, he watched as others attacked, kills were made. He, Fell, and Tynan instructed as needed.

When everyone was warmed up, Patrin resumed. "Today, the lessons are about teamwork. One wolf will divert the prey's attention while another wolf attacks. Tynan and Fell will demonstrate as we go over the techniques."

"Patrin," Jody yelled, "if one wolf is enough, why use two?"

"Good question. Honestly, if your target is unwary, not looking for trouble, unarmed, you should have no trouble. Watch now." Raven-black hair gleaming in the sunlight, Patrin sauntered across the low hillock, looking like the typical hiker. "See how easy a target I am?"

Everyone nodded.

"However, if you're up against a soldier..." He picked up a rifle from the ground. His muscles tensed. His alert gaze swiveled over the area. Each balanced step showed him ready to fight. "...how effective will you be?"

"Liable to get perforated with bullets before we get within ten feet," Van answered.

"Exactly." Patrin moved toward the brush. "Wolves are excellent stalkers—and a human's peripheral vision sucks. Unfortunately, a throat kill means attacking from the front where your target can use a weapon."

"Got it," Jody said. "So, distracting him is the answer."

Patrin pointed his finger at her. "If I had an army, I'd recruit you." He addressed the rest of them. "We'll teach an effective two-wolf method today. However, *anything* that distracts your target and points his rifle away from the attacking wolf will work."

"Tynan, play a Scythe soldier. Fell, you're the attack wolf. I'll be the diversion wolf."

Tynan walked over and accepted the rifle.

As Patrin stripped and changed to wolf, Tynan crossed

the rise, walking slowly, cautiously. All senses aware. His posture reminded Margery far too much of the Scythe guards, and she shivered.

Patrin slipped out of the bushes, stalking him from behind. Off to Tynan's right, Fell moved silently through the undergrowth.

Patrin charged, jaws closing on Tynan's left rear thigh.

With a yell, Tynan turned to the left, swinging his rifle around. Even as Patrin darted away, Fell leaped at Tynan's vulnerable neck.

Off balance, Tynan fell. And as Fell pretended to rip his throat out, Tynan died...dramatically.

Hoots and whistles and yips ran around the clearing.

Grinning, Jody nudged Margery. "Wanna team up and take Van down?"

Still seeing Tynan falling, dying, Margery had to force herself to smile. "Sounds good."

Her gaze returned to the rise where Tynan was coming back from the dead. She couldn't keep from scrutinizing his clothing for blood, watching his expression for signs of pain.

When had he come to mean so much that the mere thought of him being hurt was intolerable?

Oh, she was in so much trouble.

CHAPTER EIGHTEEN

*C*old *Creek, North Cascades Territory* - *waning crescent moon*

Tynan sniffed the air, breathing in the aroma of steak on the grill. Wildwood Lodge's Sunday party had chosen a menu that shifters would love. Meat and lots of it.

Although he'd never say no to one of Bree's desserts.

Since his alpha was stuck manning the grill, Tynan took him a beer. "Anything you need me to do?"

"Thanks—and nope." Shay smiled. "Enjoy your day off."

"Will do." Who wouldn't enjoy a sunny afternoon and a party of shifters having fun?

He dodged two teenaged cubs on their way to the soccer game, sidestepped a bevy of females comparing notes about a well-endowed male, and paused at the chess table where Thorson was locked in battle with the blademage Gawain.

Gawain was winning, much to Thorson's annoyance.

Every other Sunday during summer, the lodge held a party—one that drew the humans and Daonain in the community together. It was difficult to classify someone as "other" after sharing a beer and laughing together at youngling antics.

Considering the carousing on the mini-playground Zeb had built, there was more than sufficient youngling activity to enjoy.

Tynan spotted Meggie applying a bandage to little Luke's knee and giving him a hug...which he enthusiastically returned. Tynan smiled. She said her contentment came from being surrounded by people she could help. Being accepted.

He understood her right down to the core. Those were his needs as well.

Being loved, now that would be a bonus for him, but he was hoping...

For nearly a week, she'd spent evenings and nights with him and Donal, leaving early in the morning to make breakfast for herself and Oliver.

A glance ascertained that Oliver wasn't at the lodge party.

Tynan shook his head. He'd invited the male to join him for a drink or a forest run and had been turned down. Same with Donal. Was Meggie's littermate merely antisocial—or was he resentful they were taking up his sister's time?

Either way, they weren't going to back away from Meggie.

As Meggie took Luke back to his father, Tynan watched, remembering the feeling of her soft body against his. How she'd so easily become an important part of their lives. Talking about her day's adventures and getting him and Donal to share theirs. Teasing Donal about what she called his *bedside manner*. Even sex was different—special—maybe because this time they were with a female who really cared about them. Yes, they shared something.

And eventually, the three of them should talk about the future. Because Donal had fallen as hard as Tynan had.

Who knew falling could be so pleasant?

Smiling, Tynan wandered across the patio.

In a grassy stretch by the creek, teens were playing a vigorous game of pounce and tackle. Their agemates, Hector and Lysander, watched from the sidelines.

"Didn't they let you join in?" Tynan asked.

"They would, but Mama said no." Lysander turned up sad brown eyes. "The healer said if he caught me doing anything strenuous or climbing again, he'd rebreak my leg for free."

"Ah." The accidents from the newest teen craze—tree-ways—had sent Donal into more than one shouting fit, especially when the injured were non-feline shifters. "*Why in the Hunter's forests would dogs be climbing trees? Or bears be leaping from branch to branch? Frost-bitten sprites show more sense."*

"That grumpy healer probably never climbed a tree in his life," Hector—a werecat—said under his breath.

Tynan covered his laugh with a cough. "Actually, Donal loves climbing. Over the years, I've busted quite a few bones trying to follow."

"You?" Hector stared, then flushed, belatedly remembering Tynan was Donal's littermate.

Grinning, Tynan caught Shay's attention, motioned to the two lads, then at Shay's grill and pantomimed flipping a burger.

The alpha nodded.

"Watching people play is boring, so how about something else? If you ask nicely, Shay'll teach you how to grill burgers. You know...the cooks get special treats from Bree."

"Seriously?" Lysander brightened. Teen bears were always starving. "Thank you!"

Hector watched his sibling head straight for the grill. "Thanks, Deputy. He's been kinda unhappy—and we've always wanted to learn to grill."

As the pup followed Lysander, Tynan nodded in satisfaction. The lads were Gather-bred, their mother raising them on her own while working as a grocery clerk. Hector had recently apprenticed to Owen to learn to carve, but Lysander hadn't found anything yet.

Lacking a goal... It was a tough place to be. Although

Donal had always known his path in life, Tynan hadn't found his own trail until years later in Ireland.

Raised voices drew his attention. A cluster of male wolves in their twenties, Herne help him. He veered that direction.

"Chad was tossed out of the pack like a chewed-up bone. He deserved better." Fyodor, one of Chad's friends, scowled at the group around him.

"I know you thought his shit didn't stink." Fyodor's littermate, Emil, crossed his arms over his chest. "But, bro, Chad's an asshole. No female was safe around him."

"Shay and Zeb warned him and Patrick over and over. Patrick got smart; Chad didn't." Warren curled up a lip in a snarl. "It's wrong to bully the females. Good males protect them, not rough them up."

"It's the females' fault. Chad only gave them what they were asking for." Fyodor stopped when he noticed Tynan was listening.

"Interesting notion," Tynan stood close enough to loom over the lad. "I guess if I backhand you into the creek, I could say you asked for it?"

Fyodor went pale, then red.

"Fair question." Warren snickered. "At least Fyodor deserves getting pounded on—more than any of the females Chad pushed around. The puny asshole did it cuz hitting someone littler and weaker made him feel bigger."

"Like that wasn't obvious," someone else said from the

back. "A male who picks on a female is completely gutless. Lower than a coyote."

Fyodor looked like a badger had bitten his nose. Or like he'd had a revelation. Seems he hadn't realized the cause of Chad's aberrant behavior.

Fyodor might be salvageable, though. Maybe with some long runs and forest talks, Tynan could get the pup back on the right trail.

For now, Tynan pointed toward Breanne who was struggling with a huge platter. "Our alpha female looks exhausted. Since you're stronger than she is, can you help get the food out of the kitchen?"

"Sure," Warren said.

"Can do, Tynan."

Tynan caught Fyodor before he followed the others. "I'm going for a run tomorrow evening and could use company. Think about what you were talking about here, and we'll discuss it while we're out."

The cub's mouth dropped open.

Tynan grinned. "We'll work on your hunting skills, too."

Fyodor looked like the sun had risen. "By the Gods, yeah. Thanks, Beta!"

Turning, Tynan checked the area. Troublemakers were dispersed. Everyone else was engaged and having fun.

Time for a beer.

At the drinks table, Zeb joined him. "Beta," he said in his harsh voice.

Tynan chuckled and returned the greeting, "Beta."

Zeb's gaze was on Fyodor who was helping his littermate carry a tub of ice. "Knew you'd be good for the cubs."

Tynan frowned at his fellow beta. "You do realize that the young males admire the hell out of you."

"Aye." Zeb's rare smile flashed in his dark face. "And you. But *you* they'll talk to."

"Ah." Tynan grinned. "Maybe it would help if you didn't think a conversation consisted of growling?"

The response of a growl made him laugh.

Near the end of the evening, Margery held a sleepy boy cub in her lap as she sat at a table with Bree.

"I'd nearly forgotten how much work these parties are," Bree murmured. "And how much fun."

"They really are. Both."

"The eye-candy doesn't hurt either." Bree motioned toward Donal and Tynan.

Margery could only grin sheepishly. All her female friends were teasing her about the way she watched Donal and Tynan.

She hadn't thought she was that obvious.

Wrong.

But, dear Goddess, both males were simply captivating. Tynan, stable and strong as a mountain, watching over the wolf pack...and everyone else, too. He probably didn't know how *not* to be a protector.

Donal had arrived late, as brilliant as a lightning flash in a dark sky. People pulled him into conversations, asking for his opinions. Of course they did. The healer was incredibly smart, gave excellent advice—and Mr. Grumpy Cat was just plain fun to listen to.

Bree frowned at the side gate. "People are starting to leave. I'd better go make like a hostess."

"I'd come and help, but...cub." Margery gestured at the three-year-old on her lap.

"Stay put. Pup-tending is valued in the pack." Laughing, Bree headed off to tell people goodbye.

"There's a smart lad. Found somewhere soft to sleep after a long day of playing." Tynan put a glass of juice on the table, sat next to her with a beer in his hand, and grinned.

"You smart lads are all alike." Last night, he'd stretched out on the couch with his head in her lap. She sipped the juice and smiled. Maybe someday she'd learn to like beer or wine. That day hadn't yet arrived. "Thank you, it's wonderful."

"So are you." Tynan leaned over to kiss her, slowly, careful not to disturb the cub. Turning his chair, he settled down to watch the sun's last glow behind the mountains.

"Sun worshipper," she teased him. How many times had she seen him sprawled out in a sunny spot on his porch?

"Side effect of Seattle. There were weeks all I could see were tall buildings and cloudy skies."

"Disgusting human city." Donal took the chair on Margery's other side. "I wouldn't last two days there."

"That's optimistic," Tynan muttered, "considering your complaints before the rescue last fall. If we hadn't had you trapped in a helicopter, you'd have headed straight back to the mountains."

Donal's pseudo-indignant hiss made Margery laugh because the healer never really took insults to heart.

He propped his feet up on a chair. "Ty's a sun worshipper, aye, but it's *someone else* who sneaks out of bed to sit in the moonlight every night."

Tynan grinned. "You saw her, too? The first time, I figured she was heading home, but, instead, she plopped her curvy ass on the floor in front of the window."

"Sorry. I didn't mean to wake you up." Face warm, Margery looked down to resettle the sleeping cub in her lap. The youngling didn't even stir.

"You're a wolf, sweetheart. Stealth isn't in your skill set." Donal gave her knee a pat to go with the insult.

"I can be sneaky."

"Now there's a pout," Tynan murmured and kissed it off her lips. "Is it just our house or do you get out of bed every night?"

"You're as snoopy as Donal. Tell you what. If I share my past"—reaching around the cub, she pointed at Tynan —"then you have to share about living in the city. Balance." Balance was another of the Daonain customs she'd relearned during her time in the Elder Village.

She really did like the tradition.

"What about Donal?" Tynan adjusted her aim so she pointed at his brother instead. "No balance for him?"

She snorted. "Like he doesn't share everything already?"

Donal gave her an insulted look—which she knew was feigned. He had more self-confidence than anyone she'd ever met.

"Balance, hmm?" Tynan eyed her. "Aye. I'm in."

"Okay, then." But...was it right to push Tynan to talk about something that must have been horrendous? How could anyone live there—for a decade—after knowing the freedom of the forests?

"Meggie?"

A quick look showed Tynan didn't look upset or stressed...and he expected her to talk first, it seemed.

"Okay, fine." She blew out a breath, disturbing the cubling who snuffled a little grouchy sound. "My grandmama would sit with the Mother every night, out on the back porch where the moonlight could find her. After I was, oh, maybe around eight or so, I joined her."

Donal's eyebrows rose. "She sat with the Goddess?"

"It's a tradition handed down by the females in our line. Mama joined us sometimes." Margery shook her head. "As a Scythe prisoner, I was so angry and scared, but when I sat with the Mother, in her moonlight, even the ugliest emotions drained away. Since my cell window was tiny, I would get out of bed to catch when she shone through the window."

"And now?" Tynan asked.

"Now, when the moon lights the window, I feel her presence, like she's calling me to sit with her. So I get up."

"And fill yourself with her glow," Donal said softly. "No wonder children flock to you."

Margery looked down at the cub in her lap, kissed the silky hair, and jerked her chin at Tynan. "Your turn, Mentor. How did you manage to survive all those years surrounded by buildings and concrete and steel? With only humans? Donal said you didn't visit him hardly at all."

Tynan ran his hand through his hair in the way he did when he was herding his thoughts. "The lack of visits was... Well, if I somehow revealed the existence of shifters, I couldn't chance letting them track me here."

Margery flinched at the jab of pain. One Dogwood shifter had been careless, and her village had died.

She took Tynan's hand. "The Elders said a Daonain can't live long without shifting. It was partly why the female captives were dying. How did you...?"

"I trawsfurred often enough. On my days off, I visited the nearest forests or crossed the Sound to the Olympic Peninsula. I got a reputation for being a backpacker." He smiled. "There were a couple of forested parks within Seattle that I'd run in after closing time."

"Was it enough?" she asked.

"No. Not really." He put his arm over her shoulder as if needing the closeness. "It's why after I came here, I spent my first two months mostly in the forest. Donal wasn't happy."

"I worried you might not come back one day." Tone grim, Donal looked away.

"I'm sorry, *mo deartháir*." Tynan's eyes filled with remorse. "I should have explained."

It wasn't like Tynan to hurt someone. But knowing how hard some things were to talk about, she slipped her hand into his.

Donal huffed. "Sometimes, deputy, it feels as if you've jailed-up your own words."

The silence stretched between the brothers...and Margery could do nothing but wait.

"City law enforcement requires tight control over emotions." Tynan shook his head. "It's worse for a wolf with only humans around. Although the police are a type of a pack, I couldn't let my guard down. It's too easy to say something suspicious. I could never speak without thinking. And it was safer if I never shared anything personal."

After a long moment, Donal nodded at his brother. Accepting the explanation. The effort.

Shifting the child on her lap, Margery leaned into Tynan's side. Giving him the warmth of pack. "Maybe it's time to unlearn those habits," she told him firmly.

Laughter lit his blue eyes. "Bossy little wolf. I will if you will."

Oh, now that's just mean.

CHAPTER NINETEEN

C *old Creek, North Cascades Territory - dark of the moon*

The following Saturday, Tynan walked through the open door into Donal's clinic room. His littermate and Meggie were washing the blood off the big table in the center of the room. "Looks like a war zone in here."

"Kevin Murphy." Donal hissed his annoyance. "Idiots shouldn't be allowed to use sharp edged tools."

"That's what Mother used to say." Tynan grinned and told Meggie, "She had a tongue sharper than a blade."

Meggie smiled before a crease appeared between her brows. "She didn't use that sharp weapon on her pups, did she?"

Busy cleaning, Donal said easily, "Of course she did."

Meggie looked appalled.

Huh. Tynan had never considered how their mother's parenting would appear to someone else. Her admirable dedication to healing had left little time or energy for her cubs. She'd also been short-tempered, critical, and sarcastic.

He tried to imagine Meggie flaying a cub with her words.

She wouldn't.

Their mother shouldn't have either.

Unsettled, Tynan changed the subject. "I take it that Murphy's wounds were from a knife?"

"That's right." With a groan, Meggie raised her arms and stretched, the posture pulling her shirt taut over her full breasts—and stirring Tynan's blood. She leaned against the now-clean table. "The brothers were field-dressing a deer, and Kevin got cut."

"Nicked an artery, the dumbass," Donal stated. "I doubt butchering would lead to a wound on the inner arm. I daresay the idiots were "sword" fighting and missed."

"Sounds likely." The Murphys were good males Tynan would let guard his back any day. But they were less responsible than adolescent shifters. "Did he need help getting home?"

"His brother took him." Donal washed his hands. "He'll be fine."

"Physically, at least. His ego, though, might take a while to recover," Meggie glared at Donal. "Or, I should say, both of their egos. Your manner with the people you're caring for isn't at all polite."

This was like watching a pixie go after a bear. Tynan rubbed his mouth to hide his amusement

Donal held up his hands, palms out. "I'm nice to the ones who deserve it. Getting slashed from being stupid? They don't deserve me being polite."

"That's not your call. *Healer*." She gave him another frown and headed out.

Donal grinned. "If not for that weak ankle, she'd have stomped out."

"She has a temper." Tynan heard the front door slam. "Although it's normally used to defend someone else."

Donal had drawn a glass of water, and he paused with his hand halfway to his mouth. After a second, he lowered the glass. "You know, you're right. I'll try to behave."

Because he didn't want to upset the little banfasa.

Tynan smiled. It looked as if he and Donal were on the same trail.

"You're back early. Did you need me for something?" Donal asked.

"Both of you, actually." Tynan motioned toward the door. "Let's go—"

"She'll be back soon enough. She forgot her bag." Donal grinned, picked up the big leather medical bag, and led the way to the kitchen.

A minute later, a tap sounded on the front door.

"Come on in," Tynan called.

"It's me. I left my bag here." Her footsteps went into the clinic, stopped, then came down the hall. Meggie appeared in the kitchen.

"Donal, did you take my—" Spotting her bag on a kitchen chair, she shot Donal a quizzical frown.

"Yes, I'm holding your bag hostage." Donal smirked, then his tone turned serious. "I wanted a chance to thank you for your help in calming the idiot down and getting the bleeding stopped. Sometimes I don't have enough hands to control bleeding and do the healing."

Her cheeks turned pink. "You're welcome."

"Since that's done..." Donal grinned. "Tynan—"

"I'm glad I can help," Meggie said, then frowned at Donal, "but calling your patient an idiot isn't good."

"Stubborn much?" Donal scowled. "If I have to deal with stupid injuries, there's a possibility I won't have the power to deal with someone who really needs me."

Tynan gave his brother a sympathetic nod. It was the same with law enforcement. There were only so many hands to go around. It was frustrating to have to deal with disasters that occurred because some idiot troublemaker was dimmer than a cave at midnight.

"I understand." Meggie pursed her lips. "But our job is to heal—not to judge. Considering some of the stories Tynan's told me about you two when you were younger, well, I'd think you'd be more understanding."

Tynan snorted. "She's got us there."

"You more than me," Donal said in a superior voice.

"Really, you were the worst—"

"No, I think you get the gnome-brain prize." Tynan took advantage of Donal's insulted surprise to move closer to Meggie. "Like when you heard funny mewing noises and were convinced there were kittens buried in the snow."

Meggie's mouth dropped open. "Someone put kittens out into the snow?"

Tynan grinned, his silence forcing Donal to reply.

"As it happened, they weren't kittens." Donal shot a glare at Tynan. "It was a wolverine den."

"The mother was so fecking mad, she chased us halfway down the mountain." Tynan wrapped his arms around Meggie, bringing her slowly against his body until her breasts pressed against his chest. Tantalizing them both with the increasing heat. He kissed her, taking his time, before lifting his head. "We survived, though."

"I'm very glad you lived." Her tongue traced a path over his lower lip...and now he was totally hard. He hadn't released her, and she could undoubtedly feel his erection against her soft pelvis.

Her eyes grew heavy-lidded. "Are you home early?"

By the Gods, he did love how she responded to him—to them both.

With an approving smile, Donal glanced toward the stairs and the big bedroom.

Tempting. But that wasn't what he was here to talk about. "I'm home early because tonight is the dark of the moon. There might be a hellhound in the area, which means all the cahirs are patrolling tonight. Shay asked if we'd stay at the lodge with Breanne."

"Ah, right. She hates being alone." Donal looked at Meggie. "I don't know if she's mentioned it, but she's had ugly run-ins with hellhounds."

At the grim note in Donal's voice, Meggie turned pale.

Tynan set a hand on her shoulder. "I told Shay I'd ask you two."

Meggie blinked. "Ask Donal *and* me?"

"It's not my littermate I'm after sleeping with, now is it?" Tynan kissed her again, slower this time. "The lodge has very big beds. In case you were wondering."

She pushed him back, laughing. "You are even sneakier than the werecat."

Donal joined them, leaning against Meggie from behind. "The cat thinks this is an excellent idea. We can keep Breanne from worrying too much, have ourselves some fun, and enjoy a big breakfast in the morning."

Meggie bit her lip. "If you two were out trying to stop a hellhound, I'd be terrified. Poor Breanne. Yes, we should stay with her tonight."

Tynan kissed her forehead. He'd known that would be her answer.

"It doesn't seem right to leave Oliver here alone, though," she said.

"Bring him along. It'll do him good to be somewhere other than your house and the forest," Donal said.

"It will." Tynan exchanged a look with his littermate.

Meggie's brother hadn't done anything since he'd arrived except read, eat, and visit the forest. Rather than improving, he seemed to be cycling downward."

"I'll ask him." Meggie slipped out from between the two of them. "I have a couple of elderly shifters to see, then I'll get packed." She grabbed her bag and was gone before Tynan could say a word.

Despite the slight limp, her footsteps had a lovely bounce. "She's happy."

Donal nodded. "I've never met anyone who was more suited to be a banfasa. Me—I love the healing, the connection to the Mother, and the challenge. The people...perhaps not so much."

"For her, it's all about the people." She had so much love to give. By the Gods, he was lost because he was hoping she had enough love to extend it to a couple of unworthy males.

The dark of the moon nights, or as Donal thought of them, hellhound nights, always left him knotted into a ball of tension.

Breanne wasn't looking much better. At sundown, she'd cheerfully kissed her cahir mates as they set off to patrol the town. Then had grown increasingly apprehensive.

By the Gods, waiting was hard. Even now, the cahirs might be fighting against an almost invincible armored monster.

Breanne might lose her mates.

Donal would have to try to heal whatever bloody mess the hellhound left.

He didn't always win.

There were nights he wondered if it would be easier to be a cahir than a healer.

Seeing how Breanne was stewing, Tynan had tactfully gotten everyone into the library room to put together a jigsaw puzzle. The female needed to stay busy.

With a sigh, Donal leaned back in his chair and looked at the other five around the Wildwood's big library table. Margery sat between him and Tynan. Bree was next to Oliver. On Oliver's other side was Silas, his shifter-soldier comrade from another territory who'd rented a room upstairs.

Earlier, Silas and Oliver had shared a bottle of whisky outside on the patio. As the bottle emptied, Oliver had grown more withdrawn, Silas the opposite.

The lodge was quiet. The log walls and beams settled with muted creaks from the increasing cold of the evening. With warmth wafting in from the crackling fire in the main room, the library was pleasant.

Even better was having others close, who also were worrying about the cahirs.

"Mom loved jigsaw puzzles." Margery tried to fit a piece into the stovetop portion of the puzzle. "Oliver, remember that impossible one of the ocean and sky. It was all blue and white and nothing else."

Eyes slightly glazed, Oliver smiled slightly. "She didn't stop until she'd finished the whole thing—took her forever."

"I prefer the ones with lots of colors. And animals. But Zeb refuses to put together anything with kittens. Or puppies." Bree pouted. "Especially puppies."

The deadliest cahir in the Territory... Donal choked on a laugh. "I'll bring you a breakfast bunny if you get Zeb to work on a puppy puzzle."

Tynan grinned. "There's a bunny you'll never have to catch."

And isn't that a shame? Donal picked up a puzzle piece. "Ah, a frying pan. Probably in your kitchen section." He handed the piece to Margery.

She fit it into place and grinned. "Ta da!"

"Probably the most success you'll have on a stove." Oliver smiled at his sister, then Donal. "She burned the cake she was baking so bad it set off the smoke detector."

"It seems I can't read a good book and bake at the same time. Who knew?" Margery gave her brother a wicked smirk. "You can cook next week."

Her brother looked as if he'd like to dig a hole for his words and bury them deep.

"Learn to use a timer." Bree, the best cook in town, grinned. "It's the only reason I don't burn everything I make."

Tynan ran his knuckles over Margery's cheek. "Little wolf, I'll buy you a timer if you'll make us that shortbread again. It was delicious."

Silas snorted. "The things males will say to get a female to fu—"

Donal leaned across him, thumping their shoulders together hard enough that the offensive sentence ended in a grunt. *Gormless pixie-bait.* Donal smiled pleasantly. "Sorry. I saw a piece I wanted."

After a glare, Silas bent his attention to the puzzle.

Breanne winked at Donal and changed the subject. "Have you heard about the Summer Solstice festival the Cosantirs are planning?"

"Cosantirs. Plural?" Tynan frowned. "I'm missing something."

"This summer, the solstice and full moon occur on the same day, which is pretty rare. Some of the Pacific Northwest Cosantirs want a multi-territory festival. A chance for shifters from different territories to mingle...and to mate at the Gathering."

Tynan grinned. "And each Cosantir hopes to lure new shifters into his area?"

"Shay says Cosantirs are as greedy as flower fairies in a rose garden," Bree said.

"Have they decided where this festival will be held?" Donal asked.

"Someplace between the North Cascades Territory and Rainier Territory. Still in the God's forest but not claimed by a Cosantir."

Margery bit her lip, her shoulders hunching forward. "Are we *required* to go to the festival?"

"No." Bree gave her a sympathetic look. "Although it sounds like fun. Some crafts people will bring their stuff. Apparently, bards love festivals, so they'll come. Singing, dancing. And howling. They want it to last a couple of nights to make it worth the drive."

Why would the little banfasa be reluctant? She loved people. Donal tilted his head, puzzling it out. Ah, could she be worried she'd run into the Rainier shifters? Probably.

Damned if he'd let her fall into the trap of being afraid to leave Cold Creek. He took her hand. "Calum will probably request that we attend the festival."

His reminder that she was needed seemed to do the job, pulling her away from thoughts of Rainier where she'd been treated so badly. Her gaze cleared.

"Why would the Cosantir request Margery if she doesn't want to go?" Oliver asked, frowning.

"Because she's our banfasa." Tynan gave her a smile. "No matter how effective the Cosantirs and cahirs are, brawling and accidents will occur."

A clatter outside drew everyone's attention.

"Someone ignoring the sundown curfew?" Oliver asked.

Tynan rose. "I'll check. If it's a shifter, I'll stuff them back into their cabin."

"We have a couple of humans renting cabins," Bree stood, as well. "It's probably them."

Donal patted Margery's shoulder. "Back in a bit, wolflet." If there was trouble, he needed to be at his brother's side.

The noise turned out to have come from a drunk human in one of the cabins. That was a relief. Since the scent of Daonain was all over the area—and hellhounds preferred Daonain blood—the humans were safe enough after dark.

Shifters weren't safe at all on the dark of the moon. As they re-entered the lodge, Donal was bloody pleased to close the heavy door behind them.

Bree glanced at him and Tynan. "I'm going to swing by the kitchen and get drinks and snacks. Any requests?"

"Whatever you have is great." Tynan patted his stomach. "I haven't found anything you make that I don't love."

Tynan's compliment put a bounce in her step.

"Very clever, wolf." Donal punched his brother's arm. "Don't think your smooth-talking will get you extra cookies."

At the sound of shouting from the library room, Tynan's smug grin faded. "What in the Hunter's forests...?"

That was the shifter-soldier's shouting. "You come here to be all comfortable—and left the town with no one who knows scat about healing. My brother almost died, you lazy fucking bitch."

"I'm sorry your brother was hurt." Margery's voice was calm—but Donal could hear the tremor of fear.

Rushing into the library after Tynan, Donal felt fury well up inside.

The big shifter-soldier loomed over Margery, one meaty hand on each shoulder, punctuating each word with a shake.

"Silas, you're getting carried away." Offering an ineffective protest, Oliver was just beginning to stand.

Growling, Tynan grabbed Silas and threw him across the room. He hit the wall hard and dropped to his knees.

Not enough. Not nearly enough. Donal slammed his fist into his palm and glanced at Tynan.

Tynan nodded, then pointed to himself.

No way the wolf would deal out all the punishment. Donal pointed one finger to himself, held up the second finger and pointed to Tynan. One punch each.

After a narrow-eyed stare, Tynan nodded.

As Silas regained his feet, Donal walked over and punched him in the gut so hard he folded in half.

Gasping, the boggart spat out, "What the fuck!"

"No decent shifter pushes females around. I know you shifter-soldiers missed out on some of our traditions, but this is one you should take to heart," Donal told him.

Silas slowly straightened, his face purple. "You stinking—"

Tynan's short jab to the ribs slammed Silas back into the wall. There he stayed. His breathing sounded like sobs.

Worried, Donal took a step forward.

"Nothing's busted, healer." Tynan grabbed Silas's shirt front and yanked him forward. "The pain in your ribs will remind you to be polite to females. Now get your tail out of here."

Hand on his side, Silas stomped out of the room. A

second later, the lodge's front door slammed hard enough to shake the pictures on the wall.

Instead of going upstairs to his room, the weasel-tempered asshole had gone outside...on a dark of the moon night.

Shaking his head at the idiocy, Donal turned to Margery. She was standing, spine straight, hands in fists. Tough little female, but so pale. This was the last thing she needed, more violence from males.

Scowling, Tynan turned to Oliver. "You let someone put their hands on your sister?"

"He was just upset—wasn't hurting her." Oliver flushed. "His littermate managed to survive the Scythe and then almost died because he busted his leg and there was no one—"

"That's not Margery's fault," Donal snapped.

Oliver swallowed. His voice cracked as he said, "I know how it feels to lose my brother."

The Scythe had killed Margery's other littermate. Donal's own heart ached at the thought.

"*Wasn't hurting her?*" Tynan repeated Oliver's words, then shoved the male in Donal's direction. "Does it feel good when someone bigger pushes you around?"

"She spent years being beaten up by the Scythe. And you let another big man treat her like that?" Donal pushed Oliver away, hard. The male staggered.

How much had he had to drink?

"A brother gifted with a sister should do his utmost to

protect her," Tynan snapped, and the scorn in his expression made Oliver turn dark red.

Oliver pulled in a breath, scrubbed his hands over his face, then faced his sister. "They're right. I'm sorry, sis."

Without waiting for her response, he fled like a coyote caught stealing a cougar's kill. His footsteps sounded, going up the stairs.

Donal shook his head, feeling soiled. "That male is—"

"Is my *littermate*."

Margery's fist in Donal's gut sent a blast of pain through him.

Then she swung at Tynan who didn't try to dodge and took the punch on his jaw. "You had no right to—"

"You didn't run after your brother to comfort him," Donal pointed out softly.

"And embarrass him further?" Her bottom lip quivered. "How could you? After all he's lived through."

Tynan frowned. "Lass, you lived through worse. He should have stood up for you. Protected you."

She took a step back. "I... Oliver isn't one to get into a fight. Orson and I always protected *him*."

By the Gods, what a mess. Donal took a step toward her. "That was when you were cubs, sweetheart."

Which might be part of the reason Oliver hadn't jumped in. He didn't see himself as a protector. It'd been Margery's job—and how fucked up was that?

"You're not cubs now. He's bigger, stronger, and trained to fight." Tynan's voice was very level.

"Even if he wasn't..." Donal shook his head. "Margery, as Daonain, we protect our females—"

She ran out of the library room, fleeing much as her brother had.

Well...Donal rubbed his gut where her fist had impacted. Not quite like her brother.

That did not go well. Tynan pulled in a breath, feeling like someone—a little wolf—had taken a bite out of his heart.

When Donal started to follow her, Tynan gripped his arm. "Let her go. She needs some time."

And face it, a snarky cat wasn't a good choice at soothing a female.

When Tynan finally led the way out of the library, he didn't see her and had a moment of worry.

Please tell me she didn't leave the house on a dark of the moon night.

Hearing female voices in the kitchen, he relaxed. She was with Breanne. *Good.* Bree was a soothing person.

Unsure what to do next, he took a chair in the sitting area. "We could have handled that better."

Looking as unhappy as Tynan felt, Donal sat on the couch and held his hands out to the fire. "Punching the mangy-tailed maggot was the right thing to do. Reprimanding her brother though..."

"Aye, her brother." That was the problem. Tynan rubbed the ache in his neck. "She hurts for him."

"Aye. She might not forgive us for making him feel bad. Not any time soon."

There was no answer for that truth.

The low sound of conversation came from the kitchen. Maybe Meggie would confide in the alpha female. Breanne might condemn Tynan and Donal, but he had a feeling she wouldn't approve of Oliver's inaction, either.

In the fireplace, a salamander pirouetted in the flames. Only one fire lizard tonight. Did salamanders get lonely?

Absently, Tynan rubbed his chest. The altercation with Meggie had lodged there with a dull ache. "We should have talked with her before tackling her brother."

Donal snorted. "I figured that out right about the time her fist hit my gut."

Angry female shifters could stay angry for quite a while. "I've seen human males try to placate their women with flowers or chocolate."

Donal brightened. "Is it effective?"

"Maybe in decreasing the time to resolution. Not the ultimate results."

"As in, if the relationship was doomed, it would still be doomed?"

"Alas, yes."

"Still..." Donal turned to look at the kitchen. "What kind of chocolate would—"

A loud yell interrupted him.

That'd been Silas's voice. Just outside the lodge. He

screamed—a rising shriek that broke off with the gut-wrenching finality of death.

Fuck.

Tynan ran to the door, Donal behind him. He slapped Donal's hand away from the handle. "Wait."

Tynan edged the curtains apart. Metal bars covered the lodge's front windows. A light over the door illumined an empty parking area. Vehicles were parked near the porch, off to one side.

There. On the far side of the gravel lot. Something the size of a grizzly moved. No fur. The light glinted off bony spiked plates and a shark-like head.

Tynan's breathing stalled.

That was a hellhound, something he'd never seen before.

It stood over a body and a pool of black liquid. Blood. The amount indicated the victim was very dead. Tynan recognized the lime-green shirt that Oliver's friend had worn.

"Yes, that's Silas," Donal murmured.

By the Gods. Every instinct Tynan had shouted for him to attack and kill the demon hound. It was his job to protect. But even the God-called cahirs didn't take on a hellhound alone.

"Call Alec," Tynan said quietly.

"Already on it," Donal snapped, phone in hand.

To the left of the parking area, Shay in wolf form slid through the underbrush.

Thank fuck, it appeared the cahirs were already here.

Zeb in human form followed the wolf.

As the hellhound devoured its kill, Zeb and Shay separated for the attack, the wolf to the rear, Zeb from the side.

Suddenly, a shout came from a cabin down the lane. "What was that yelling?"

The hellhound turned...and spotted Zeb in the open. It charged, an unstoppable force. Even as Zeb shot his pistol, the demon hound ploughed into him, knocking the cahir onto his side, ripping at his shoulder and neck.

Snarling viciously, Shay attacked from the rear in a frantic effort to save his brother.

The hellhound spun, latched onto Shay's front leg, and threw the wolf halfway across the lot. The wolf didn't rise.

Gods help them. Tynan's gut tightened. *No choice.*

"Lock the door behind me, *mo deartháir.*" Ignoring Donal's protest, Tynan stepped silently out onto the porch.

Shadows moved in the forest on the right side of the lot, and a glimmer of hope awoke. The other three cahirs were coming, two on one side, one on the other.

But the hellhound was already stalking toward Shay to finish him off. Shay wasn't moving.

The other cahirs would arrive too late.

Yelling, Tynan leaped off the porch to land right in front of the hellhound. Then he ran...ran faster than he ever had before.

No predator could resist fleeing prey.

As he tore across the lot toward the three cahirs, the

scrabble of heavy claws grated in the gravel behind him. Closing on him.

What is going on? Who had screamed? Even as Margery ran into the living room, Donal shouted, "Lock the door," and disappeared outside.

Outside. She reached the door, looked out, and horror met her eyes.

Tynan tore across the parking lot with a ghastly monster after him. Huge and gray and...it was a hellhound. *Oh Gods.*

Closer to the lodge, Donal sprinted toward someone on the ground. Blood spurted upward in rhythmic fountains— an artery had been torn open.

Zeb—it was Zeb. At that rate, he'd bleed out quickly.

Donal would save him.

But no, Zeb was growling, fighting Donal, pushing his hands away. The cahir was disoriented.

Margery's hands closed into fists. Donal needed help. She took a step forward, and terror seized her. *Hellhound.*

But Zeb would die.

Her heart slammed so hard against her ribcage she couldn't draw a breath. Hideous growling came from the other end of the lot.

She couldn't help Tynan. Must help Donal.

Pulling in a breath against the constriction in her lungs, she abandoned safety and scrambled to Donal. She skidded the last inches on her knees and bumped against Zeb's hip.

"Zeb. Easy, Zeb. Peace, cahir." She took his hands
—*please, Mother of All, help*—and pushed the calm of the
Goddess into the cahir. "It's all right, Zeb. You're safe.
We're all safe."

Such a lie.

But Zeb stilled, letting her hold his hands. His dark eyes
were dazed.

"Bless you, banfasa." Donal put his hands lightly on
Zeb's neck, stopping the arcing blasts of blood, and with a
blast of power she could feel, healed the artery.

A ghastly shriek split the air.

Donal turned to look across the lot.

Terrified of what she'd see, she followed his gaze—
although she had to lean forward to see past a pair of legs
standing between her and the sight.

The hellhound was down.

Thank the Gods.

A grizzly and panther circled the hellhound's still figure.
As Alec stood over it, the hellhound shimmered and
trawsfurred into human form. Dead.

Tynan was bent over, hands on his thighs, gasping for
air. When Alec slapped his shoulder and said something,
Tynan's response made the sheriff laugh.

Males.

But Tynan was alive. Was safe. As the pressure around
Margery's ribs eased, she could breathe again.

Hearing a whine, she squinted at the shadows. "Donal,

there's a wolf over there. Shay. It's Shay, and he's hurt. I'll take care of Zeb."

Donal eyed Zeb. "That'll work." He rose, squeezed her shoulder, and headed for Shay.

Zeb tried to rise, too.

"If you move, you idiot, I'll shoot you," Breanne said in a very calm voice.

Margery blinked, realizing that the pair of legs between her and the hellhound belonged to Bree. The alpha female held a big pistol in one hand and a dagger in the other.

"Where'd you come from?"

Breanne smiled tightly. "I followed you out."

Tynan walked up, his eyes narrowing. "By the Gods, what are you two doing out here? Don't you—"

"Perfect timing, Deputy," Margery interrupted the forthcoming lecture. "Can you help Zeb inside? I think he's concussed, and I know he's lost a lot of blood."

The look Tynan gave her said the lecture was only postponed.

"Let's go, cahir." He pulled Zeb to his feet, supporting him when the cahir's knees buckled. Breanne stuffed the pistol under the waistband of her jeans and took his other side.

Closer to the trees, Donal was trying to hold Shay's leg to heal it and failing.

The wolf was riled up. And, Gods, Shay sure had a scary growl.

Margery eased herself down to kneel beside the wolf,

then tangled her fingers in his fur, past the undercoat, against his skin.

Don't bite me, please, Alpha. She kept her voice to a low murmur. "Hey, Shay, you know Donal, let him heal your leg so we can go inside. Breanne's waiting for you, and she won't let you come inside if you're bleeding. I bet you can have some cookies if you're a good wolf."

Donal flashed her a grin. "There's a lure."

She smiled and kept talking, knowing it didn't matter what she said. The words helped her connect more deeply to the calm at her center. There was the slow lap of the peaceful waters and the moonlight sparkling on the dark surface. How could she not share such tranquility?

Under her hand, muscles relaxed, and with a heavy sigh, Shay laid his head in her lap.

"Margery, you're a treasure," Donal said quietly. "I'll be done in a minute, Shay."

Donal's face went still, his eyes distant as he concentrated.

Oh, how she'd love to have his talent. But—she looked down at the quiet alpha—she had a Mother-given talent and her own hard-won skills.

So, as she stroked the soft fur, she offered her gratitude for the blessing of being able to help when needed.

"Thank you, sweetheart." From his seat on the couch, Donal took the glass of apple cider from Breanne and glanced around the lodge's sitting area. Everyone had shifted back to human and dressed.

On the other side of the room, Margery's littermate was serving coffee. Although a bit unsteady on his feet from the alcohol, Oliver had run out to help everyone into the lodge. Donal had been pleased to see him search out Margery to make sure she was all right. Now he was quietly helping where he could, despite his grief for his comrade in arms.

When Oliver was told it was Silas who'd died, he flinched. Apparently, Silas never stayed inside during the dark of the moon. Since he'd never seen a hellhound, he didn't believe they existed. And so, Oliver had taken another wound to a heart that had already received far too many.

Despite Donal's anger earlier, he could only feel pity for the young male now.

Turning his gaze away, he drank the apple juice, the icy cold sweetness a surprise after the bitter taste of futility in his mouth. But life had its own balances. He was alive. Tynan and Margery were alive. Against the odds, they'd all survived, even if a bit battered.

Shaking his head, he concentrated on healing the mangled flesh on Ben's shoulder. "How'd you make such a mess?" Then he knew. A hellhound's plated armor had razor-sharp points that abraded everything. "You shredded your shoulder on the armor?"

Ben grimaced. "Yep."

"What happened over there?" Donal's throat tightened until he had to force the question out. "I saw Tynan playing prey but missed the rest."

"Tynan baited it? Is that why I'm not dead?" Zeb put an arm around Breanne. He was sitting on the blanket pile next to the fire with Shay on Bree's other side. "When our attack went to shit, I kinda figured we were hellhound fodder."

"You should've been. We were too far away to reach you in time. But Tynan jumped off the porch so close to the damned thing, he could've slapped it on the snout. He drew it right to us." Cross-legged beside the couch, Owen bent forward to let Margery put pressure on his back wound. "You're incredibly fast, cop."

Shoulder against the wall, Tynan laughed. "I had incredible motivation. Those teeth were only a foot away when Ben crashed into it from the side."

Too fucking close. Donal closed his eyes for a moment. A glance at Margery showed she was equally shaken.

Ben rumbled a laugh. "Yeah, I knocked it off its feet, but if Owen hadn't chomped onto its hind leg, it would've gotten me."

"I think I bit the same leg as Shay did. The armor plating there was already damaged," Owen said. "It didn't appreciate the second bite, I'd say."

"Was that the horrible shriek I heard?" Margery asked with a shudder.

"Not horrible. Really, really satisfying." Owen grinned.

Bloodthirsty cahirs.

After one more surge of power, Donal straightened and checked Ben's shoulder. Only pink lines marred the skin along with a lot of blood. Nothing was open. "Done here."

He moved to the other end of the couch to work on Owen's wound. A bite. "You bit the hellhound. Looks to me like it bit you back."

"Fucking monsters," Owen grumbled. "Yeah. While I sacrificed my skin for the cause, Alec rolled under it and sliced open its belly."

"Rolled under it. Why am I not surprised?" Were cahirs born crazy, or did the God make them that way?

Hand on Owen's back, Donal ran his gaze over the sheriff. Jeans and shirt ripped, no massive bloodstains. "Did it get you, too?"

Alec was as relaxed as Tynan. The two were much alike. "Nope. Just a few scrapes from sliding on gravel, and those will earn me a warm welcome from my mate."

"You're gonna play the *wounded-while-saving-the-world* card." Owen looked thoughtful. "I'll have to see if that works."

Ah, new love. Previously distrustful of females, the cahir had turned completely around after he and his brother lifemated Darcy.

That didn't mean his tail shouldn't be pulled now and then. "Owen, my friend, if your female won't drag you to bed unless you've almost died, you're doing something wrong."

As the other cahirs started to tease Owen, Donal winked at Margery. Because last night, she'd dragged him and Tynan upstairs, saying it was her turn to have her way with them.

Catching his look, she blushed the prettiest of pinks.

"While we're all here, let me make sure I have this straight—since I'll have to explain to Calum." Alec folded his arms over his chest and frowned at Tynan. "You were unarmed and decided to bait a hellhound? To get it away from Zeb?"

When Tynan simply shrugged his agreement, Donal grinned. If his littermate saw something needed to be done, that's what he did. He didn't second guess his actions—or defend them.

"Then, even before the hellhound was killed, Donal ran into the open, followed by our banfasa and Breanne." Alec gave Donal an irritated stare. "Healer, you know better."

"I do, and normally, I'd wait. Zeb had an arterial bleed, and there was no time."

After a second, Alec nodded and turned his displeasure toward Margery. "There was no need for you to—"

"There was." Her chin lifted. "Zeb was dazed and fighting Donal. He needed to be calmed down so Donal could work." She repeated Donal's words. "There was no time."

Donal had almost had a coronary when she appeared, but...she'd been right to do so.

"Sorry, Donal." With a rueful look, Zeb admitted, "I thought you were the hellhound."

"I'm confused." Alec rubbed his forehead. "Margery, why would you think you could calm him when Donal couldn't?"

"She has a gift," Donal murmured. "A miraculous gift. Many banfasas can ease a shifter to some degree, but I've never met anyone with Margery's skill."

Margery stared at him, the surprise in her gaze heartbreaking. Which was just wrong. She should know how much her clan appreciated her.

He and Tynan would work on that.

Sitting back, Donal slapped Owen's arm. "Done here. Go clean up."

"Thanks, healer." Owen rose.

Alec turned to look at Zeb and lifted his eyebrows. "Is that how you see it?"

"You know how when we shift, the Mother blesses us?" Zeb asked. "When Margery joined us, it felt like that. Like a hug. I still couldn't think, but I knew everything would be all right."

Alec scowled up at the ceiling, maybe to see if that's where they'd all left their common sense. Finally, he sighed. "In that case, thank you, healer. Banfasa. Although when I tell Calum about you two being in harm's way, he'll leave claw marks on my hide."

Alec's gaze turned to Breanne. "You, however, have no excuse for setting foot outside the lodge."

Her lips quirked. "On the contrary. Someone needed to guard our healer and banfasa. I was there, *and* as it happens, I've killed a hellhound before."

"I knew she'd use that on him," Zeb said in a low tone to his littermate.

"Give it up, Alec." Shay kissed Breanne's fingers. "Breanne won't hide when her mates are down. If you can win a battle like that with Vicki, let us know how."

"You win." Alec huffed a laugh, then straightened. "Owen, Ben, let's finish patrolling. Shay, Zeb, take it easy for a couple of days, or we'll all suffer through one of Donal's diatribes."

Donal stiffened. "My *what?*"

"You mean his rabid ranting?" Ben grinned.

"No, I think it's called the healer's harangue." Shay tilted his head, baring his neck like a submissive wolf. "No worries, Donal. We'll behave."

"You'll regret the insults, you maggot-ridden, mangy-tailed, minnow-dicked mongrels." Donal turned a narrow-eyed stare on the entire batch of idiotic warriors...then heard the little female beside him trying to smother giggles.

And he smiled.

She'd gotten past being mad at him. Maybe now she'd accept his and Tynan's apologies?

Maybe. She was stubborn. A banfasa. *Female.*

Groveling might be needed.

CHAPTER TWENTY

C old Creek, North Cascades Territory - dark of the moon

A while later, upstairs in the lodge, Margery got out of the shower. She'd insisted on going last because she knew she'd need time to cry. Just cry.

Tears had helped, although not enough.

As she dried off, her hands trembled. It felt as if she hadn't eaten for a day, only the hollowness was in her chest.

Tynan might so easily have been slaughtered by the hellhound. Her brain kept replaying the sight of him running, the monster so close behind.

And Donal—he'd gone out to save Zeb, knowing the hellhound was there.

Oh, she wanted to just...just yell at them. Didn't those males know how easily people died? One moment alive, the next dead. The bonds would snap like a dry twig as the Mother gathered in a shifter's spirit. Margery could still feel the broken-off tie to her littermate Orson.

Yet...Donal and Tynan did know of the fragility of life. A healer. A cop. In their own ways, they dedicated themselves to saving people. To dealing with death.

Despite her hot shower, the coldness lingered inside, as if her bones were made of ice. Donal and Tynan had almost died, dammit. The thought kept circling back. Didn't they understand how much she lo—

She shook her head hard. No, love wasn't what she could possibly feel. She hardly knew them.

Yet the thought of losing them was wrenching. Unbearable.

She tossed the towel on the rack. She needed to see them, to feel the warmth of their skin, to hear their voices.

The bedroom was dark, the only light came from flickering candles around the room. There was enough illumination to see Tynan sprawled on the immense bed, Donal on the small couch. Both wonderfully naked. Tynan so powerful and broad-chested. Donal all hard contoured muscles.

Smiling, they rose as she walked closer.

"Meggie." Tynan's smile faded. He touched her face gently, then silently gathered her into his arms. He laid his cheek against the top of her head. "What's wrong, little wolf?"

For years, she'd dreamed of going home to Dogwood, of having everything back to what it was when the world was safe. His embrace gave her that feeling.

"I just..." Why was it so difficult to ask for what she needed? "Can you hold me for a minute? Both of you?"

"That we can do," Donal murmured. He leaned against her from behind, his body warm and hard. He slid his arms between her and Tynan, his palms warm against her abdomen.

The males radiated heat. Her shivers faded. "I was so scared."

"We were all scared." Tynan stroked a hand over her hair. "Terrified, actually. But we're alive, Meggie, and unharmed."

"Can we—"

"Wait." Donal's grip tightened around her. "Tynan and I talked. We'd like to clear the air between us."

What did he mean? "Clear the air about what?"

"About taking Oliver to task." Fingers under her chin, Tynan tilted her head up to meet his eyes. "Sure, and it's easy to forgive people when there's life-threatening danger, but that seems too much of an easy out. What we'd like is this—"

"We stand by what we said—he should have protected you." Donal kissed her hair. "But...we can see he's having a rough time with all the changes in his life."

Tynan's thumb rubbed over her chin. His eyes were intensely blue—and honest. "We jumped in without talking with you first, and that was wrong. We hope you'll forgive us, and we'll try to do better next time."

The resentment and anger toward them had still been there, buried down deep. As the tiny knot in her chest released, Margery leaned back against Donal's hard body. "You're forgiven. And...thank you."

She smiled up at Tynan and hugged Donal's arms closer around her. "Thank you for caring."

"*A cuisle mo chroidhe*, that's not something you'll ever have to worry about." Tynan's words were an Irish-accented rumble. He bent to kiss her ear. Her neck. Her shoulders.

The Celtic endearment—*pulse of my heart*—blossomed inside her.

And under his touch, desire rose within her, as inevitably as the sun's warmth brought flowers in spring. "Ohhh."

Behind her, Donal's hands cupped her breasts as he nibbled on her arm. "Mmm, you smell like cinnamon and apples. Very edible."

Apple pie scented bath soap had been in one of the dispensers. As Donal kissed up her shoulder, her thoughts fragmented.

She ran her hands over Tynan's thickly muscled chest, laying her palm there, on his sternum, to feel the beat of his heart.

A big heart to contain all that protectiveness and caring.

So much like his brother. And she wanted them both so badly she started to shake.

She swallowed. They'd been making her ready, slowly, helping her to adjust to the idea of taking them both at once.

No more waiting.

Reaching back, she put an arm around Donal's neck. "Tonight, I want you both. Inside me."

Under her palms, she felt their muscles tense.

Donal paused. "Margery, I don't know..."

"Tonight." She made her voice firm.

Tynan studied her, his gaze darkening to the blue of a twilight sky, then he smiled slightly. "We'd hate to deny our female anything that would make her happy."

"Ah, well, when you put it that way." Behind her, the werecat laughed, then soundlessly moved away, and coolness drifted over her skin where his warm body had been.

Taking a step back, she ran her hands over the mesmerizing ridges of muscle on Tynan's abdomen. Moving back up, with a finger, she circled the flat, coin-sized nipples, so different from hers. "You're such a male."

A corner of his mouth tipped up. "And you're such a female." He ran his finger around her nipples.

The heady sensation as the tips pebbled into aching peaks made her stomach quiver.

After dropping something at the foot of the bed, Donal returned. He ran his hands over her ass, squeezing and massaging the cheeks. "You look tired, wolflet. As your healer, I think you should go to bed now."

Despite the waves of heat running over her skin, she giggled and answered in a virtuous voice, "I always listen to my healer."

Especially when the healer agreed with her. There was nowhere in the world she'd rather be than in bed...with her males.

"Come along, Beta. It's bedtime." She wrapped her arms around Tynan's neck and pulled him down for a kiss.

Rumbling his pleasure, he took control, rough and deep, demanding a response, making her knees sag. He moved her backward until the mattress touched the back of her thighs.

Unbalanced, she sat down. The quilt was cool under her bottom.

Tynan glanced at Donal in an unspoken command.

Donal joined her on the bed. "Come here, sweetheart." He drew her down beside him.

She squeaked as he flattened her out on her back. He slid his arm under her neck to provide a pillow, even as his lips covered hers in a sensuous kiss, full of nips and teasing tongue.

Her bloodstream felt as if it was filled with searing lava.

As Donal nibbled on the corner of her mouth, Tynan's unyielding hands parted her legs. Opening her.

She tried to sit up, to see—but Donal leaned over her, his weight pinning her down, even as he kissed down her jaw.

Trapped for their pleasure.

A series of gentle bites ran up the inside of her left thigh, then her right, stopping just short of her pussy. As if Tynan was painting a target with her clit as the bullseye.

Blood swept to her core, engorging her clit until it tingled and throbbed with need.

Need more.

As she ran her fingers through Donal's silky dark hair, he kissed under her chin, then down her neck, over the tops of her breasts. His hot, wet tongue made circles around each nipple, then his teeth lightly bit the sensitive jutting peaks.

Too many sensations from hands and teeth and tongues and lips.

She felt her labia being opened, exposing everything, then Tynan's tongue flickered over her clit, dancing like a butterfly's wings. Her gasp made both males chuckle, and then Tynan rubbed more firmly, one side, the other.

When he paused, Donal closed his mouth over her nipple. He sucked strongly, then lashed the swollen nub with his merciless tongue, before sucking again.

Oh Gods, it felt as if her blood was surging up and down her torso, swirling faster each time.

Kneeling at the foot of the bed between Meggie's legs, Tynan slid a finger inside her cunt. He chuckled as she wiggled uncontrollably. By the Gods, he loved how she responded to them.

She was already hot and slick. Tiny contractions battered his finger each time Donal sucked on her nipples. Looking up, he could see the skin on her swollen breasts was tight. Her nipples had turned gorgeous pink-red.

He'd never seen a more beautiful female.

With one finger still inside her, he ran his hand over her thigh, opening her even more. Her glistening clit strained out from under the hood, demanding his attention.

Leaning down, he flicked his tongue over the hot little pearl and added some long, slow licks. She tasted like the wind off the sound, salt and sea breeze, and he could feel his blood rising like the tide.

Between his legs, his balls hung heavy with urgency.

Soon.

But not until she was desperate with need.

Because tonight, he and Donal would share their female in their favorite way, the most intimate of ways.

Slowly, he slid his finger in and out between the hot silk of her pussy lips...and teased her clit with teeth and tongue.

Donal was alternating his attention between her mouth and her breasts.

When he heard her beautifully high little whines, Tynan smiled.

There was nothing more satisfying than overwhelming the little wolf with a maelstrom of sensations until she surrendered...everything.

Her hips rose with each slow movement of his finger, and her legs trembled against his shoulders.

It wasn't time for her to come. No, not yet.

He rose and took her hands. "Come here, lass." Pulling her to her feet, he put an arm around her to steady her.

"But..." She blinked up at him.

"No worries, little wolf. We're not done." Not even close. To please himself, he cupped one swollen breast in his palm. So heavy.

When he tugged at the nipple, rolled it lightly between his fingers, her whimpering, needy sound made his cock strain upward.

Control, Tynan.

"Donal." He nodded toward the end of the bed.

With a flashing smile, Donal moved to the center of the bed. He lay on his back, legs dangling over the end, toes touching the floor. Cock jutting up.

Meggie stared at him—and the slight tensing of her muscles showed she remembered what she'd asked them for.

Tynan smiled down at her. Her face was flushed, her lips reddened. He couldn't help but take another demanding kiss—and then he lifted her onto the bed, settling her on her hands and knees so she straddled his littermate's hips.

"There you are." Donal pushed her hair behind her ears, bracketed her face with his hands, and pulled her down for a kiss. And, of course, started to play with her dangling breasts.

When her hips began to make small squirming movements, Donal laughed. "Let me inside you now, sweetheart." Reaching down, Donal helped her lower onto his cock.

Her moan was like fire in Tynan's veins.

Slow. They had to go slow. He opened the jar of coconut oil Donal had left at the end of the bed.

Donal caught his gaze and smiled. Taking Meggie's wrists, he pulled her forward and set her hands on his chest. "Hold still for a second, *cariad.*"

Scooping some coconut oil into his hands, Tynan let it warm, then slicked up his dick before smearing more onto her pretty puckered arsehole.

Gasping, she jerked, but was held in place by Donal's grip on her hips—and his dick in her cunt.

He and Donal waited.

Panting slightly, she looked over her shoulder at Tynan. Her hazel eyes were anxious, yet warm with desire...and more. After a second, it obviously dawned on her he was waiting. "Yes. This is what I want."

"If you don't like it, *mo leannán,* we'll stop." He ran his slick hand over her shoulder, down her back and side, needing the contact to assess her feelings. He'd have to check often; the little wolf tended to disregard her own needs for others.

Bending, he slid his arms around her. She turned her head so he could capture her lips. The long slow kiss told him his fate.

By the Gods, she's stolen my heart.

Huffing in pleasure, Donal ran his hands down her torso.

"I love this position." Without moving his hips, without thrusting, he played with Meggie's breasts.

And she started to squirm.

There we go.

Donal's hands on her breasts were driving Margery crazy—because he was inside her, so hot and thick, yet wasn't moving.

Move, please move, now.

Her whole lower half pulsed with an urgent hunger. She tried to rise off his cock, managed a heavenly inch before Tynan held her in place.

"Nooo," she whined.

"Are ye ready then?" He leaned over her, his deep voice a tantalizing whisper next to her ear.

"I *was* ready." She nodded frantically. "Now, now, *now*."

"Now it is."

Donal reached down, pulling her buttocks apart, half-massaging them at the same time.

She felt Tynan's finger making small circles around the rim, pressing inside briefly, out again, awakening all the nerves in that area. One finger penetrated, then two, in and out.

Hot shivers ran through her body like waves of lava as he eased her open. As he'd done before on other nights.

Setting one foot on the mattress next to her right calf,

Tynan replaced his fingers with his shaft. The head pressed against her rim, and her eyes widened.

Oh Gods, he's a lot bigger than a couple of fingers.

Her fingernails dug into Donal's chest at the uncomfortable pressure.

"Push out, sweetheart," Tynan murmured.

As she complied, he slid in, out, each time a little farther, stretching her muscles widely, almost painfully.

She whimpered, and then the biggest part of the head was in, and he paused. The feeling of being...penetrated... back *there* was so different from anything she'd ever experienced.

"Breathe, Margery." Donal ran his hands up and down her arms, silvery gaze on her face.

She tried to breathe. Surely there was air somewhere.

Tynan didn't move.

She was throbbing around his dick—around them both, because Donal's cock was still deep inside her.

Then somehow, everything inside her relaxed. Adjusted.

She pulled in a slower breath.

"There's a good wolf." The approval in Tynan's low voice was like a warm hug. Ever so slowly, he pulled back and added more of the coconut oil.

The next time he thrust in, she gasped at the excruciatingly intense pleasure. He went deeper, deeper until his warm thighs pressed against her bottom. "There we go."

Panting with nerves, she froze as *both* cocks moved

inside her. How could she be so full? Every nerve was firing, lashing her with unfamiliar sensations.

Incredible sensations. "Oh, oh, oh."

"Easy, wolflet. It's all right." Donal's hand brushed over her face, and the concern and love in his touch made her eyes prickle with tears.

Gently, he drew her down for a kiss.

But her movement forced Tynan's cock deeper, and she squeaked, feeling impaled—unsure if it was pleasurable or not.

Chuckling, Donal kissed her slowly, deeply, then, keeping one firm hand on her hip, he used the other to cover her breast. Her nipple was tender, almost too sensitive as he tugged on it. Her body tightened in reflex—and clenched around the huge erections inside her.

Burning shivers coursed over her skin.

And then they started to move.

The hands on her hips lifted her up and off Donal.

As Tynan thrust in fully, the thick slide of his erection deep within her was the most exciting thing she'd ever felt.

Heat lanced through her body as he slid out, and she was pulled down onto Donal's cock. The two shafts worked her, driving her up and up. The merciless rhythm became her world until the only thing she could feel was the brilliance of them within her. Them holding her. Touching her.

Loving her.

As they sped up, Donal reached down and rubbed his thumb over her engorged clit.

One more impossible sensation.

Too many sensations. Her body gathered, tightening around the rigid shafts harder and harder as the thrusting drove her to an unbearable height.

And over.

"Ooooob." Wave after wave of scalding ecstasy roared through her. Her eyes went blind, the entire world turning to the silver of a full moon.

And the pleasure went on and on.

Donal had never seen anything so beautiful as when Margery came apart in their arms. Face flushed a deep red. Her nipple a hard point on his palm. Her cunt squeezed his erection in rhythmic spasms until he couldn't hold out.

When he met Tynan's gaze, his brother nodded. *Go ahead.*

Donal gripped her hips and drove in fast and deep. The pressure inside him rose to a staggering level for one long, blissful, agonizing moment, and then the pulsing heat flowed from his balls to his cock in piercing jerks of pleasure.

Giving her all that he was and joining them together in the most primal fashion.

With a low growl, his littermate climaxed, too, sharing the moment with him, with Margery. Their female.

A sweetness, a rightness, like he'd never felt before washed through Donal.

After a moment, he lifted his gaze to Tynan, and they both smiled. *Yes.*

Before Donal even thought of moving, Tynan kissed down Margery's back and pulled out.

Her sharp inhalation at his loss made him smile. After stroking her hair, Tynan whispered, "You're beautiful, *a leannán*. Thank you for this gift," before disappearing into the bathroom.

At his words, her lips quivered slightly, and Donal's heart ached. Tynan was right. The wolflet needed all their tenderness.

"Come here, *cariad*." Gently, Donal eased her down on top of him so he could run his hands up and down her back. So he could kiss her.

Her lips were sweet, and her curvy body was the sweetest weight. Had he ever known anyone so giving?

By the Gods, it shook him how close he'd come to losing her, to losing Tynan. This time together had been more than a mating; it was a celebration of joy that they'd survived.

And with a sigh, he admitted the truth simmering in his heart.

He loved his brother...and he loved Margery.

After cleaning up, Tynan crawled into the bed and grinned. Looking boneless, Meggie was draped over Donal like a blanket.

Tynan grinned at his brother. "Share, greedy cat." He pulled her off Donal onto the mattress so they could tuck her between the two of them.

Snuggling down with her head on Donal's shoulder, she pulled Tynan's arm over her waist and cuddled his hand between her breasts. Her fingers twined between his.

Within seconds, her breathing slowed, and she went limp again.

"I think we wore her out." Donal stroked her hair, his expression soft.

"I'd say the entire evening did that." By the Gods, it had been a terrifying night.

He'd been one second from death.

Silas had died.

Meggie and Donal had been out there with the hellhound. The thought of losing them...

Unable to help himself, he rolled Meggie onto her back, gripping her hand as if he could hold her back from her reckless courage.

He looked over at his littermate. "I understand why you went out there, *mo deartháir*." His voice came out a low rasp. "But by the Gods..."

Donal's gaze met his. "How do you think I felt, seeing you jump in front of a hellhound? And then realizing Margery followed me?"

Without opening her eyes, Meggie stirred and bent her head to kiss Tynan's fingers, her lips soft on his callused hand. "'Course I did. You needed help."

Braced on an elbow, Tynan kissed her cheek, then her lips. The words weren't easy to say, but he offered them like a wolf bringing a breakfast bunny to his mate. "It's not easy to see someone I love risking her life, *mo chridhe*."

Her eyes flew open. The way her body went still told him she hadn't considered that he might actually care for her.

That was his failing...not sharing his emotions. He nuzzled her hair and tried again. "I love you, Meggie mine."

His littermate grunted as if he'd been punched.

After a second, Donal went up on an elbow, mirroring Tynan's pose, and kissed Meggie. "I love you, too, you know."

When she made a sound like a startled mouse, he shot Tynan an amused look—because nothing kept the cat down for long.

Donal pushed a strand of hair out of her face. "As it happens, I know you love us back. Don't you?" The light way he said the words couldn't conceal the longing beneath.

Aye, we're both lost, aren't we?

Tynan ran a finger over her cheek. "Give us the words, little wolf."

She was incapable of holding back when someone needed her...and there was no way she could miss how much they needed to hear how she felt.

Tynan's heart swelled painfully as she whispered. "I love you, Tynan."

She turned to Donal, "I love you, Donal. Both of you."

Reaching out, she pulled them down to her, hugging them tightly.

Tynan put his arm over her and his brother. The satisfaction of holding the ones he loved—his family—filled him to overflowing.

This...this is right.

CHAPTER TWENTY-ONE

Unclaimed territory, Washington - waxing gibbous moon

Nerves had Margery tapping her fingers on the steering wheel as she drove south on Highway 9. The last month, since the first night she'd spent with Tynan and Donal to now, had been like an amazing dream. Work, friends, and a home. Tynan and Donal.

They loved her. She pulled in a breath, hearing their words again. Seeing Tynan's clear blue eyes so filled with emotion, hearing the catch in Donal's voice.

They love me. Me!

She'd never dreamed life could hold so much happiness.

A growl broke into her thoughts.

She frowned at Tynan in the passenger seat. "Am I doing something wrong?"

"Not you, lass." He pointed to the car in front of them on the highway. "They're moving slower than a pixie after a hard freeze. If you stay behind them, it'll take us all day to get to the festival grounds."

"Oh." That sounded fine to her. Because she had a feeling this weekend was liable to turn a dream into a nightmare. The Rainier clan would be at the summer solstice festival.

Grumbling came from Oliver in the back seat, and her mood lightened. It was good to have him here.

After disappearing for a week after Silas's death at the lodge, he'd returned and apologized for his behavior that night. They'd talked and then talked some more. He'd shared what he'd experienced as a shifter-soldier. That he was having trouble coping. That he'd been drunk that night and a few other nights.

For the last week, things between them had gotten better.

Which was good. Neither of them liked conflict—one of the few traits they had in common. Over the years, she'd forgotten how different she was from her littermates. She was the even-tempered, practical, and affectionate one. Being a banfasa suited her.

If he'd lived, tough Orson would have probably been a warrior—a cahir, even. Her last memory of him still hurt:

him charging the Scythe, the soldier's gun firing, the life draining from his eyes.

The Mother guard you, Orson.

Oliver was the sensitive, creative one. Grandmama had once said that a vivid imagination made it difficult to be brave...and Oliver had been awfully cautious as a cub. Being forced to become a Scythe soldier must have been such a nightmare. And during their talks, he'd said the Scythe considered killing him for being a *"waste of time and effort"*. His self-esteem had been shredded. He had nightmares from what he'd witnessed. What he'd been forced to do.

She understood, oh, she totally did. And she'd help him all she could.

Although if he kept grumping in the backseat, she might turn around and smack him one.

"I hate the fucking human vehicles," he muttered. "Go faster, sis."

The sound of him scratching set off her own itches. She rubbed her arm vigorously before frowning at Tynan. "Why aren't you itching?"

He shrugged. "I'm more immune than most to metal. It's why I could survive in the city."

"Oh." She sure wasn't immune and didn't want to be in the car. At all. She studied the slow vehicle in front. "I need to go around—*pass* him. Right?"

"Aye. Turn on your signal, check the left lane with the back mirror and side mirror, then turn your head and look, as well."

She followed instructions. "All clear."

"Move out as you speed up and go around."

Learning to drive a car was tricky. Everyone she'd watched made it look so easy. At least Tynan was incredibly patient. Donal...well, Donal wasn't. Perhaps it was just as well that Donal was staying in Cold Creek until tomorrow. He'd said he didn't want to leave the town without a healer for too long...but that was after Tynan mentioned she would be the driver on the way down.

As she completed the maneuver and returned safely to the right lane, she chuckled.

"What's so funny about passing?" Oliver asked.

"It reminded me of my first drive down Main Street." She'd practiced in the Wild Hunt parking lot and the tiny Wildwood Lodge lanes. Main Street had been her first experience with other cars, pedestrians, and stop signs. "The trouble is...Donal *hates* cars. He said Karl Benz and Henry Ford were hellhounds in human form."

"Wait, wait, wait..." Behind her, Oliver was laughing his ass off. "You asked the *healer* to teach you? Are you suicidal?"

"He volunteered." She sniffed. "Really, he was fine...until Irma Neilson and her dog stepped right in front of the car." Thank the Mother someone had invented seatbelts.

"Mmmph. If you'd run over her fat poodle, you'd have had two people upset," Tynan said in an odd voice. His hand was over his mouth, his shoulders shaking.

"You're *laughing*." She gave him a disgusted look.

"I'll bite—what happened then?" Oliver choked out.

Margery rolled her eyes. "That Donal. He threw his hands in the air and said I was as unaware as a drunken dwarf during mead season. Thank the Gods the windows were up so Irma didn't hear what he called her."

Tynan was carefully looking out the window. "Mmmph."

"*Mmmph* my tail. Our illustrious healer sounded like one of Emma's preschoolers having a tantrum."

Weird snorting sounds came from the back seat, and Margery almost grinned. Oliver hadn't laughed like this since they were younglings. He sputtered out, "I'm going to tell Donal you said that. Oh yeah."

"Don't you dare, bear." But she giggled. Her littermate sounded...normal. So normal. Carefully, she passed another slowpoke.

Tynan's murmured, "Very well done," made her beam.

Driving. I got this. No matter what Donal said.

Highway 9 gave way to smaller Highway 2, and then even narrower roads. The curves grew sharp as the land rose from foothills to mountains. Few vehicles traveled this road.

Probably other shifters.

"Slow down." Tynan pointed to a tiny path through the grass. "Pull onto the shoulder there."

When the car stopped, Tynan turned. "Oliver, can you take our packs to the clearing, please? The festival location is a short walk down that path. We'll take the car and park it farther away."

"Sure." Oliver got out, sniffing the crisp mountain air. "It'll be fun to explore around here."

"Good enough." Tynan opened the back and pulled out the soft packs. "We'll see you later then...or will you be in the shifter-soldier meeting with Wells?"

"Nah, that's tomorrow." Oliver's face tightened. The shifter-soldiers had been summoned by Arthur Wells, the human spymaster who was hunting the Scythe.

Margery was hoping he'd called them together to report that the entire Scythe organization had been eliminated.

I can hope, right?

As Oliver hefted the packs and headed down the trail, she looked around. No cars were parked in sight, although there was room for perhaps two vehicles on the shoulder. "No one else is here?"

"To avoid attention, everyone's parking elsewhere on the road and hiking in through the forest." He smiled at her. "Once we find a spot, we'll shift and go furry. Maybe even find a sunny patch of grass to...enjoy." His masculine voice held a suggestive growl, and her whole body went soft and needy.

"We're here to work," she made a token protest, but from the light in his eyes, he could scent her desire.

"No problem, Meggie mine." He ran a finger over her lips. "I'll make you work for each and every orgasm."

A couple of hours later, Tynan slowed as the trees opened into a meadow. He could scent other shifters, hear the sounds of conversations, of a guitar, of a fire.

They were arriving somewhat late. Having found that sunny patch of grass, he'd...had fun. Meggie had come so many times that she'd wobbled when she stood. It was good they were in wolf form—she'd needed all four legs.

And she'd nipped him when he laughed.

After a quick glance at the festival grounds, Tynan skirted the tree line and entered a big tent. The back flap opened to the forest so those in animal form could slip in and shift to human.

Meggie followed him in.

Around the sides of the tent, personal backpacks and duffels were meticulously organized by territory. He found the North Cascades section and, after a few sniffs, located where Oliver had left their bags. Dropping the small pack of their clothing he'd carried, he shifted to human.

As they dressed, he watched Meggie. Her nipples were still swollen and red, her cheeks beard burned.

She caught him looking and flushed.

So loveable. Drawing her into his arms, all silky skin and soft flesh, he nibbled on her shoulder.

She leaned against him. "I just realized we forgot to pack sleeping bags."

"We didn't forget. For non-human events, most of us spend the night in animal shape. Our pack will make a big furry pile."

Her eyes lit.

Poor little wolf that something so commonplace hadn't been part of her experience. Being Daonain, she'd been targeted by the worst of humanity.

Now, he and Donal would have the joy of showing her the best of being a shifter.

And in that light, he needed to talk with his snail-slow littermate. Sure and his brother was thicker than a stump when it came to relationships. Nonetheless, it was time—past time—to take the next step. After all, Meggie was practically living with them.

Of course, many shifters never took it further, content to love each other, yet still participate in Gatherings every full moon. Tynan shook his head. He wanted more than that for them.

He wanted to see their lifemating bracelets on her wrist. Wanted a lifetime of waking with her snuggled between him and Donal, breathing in her scent, giving her everything that was in his heart.

Yes, it was time to have that talk with Donal.

Under the biggest trees at the edge of the meadow, Margery pushed to her feet. Stretching her arms over her head, she groaned. Driving a car could sure knot a person's muscles.

Driving, then lots and lots of sex, then helping set up the dining tent, and now, tending wounds. Her lips quirked as she watched the two troublesome cubs dash toward the dining tent as if they'd never gotten all scraped up falling out of a tree.

When Donal arrived tomorrow, he'd have a fit when he learned the Cold Creek teens had shared their favorite hobby with the other territories' cubs.

Treeways were being created in the forest all around the festival grounds.

Grinning, she boosted herself up into one of the trees to look. Yes, there it was. The tops of the larger branches had been smoothed to make secure landing spots and were marked on top with a dab of light paint. One easy to use tree path that was invisible from below.

The tree next to hers shook as a cub jumped to it.

Athol shifted to human, balancing easily on the branch. "You like our treeway?" After his rough first shift when he'd panicked and slashed the cublings, he'd worked exceedingly hard to gain control over his forms.

"It's very cool," she said honestly. "Makes me wish I were a cat."

Athol puffed up at the compliment before heading back to join his friends without bothering to shift.

Margery winced. All that bare skin. But the teens played up here in both forms.

Donal would be displeased that she hadn't scolded them. *"You're encouraging that Gods-benighted, pixie-brained behavior?"*

Hypocritical feline. Last week, she'd spotted him and

Alec playing tag high up in the Cold Creek treeway. They'd moved far faster than the youngsters—and had a wonderful time.

Smiling, she dropped out of the tree and picked up her first-aid bag. A small healing tent was being erected near the center of the meadow. Supplies were already there. Since Donal wasn't coming until tomorrow, he'd asked her to get everything organized.

He trusted her to do that and simply assumed she'd be working in the tent with him. The compliment was...everything.

"Hey, Margery." Jody, accompanied by her three mates, was loaded down with firewood and heading for one of the firepits set up around the meadow. "Let's practice some takedowns tomorrow before breakfast."

"Sounds good." Margery smiled back as the males all nodded to her. And okay, she was just a little grateful that Tynan and Donal didn't have another littermate. Although Daonain triplets weren't uncommon, most times the third littermate was female.

Three males as mates? Margery grinned. *You go, Jody.*

As she walked, Margery saw shifters loaded down with blankets emerge from the path to the road. By tomorrow morning—when the festival officially started—everything would be in place. She'd been pleased when Vicki and Angie asked her to come and help set up. Being part of the community...she loved it.

"By the Gods, I hoped to find you here, banfasa." The

ugly note in a male's voice brought her to a halt a second before she recognized who was speaking.

Pete, the Cosantir from Rainier Territory.

Two older males stood beside him, a slight aura of power around each. They were all Cosantirs.

Angie had mentioned that the attending Cosantirs hoped to have a meeting. But, cat-scat, why did Pete have to be one of them?

Stomach tightening, she nodded politely to Pete. One was never rude to a Cosantir. "Cosantir."

"Margery." The werebear was big-boned, slightly pudgy, and his yellow-gray hair was receding. His smile didn't reach his eyes. "How is North Cascades Territory treating you?"

"Everyone has been wonderful." She took a sideways step. "I need to go and—"

"You need to return to my territory. North Cascades already has a healer, a powerful one. Skilled shifters should be spread out, especially banfasas and healers. Otherwise shifters die from lack of care. Some of our wounded can't go to human hospitals, after all."

She stiffened. "I won't return to Rainier Territory. Ever."

"You don't have a choice. Calum can't keep you if—"

"You treated me like a slave. After a decade as a captive, I won't willingly enter another cage."

The other two Cosantirs were frowning.

"A *slave*." Pete's face turned an angry dark red. "That's no way to talk about free room and board."

"You kept me penniless. Without transportation. With

no choices in food or lodging. You told me I *had* to be a banfasa, wasn't allowed to do anything else. My clothes were rags, with no way to replace them since I wasn't allowed to earn any money." She drew herself straight. "That's a slave."

When his hands fisted, she forced herself not to retreat. If he hit her, well, she'd find out what happened when a shifter fought a Cosantir.

Because she'd found her fangs.

Someone crowded Margery on the side, and she almost swung at them. But—it was Vicki beside her.

The petite brunette radiated anger, and her stance said she was ready to take on Pete all by herself.

Mother's breath. The unbelievable sensation of not being alone shook Margery, and she looked down at her feet, fighting against tears.

Vicki bumped her shoulder against Margery's to get her attention, then nodded at the Cosantirs.

Focus. Right. Margery lifted her chin. "When I *escaped* to the North Cascades, your shifters spread lies about my skills to try to keep me from being able to survive."

"Lying? I'm appalled." Pete shook his head. "Or perhaps they knew something we don't?"

Even as he spoke, Margery realized she didn't need revenge. His past manipulation didn't matter. Being able to tell him how she felt, to confront him, this was enough.

As long as he couldn't drag her back against her will. The thought made her fingers clench into fists.

"Her talent isn't in question in my territory." A deep

laugh came from behind her, and the words had a slight British accent. "Margery is extremely skilled, and my clan is delighted to have her. Donal has already put her to work."

Coming up behind her, Calum squeezed her shoulder and moved past. He motioned to the other Cosantirs. "Since Pete introduced the subject, perhaps we can discuss how to encourage skilled Daonain to settle in a territory."

The other Cosantirs followed Calum like wolves after their alpha.

Pete's hands opened and closed as he stared at her.

She stared back, unmoving. Her own hands were still in fists.

Huffing, he scowled. "Fine, stay here, then. You're not worth my time or effort." Turning on his heel, he stomped after the other Cosantirs.

Oh, my Goddess. She'd...she'd *won.* Shivers were lodged in her bones, and she had to force her fingers to open. But it was over. She'd stood up to him.

Pulling in a hard breath, she turned to Vicki. "Thank you. I felt really alone for a minute."

"Not even close." Vicki grinned. "Next time, scope out your surroundings." The ex-military female pointed to the left.

Hands on hips, staring after the Cosantirs, Angie stood in the door of the cook tent with Breanne and Darcy beside her. Darcy held a pot like she planned to wallop someone.

Vicki pointed to the right.

Tynan stood beside Joe Thorson and the North Cascades cahirs, including her pack leaders, Shay and Zeb.

Margery stared. Mother's breasts, but they'd all been standing by. Ready to help if she needed it. The knowledge took her breath away.

After a second, she managed to blink back tears and find a smile instead. "Thank you. Thank you all."

Tynan gave her an approving nod.

Angie brushed off her hands. "Good job of standing your ground, girl."

Darcy winked.

And everyone returned to what they were doing. Because they hadn't thought they'd done anything special.

She knew better.

"I have to admit, I'm surprised Tynan didn't jump in," Margery said.

"Actually, when the cahirs moved to intervene, he told them to wait. That it would be good for you to bare your fangs and confront the asshole."

"I..." Margery blew out a breath. "He was right. It felt good."

"Even better, the way you stated your case to all the Cosantirs means Pete can't claim we stole you. You're safer this way."

"Huh. That's...smart."

"That would be Calum. He was beside Tynan when you started raising hell with Pete."

A good, protective Cosantir. Friends on her side. Tynan

and Donal. "I'm really glad Heather brought me to Cold Creek."

"So are we. Now, come on, we have somewhere we need to be." Vicki motioned toward the other side of the grounds.

As they headed that way, Breanne and Darcy fell in behind them.

Halfway across the meadow, Margery heard someone say, loudly, "Oh, cat-scat, it's the scarred-up gimp. Honestly, why does she bother to attend Gatherings? Does she really think any male would want her?"

The words made Margery flinch. Made her remember the scar on her face. Her limp. Made her feel...less.

Vicki hissed under her breath and turned.

So did Margery.

The female talking was Sarah, the brunette who been with Donal at Margery's first Cold Creek gathering. Beautiful, petite, curvy. With a tongue sharper than a razor.

Deal with it now. No hiding in caves, remember?

Margery made her voice strong—and spoke to Sarah and her companion. "In case you forget, Daonain Law says all single shifters must attend Gatherings. That's why I attend." Then she remembered what Oliver had said about beauty hiding an empty heart. "As for being wanted, I've noticed many males prefer inner strength and compassion to outer beauty."

A low masculine laugh from the side startled Margery. Two males had stopped to listen.

One had dark hair and even darker eyes. "I far prefer compassion, aye."

The other, cahir-sized with long flaxen hair, gave Margery a slow perusal, taking in the scar on her face and those on her bare arms and hands. His lips turned up for a second. Then he turned to Sarah and said, "Any male who has fought recognizes battle scars like those, and any male worth the name honors courage far above shallow attractiveness."

Both males tilted their heads at Margery, and the dark one murmured in a French-accented voice, "We will hope to win your favor at the Gathering tomorrow night."

Without another glance at Sarah, the two strolled on.

Speechless, Margery stared after them, but Breanne and Darcy were snickering.

Red-faced, Sarah stomped away in the other direction, trailed by her friend.

Grinning, Vicki started walking again, pulling Margery along. "We're running late, crew. Let's go."

"Late for what?" Margery's question was answered when Vicki stopped at a rock-enclosed firepit. Big logs around the pit created benches to sit on.

"Here you are. Finally." Emma, the bard, was comfortably seated on one log, and Breanne dropped down beside her.

Heather was on another log. "I was beginning to think you got lost."

Darcy tossed a blanket on an empty log and sat down.

She extended her legs to toast her boots. "Boy, don't go wading in the creek. The water's freezing."

Laughing, Heather motioned with the mug she was holding. "How about a warmer-upper to get rid of the chill?"

"But—aren't we supposed to be setting up?" Margery glanced back at the camp.

"Everything's finished," Heather said. "We've been waiting for Vicki and team to find you."

They'd been looking for her. Wanting her.

How many times could they reduce her to tears in a few minutes? Blinking hard—again—Margery joined Heather on the log and accepted a mug from the batch near the fire.

Vicki sat on her other side and picked up a mug.

Catching the fragrance, Margery smiled. "Hot chocolate's a great idea."

After a sip, Darcy widened her eyes. "This is hot chocolate with a major kick. Really nice, Heather."

"We've corrupted Darcy," Breanne said. "She's learned the wonders of Baileys, Kahlua, and Amaretto."

"I don't even know what those are," Margery admitted.

"Oh, you will." Emma laughed. "Be aware, though, that your hot chocolate has a lot of alcohol in it."

"Fuck yes. I love drunken sex in the moonlight." Vicki took a hefty gulp as everyone snickered.

Drunken sex with Tynan sounded like a lot of fun. It was a shame Donal had stayed in Cold Creek. Margery took a tentative sip. "Oh, my Gods, this is really good!"

Laughter rippled around the fire.

As if the sound had drawn it, a salamander appeared in the flames, rising to do a swirly dance.

"There's a pretty guy," Emma said in approval. "And, look, he brought a friend."

Well above the flames, where smoke rose into the air, a sylph mirrored the salamander's dance.

Margery breathed in the cool, clean night air, holding the scents of wood smoke, of deep forest, of chocolate and shifters.

The air of freedom.

For a moment, the past crept closer: *The loneliness of the tiny cell. The pain of bruises and welts. The slow exhaustion of impending death. The hard cell floor where she'd sit beneath the narrow window so the moonlight could wash over her.*

But she was here now.

Overhead, the stars were appearing in the darkening sky as a silvery glow lit the rim of the mountains. Tonight, the moon would cast her light over the entire world.

Tears prickled her eyes at the beauty.

"I love this. All of this," she whispered.

Hearing her, Darcy looked around. At the forest, the tents, the females gathered around the fire. She nodded. "Home. Back with our people. Friends."

Then, being the irrepressible Darcy, she snickered. "And the males aren't bad either."

Cheers greeted her statement.

Darcy waggled her brows. "Have you noticed that Margery agrees with me—at least about two of them?"

That got even more hooting. It seemed everyone had noticed.

"Well, honestly. I barely get a newbie broken in, and they go off and get mated." Heather huffed. "It's very annoying."

Her light tone couldn't conceal the unhappiness beneath it.

Margery took her hand. "I'm sorry." Because she'd felt the same way in Ailill Ridge when it seemed everyone else had friends and mates and family.

"No, don't be, sweetie." Heather leaned against her. "I'm just crabby that I can't find anyone for myself."

Vicki frowned. "Considering that you're strikingly attractive, intelligent, fun...and nice, I always figured your lack of mates was your choice. It's not?"

Did the human military teach bluntness as a weapon?

Emma frowned at Vicki, then sighed. "All right, I have to admit, I thought the same thing."

Although the redhead didn't upset easily, Margery patted Heather's shoulder in wolfy support.

"Okay, yes, I'm fussy. Potential mates get rejected...for lots of reasons." Heather stayed, shoulder to shoulder with Margery, obviously needing the contact. She turned to Vicki. "For example, I adore your Alec and Calum, but I grew up with them. They're like littermates."

"That makes sense." Breanne frowned. "My Shay and

Zeb were in Rainier with you for a long time. How did you manage to resist *them?*"

"Girl." Heather waved her hand dismissively. "In Rainier, Zeb's idea of conversing was to growl. You and Shay have been good for him but still..."

"I love this!" Emma pointed her mug at Heather. "Now mine!"

With a roll of her eyes, Heather said, "Ryder wasn't here. Now, Ben is appealing. I love his size and easy-going personality, but my two littermates are bears. When Ben goes bearish, he feels like another brother."

"You *are* fussy," Darcy said in disbelief and offered up her males. "Owen and Gawain?"

"I didn't know Gawain. But Owen? The only time he said more than two words to a female was at Gatherings."

Margery grinned. Breanne said Owen used to act like females were a scourge of mosquitoes. Wasn't it cool that Darcy had snuck in under all his defenses?

The other females were looking at her, waiting for her to ask.

"Um, Donal and Tynan?" Margery tensed. It would be horribly awkward if Heather had wanted them.

"Tynan lived in Seattle, so I hardly knew him. As for Donal, we'd kill each other within a week—and not in a sexy way." Heather snorted. "If he ranted at me, I'd smack his nose and then he'd probably rip my intestines right out."

"But it's fun when he goes on one of his spiels," Margery protested.

"*Not.*" Heather lifted her hand and her *smack-a-snout* motion sent Margery into giggles.

"Speaking of the cop and the healer"—Emma strummed some introductory chords on her guitar—"what's going on there?"

All eyes turned to Margery.

"Wow, you're all so snoopy."

"Yep." Vicki pointed to herself and Darcy. "Curious cats." She motioned to Heather and Breanne. "Nosy pack members."

Emma raised her hand. "Story-loving bard."

"Fine." Margery took a sip of chocolate, stalling for time. Then another sip because it was so very good, like a creamy dessert. "We're, ummm, together at night."

"That long *ummm* means sexy times, right?" Heather waggled her eyebrows.

"Every clever man knows what *ummm* means." Vicki nodded.

Laughing, Emma smiled up at an imaginary male. "Hey, Ben, you want to...*ummm?*"

The rest of them broke up.

"Morning *ummms* are sure a nice way to start the day," Darcy murmured.

"There are times, though. Two cahirs after they've been in a battle?" Breanne shook her head, saying to her imaginary males, "No, guys. If we *ummm* again, I won't be able to walk."

"I have to admit, I've never had such excellent *ummming*

as I get now," Vicki said. "Calum and Alec are infinitely creative."

"By the Gods," Margery muttered. "I'm never going to be able to use that word again."

"Ummm, what?" Heather asked with a smirk, then turned serious. "Be aware, new wolf, *ummming* outside of Gatherings can lead to expectations."

"Expectations?"

"Like getting serious." Vicki ran her fingertips over her lifemating bracelets—the Daonain equivalent of a wedding ring.

Margery frowned as she sipped her drink. Were Donal and Tynan...serious? They said they loved her, but did they want more than what they had right now? Would they want to mate for life?

She imagined the feel of two lifemating bracelets on her wrist, one from each male.

What would it be like to know she'd be with them forever?

She'd live with them...although she almost was now. They were together every evening, especially when Oliver was out.

They'd make supper together.

Tynan popping a strawberry in her mouth and following with a kiss. Donal sliding past, rubbing against her—such a cat—and purring in her ear as he sneaked in a quick feel. They'd talk about their days, about patients, about criminals, and discuss ways to help the people in town.

The days since they'd said they loved her had been more than joyful.

She put her arms around herself as if to hold the dream in, then went a step further and imagined the future. Imagined cubs crawling on the floor. One would look like Tynan, one like Donal. Maybe even one like her. Would their personalities hold true, too? *A stack of blocks falling, and one pup babbling in a toddler-Donal rant. The other with a Tynan-frown before he determinedly started over and was joined by his littermate. Working together.*

Until she swooped in to give them mommy hugs.

The dream seemed to snap into place, as if she'd had it forever without realizing it. Because...she loved Donal and Tynan, and they loved her back.

She knew it now. Accepted it. Delighted in it. But where were they going with their lives?

Because...with all her heart, she wanted to be with them forever.

CHAPTER TWENTY-TWO

C *old Creek, North Cascades Territory - waxing gibbous moon*

Answering dispatch's call, Donal drove through the dark night up into the mountains. Although it was past midnight, he hadn't retired for the night. The empty bed hadn't appealed—not without Margery and his littermate. He'd agreed the two should go early to help set up the festival grounds, but by the Gods, he hadn't realized how lonely the house would be.

Especially without Margery. It felt as if she'd always been in their lives, sleeping in their bed, working with him, but really, it'd been less than a complete month.

He'd fallen fast, hadn't he?

One of these days, they needed to discuss what came next. Somehow.

Ahead, the incline steepened. As he rounded a curve, ominous red flares on the road flagged the accident. His stomach tightened. There must be shifters hurt, or the dispatcher wouldn't have called him.

By the Gods, shifters shouldn't be permitted to use cars. Or trucks. Or anything with wheels.

Spotting Alec's white-faced deputy, Donal pulled over and joined him. "How bad?"

"Nobody's dead, yet, but it's ugly. The cars went over the side." Jenkins swallowed hard. The stink of vomit came from the shoulder where the younger male had been sick. "Alec is down there. Sent me up here to wait for you. The Murphy brothers are on the way."

"Good." The brothers volunteered at the firefighting station.

If it was this bad, he'd need added power, and it'd take a while for the females to arrive. Donal pulled out his phone. No signal. Of course not. "Contact dispatch and have them send me"—who were the two females he'd mated last Gathering?—"Nia and Francesca. Or Farrah as third choice." He'd mated with Farrah two moons ago. She lived close and had a fair amount of power.

"Got it." Jenkins pointed to where skid marks went off the road. Farther down the bluff, destroyed brush showed the appalling fall the cars had taken. "Watch your step. It's steep."

Of course it is.

Because nothing about this night was going to be easy.

Sourly, Donal pulled on a backpack of medical supplies and followed the trail of destruction, past broken-off trees and flattened undergrowth. It was good the forest was still damp, or fire would be a concern.

When the slope evened out, he spotted a sedan bent sideways around a tree. The second vehicle had hit the sedan near the trunk. Whimpering and moaning came from both cars.

A camp light sat on a bare patch of ground to illuminate the area.

"Donal." Alec was half-inside one vehicle. "Got Tina here with Griffin. She's bleeding badly. If you check for spinal injuries in the sedan, then I'll trade places and get them out while you're fixin' Tina." His southern accent surfaced with the tension.

"Good plan."

Opening the sedan's driver side, Donal saw why Alec was concerned. Neither of the pigeon-brained males wore seatbelts. One was half on the floor, the other tangled with the steering wheel. Broken bones, bleeding, dazed, struggling.

"Cubs. I know you hurt, but I need you to stay still. No moving." Donal kept his tone firm and kind. Hearing the voice of someone in charge would give them the hope that everything would be all right.

Hopes were so often wrong.

Focusing, he ran a hand down the driver's back. Spine was intact. Youngsters were so fucking flexible. A quick sweep of his front exposed no major internal damage. Broken ribs. Broken arm. Donal could assess better once he was out of the vehicle.

It took all his strength to yank open the warped passenger door. The male was lucky the back half of the car had impacted the tree.

Donal checked him over. Muscles alongside the vertebrae were strained. A hip was dislocated. Broken right leg, right humerus, ribs. Concussion.

"Stay put and we'll get you out of here."

A groan was the only answer.

"Alec." At the other car, Donal waited for Alec to emerge, then slid in as he reported the damage and what to watch out for. "You might want to wait for more help to move them."

"Will do. Looks like help is here." Alec headed back toward the other car.

On the road above, flashing lights heralded the arrival of the fire truck. The Murphys loved those damned lights.

"Is Griffin all right?" Tina whispered. Ah, right—she'd lifemated Griffin and his two brothers last fall. No wonder she was worried.

Donal checked the unconscious driver. At least these two had worn seatbelts. The male had bashed his head against the side window when the car rolled. Nothing major. "He'll be all right."

Despite her obvious pain, she smiled. "Thank the Mother."

After assessing her quickly, Donal gripped the sharp branch that'd come through the shattered windshield and penetrated her shoulder. "This is going to hurt, Tina. Don't move, please."

Smoothly, quickly, he pulled the branch out.

She gave a short, cut-off scream. Her hands clenched in fists.

Bending his head, Donal covered the wound with his hand and healed the severed blood vessels before she bled to death. An incredible amount of damage there. Carefully, he positioned her so he could repair her splintered collarbone. And the muscles around it.

Good enough for now.

Next patient...

As he determinedly worked through the bleeding wounds and the broken bones, energy poured out of him. By the Gods, he hated human-made machines. Especially cars.

Demon boxes on wheels.

He started on the driver of the sedan.

"Where's the banfasa?" Kevin Murphy asked as he helped pull the male's arm straight so the bone could be repaired.

"Helping set up the festival area."

"A shame. We sure could use her here."

At the sedan, Cody Murphy and Alec tried to calm the passenger so they could maneuver him off the floor. "

Kevin snorted. "Alec should just punch the idiot and knock him out."

"He already has a concussion." As Donal spoke, his eyesight blurred. Gods blast it, just one more second. He managed a last blast of power that knitted the male's arm. Mostly.

Then he fell back against the side of the sedan.

"*Healer.*"

His head buzzed like he'd upset a beehive inside his skull. His words came out slurred. "Splint the break. It's only partially healed."

"Donal. You look terrible." Farrah knelt and hugged him from behind in the way he'd taught her when she shared power with him before.

"Thank you for coming." He put his hand over her arms and drew...nothing. No power moved.

Surprised, he tried harder and received merely a trickle. There was power in her, but the bond between them felt like a string rather than a rope.

Two months wasn't that long. He often pulled power from females he'd mated even three Gatherings prior. He'd never had a problem before.

Farrah held him patiently. "Bonnie said to tell you Nia and Francesca aren't in town."

Gnome-nuts. They'd probably gone to set up the festival area like Margery.

Out of power and out of options. He set his jaw. "I understand. I'm afraid this will take longer than before."

It did. Pulling power from her was like using a rusty pump to get a cup of water rather than standing downstream in a surging river.

Eventually, he had enough to continue.

Barely enough.

Horror unfurled in his guts.

If someone had been critically injured, they'd have died.

Pulling himself together, he patted Farrah's hand. "Thank you, sweetheart. I appreciate the help."

"Sure." She kissed his cheek. Keeping her gaze away from the injured and the blood, she scrambled away and up the hill.

Rising, Donal waited a second for his head to stop spinning, then went back to work.

CHAPTER TWENTY-THREE

*U*nclaimed territory, Washington - one day before the full moon

Early Sunday afternoon, there was activity and noise everywhere.

Last fall, as a Scythe shifter-soldier, Patrin MacCormac and his brother had been confined in a barracks in an isolated compound and only allowed off-base long enough to assassinate someone. A hellish life, it had been. Their sister held hostage for their good behavior, trackers embedded in their bodies. Trapped.

Who could have imagined their sister, Darcy, would be the one to pull together the forces that had attacked the Scythe compounds? Fuck, but he was proud of her.

Now, he and Fell were free. Well, almost free. There *was*

the small matter of eradicating the organization called the Scythe.

That...might take a bit of a while.

Over the course of the day, the festival grounds had filled with shifters. Old friends from different territories were exuberantly meeting again. New friends were being made. Under the waxing moon's influence, hopeful males postured to win females.

Near the firepits, the bards were taking turns playing instruments and singing.

After dropping off food at the footpath, shifters parked elsewhere and came through the forest. Delighted to be the first to sniff out good eats, cubs were carrying the food from the road to the festival grounds.

So many people. So much movement. This shit was fucking overwhelming.

Fell hated it; Patrin loved it.

With Fell behind him, Patrin strolled into the largest tent on the festival grounds. They were early for the meeting, but life had taught him that a wise wolf surveys the terrain before calling the pack.

Filled with rows of folding tables and chairs, the tent space was almost empty. At one side of the tent, a space was open for entertainers or speakers. Being a good littermate, he chose a corner table at the other side so Fell would feel comfortable.

The light dimmed as a cahir blocked the entrance, positioned to check whoever entered the tent.

Fell studied the huge male. "Damn. Bet he's a grizzly."

"Glad he's on our side."

Shifters filtered into the tent. Pack leaders arrived. Cahirs took up an area on the left side of the tent. Owen, one of their sister's mates, was there, and gave Patrin and Fell a nod.

"Darcy chose well," Fell muttered. "Good male."

"Aye, he is. So's Gawain. Not that we'll ever admit that to Darcy." Doing so would flout the *tease-your-sister* tradition. *Can't have that.*

Fell grinned.

Patrin leaned back, stretching his legs out. He rather envied Darcy for her new life. Rewarding work. Belonging. And she'd found mates to love.

Someday...

It was a shame Darcy's friend, Margery, was already involved with the healer and cop. Such a sweetheart—and she was from Dogwood. Understood what they'd all been through. Would understand the dark places in a soldier's soul.

"Patrin, Fell." The greeting came from a group of their fellow soldiers. More and more entered the tent. With grins, comedic insults, shoulder buffets, the shifter-soldiers settled at tables and chairs around Patrin and Fell.

By the Gods, it's good to see them again.

All the shifter-soldiers in the area had come to the festival in answer to the summons from Wells.

Since the Scythe were eager to capture more Daonain—

especially those who'd escaped them, Wells was wise to arrange a meeting far away from shifter towns. This remote festival was a perfect location.

Near the open space for speakers, the Cosantirs settled in a cluster of tables. Calum, the North Cascades Cosantir was there, seated with Alec, and their mate, Vicki. Patrin had come to respect the small brunette female who'd served in the human military and as a spy before being turned Daonain.

Wells sat with Calum. Older, medium height, lean as a wolf after a hard winter, he had the eyes the color of ice and a mind more calculating than any feline. The human spymaster had been Vicki's boss when she was human and was now the *caomhnor* of one of her cubs.

Wells wanted to destroy the Scythe almost as much as the shifter-soldiers did, and since the Scythe were human, the Daonain had let him take the lead.

When the spymaster rose, everyone went silent.

Wells didn't bother with pleasantries or welcomes. "When the Scythe Seattle compounds were destroyed, the Director and the Colonel escaped."

Patrin scowled at the reminder. That night, the Director had been called from his supper to meet the Colonel in downtown Seattle—and missed being trapped and killed in the compound by only a few minutes.

Wells continued. "Thanks to the shifter-soldiers' effectiveness as assassins, the Colonel has a lot power. He was— and has been—careful that no one outside his Pacific

Northwest division learned that his assassins were anything other than skilled humans."

"Secrets have a way of coming out," someone said.

"Yes," Wells agreed. "The Colonel's reputation suffered when the compounds were destroyed and the hostages released. He's now scrambling to regain his influence."

"What does that mean for the Daonain?" Patrin asked.

Wells gave him a nod. "First, the Director and Colonel have prioritized capturing shifters. Your territories, especially in the Pacific Northwest, already know this."

The Cosantirs were nodding.

"Second. Because the information about you hasn't been shared, if we can eliminate the Colonel's division, a major danger to you would be gone."

The Cosantir from Colville Territory frowned. "They're manipulating your human government, breaking *your* laws. Why haven't you eliminated them already?"

Wells' mouth flattened. "I would if I could find them. Because of the risk to the Daonain, I haven't called on my own resources to locate them. But, gentlemen, I can't justify that for much longer."

"You need help," Alec said from where he sat.

"Exactly. I have leads. I need trained help to pursue them."

Patrin eyed the spymaster. The human had proven his worth during the battle in Seattle. He was a canny fighter with a catlike talent for sneakiness.

Patrin glanced at Fell.

Gaze dark, Fell nodded. Even more than Patrin, Fell craved vengeance. Neither of them could move on with life until the danger to the Daonain was eliminated.

And they were experts at elimination.

"We're in," Patrin called.

A few of the cahirs added their voices. Almost all the shifter-soldiers did.

Patrin noticed one who was silent.

After meeting Patrin's gaze, Oliver looked down. Physical strength, fighting and warfare skills—the werebear lacked them all. He wasn't stupid. He just had more of a prey than predator personality. From the way his shoulders curved inward, he hated that about himself.

Guilt was a stupid emotion.

Patrin slid his chair over. "Oliver, we've had this talk before. You're not a fighter. You won't be useful for this kind of hunt, but there are other things you can do to help. Even when the Scythe are dead, the Daonain won't be safe in this technological human-ruled world. If you want to defend our people, learn that technology. Fight with your mind. That's where your strengths are and where you will have victory."

Without waiting for a response, Patrin slid back to the table.

Fell nodded his approval.

The two of them had been the leaders of the shifter-soldiers, and although no longer in charge, it was difficult to let go of the responsibility.

Oliver was smart. Creative. He simply needed to use those talents to make a new life for himself.

Sympathy was an edgy weight in Patrin's heart because starting over was easier with a littermate at one's side. And Oliver had lost his.

Patrin bumped his shoulder against Fell's. If Patrin ever faltered, his brother would be there. Together, they could face anything.

And when the Scythe were gone, if they were still alive, they'd see where the wind would take them.

Having left his vehicle at a trailhead parking area, Donal loped through the silver fir forest, heading for the festival grounds. The mid-afternoon sun was bright, the air warm and dry with the dusty tang of evergreens. Fir needles were soft underpaw.

Yet he couldn't really enjoy the day—not with last night preying on his mind.

Aye, maybe it shouldn't bother him so much. He might have more power than most healers, but it could still run out. Like last night.

That had been far too close.

All the remainder of the night, he'd stewed over the difficulty in drawing power from Farrah. She'd shared her energy with him before. It hadn't been that long since he'd mated with her. The only thing that had changed was the bond between them.

Aye, when he thought about it, the bond between him and the females with whom he'd mated had narrowed. All except for one female—Margery.

His feelings for her were impacting the bonds he had with other females. The knowledge was a swamp of unhappiness within him.

Because if he couldn't recharge, shifters would die. He'd fail them.

By the Gods, he wouldn't let that happen. He couldn't.

He needed to back away from Margery. Create some distance so he wouldn't lose those connections.

At the Gathering tomorrow night, he'd mate with as many Cold Creek females as possible. No matter how unhappy it made someone else...or him. He had enough control over his dick to get it to rise.

Reaching the festival grounds, he slid into the storage tent from the back and trawsfurred to human. After sniffing out his and Tynan's pack, he dressed in jeans and a flannel shirt.

Outside, the scattering of large tents on the north and south edges created a token street. There was a dining tent. A sleeping tent for the elderly and cubs in case of rain. An entertainment tent. A smaller healing tent.

"Hey, healer."

At the rough-sounding voice, Donal turned and spotted Owen inside the crafts tent where artists could display their wares. The brown-haired cahir hadn't bothered to shave, and dark scruff shadowed his jawline. He was seated on a blanket with his carvings arranged on another blanket.

Donal studied the wood sculptures: A wolf led a small pack. A panther perched on a limb above a rabbit. There was a female wolf with her head tilted, paw raised.

She looked almost like Margery. And wouldn't that carving be perfect for the shelf in his bedroom? "You do good work."

"Thanks." The cahir gave Donal a half-smile. "It's good you weren't here earlier. The females were lapping up alcohol-laden hot chocolate last night—and some hadn't realized the after-effects of drinking."

Shifters didn't suffer hangovers as badly as humans did, but since most Daonain weren't used to feeling ill at all, the first few times could be a shock. "Good to know."

Owen snorted. "When Angie dropped some cast iron pots this morning, Bree let out a sound... I haven't heard screeching like that since a werecat caught her tail in a forked branch."

Donal winced. Tails were almost as sensitive as testicles. "Thanks for the warning."

"Margery's pretty much recovered." Owen nodded toward the right.

Donal followed his gaze and spotted Margery talking with Darcy near the back of the tent. Gawain, a blademage, was showing her a bracelet he'd made.

A *lifemating* bracelet.

Fucking, sprite-cursed irony. Donal could feel the blood draining from his face.

Owen gripped his arm. "Is something wrong?"

"No." Donal shook his head. "Nothing."

He stiffened his spine. It had to be done. Letting their female—*no, not theirs, she couldn't be theirs*—letting Margery get her hopes up wouldn't be right. Would be cruel. "See you later, cahir."

Everything in him wanted to pretend it was all going to be all right.

No. He was an honorable male—*act like it, cat.*

He walked across the tent. "Margery."

"Donal, you're here!" Face lighting, she wrapped her arms around him and hugged.

Unable to help himself, he bent his head and took her lips in a warm kiss. By the Gods, he'd missed her, last night at the accident, in his lonely bed, at his silent breakfast. Her laugh, her scent, her joy, the peace that pooled around her— she was buried in his heart so deeply he'd never be able to remove her.

Maybe it would be all right. Even if he couldn't lifemate her, he could still love her. Maybe love her a little less. That would work, wouldn't it?

Would she see it that way?

Dread made his bones feel as if they'd shatter at a blow.

"Are you feeling all right, Donal?" She stepped back, holding his hands between hers.

"Sweetling, we need to talk." He squeezed her fingers and led the way out of the tent.

A hemlock and Douglas fir grove at the tree line provided shade from the afternoon sun.

Finding a flat piece of ground, she sat down beside him and waited. The light teased red glints from her rich brown hair. Her nose and cheeks were pink from sunburn.

After a second, as peace seeped into him, he realized she'd taken his hand again. He could feel how much she loved him.

The knowledge might break him into pieces.

"Can you tell me what's wrong?" she asked softly.

"There was a two-car accident last night..." He went through the injuries. The whole mess.

"Oh, Donal, did one of them die?" Her hand tightened on his.

His unhappiness had led her to believe he'd lost someone.

In a way, he had. He might lose *her*.

"No, but it was far too close. You know I get power from females I've mated with—which is why I mate a number of females at every Gathering."

She nodded briskly. "Right."

Then she realized exactly what he was saying. Her expression went blank in a way he hadn't seen in a while—because it was a defense she used when she was afraid.

He grimly continued, setting it out for her. Eliminating his own happiness. "There are times I need power from more than one female. When there are multiple injuries, if I can't get enough power, then shifters will die."

She swallowed. "You saw me talking to Gawain."

"Yes."

"Lifemates don't attend Gatherings because they mate only with each other. If you lifemated, you'd have only one female for your source."

Unable to speak, he nodded.

The pain growing in her eyes was echoed by the pain in his heart. The bond between them—and it was there—felt as if it was being pierced by sharp fangs.

"What the fuck is going on?" Tynan's voice was the harshest growl Donal had ever heard.

Pressing a hand to the ache in his chest that had drawn him to this spot, Tynan looked at his brother and saw only misery. He turned to their female and saw the same expression in her face.

"What's happened, little wolf?" Going down on a knee, he reached for her hands. The soft little hands that had been all over his body last night even as she'd giggled and told him they were *ummming*. Drunken ummming, no less.

He'd never laughed so hard during a mating before.

Now, she looked as if someone had gutted her. Instead of taking his hand, she rose and backed away. From him. Tears filled her eyes. "To see you two with others... I don't think I can handle that."

"Handle what?" Rising, Tynan saw her gaze was on Donal. "Donal?"

"I had to explain." Donal stared at the ground.

"Explain what?" By Herne's hairy hocks, someone had better—

"I...I need to think." And Meggie fled as if a grizzly was on her heels.

Tynan turned to his littermate. "What did you say to her?"

The way Donal rubbed his cheek with his palm said he was equally distressed. He pushed to his feet to look at Tynan. "We had a two-car accident last night. The cars skidded off the road and down a steep ridge. Multiple breaks, lacerations, internal injuries. I ran out of power, brawd."

Tynan winced, a sick feeling in his gut. Donal worried about losing his patients. Tynan worried about losing his littermate. Last time that'd happened, Donal had almost joined the dead.

"Besides Margery, I only mated two females last Gathering. Neither of them were available—they're here." A muscle jumped in Donal's cheek. "I got help from a female I'd mated two Gatherings ago. But drawing power from her was like pulling a tooth. It didn't flow. I only got drops instead of a lake."

"Because it'd been too long since you'd mated her?"

"I don't think so." Donal's mouth compressed. "I think

my...feelings...for Margery are affecting the bonds to other females. I'm getting too attached."

Wait, wait. Tynan stiffened and asked again, "What did you say to Meggie?"

"I told her about the accident and lack of power." Donal pulled in a breath. "And I explained I couldn't lifemate anyone. Her. Ever."

What the fuck?

Anger was a sharp blade severing the control of his temper. "You made a decision that affects both of us without talking to me first? Without any discussion or having me present?" The memory of her face, of the tears in her eyes stabbed into his heart. "We found a female we both love, and you tossed her away?"

"Tynan, I... Yeah."

Tynan growled as the ache in his chest grew, filling his world with pain, with despair. He looked up, thinking the sun had gone behind a cloud. But the sky was clear, the air clear. But his world had gone dark.

Gone, all the hopes he'd nourished, the future he'd wanted.

He pulled in a breath.

His brother's silvery eyes were dark. Haunted. His face strained, his black flannel shirt wrinkled. Donal was hurting.

Good.

Tynan swung and punched Donal right in the jaw.

Donal landed on his ass on the stubbly forest grass. "What the *fuck*."

"No, fuck *you*," Tynan growled.

Face darkening, Donal rolled up and dove forward. His shoulder hit Tynan's gut, knocking him back.

And then they fought.

Donal's moves were feline quick. Growling, Tynan moved faster. Hit harder.

His future was gone.

They were fighting. About her.

Having heard the shouting, Margery had turned in time to see ever-so-controlled Tynan hit his brother. Other shifters were watching but not interfering. Letting the males fight.

Fight.

Watching them, she pressed her hand to her mouth to silence the protests, the screams.

To keep from crying.

They were as close as any littermates she'd ever seen, and they'd been through so much already. Separated for a decade. They'd each said how much it meant to be back together.

Now they fought—because of her. Not from anything she'd done, but simply because she was here.

Donal would never lifemate anyone.

Funny how she'd only now realized how much she wanted that dream.

Could she ignore her hopes and settle for less? Not all shifters lifemated. Some never formed a bond. Some didn't want such a demanding type of love. Didn't want to know they'd be with those mates until death and beyond.

Because a lifemating was forever.

Leaning against a tree, she felt the strength of the trunk, rooted deeply, lifting its branches high into the air. Surviving blizzards and drought, fire and freezes.

But trees stood alone.

She loved them, Donal and Tynan. If she stayed, she might still be with them, together, like they had been over the past month. Not alone.

But with every full moon, she'd attend the Gathering and have to watch them mate with other females.

Gatherings were sacred. No jealousy, no territorial displays were allowed. She'd be expected to mate with other males. Although, if she had no interest, it wouldn't happen.

Could she handle seeing Tynan's lips on another female? Seeing Donal take someone's hand and lead her upstairs.

How long before she broke and hit someone in a Gathering. Or even caused more fights between the males?

Eyes blurred with tears, she saw Tynan knock Donal to the ground. They were bleeding. Both of them.

And she ran.

Halfway across the festival grounds, she heard Angie

yell, "Margery!" She slowed and reluctantly headed for the firepit where Angie was grilling various meats.

"Yes, Angie?"

Her boss gave her a careful perusal. "Are you—" She halted when Margery shook her head. She held up a folded-over paper. "All right then, your brother asked me to give this to you."

"Oliver?" Frowning, Margery took it, opened it.

Margery,

Wells had a meeting with the Cosantirs, cahirs, and shifter-soldiers. He asked for help in hunting the Scythe. Patrin and Fell, hell almost all the shifter-soldiers volunteered to help.

I can't.

I'm a shit soldier, and I can't go back to that."

Margery closed her eyes at the horror of what she was reading. Asking Oliver to be a soldier, to fight again. No, that was so wrong. Once again, he'd been left feeling inadequate.

She kept reading.

I'm going to leave. Get out of here, out of the States. Go to Canada.

I'm sorry I'm messing up your plans for us living together, but I can't stay here.

I love you, sis,

Oliver

He was leaving? The bond that connected them pulsed with her hurt.

Angie's hand closed over her arm. "Margery, what's wrong?"

"Oliver. He's leaving." She looked around frantically, then down at the note. "No, he's already left."

Everything—everything was breaking around her. Eyes filling with tears, she shoved the note into Angie's hands and walked away.

On his knees, Donal swayed as he raised his fist for another punch. It didn't happen. The strength in his muscles had drained into the ground.

Tynan was trying to stand. With a low growl, the stubborn wolf pushed to his feet, staggered a few steps, then straightened. A bruise reddened one cheek; his lower lip was bleeding, and one eye was swollen.

Herne's horns, he'd given his littermate a black eye? What the fuck was wrong with him? With Tynan? They weren't new shifters with no control over their tempers.

But they were shifters in love with a female.

Tynan's cop-face was unreadable, but the pain in his eyes couldn't be hidden.

I put that there. Donal bowed his head. If Tynan wanted to kick him in the head, he wouldn't block the blow. Guilt piled onto the grief of losing Margery until the combined weight threatened to crush him. "I'm sorry, brawd."

"Yeah, me, too."

His littermate's hand appeared in Donal's field of vision. Grabbing it, he let Tynan pull him to his feet.

And hold him up until his head stopped spinning.

With a sigh, he shook his head. Yeah, that hurt, too. "Want me to leave?"

"No, let's talk." Tynan shot him an unhappy look. "Something we should have done first."

"I know. I was wrong." Donal touched his throbbing cheekbone gingerly, feeling the warm liquid on his fingertips. Blood. The gash didn't hurt nearly as much as the pain under his sternum. "I was afraid to wait—I wasn't sure I'd have the courage to tell her."

People on the grounds glanced at them, detoured away from them, but didn't interfere. Merely one more fight in the hot-tempered shifter world.

"Let's clean up." The sound of a babbling creek drew Donal toward it.

Near the water, the air was cool and moist under a canopy of the alders and willows. Farther upstream, cublings were trying to catch minnows in the clear stream.

Going down on one knee, Tynan splashed water over his face and hands. Head tilted, he listened to the laughter, then sighed. "I wanted a mate...and to raise cubs if the Mother so gifted us."

Wanted. Past tense.

Tynan rarely asked for anything for himself. He gave and gave. To Donal, to the wolves, to the Daonain. To the God. Ten years in a human city.

Of course, now he was home, he would want to have a family. To find a mate to share with Donal.

And they had.

They *had*.

Donal rinsed the blood from his cheek.

"You told Meggie you wouldn't lifemate her," Tynan said slowly. "That we wouldn't. Can you explain this to me?"

"I mate with multiple females to have enough power for emergencies. I told you this before." Donal sank down onto the ground, his back against a tree trunk.

"Aye." Tynan frowned. "But I didn't realize if we found a female to love that you'd reject her."

Cat-scat. "One...one isn't enough, brawd." Donal scowled. How could he explain this? "You know how Mother never lifemated but had numerous matings at every full moon. To ensure she had shifters available to give her power."

"Yeah." Tynan paced across the tiny space between the trees. "Go on."

"You were in Ireland when she reached the change of life, and her tie to the moon was broken. No longer fertile, she attended no Gatherings. No one wanted to mate her."

She hadn't been a likable female. "Without a full moon heat, she wasn't interested either."

"Not surprising." Tynan sank down onto his haunches. "How'd she acquire extra power?"

"She didn't." Donal ran his finger through the dry dirt under the tree. It had rained days before. Under the dry top layer was the one filled with moisture and life.

He continued, "After you left, I spent time with the Visser littermates. Three years older, remember? Roel is crazy, but Senne was quiet. Kind. I was lonely, and he let me tag along with them." Red hair, freckles, gentle blue eyes. A balance for his frantic littermate.

The werebear had taught Donal how to raid beehives.

With a sigh, Tynan settled on the ground, his back against a tree. "*Was* quiet. What happened to him?"

"A cliff crumbled out from under a bunch of young shifters. I was healing then but didn't have any reserve. No matings yet." Males started attending Gatherings when younger than their female agemates, but he'd not reached that point then.

"I healed Roel and another one, then was out of energy. Mother was the same, depleted before she got to Senne. With no one to give her more power, she couldn't save him."

Kind, quiet Senne had died. Because the healers ran out of power.

The guilt had never left.

Donal's throat was dry as the dirt under his fingers.

471

"Letting our people down...I can't do it. Even if it means the rest of my life gets fucked up."

"I know all about that kind of reasoning." Tynan gave him a wry smile. "It's hard on the people who love you."

Gnome-nuts. Donal rose and sat back down beside Tynan. For the ten long years Tynan was in Seattle, Donal had missed him with an unending ache. All too often, he'd yelled at the wolf for his idiotic guilt that drove him to serve the God. For damaging both their lives."

Now Donal had smashed Tynan's hope and dreams.

For guilt.

Donal's shoulder rubbed against Tynan's. Here was warmth. The rightness of the brother-bond. "How do I make this right for you, brawd? Without power..."

"If a healer doesn't have enough power, some shifters will die." Tynan's voice was dispassionate. Level. "You have more power than Mother ever did. Why is that?"

Donal blinked as the question went a different direction than his well-reasoned, too-familiar arguments. "No one knows why healers have different levels of power. It's not because of size or gender. I always thought it was partly from how much a healer cares."

"I heard Mother had a lot of power when she was younger."

"So she said. Maybe storage diminishes with age." Donal frowned, thinking of his apprenticeship. Master Quany had been ancient—and immensely powerful.

"Doubtful. I met healers in Ireland whose powers

remained the same or grew as they aged. Most were lifemated."

"Lifemated?" Had he ever met lifemated healers? After Mother grew too irritable to teach, Donal had apprenticed with Master Quany. The old male hadn't been mated. When traveling, Donal had met a few healers in passing, but hadn't bothered to ask if they were mated or not.

Still... "Lifemating means only one person provides additional energy."

"Aye, that's what it means." Tynan studied Donal. "Let's play with numbers. As she grew older, our mother possessed little energy of her own, had no lovers to supply more, and she died younger than most Daonain. Probably because she felt useless and unloved."

The thought of being so reduced as a healer and as a shifter was painful. Donal could understand why she'd simply let herself die. "Go on."

"The two Irish healers in my village were over a hundred. Strong and stable in power. Lifemated and able to draw on their mate."

Where was he going with this?

Tynan nudged his shoulder. "I assume the lifemated healers might lose some patients in a disaster since they have only their bonded mates to call on. But, Donal, how many were lost because our mother had no one, died early, and left no healer in the village at all?"

Donal pulled in a breath. "That's a different way of looking at it."

Hope sparked to life inside him.

Tynan's voice softened. "The Irish healers were happy, Donal. Beloved by the town and their lifemates and their cubs."

Their cubs. He'd always wanted cubs. A mate to share with Tynan. The idea of such a gift was...impossible.

"I'm not giving her up—or you, either." Tynan rose. "Think about it."

The water was cold on her paws as Margery splashed through the stream toward the black bear on the other bank.

Oliver.

She gave a yip to tell him it was her and saw him freeze.

After slowing to lap up some water, she scrambled up to join him on the soft grass.

What a mess. With every step farther from Donal and Tynan, she felt her chest hurt more. Like it or not, there were bonds between them, and oh, the ties ached like a badger was chewing on them. Leaving everything unresolved was tearing her to pieces.

Then there was Oliver...

She'd been following his scent for an hour or so, grateful that as a bear he tended to move far more slowly than a wolf.

With a sigh, she shifted, pulled off the bag she wore tied

to her neck and stomach, and pulled out the ultra-thin clothing. The bag was the same color as her chest and belly fur, the straps thin enough to be hidden beneath her thick ruff. She pulled on bike shorts that held her money and ID in the pocket, an elastic tank top, special slippers that compressed with hard enough soles to finish a hike. Such very light-weight clothing—the humans were good at the oddest things.

Once dressed, she straightened and gave her silent littermate a frown. "A note? Seriously?"

His face crumbled. "I'm sorry."

"Oh, Oliver." She put her arms around him, feeling the tremors in his body, hearing his breathing shudder with unspent tears.

"I'm sorry, sis," he whispered. "I couldn't face you."

By the Gods, how many times would the Scythe destroy his life? "Well, you're stuck now."

She pushed him back far enough that she could look at him. "Bro, I only wanted a chance to say goodbye."

"You don't think I'm a coward?"

"Not hardly." She shook her head. "Patrin and Fell are intent on getting revenge. That's not your way. Not how we were raised. But why Canada?"

"The Scythe are mostly US-based." He hesitated. "And last night, a Canadian told me their town has a counselor— a shepherd. He said talking through things might help me move on."

She blinked. "How did he know…"

"Know I was having trouble?" Oliver averted his gaze. "I was...drinking. Drunk. And he and his littermate, I guess they were worried. We talked."

Bless the Canadians. "You found a destination and a goal." Her muscles loosened as her worries eased.

"Yeah." He glanced at her. "Want to come with me?"

Surprised, she sat down on the bank.

He joined her...but not shoulder-to-shoulder like a wolf or a cat would. Not as touchy-feely, bears were often more solitary, but Oliver took it to a whole new level.

"Bro, I can't leave. I have a job, friends." Tynan and Donal...only, she didn't have them, did she? They weren't hers, would never be hers.

All the way on the trail, she'd gone over and over what she should do.

Because, even if Donal didn't—couldn't—love her, she had a feeling Tynan might not agree. The fight showed that. Only, as a banfasa, she knew exactly how Donal must feel.

How could he risk his patients' lives?

So, she'd back away from them if that's what it took. And she absolutely wouldn't come between the brothers. She wouldn't let their feelings toward her turn their love for each other into something ugly. Even if the thought of not having them in her life scorched through her like the worst of burns.

"You could work in Canada," Oliver said after a moment.

She leaned over to give his shoulder an affectionate shove. "Stubborn bear."

By the Gods, she was going to miss him.

As a cloud cut off the warmth of the sun, she brought up her knees and wrapped her arms around them. "I'm a wolf. And a social sort of person. I need companions, touch, a pack. You don't. What are you planning to do when you get to Canada?"

"Uh." He shrugged. "Hang out in the forest. Enjoy the quiet. The mountains."

"With me beside you all the time?"

His appalled expression was her answer. And his. "That...wouldn't be good for you, would it?"

Her brother did have a good heart. He'd simply lost his trail and needed to find it again. But it wouldn't be with her.

Tears burned her eyes. First, Donal's rejection. Now, having to watch her littermate head north.

"No. I love being a banfasa—I have a gift for it—and the Mother of All expects me to use my skills and talent. Oliver, you get unhappy when you're stuck around too many people, and I get the same way if I'm alone too long."

He scrubbed his hands over his face. "Are you going to be all right in Cold Creek? Guess you'll probably end up lifemating Donal and Tynan?" The concern was obvious in his voice.

The question was like being stabbed through the heart. "Eh, who knows the future? I love them, though." That answer she could give without any hedging. "And I love Cold Creek—the people, the town."

"Okay. Guess that'll do."

It would have to. She pulled in a breath. "I'll miss you."

"Yeah. I'll miss y—" He stopped abruptly, and his nose lifted. He sniffed.

All the color drained from his face.

Before she could speak, he scrambled up the nearest tree. With his dark green shirt and brown shorts, he disappeared into the canopy.

A sniff of the air brought her nothing much. Perhaps a faint hint of something nonorganic. As a bear, Oliver's nose was better than hers. What had he smelled?

Unable to sit, she paced until he dropped down. "What is it?"

His voice was low, almost panicked. "Humans—a whole fuckload of them. Armed and wearing camo."

Her breathing stopped. "No."

"They have to be Scythe, sis." Oliver pulled in a breath. "They're moving in a line. Toward us."

"Oh Gods, they must have found out about the festival." So many Daonain, all in one place.

"Yeah." Oliver pointed east. "They probably used a back road, then hiking trails for this bunch. Bet they'll send another attack up the main road—and time it so they all arrive together. Envelop the festival from two sides."

Margery yanked off her clothes, jamming them into the bag. "We have to warn everyone."

"*No*. If we go back, we can't escape before they attack."

The stench of his fear woke her own terrors. Revived her memories of that night they attacked Dogwood. *Killing and killing. Shoving children into trucks. Blood everywhere. Screams. Fires.* Chills ran up her arms as she fought against her churning stomach.

"We must warn them." She forced the words out, trying to convince herself. "There are cubs. Young ones. Mothers."

Young Athol who'd just learned to shift. Vicki's Sorcha, Artair, and Toren. Emma's adorable Minette. Bonnie's feisty cubs.

No, she would never let the Scythe have them, no matter what it took. "I'm going back."

She secured the bag to her chest, trawsfurred—and hesitated.

Despite the fear in his eyes, Oliver nodded. "We'll warn them together."

Brother at her side, Margery tore through the forest as the sun edged toward the west.

The forest creek to the west of the festival grounds had turned into a cub play area. And Heather had managed to steal Sorcha away from her mama. Smiling, she flicked droplets of the icy water onto her favorite cubling's bare legs.

Around seven months now, the little girl squealed her laughter, hands waving and feet kicking.

A quiet chuckle came from the intimidating human standing beside Heather—something rarely heard from Wells. Sorcha's littermate, Artair, was fast asleep against the spymaster's shoulder.

On Heather's other side, Joe Thorson held his namesake, Toren, between his legs. Sitting proudly, the cub beat on the grass with a wooden rattle, then waved it at the tree fairies swinging from the nearby branches.

Pixies adored cubs, no matter the species.

A cool breeze off the mountains made Heather shiver. "Well, my sweet lass, I think it's time you put on some clothing." Dressing the kit in a dark green romper, she blew a noisy raspberry on the little round tummy before doing up the snaps.

Sorcha had the greatest laugh.

As Heather lifted her for more kisses, love filled her heart. *Thank you, Vicki, for sharing with me.* Even if it made the lack of her own pups so much harder.

Maybe, someday, the Great Mother would bless her.

Thorson said in his raspy voice, "Toren, time to leave."

Hearing his name, Toren clapped his hands—his newest skill—and gurgled happily.

The sun was hovering over the treetops as if reluctant to leave. Summer Solstice was tomorrow—the longest day in the year—and sunset wasn't until a smidge after nine pm.

Heather nodded at Thorson. "The Cosantirs' meeting should be done soon."

Heather grinned, thinking of when Vicki'd been told about the plans for today. "*Another fucking meeting? For fuck's sake, Calum.*"

Her poor friend had wanted to spend the day outside. Instead, she'd been stuck in a meeting with Wells and the shifter-soldiers. And now, the various Cosantirs, their mates, and their cahirs were using the meeting tent. Calum was there as well as Pete from Rainier Territory. There were Cosantirs from Gifford to the south, Colville to the east, and Garibaldi over the border in Canada. It wasn't often the guardians left their territories, so they'd welcomed the chance to discuss common problems—the increasing human threat, the Scythe's attempts to find them, human laws that might affect them. New ways of evasion. Technology and precautions.

Ryder who had mad skills with computers had been drafted to speak with them.

Heather knew the Daonain must become more tech savvy. Being the CEO of a software company, she had a head start, but she'd always been an outlier when it came to liking computers. Too many shifters, like her Cosantir, Pete, refused to acknowledge the changes in the world. They believed the Daonain could simply hide in the forests if threatened. Even worse, they used human technology like phones without understanding the dangers.

Such shortsightedness endangered everyone—including

the cubs. A cold shiver ran up her spine, and she held Sorcha closer.

Resettling Artair on his shoulder, Wells did a quick survey of the surrounding forest. The man never let down his guard. Was that because he was in the midst of shifters or because he'd been a spy for too many years?

Eyes narrowing, he tilted his head to hear better.

Heather listened. Even in this form, her ears were better than a human's.

From the north, an animal was approaching at a fast pace. More than one. New shifters playing nip-the-tail?

No, there was a desperate urgency to the sound.

A chocolate-brown wolf shot out of the underbrush and sprang across the creek. The female stopped in front of Wells, hind leg raised slightly.

"Margery?" Heather stared. Her friend's muzzle was covered in froth, her sides heaving with her breathing.

"You're Oliver's sister." Wells' face darkened. "What's wrong?"

Margery shifted and knelt at his feet, gasping for air. "The Scythe. They're coming. Many of them—dark camouflaged clothing, weapons."

A bear charged out between two trees, splashed through the creek, and trawsfurred into a young male. Kneeling beside Margery, the resemblance was plain.

Oliver spat out between breaths, "A long line. Got night-vision goggles. Gear doesn't match—maybe mercenaries.

Coming slow, about two hours out. Probably move on us after dark."

Wells turned his head to the south. "If they're smart, they'll bracket us with an attack from the road."

"Wells, give me Artair." Heather held out her free arm. "Go warn the Cosantirs while they're all together."

Placing the cub into her arms, Wells said, "Oliver, come with me. I'll warn the Cosantirs while you round up the shifter-soldiers. Send Patrin and Fell to the meeting tent."

"Yes, sir." Oliver pushed to his feet, staggered sideways a step, then yanked the mini pack off his back. He pulled out shorts and put them on. "Sis."

Margery's lips quivered as she smiled at him. "Be safe, bro."

"You, too."

Oliver sped after Wells, who'd already headed for the festival grounds.

Thorson turned toward Heather. "We need to send the cubs somewhere safe."

"Yes." Heather's gaze met Margery's, and she saw the same determination there. Time to get moving. Get a head start.

No Scythe soldier was going to get anywhere near the little ones.

Tynan didn't want to be stuck in the fecking Cosantirs' meeting. By the Gods, he needed to go after Meggie, not listen to Ryder talk about computers.

Earlier, Angie had grabbed him and told him about Meggie and her littermate. Had handed him Oliver's note that said he'd headed to Canada.

Meggie had gone after him.

Tynan rubbed his chest, feeling as if she'd had taken a knife and stabbed him.

Before he could grab Donal and follow her, his brother was called to deal with a clawing. Stupid young males.

Then Alec dragged Tynan into the Cosantirs' meeting, saying, "*You're a deputy and a pack beta. You're part of the shield that protects the Daonain.*"

So here he was, listening to the idiot Rainier Cosantir say he had no idea humans could eavesdrop on cell phone conversations or that a human might notice the flyer he'd posted in the grocery store about the festival.

That thick *gobshite* had put a target on his town and on this festival.

Appalled, the others in the meeting—except for Pete's own people—were shouting at the idiot.

Tynan shook his head. While they yelled, he'd go make sure the festival was safe. Instinctively setting a hand on his firearm, Tynan headed for the door. He'd ask Patrin and Fell to post the shifter-soldiers as sentries until something better could—

Blocking the exit, Wells stepped into the tent. "Cosantirs, you're going to be under attack. Probably at dark." The spymaster's loud voice stilled the arguing shifters. "The Scythe are on the way."

Everyone jumped to their feet, yelling.

"Silence." Calum's voice slashed through the noise like claws across a snout.

"Do we have time to get our people out?" one of the Cosantirs asked.

"Doubtful," Wells answered. "The road will be watched —possibly blocked. In animal form, the fastest shifters might escape the approaching line."

Calum motioned Wells forward. "Spymaster, you know our skills, our numbers. Show us what we're up against and make us a plan."

Beside the poster board, Ryder ripped off the paper he'd been using and handed Wells the colored markers.

Using black, Wells drew a circle for the festival grounds, then a double line for the blacktop road to the south. Dashes marked the footpath from the road to the grounds.

"This is where the Scythe were spotted." A line of red Xs crossed the forest to the north. "Their mismatched gear implies we might be facing mercenaries. If the Colonel is keeping this quiet, he won't pull from the normal Scythe resources."

Wells traced his finger from the grounds, around the side of the Xs, and back down. "We can send wolves to attack these soldiers from the rear. Quietly."

Calum pointed to Shay. "Shay, take charge of all the wolf packs. The other alphas will take orders from you."

The Rainier pack leader, Roger, opened his mouth to object.

Calum's eyes were turning dark, the mark of the God, and Roger sat back quickly.

Wells made green Xs behind the northern line of Scythe. "Wolves, get behind them. Don't wait for dark. Night-vision goggles are highly effective, which means the shadowy time before the goggles are useful will be your best choice. With thermal vision, it's difficult to tell friend from foe, so if they're carrying that technology, we'll hope they save it for clean-up."

"If the wolves take out the attackers, everyone at the festival should be fine." Pete's face was pale.

"No, you won't be fine." Wells gave the Rainier Cosantir a look that Tynan recognized from his new shifter days— one that said the elder would be surprised if this idiot could find his way out the forest on a wide trail at high noon. "When capture is the objective, forces attack from all sides to prevent any escape."

"The road," Zeb muttered.

Wells nodded and drew red Xs along the road to the south. "An almost unused road means they can block it without attracting much attention. As soon as it's dark, they'll attack from the road and the north to bracket you."

Tynan frowned. "Won't they try to coordinate in some way?"

"Good question. I have a jammer on the Hummer that'll wipe out any communications tech in the immediate vicinity. I'll set it off before it gets dark." Wells gave him a thin smile.

The spymaster had parked his big Hummer on the shoulder of the road...right at the end of the footpath. He'd left only enough room for one person at a time to get past his vehicle.

The human's paranoia was justified, now wasn't it?

Wells ran his finger along the depiction of the road. "The south roadside is a steep drop to the river. Very little parking—so they might even disembark troops right on the road."

Calum frowned. "We need to get younglings away."

"Yes." Wells motioned to the left and right of the festival grounds. "Take those too old and too young to fight out of here. East and west. Find hiding places that will block thermal scanning."

Ben walked up to the map and tapped the northeast section. "Partway around this rise is an exposed cliff with caves. Good hiding for the least mobile shifters."

Shay rose and pointed to the southwest. "The pack ran that area last night. Looked like it had a landslide a while back. There are uprooted trees, hollowed-out areas, and overhangs. It's rough terrain, and good hiding for agile youngsters and their protectors."

Calum studied the map. "All right, then. Pregnant females, new mothers, anyone who can't move well, and the youngest cubs to the east. Ben, take who you need to get them there along with Donal. Once they're situated, return with the healer. Go now."

"Your will, Cosantir," Ben said.

Calum met Tynan's gaze.

Tynan nodded agreement. Helping hide the females would keep Donal from the first outbreak of fighting and let him return in time to tend the wounded. Unfortunately, he was the only healer here. Not surprising since healers had an intense sense of duty to their own clans and rarely strayed far from their territories.

A thought occurred to Tynan, and he caught Ben's attention. "Griz, while you're getting the females together, have Donal stash medical supplies around the perimeter. Until the battle is over, the healing tent will be a target."

"Fuck," Zeb muttered. Then frowned. "Hide the supplies?"

Tynan couldn't quite manage a smile. "He can mark the locations in the traditional manner—by peeing on the closest bush. Most of us know our healer's scent."

No human would notice.

Grins appeared.

"I'll see it done." Ben headed out the door.

Calum turned back to the map and pointed to the west side. "Owen, you're in charge of the cubs and non-fighters who can scramble over rough terrain. Take who you need to get them there. Put Emma in charge, then return. Go now."

"Your will, Cosantir." Owen strode out the tent door.

Nodding to Wells, Calum stepped away. "Continue, please."

"I could've used you in the military," Wells murmured, then addressed the group. "We want the insides of the tents lit up. I'll set my tablet to play a loud lecture in the dining hall."

"You'll make it look as if we're here. To lure them in." Alec's smile was grim.

"Yes, we'll focus their attention on the tents." Wells ran his finger around the festival grounds circle. "Hide your fighters in the forest, both close-in and farther out. Go high and low."

Vicki studied the map. "Give me a weapon. I'll—"

Two cahirs from out of state spoke at the same time. "The females need to be sent away. All the females."

North Cascades shifters who knew the Cosantir's mate braced, knowing what was coming.

Vicki straightened—and set her feet. Fighting stance. Ice filled her low voice.

"'*When Nag the basking cobra hears the careless foot of man,*

He will sometimes wriggle sideways and avoid it if he can.

But his mate makes no such motion where she camps beside the trail.

For the female of the species is more deadly than the male.'"

She shot Calum a look. "I fight."

Even as Alec sighed, Calum closed his eyes for a second, then nodded.

Every male shifter in the room felt the two mates' pain.

Females were to be guarded. Protected. Not assigned a place in battle.

Yet a person had the right to determine their own fate.

Vicki scowled at them all. "Shifters, it works like this. If the females want to fight, they will. If they fucking wish to join the fucking noncombatants, they will. It's. Not. Your. Fucking. Choice."

The two cahirs stared at her in shock, then—most wisely—nodded. As did the Cosantirs.

"Good." Vicki ran her hand over the road on the map. "Once I'm armed, I'll find a spot on the road to the west and deal with incoming vehicles and disembarking troops. I'll try to direct my fire away from the forest and fighting. Wells?"

"I'll take the road to the east."

She nodded and addressed the shifters again. "When setting up positions, consider the road itself as a kill zone and stay the hell off of it."

As Tynan studied the map for where the wolves would best be useful, an icicle of fear stabbed into his guts.

How long ago had Meggie headed north with Oliver? He'd been grateful she was well out of the fight, but if the Scythe didn't plan to attack until sunset, they could be positioned miles north.

By the Gods, he'd give anything to have her close where he could protect her. Know she was safe.

But at this point, the farther away she was, the better.

Stay safe, little wolf.

CHAPTER TWENTY-FOUR

*U*nclaimed territory - one night before the full moon

On the west side of the meadow, shifters milled around. These were the agile noncombatants, Margery thought, as she helped line up the younglings. Owen's group had the cubs who were too young to shift, but old enough to traverse bad terrain as well as females and elders who weren't up to helping with the fighting.

Emma and Ryder waited in the line, each assigned a batch of children. Minette had a tight grip on Emma's hand. Once they arrived, the bard would take charge of keeping the cubs calm and hidden. Many mothers were remaining to fight.

Oliver joined Margery, a pack with food and water on

his back. After smiling at her, he looked at Owen who stood nearby. "Cahir, I'll go with your group. I'm crap at sneaking around, but effective at fighting from a fixed location. Guarding is where I'll do the most good."

Owen eyed him, then nodded. "I can use you. Bring up the rear and make sure no one falls behind."

With the cahir leading, the line of shifters headed into the forest.

"After you." Oliver motioned to Margery to take up the tail end in front of him.

She shook her head, her heart aching. "I can't. My ankle makes me a liability on rough terrain." She was already limping from the run to warn the shifters. "My place is here where I can help with the injured."

"But..." He scowled, then shook his head. "Arguing with a banfasa never works. Be safe. Please."

"You, too." She hugged him and gave him a push to join the line.

As he followed the others into the woods, she leaned on a tree to figure out where to go next.

On the other side of the grounds, Ben's huge shape in his grizzly form led away the pregnant shifters also in animal form, followed by females carrying the youngest cubs and infants. Heather was there, Sorcha in her arms.

Margery spotted Donal who held Vicki's other cubs. Attention on the footing, he hadn't seen her. The ache in her chest grew.

Donal. Be safe. I love you.

Near the dining tent, the wolves were dividing into three groups. On the left, Shay and Zeb had charge of Cold Creek's pack as well as the Rainier wolves.

On the right, Tynan stood with Warren, a younger male. The wolves from other territories gathered around them.

Patrin and Fell would lead the shifter-soldiers who were wolves. As they all formed up, Patrin was giving hasty instructions on how to pair up and attack a human, much as he'd taught Shay's pack last month.

Gods, she wanted to go with her pack. Or to be with Tynan. She could fight—or at least be the diversion team-mate. But the wolves would be traveling fast to get behind the attackers. And, once again, her damned ankle would slow her down.

No, she was best staying here.

"Let's go." Shay motioned. The leaders trawsfurred, and the three groups of wolves filtered into the forest, heading north.

Be safe, Tynan. I love you.

He hadn't seen her either. He and Donal probably thought she was well on her way to Canada. That was good. They didn't need to be worrying about her right now.

She was worried enough for all three of them. How foolish she'd been to decide she couldn't handle watching them mate with others. Right now, she'd be delighted to see them at a Gathering, no matter who they flirted with. Knowing they were alive would be enough to keep her happy.

Funny how the threat of death rearranged priorities.

"Hey, Margery."

Margery looked around and then up.

Above her head, Darcy perched on a tree branch. The female was naked, ready to shift into her cat form.

Margery puffed out a breath. "Well, isn't this like old times? The Scythe with their guns. Darcy playing cat games in a tree."

Despite the fear in her eyes, Darcy grinned. "And Margery, who lets nothing get her frazzled."

Looking past her friend, Margery saw a whole batch of young werecats up in the trees. From new shifters to older teens. Athol. Jamie. *Gods, no.* She suppressed her protest and asked carefully, "Shouldn't the cubs have left with Owen?"

"He tried to tell them that. I tried. They refused."

Herding teenaged werecats was an impossibility. "I see."

"They want to fight." Darcy thumped her forehead on the tree trunk in frustration. "If I keep them up here in the treeways, they'll be out of the worst of the fighting. I hope. But we need a way to carry big rocks. Ideas?"

Rocks? After a second, Margery got it. Any Scythe underneath a cub's tree would get a concussion. By the time the rock hit, the kit would be in a different tree. "Sure. The craft tent has baskets. The storage tent has small backpacks and mini packs. Give me two kids and I'll load them up with carriers."

Athol and Jamie dropped down in front of her.

"Good, let's go." Glancing back at the younglings in the branches, Margery knew where she'd be fighting.

As Patrin and Fell's shifter-soldiers broke off to reach their designated place in the center of the attack, Tynan stopped his own group. They were well to the north of the Scythe line of soldiers. Before advancing, he needed to get his temporary pack arranged.

After they shifted to human, he had them pair up, pushing for older-younger teams.

His own team-mate was a young male from the Cold Creek pack. Shay had ordered Warren to be Tynan's partner, to give him someone he knew and could trust. Bless the alpha.

Shay and Zeb were leading their pack and the asshole Rainier pack around the Scythe from the west side.

Patrin and Fell would attack the Scythe from the center.

The attack on the eastern third fell to Tynan who'd lead wolves from east Washington, Canada, Montana, Idaho, and Northern California. His group wouldn't be as cohesive as Shay's pack—but since only the toughest wolves traveled far from home, he was pleased with the quality of the wolves he had.

He gave the newly teamed wolves time enough discuss attack methods and signals, then got them sorted into a line.

The sun was behind the mountains now, the lingering rays filtering sideways through the branches. "Twilight is hunting time. Our time," Tynan said to his made-up pack. "Leave none of them alive."

Resolved nods answered him.

Obviously fearful of being spotted, the human mercenaries were avoiding the trails and filtering through the forest in a wide wave.

Shifting to wolves, Tynan's group fanned out and moved forward after them.

With Warren on his right, Tynan padded forward.

Silently covering the ground to the rear of the Scythe line took a while.

As they advanced, Tynan caught sounds from in front of his wolves—the noise of clumsy-footed humans. His fur rose on his back.

From the distant festival grounds, an odd noise drifted through the trees. After a second, he recognized it as cheering and applause. Wells had set off his recording from some conference as a red herring to keep the attackers focused on the tents.

By now, the civilians—no, the *noncombatant* shifters—should be hidden. The werecats and werebears assigned to the perimeter of the festival grounds would be in their ambush locations ready for any mercenaries not caught by the wolves.

Tynan raised his nose to scent what was ahead.

There it was—the metallic stink of weaponry and body armor funk.

Warren sniffed, and his ears went back in disgust.

Invisible in the thick forest undergrowth, the team to Tynan's right caught up to their prey. He heard a soft curse, a thump, and a low growl. Something or someone fell. Scrambling noises. Silence.

Tynan kept moving, Warren off to his side.

Ears flickering forward, paw raised, Warren alerted.

Tynan paused and could make out the form of a Scythe in front of them. A tall bulky male in camo body armor. The mercenary's head was turned to the right. He must have heard the kill.

As Warren moved straight toward the human, Tynan circled to the side.

Closer.

As planned, Warren lunged and savagely bit the back of the human's leg.

With a panicked grunt of pain, the human turned left and swung his rifle toward Warren's head.

Tynan sprang upward from the right. His jaws closed on the throat and clamped down, tearing flesh and cartilage away.

Blood splattered across the brush and ground as the soldier fell. His rifle thudded against a tree trunk. As his boots hammered in the soft dirt, he seized...and died.

A faint whine came from Warren. Shivering and panting, the young male stared at the dead body.

First kill.

Tynan had been about Warren's age when he'd helped his Irish uncles kill a feral shifter. Afterward, he'd puked up probably every meal he'd eaten in the previous few days, then been too shaky to stand.

Knowing the lad would always carry the ugly regret of having taken a life, Tynan padded over, leaned against the other wolf, and licked his nose. Reassuring Warren that he'd done well.

After a minute, Tynan lifted his head. Ears swiveling, he listened. Stealthy movement. The crunch of human boots farther ahead. Time to go.

No whines or whimpers indicated a problem with the rest of his wolves, although no battle went without casualties. Tynan stiffened his resolve. Shifters would die tonight, but if they didn't act, they all would be captured or die. This was the task before him.

Warren shook hard, fur fluffing, then looked at Tynan. Ready for the next.

Good lad.

Tynan led the way forward.

The pregnant females, elderly, and young were safely hidden in the caves. Donal hated to leave them. Every instinct said to protect the most vulnerable of them all.

But the labyrinth of caves could be easily defended by

the two older cat shifters who remained as guards. Breanne, one of the clan's best shooters, would stay, too. Wells had supplied her with three pistols and a wealth of reloads.

The shifters who'd carried cubs here had already started back. Donal had lingered to heal a baby's scraped arm so the pup would stop crying and not give the location away.

Outside the cave entrance, Donal circled to the right, looking for Breanne.

Well concealed, she was located with an excellent field of fire to defend the caves. As he approached, she went white and staggered. Her hand pressed to her chest.

He hurried over and took her hand to assess. No injury. "What's wrong, Bree?"

"Oh Gods, Donal, one of our wolves just died." Her skin was clammy. "I *felt* him die."

The alpha female's pack bonds would tell her if a wolf had returned to the Mother. Fear shot through Donal. No... no, it wasn't Tynan.

His gut unclenched. Their littermate bond was intact; his brother was all right.

But a wolf had died.

"I'm sorry, sweetheart."

She leaned against him, tears glimmering in her eyes. Then her mouth firmed, and she straightened. "Get going, healer. The clan is going to need you."

The sun's rays were dimming. Under the trees, darkness grew, even as the moon rose in the east.

The shifters had started their attack, Herne the Hunter aid them.

How many would die tonight?

"Watch carefully—and stay safe." Donal gave Bree a quick squeeze around the shoulders and shifted to cat form.

Partway back, Donal veered onto a deer trail that paralleled the bigger path between caves and festival grounds. Because there might now be humans hunting them.

Anger burned inside him, hot and hungry.

Over the winter, he'd cared for survivors of the Scythe compounds. Seen the damage, mental and physical.

He'd held Margery after her nightmares. Seen her scars. Watched her limp. No matter how foolish he'd been about healers not lifemating, there was a bond of love between them.

Right now, he was grateful she'd taken off for Canada with Oliver. At least she would be safe. If he and Tynan survived today, they'd go after her. Track her through the forest. Follow her all the way to Canada if need be. He'd beg her forgiveness for being slower than a squashed snail at figuring out the truths between love and duty.

He paused, catching a faint sound. A rhythmic crunch, like what a boot-clad man might make on the thick forest duff.

None of shifters would wear boots today.

The human was on the wider trail and headed toward to the caves. The noise came closer and passed him to his right.

Lowering his body, Donal stole through the undergrowth to that trail and spotted his prey. The dim light was no problem for a werecat. Unfortunately, the human wore odd-shaped goggles—probably night vision enhancement—and was studying a handheld device. Flickers of red showed on the display.

Could he be tracking the elderly and pregnant shifters by the lingering heat in footprints?

Exposing his fangs in fury, Donal stalked forward—and spotted movement in the underbrush left of the soldier.

Moonlight reflected on yellow eyes. A wolf. Red-brown fur with darker saddle and tail. The rare white tip on the tail identified Heather.

Focused on the human, she didn't see Donal. Before he could catch her attention, she leaped at the soldier's throat.

Brave wolf.

The human had fast reflexes. Blood pouring from his neck, he dropped everything and grabbed her fur. Her weight sent him staggering backward.

Donal sprang from behind. His jaws closed on the human's nape to sever the spine. At the gut-wrenching crunch, Donal dropped...the body.

Heather backed away. Shifting to human, she dove into the bushes. Vomiting.

His own stomach unsettled, Donal pulled in calming breaths. He'd be all right. This wasn't his first kill. And death was a familiar companion to a healer.

Clamping his jaws around a boot, he dragged the corpse

behind a thicket of huckleberries. The device followed. Back on the trail, he scuffed up the evergreen needles to hide the signs of combat...although if the humans used heat sensors, his precautions would fail.

Heather returned in wolf form. Ears forward, she bobbed her head in a thank you, then trotted toward the festival grounds.

On the parallel trail, Donal went the same direction.

A minute later, gunfire and screaming broke the silence of the night.

Gods, Gods, Gods, how many had she killed? The taste of blood was like a foul paste in Margery's mouth.

Gunfire and screams echoed off the mountains and tree trunks, seeming to come from everywhere. Her sensitive wolf's ears rang until she felt half-deafened. The acrid stink of gunpowder created nose-wrinkling eddies in the air.

The ugly sounds and scents revived memories of the attack on Dogwood, over and over. Her muscles twitched, wolf instincts ordering her to flee. *Run away! Far, far away.*

She couldn't.

Here, on the east perimeter, she was one of the ground fighters for several treeway cubs. Stationed on branches above, the young shifters followed her, waited until she was positioned near the enemy, and cast their big rocks.

While she attacked from below.

Her nose caught the stink of another, and she sank lower. Saw the human's uniform, weapons. Again, she fought against panic. Again, she won.

The man's camo clothing blended into the foliage and shadows...but foliage didn't move in a straight line. And even when a human tried to be silent, hard-soled boots made noise.

She stalked him. Assessed his equipment—helmet, the goggles that let him see better at night yet hindered his peripheral vision. A rifle.

From where should she attack?

Her stomach twisted. *I'm not a killer.*

But she was now. Deep within, bonds ached where some had been broken. Members of her pack were dead. Grief firmed her resolve, even as her wolf instincts surfaced, and she bared her fangs at the cub-killer.

Because above her, a tree branch creaked under a young shifter's weight. Athol. Hector was in another tree. And Jamie.

The cubs were prepared. This part was hers to do. To keep them safe. Ignoring her fear, the pain in her side, the soul-deep sickness, she moved her tail.

Ready.

A rock hit the soldier's jaw from the side, two more struck his bizarre goggle things.

He grunted—"Fuck!"—and staggered back. His rifle barrel dropped down as he grabbed his face.

Springing upward, Margery ripped his throat open, pushed back, and darted away.

Never stop moving.

The first human she'd attacked had stabbed her. Only her ribcage had kept the knife from finding her heart. The long painful slice along her side still burned. Still bled.

Behind her, the mercenary hit the ground with a thud as he choked on his own blood. The body spasmed, gurgled, and went still.

Panting, sickened, Margery dragged the body off the trail.

Leaving her kill, she moved farther—enough she couldn't scent the blood—and sank beneath a thimbleberry bush. If she'd been human, she'd have been sobbing. *I'm supposed to heal.*

She barely kept from whining.

Slowly, she regained her composure. The cubs would be waiting—and if she didn't do this, they would.

A scent drifted to her. A panther—adult male. No, two of them. Approaching her hiding place.

The brush moved as the two shifters joined her. Owen and Ryder. Owen shifted, edging close enough to whisper into her ear. "Good technique with the cubs but let us take the groundside part now. Go deeper into the bushes and stay safe. There are injured, banfasa. We need you alive to help them."

He stroked a hand down her fur, and she almost whimpered at the sense of companionship.

When she nodded, he shifted back to panther and moved out. As he and Ryder split up, several treeway kits followed each male.

Leaving her alone.

She squirmed deeper into the brush and simply... stopped. Everything stopped. The black haze of exhaustion engulfed her. How long could someone be terrified and sick and angry?

Paws quivering, she lay there, feeling the cold dirt under her belly. Wanting only to be home, to be lying in bed, Tynan's arm over her waist, Donal's shoulder under her head, surrounded by their scents.

Instead, she heard the rustle of clothing. The crunch of conifer cones and needles being crushed underfoot.

Humans on the trail. Two of them.

How could they not smell the stench of blood? Of death?

"Hear that?" one whispered as a rifle fired: *crack, crack, crack*.

The gunfire was distinctive. Heavier. Purposeful.

"Sniper," the other whispered. "Probably on the road to pin down our reinforcements."

"Take him out, and we'll get a bounty."

They moved away, not toward the festival grounds, but southward toward the road.

A sniper? Vicki was guarding the road on this side. In human form so she could shoot.

Margery slid out of the bushes and moved silently after the mercenaries.

They circled to the east of the *crack-crack-crack* noise. They'd be behind where Vicki was aiming.

Fear trickled like icy water into Margery's veins. She had to stop them, but...two armed soldiers. No help to take them down. Not even the diversion of a cubling in a tree. Gods, how could she do this? She was a small wolf, not a panther or bear.

But it was Vicki...

Her memory held up the picture of Vicki cuddling her tiny cubs. Laughing about drunken sex. Standing beside Margery to face Pete.

Margery growled, low and deep. No one was going to kill her friend.

The Scythe had attacked. So many, many of them. Fear iced Heather's veins, even in wolf form. All she wanted to do was flee the area.

On the way to the grounds, she and Donal had attacked and killed two more mercenaries.

The second time hadn't been any easier than the first, and she'd thrown up again.

How could anyone *do* this for a living?

Then they'd come across a wounded werebear. The bear had killed its target, but apparently the human had gotten off a shot first. After she and Donal pulled the bear off the trail, the healer shifted to human and went to work on the appallingly gory bullet hole.

Heather rested a hand on Donal's shoulder and leaned down to whisper, "I'm going to circle this area to make sure there's no Scythe nearby, then join the perimeter guard."

He gave her an assessing look, undoubtedly seeing the blood streaking her skin and face, the bruises from where a fist had caught her. The horror in her eyes at having killed.

How she was barely holding on.

But he simply gave her a half-smile of acknowledgment. They'd do what they had to do.

The werebear was conscious and almost healed. She caught his gaze, then motioned to Donal.

The bear nodded a silent agreement. Once the healer finished, the bear would guard his back. Because bears were exceptionally good at that sort of thing. And healers were precious.

Shifting to wolf, Heather moved out to circle around Donal.

East. Clear.

North. Clear.

West. Clear.

South...not. There was a faint scent of gun oil, sweat, chemicals. Human.

She followed a tiny trail through the brush, sliding up behind a Scythe mercenary. He hadn't found Donal. No, he was kneeling at the edge of the festival grounds, rifle to his shoulder.

Planning to shoot across the grounds at the shifters on the opposite side.

To scat with that.

She attacked him from the side, going for the throat—the only quick way to kill. He threw himself back, so it wasn't a clean bite, but her fangs punctured an artery.

She darted away, wary in case he went for his rifle that he'd dropped. But, blood spurting between his fingers, he was only half-conscious. And then dead.

Sickness churned in her guts, but this time she held it down.

By the Mother... She'd always considered herself a tough bitch, but this was ghastly.

Panting, she gave herself a shake.

No time to have a breakdown. She could see and smell the mercenaries. Too many of them closing in on the festival grounds.

Fine. They might have fancy technology to use at night, but she had a nose and good ears.

Silently, she worked her way through the forest, pleased for once to be on the smaller side. There was better cover lower to the ground.

On the way around the perimeter, she heard a struggle and found a mercenary grappling with a male wolf. She lent a hand—well, her fangs—and the human lost.

The wolf flicked his ears in thanks, and they went their separate ways.

On the west side, she caught Owen's and Ryder's scents, and her tail made a wagging motion. If they were here, Emma and the young cubs they'd escorted were away and well hidden.

Sniffing out the trail toward the children, she hesitated. Minette was there with the feisty small pups. Maybe she should guard the trail that led to them?

Then she caught a different scent, a wolf moving away from the trail. *Margery*. Dropping her nose to the ground, Heather made a circle as she smelled out the information.

Margery was trailing two humans.

By the Gods, what was the banfasa thinking? *Girl, you can't take on two armed men by yourself.*

Heather followed the trail.

Carefully, quietly, Tynan walked through a dense thicket of brush to the flat area within the deep cover. With a grunt of effort, he lowered Warren to the ground.

The lad was groggy, still bleeding sluggishly from the knife wound to his chest.

After the first wave of kills, the mercenaries had realized wolves were attacking from behind, and they'd lain in wait.

Warren had blundered into a soldier crouched behind a

tree, surprising them both. Even as Warren attacked, the soldier stabbed him. Tynan had been a second too late.

But the young wolf was still alive. He had a chance.

Tynan bent and caught the wolf's muzzle in his hand. "Warren, listen. Stay here. Stay silent until the fighting's over. If we win, we'll be looking for survivors. You be one of them, you hear me? Hide and hold out. Promise me."

Warren sighed. His ears flickered agreement.

Leaving his packmate was one of the hardest things Tynan had ever done.

The fighting was close to the festival grounds now. The packs had killed many, if not most of the humans coming from the north.

Wolves had died.

Tynan rubbed his chest over the ache. Some of those killed were from his Cold Creek pack. And three were from the wolves he'd led. There was nothing he could have done for them or to keep Warren from being hurt. His head knew that.

His emotions said there should have been *something*.

After assigning his wolves to maintain the line, he headed east and found Patrin and Fell, then Shay and Zeb. They moved into a copse of trees to talk.

"Sounds like some mercs arrived from the road. It's time to get rid of them all." Shay motioned toward the open meadow.

The festival perimeter was active with the sharp crack

of rifles. Growls. Groans. Screams. No one was foolish enough to venture onto the open grounds.

Tynan nodded. "They must know their attack from the north failed. At this point, they're probably hoping to capture a few shifters and retreat with what they can get."

"They'll get nothing." Patrin's gaze was dark. "And we can't let any get away to report back."

Tynan pulled in a breath. It was an ugly truth. Yet these mercenaries had come to capture females and cubs. For the good of the whole, they must be sent back to the Mother.

"In that case, the road needs to be secured to prevent them from escaping," Tynan said.

"Agreed." Shay eyed the south. "Since the cats and bears are handling the east and west, let's leave half our wolves here to keep the north safe, then move through the other shifters to take the road. Patrin, Fell. Take your wolves on and deal with the roadblocks."

A minute later, they were moving again.

As Tynan joined his wolves, heading south, he sniffed and watched for his littermate who was undoubtedly trying to keep people alive.

Tynan rubbed his chest, feeling the intact bond to his brother. *Stay safe, Donal.*

There'd been no opportunity to attack the two mercenaries before, and now Margery was out of time.

Hidden off the trail, she watched as the soldiers knelt behind waist-high boulders on the roadside.

Not nearly far enough away, gunfire sounded from a cluster of tall, wide-trunked redwoods on the south shoulder. The shooter was short and slender and dark haired.

Vicki.

The female directed her fire at a transport vehicle parked behind another one in the road. The second vehicle still had soldiers inside—who couldn't get out without being shot.

They were shooting back at Vicki, who changed positions frequently.

More gunfire came from farther down the road to the east. And Margery could see more vehicles there. Wells must be there.

Between pinning down the soldiers in the transport and dodging return fire, Vicki couldn't watch her back carefully enough.

With all the gunfire, screams, and shouting, she wouldn't hear a yell of warning. She wouldn't realize the danger until the two Scythe mercenaries shot her.

There was only one way to keep the brave female safe. Margery shivered. Two mercenaries. No diversion.

She wouldn't survive this.

Regret washed through her—and anger. She'd barely found her life, found love. She almost whimpered as the ache of wanting to be with Donal and Tynan squeezed her heart.

But her time had run out.

The tallest merc leaned forward, his rifle coming up. Vicki was rising for her next shot.

With a howl of fury, Margery charged the closest soldier. Her shoulder struck, knocking him sideways. She lunged at the one with the rifle.

He wasn't braced against her, and her weight hit him in the side. He landed on his back.

Spinning, she dove for his throat.

"Get clear, man!" the other soldier yelled.

Even as she ripped at her prey's neck, he rammed a knee into her ribs and threw her back.

She saw the other human's rifle pointed at her.

Something sprang at him. The muzzle of his rifle flashed.

The crack of the gunshot accompanied her into darkness.

The night was interminable. By the Gods, time seemed to flex and contract, seemingly only breaths between healing one wound and when another shifter was brought to him.

Earlier in the night, Donal had followed the scent of blood to find each wounded shifter and healed them there. But a while back, Tynan had found him and helped set up a healing station a short way north of the festival grounds. The clearing was surrounded by densely packed trees, so the injured were somewhat protected from stray bullets.

After positioning wolves to guard the area, Tynan had returned to the fight.

Donal scrubbed his hands over his face. There were too fucking many injured. They kept coming, and he had little power remaining, even though he was healing only the most critically wounded, leaving the less serious damage for others to bandage.

Nia, a female he'd mated last moon, carried in a young wolf, then frowned at Donal who was moving to the shifter. "Goddess bless, you look terrible, Donal. You need energy."

He nodded, but...she wasn't the first to try to help. He had no hope.

And, when she hugged him, he tried again, seeking the bond that should be there from the mating. There was no bond. None at all. "Thank you, sweetheart," he said gently, not willing to tell her she hadn't helped.

She kissed his cheek, shifted, and headed back out into the fighting. *Mother of All, watch over her. Over every shifter.*

And while you're at it, the gift of some extra power wouldn't hurt, he thought cynically.

Groans and whimpering came from the wounded lying on the ground around him. This was his worst nightmare— not having enough power to save everyone.

He went down on one knee beside a rough-looking werecat from eastern Washington.

"Sounds like the gunfire's moved." The shifter turned his

head to hear better. "Gone farther away to the southeast and southwest."

As Donal put a bandage on the bleeding thigh wound, he listened. "My littermate said the wolves plan to attack any Scythe roadblocks."

"Ah, that's it. Good." The male's voice was weak. Too weak for only that knife wound.

Donal frowned. "Roll over."

With a groan, the male tried, needing help for even that.

Donal ran his hands across the male's back. *Ah, there.* "You got struck here?"

"Rifle butt." A smile. "Before he died."

"He got revenge. Your kidney's hemorrhaging." Hands positioned over the area, Donal concentrated, repairing the intricate blood vessels and tubes of the kidney. Normally, he'd mend the damaged flesh over it as well.

Not this time. "You're going to piss blood for a day or so, but you'll live."

"Thanks, healer. The North Cascades is lucky to have you."

Luck? It seemed in short supply this night. "Get the cubs to bring you water and drink it before you sleep." With an effort, he pushed to his feet, although his knees felt like stems too thin to support his weight.

His shoulders sagged as moonlight revealed all the wounded in the clearing. Some lying on the ground, some sitting. He wished to hell Margery was here to help with first aid, to calm them, even to tell him which one to see next.

Each few minutes, he had to reassess the injured and assign priorities. And take the time to give instructions to the uninjured on how to help the ones he couldn't see yet.

Given the way he felt, he doubted he'd get to them all.

He staggered toward the one he thought was most urgent.

Tynan's hand under his arm kept him from falling.

"Where'd you come from?" Donal muttered.

"Stubborn cat, take a break or you'll be dead and no use to anyone."

"I just..."

"Need a break, yeah, what I said." Tynan guided him to a bare spot, away from anyone. Because if there was someone wounded nearby, Donal couldn't hold back from trying to help.

"I'm sitting, all right?" The ground felt softer than a mattress, and he slumped, his back against a tree trunk.

"Good. I'll stay for a while and slap dressings on people."

And undoubtedly keep an eye on Donal.

Frustration at being helpless boiled up inside. Sure, he knew better than to continue when the power was gone. All healers were taught that once the Mother's power was exhausted, the energy came from the healer's own body. And if too much lifeforce was used, the healer died.

Stopping, though? Hard to do.

He would. He had to. With an exasperated huff, Donal sat quietly, running his fingers through the stubby grass. Delicate stems, but not fragile. If walked on, the grass would bend, even break, and then send up new growth. Extremely optimistic was grass.

Reminded him of Margery.

Despite her past, she lived joyously. Even after so much loss, she'd been willing to open her heart and love him and Tynan.

After this mess, we're going to track you down and find you, sweetheart. We belong together, the three of us.

The sound of running caught his attention.

A shifter-soldier rushed into the clearing with someone slung over his shoulder. Bending, he gently laid the wounded male down.

It was Alec.

Even from across the clearing, Donal could hear Alec's strangled wheezing.

The shifter-soldier looked around frantically. "Where's the healer? The cahir can't breathe."

Donal managed to stand, to lurch over to where Alec lay. He set a hand on the broad chest that was covered in blood. The cahir might survive the gunshot wound to the lung— but not the nicked pulmonary artery. Bleeding, inside and out.

No power.

No time.

They'd been friends since the day Donal arrived in Cold Creek.

Knowing how the healing session would end this time, Donal set his hand on Alec's throat. "Easy, cahir, it'll be all right."

Reach deep, stop the bleeding, mend the slashed artery. Then... the lung, so vascular, so torn.

Power flowed, painfully dragged from Donal's own cells. Almost, almost...

The blackness hovering at the edges of his vision closed in like a raven diving for the kill.

Growling and shouting.

Too close. Fear ripped through Heather as she shook the fog from her head. She tried to scramble to her feet, but the ground tilted beneath her. She dropped back into the dirt.

Where...? What...?

The last few memories returned—along with a burst of adrenaline.

Scythe attacking the festival, killing. Margery's tracks. Trailing her. Seeing the small wolf charge two mercenaries. One aiming his rifle at Margery.

Heather had leaped onto his back, but the weapon fired. Margery fell. Heather bit down on the back of his neck even as he'd rolled to knock her loose. She'd seen the rifle barrel swinging toward her head.

More shouts. What was happening? She had to *move*.

As she rolled up onto her paws, her vision blurred—and pain stabbed into her brain. So much pain. Whining, she forced herself to stand, swaying despite having four legs.

She tried to get her eyes to focus.

The soldier she'd attacked was fighting a cahir-sized, naked shifter. The blond cahir hit him—left, right, left. Grabbing the stunned human, the shifter broke his neck as easily as a wolf would snap a rat's spine.

Farther away, a panther rose from the bloody body of the other soldier and then trawsfurred. Dark hair, dark eyes, like the deadliest of night creatures.

Heather shook her head and cringed at the pain. Where...where was Margery?

"She's alive." The English-accented voice came from behind the dark shifter. Calum was there, kneeling next to a wolf. Next to Margery.

Heather took a step in that direction.

Cat-graceful, the dark male stepped between her and her goal. He glanced at his kill, the rifles lying on the ground, then down the road. "I believe the mercenaries were targeting your mate, Cosantir." His voice was as dark as his hair—with a soft French accent.

Shivering, Heather felt her legs give out. She collapsed.

"It's good the wolves ruined their aim." The dark one moved toward her.

The blond cahir frowned at Margery, then Heather. "Two little female wolves took on armed humans?"

"And kept my mate from getting shot in the back." Calum's British accent was sharper than normal. Vicki was going to be in trouble.

With a sigh, Heather laid her muzzle on her paws. Moving was way too much work.

"I think I like your country, Cosantir," the dark one murmured.

The blond cahir laughed. "Good mountains, lots of danger, courageous females. What's not to like?"

Calum gathered Margery up in his arms. "The healing area is north of the grounds. If you could assist?"

The blond cahir walked over and stroked a hand over Heather's fur. "Come, little female, it's to the healer with you."

Although he was so incredibly careful as he picked her up, the movement shot daggers into her head until she could do nothing but shiver and try not to whimper.

The dark one joined them, easing one of her paws to a more comfortable position. He ran his hand down her side. "She's covered in blood." He sniffed and made a huffing sound. "From several humans."

The blond chuckled and started walking. His voice was a low rumble under her ear. "Been busy, have you, pretty wolf?"

His arms were like iron bands, holding her tightly to his

huge chest. He radiated heat. And his scent, oh, his wild, masculine scent played havoc with her senses.

She bent her head to his forearm and gave him a little lick. Salty, sweaty, wonderful male. She licked him again.

Even as the dark one laughed, the blond strolled along beside the Cosantir. His deep rumbly voice was quiet and assured. "Calum, the little female licked me. I think that means she's mine."

The dark one chuckled. "Ours."

"Bloody Canadians." Calum huffed. "No."

CHAPTER TWENTY-FIVE

*U*nclaimed territory - one night before the full moon

Something hurt. No, *everything* hurt, but something hurt worse than the rest.

The intense, aching pull in the center of Margery's chest felt like someone had roped her heart to drag it through a too-narrow opening.

Fuzzily, she blinked. Why was she lying on the ground? In the dirt. When she moved her head, her skull felt shattered.

She whined. Had a grizzly bit her, trying to crack her head like a walnut?

Trying to check, she lifted her hand—no, her paw. That wouldn't work. Panting, she trawsfurred to human.

Even shifting hurt.

Her hand shook as she gingerly touched the burning area above her right eyebrow. The flesh was all swollen around an incredibly painful furrow. Sticky, half-drying blood covered the side of her face.

What...? Flashes of memory strobed her brain.

Two mercenaries aiming at Vicki. She'd charged them. And, Gods, one of them shot her. That was a bullet furrow.

No wonder her head hurt.

As she pushed to a sitting position, nausea roiled in her belly.

Was Vicki all right? And wait, a reddish wolf had attacked the one who'd shot her. Was that Heather?

By the Gods, her memories were messed up worse than Breanne's jigsaw puzzle.

What about the pain in her chest? Had she been shot there, too? She ran her hands over her sternum, breasts, and ribs. Aside from the long knife slash—and a lot of bruises— she was just bloody and dirty.

Carefully, she looked around, sucking in air against the stabbing in her head.

A clearing. Moonlight shone into the center. The tree-lined edges were in shadow. Bodies lay and sat everywhere.

Captives? Terror froze her until she sniffed and found only the wild scent of shifters, blood, and pain. No firearms or armor or humans.

She wasn't a prisoner.

She was surrounded by the wounded.

If the injured were here, where was Donal? There was no healer moving around, no deep calming voice—or ranting.

The pain in her chest grew, inexorably dragging her attention to her right.

Tynan was kneeling next to...next to Donal who lay so very still.

No. No, no, no.

The ache in her chest was from him. Her bond to him strummed with agony. She tried to stand, failed, and shifted to wolf so she could stagger on four paws between the injured to get to Tynan. To Donal.

Tynan lifted his head before she reached him. "Meggie?" He stared at her in disbelief.

She collapsed next to Donal, whining her questions. Her fears.

"He did too much." The grief in Tynan's voice bit at her with sharp fangs. "I tried to give him power. So did Francesca who should have a bond with him. Nothing helps. His breathing is..." His voice went ragged. "Is slowing."

No. No, he couldn't die.

Fear shook her and the beginning of grief before Tynan's words truly registered. Francesca had tried to give him power. A female he'd mated with.

Margery had mated with him...and there was love there. They had a bond. A bond big enough to hurt like fire right now.

Lying next to him, she rested her muzzle on his bare

chest. His skin was cool. His ribcage barely moved with each breath.

Closing her eyes, she found her lake of calm, turned it into a river...and poured power into him.

Donal had fallen into a universe of cold darkness.

He woke to sunlit warmth.

He took a breath, then a deeper one, feeling as if his lungs were stretching, as if he'd been moved out from under a massive boulder.

Scents drifted to him. Tynan was close. There was the soft fragrance of flowers. *Margery?* Was that her weight? Her furry head lay on his shoulder, her paw on his chest.

No, he knew better. She was headed for Canada.

Yet he didn't move. Right now, he'd prefer the fantasy to reality.

Then he realized the smell of blood that filled the clearing included the scent of *her* blood.

His eyes snapped open, and he sat up so quickly his head spun. "Are you hurt? Where are you bleeding?"

On his other side, Tynan gripped his shoulders and steadied him. "There you are. I wasn't sure you'd come back to us." Tears glinted in his eyes. "Don't do that again, *mo deartháir.*"

Donal pulled in a breath as he heard the pain. "I'm sorry, brawd."

Slowly, he looked down—and yes, she was there.

Margery. Obviously dislodged when he moved, she gave a pained whine and shifted to human. Slowly, carefully, she sat up.

She really was there.

In fact... The realization came slowly. She was the reason he was alive at all. "You shared power with me."

Her hand was on her forehead. Her face was bloody, and her brows were pulled into a pained frown. Yet her lips tilted upward into a smile. "You're welcome."

By the Gods, he loved her. Gently, he pulled her closer and chuckled. "That's what I meant to say. Thank you. You saved my life, you know."

Her curvy body stiffened. "I know." She gave him a dark look. "Like Tynan said, don't do that again."

He wanted to talk with her, tell her how much he loved her. But this wasn't the time. "We'll talk later, *cariad*." Donal rubbed his cheek against hers. "Just don't leave us again. Aye?"

"Aye."

She'd come back to them. His heart felt swollen with the knowledge.

Even as he grappled with the emotions, he frowned and moved her hand from her head. The long furrow was too clean to be from a branch. "By Herne's holy prick, what is this? No, don't bother to try to snow me with pixie dust; I know what that is. You put your brain-pan, you know, where your brains are, in front of a Gods-benighted, buggered-up bullet."

Even as his mouth kept moving, he laid his hand over the wound and healed the bruised, bleeding tissues inside her brain, the cracked skull, then the furrow.

"There are others who are worse off," she protested.

As if he'd ever let her be in pain if he could help it.

But she wouldn't accept that answer, so he gave her the other truth, the harder one. "I need you able to move. To help." Frowning, he healed the knife wound over her ribs.

"Oh. Of course. What do you need?"

And he could only smile because the response was simply...Margery. If she could help, that's where she'd be.

Tynan chuckled and kissed her hair. "I'll find you some clothes, then go back to search and rescue. You okay now, cat?"

"I am." Donal did a quick internal assessment and felt his eyes widen. "In fact, I'm full up."

Margery snickered. "Healer, that sounds more like a car than a shifter." Rising, she looked around the tent, eyes narrowed. Assessing. Triaging.

She filled his heart to overflowing.

As Tynan pulled him to his feet, Donal exchanged smiles with him. Their mate was back where she belonged.

Hours later, Tynan and his crew carried the last of the wounded to the dining tent on the festival grounds.

The battle was over. Was won—but at such a cost. His

chest ached where bonds to several pack members had been severed by violent death. Dread lingered inside him because he didn't know who'd survived...and who hadn't.

It wasn't only wolves. The cats. The bears. They'd died fighting for their people. Their clans.

With a sigh, he bent, eased the groggy panther off his shoulders and onto a blanket. He stroked the cat's fur and murmured, "I'll get someone over here to see you."

Looking around, he spotted one of the injured, and his heart lifted. "Warren."

"Uh. Hey, Beta." The young male was curled up on a blanket. Bandages around his chest were bloodstained, and he winced when he tried to sit up. "You made it."

"As did you. I went back for you, but Donal said Ben found you first." Tynan looked away until the stinging in his eyes diminished. "You looked pretty bad when I left you."

Warren gave him a rueful smile. "You told me to hide and hold out. Figured you'd bite me if I fucked that up."

"You figured right." The words came out a growl Tynan hadn't intended.

Warren's gaze dropped. "I wasn't watching close enough. I almost stepped on that human."

"What happened was simply the way things go sometimes in a fight." Tynan shook his head. "What no one ever tells you is how fucking exhausting a battle is. We ran for miles. Stalked, fought, killed—for hours. That kind of fear, the intensity of fighting for your life—it's draining."

"Oh." Warren rubbed his face. "I guess, yeah, I was dragging. Still..."

"Pup, we took out six well-armed, experienced soldiers. If you hadn't been doing an excellent job, the first one would have killed us."

"Six?" Warren's mouth dropped open. "I...after the first couple, the rest are kind of a blur."

"You did good; You can be my battle-mate anytime."

The worry cleared from Warren's expression. After helping the lad lie back down, Tynan started across the tent, looking for Donal.

Instead, he spotted Patrin and Fell who were teasing Joe Thorson for being wounded.

Tynan almost smiled. When the two shifter-soldiers had blundered badly upon first arriving in Cold Creek, Joe was assigned to teach them. It seemed they'd learned the were-cat's gruffness covered a caring heart.

"Tynan," Patrin greeted, and Fell nodded. The two looked tired but...satisfied. How much anger had the shifter-soldiers stored up for the Scythe in a decade of captivity?

"Road blocks gone?" Tynan asked.

"Yeah." Patrin shrugged. "It got a bit dicey, but we got it done. No one escaped."

"We wondered..." Fell frowned. "Are we sure we got all the mercs in the forest?"

"Calum asked the bears to spiral outward and around the area," Tynan said. Bears had better noses than other shifters. "They'll sniff out any human still in the forest—and ensure we have no wounded left out there."

Patrin smiled. "Perfect."

Tilting his head at the white dressing on the old were-cat's side, Tynan asked, "You all right, Joe?"

"Caught a bullet. Donal repaired where it'd nicked the intestines, and Margery slapped a dressing over the hole. They're a good team," Joe said.

Tynan looked around.

Meggie was teaching a younger shifter how to elevate a leg and apply groin pressure to control leg bleeding until Donal could get there. A young shifter stood at the wounded female's feet. Doing...nothing.

To Tynan's surprise, he spotted Donal on the other side of the tent. The cant of his head showed he was healing someone. "He's still moving? Even with Meggie's help, I thought he'd be flat out by now."

"I saw him reeling, but the banfasa hugged him, and he was all right again," Patrin said.

"She's done that a few times," Thorson agreed. "And she got this tent organized faster than a brownie on cleaning day. When the treeway cubs came in, she nabbed them for assistants and—see the one at the foot of the bed? In the red shirt?"

"Yeah, just standing there."

"He's the flag-pup. Shows Donal which shifter to heal next. Got a red one and a yellow, and Margery rearranges them so the healer never wastes his time figuring out who's the worst off. She has it covered."

"That's brilliant." Tynan smiled. "Knowing her, she's also keeping everyone calm, too."

"I thought that was my imagination." The werecat's eyes narrowed. "When she sat next to me to patch me up, it was like I knew everything would be all right."

"She has a gift."

"That's why the younglings stick so close to her, isn't it?" Patrin said.

Donal joined the red-shirted cub, said something that made him laugh, then knelt and started healing the female's leg wound.

Meanwhile, Meggie rearranged her red and yellow-shirted cubs.

When the yellow-shirted one said something, Meggie grinned and hugged him.

The cub's face lit.

Thorson nodded. "Aye, she has a gift, and the clan is the stronger for it."

They were. So was Tynan.

Silently, they watched her tending the injured, dispensing peace and help in equal measures.

Tynan smiled. Because the three of them had made it through another battle alive and soon, they'd be together.

As Meggie moved toward the other end of the tent, Thorson gave Tynan a hard stare from under grizzled brows. "You serious about our banfasa?"

"Joe, you have no idea."

Margery woke, stiffened, and lifted her muzzle slightly to sniff the air, catching the stale scents of blood and sweat. No fresh smell of fear. Her ears flicked forward. There was soft breathing all around her, a few whines. Farther away, someone was talking in a low voice. She relaxed. Throbbing all over her body told of battles fought

With a soft sigh, she let herself sink down into the warmth of the shifters surrounding her. Last night, as the younglings grew exhausted, the adults had tossed blankets into a corner and sent them to sleep there in a puppy pile.

As the adults in the tent wore out, they'd shifted to animal and joined the pile of sleeping furballs.

Eventually, she and Donal ended up there, somewhere close to dawn, and later, she vaguely remembered Tynan squirming his way in to join them.

In fact, the big panther paw resting on her ribs was Donal's. Contentment filled her at the sight of him, lying on his side in front of her, his hind legs tangled with hers. Tynan was curled around her from behind, his muzzle resting on her nape.

Her males.

Not lifemates, of course, but they were hers, no matter what they thought.

She eyed the angle of the sun against the tent wall. Early

morning. The night had been long and ugly. The Daonain had won the fight, but at a cost of lives, of injuries.

The bodies of the shifters who'd been killed would be taken to Cold Creek and Rainier for the Daonain's rites of passage—the Return to the Mother.

The spymaster with the shifter-soldiers' help had used a portable fingerprinter on the Scythe bodies before trucking away all trace of their presence. He even said he had a way to dispose of corpses. Having met him, she wouldn't put it past the devious human to own a crematorium or something.

Most of the shifter-soldiers went with Wells to continue the hunt for the Scythe Colonel. Not Oliver, though. The group he'd escorted hadn't returned yet. Her chest ached because when his duty was done, he would leave for Canada.

When a tiny whine escaped her, she felt a wolf paw land on her shoulder, and Tynan took a comforting lick of her ear. Donal's purr swept over her, and he rubbed his big head against her furry cheek.

Not alone. I'm not alone.

Smiling, she breathed in the scents of her males, of her pack, of her clan. And drifted back off to sleep.

When she woke again, Donal and Tynan were gone, and the puppy pile had diminished. A quick glance showed the tent was almost empty. Donal must have finished healing the injured.

Rolling up onto her paws, she almost whimpered. Her

ribs and shoulders were bruised, and the healed knife wound was still tender. *Ow, ow, ow.*

Slowly, carefully, she picked her way out of the pile of sleeping shifters, ignoring the grumbling.

Hey, she didn't step on more than a paw or two.

After shifting to human and washing in the icy stream, she dressed and stretched. The sun had warmed the air, and a breeze swept away the last stench of battle.

It was a new day.

Returning to the grounds, she saw shifters leaving, some being helped down the path to the road. The sound of vehicles picking them up came and went.

A youngling ran past her, carrying a backpack.

The cubs were back?

Margery looked around, seeing that the noncombatants had returned.

"Margery!" Oliver stood by the firepit, drinking from a mug. He handed the cup to Angie, then caught Margery up in a warm hug. "Fuck, I was worried about you all night."

"Are you all right?" She held him at arm's length to give him a quick perusal. Scratched, dirty, tired, but intact.

"Yeah. A couple of the mercenaries got close, but I decoyed them away and up to the top of a cliff." He grinned at her. "Bears don't sneak worth shit, but I can sound like a whole bunch of people."

"You didn't get hurt?"

"Nah. Owen came up behind them—fuck, but he's, like, totally silent—and smacked them right off the cliff."

Owen was one of Darcy's mates. A werecat cahir. "Sounds like perfect teamwork."

"It worked all right." His smile said he was feeling better about himself. He gave her the same careful study she'd given him. "You're all right? Angie said you were in the fighting before the healing tent was set up. That you got hurt."

Margery shot her boss a glare that made her laugh. "I got thumped on the head"—a gunshot was a thump, right? —"but Donal put it to rights."

Oliver's sigh was relieved. "It's good to have a healer at hand."

"It is."

A noisy family group headed for the firepit, and Margery pulled Oliver out of their way. "So, bro, what are you planning now?"

"Heading for Canada. I wanted to make sure you were all right and say goodbye before leaving."

The bond to him didn't even hurt—because it was the right choice for him. What he needed to get himself back on the right trail. Pulling in a breath, she found her calm. "I'm glad you waited to see me. I needed a hug before you left."

Blinking back tears, she wrapped her arms around him.

He squeezed her so hard her injured ribs set up a protest —and they both stayed for a moment, feeling the pain of loss.

"Goodbyes suck," he muttered and let her go.

She wiped her eyes. "Yeah. Well. You know my address, my phone number. You call me when you find a place to den."

"I will. Yeah." He pulled in a breath. "Love you, sis." And then he was walking into the forest—his haven as the moon was for her.

"Love you, bro," she whispered.

After a minute, an arm encircled her waist. "He's off to Canada, like he said?" Angie asked.

"He is. It's good." Margery heard the quiver in her voice and firmed it up. "He needs to go."

"It's good when someone knows what to do next." Angie gave her a squeeze, then poured a mug of coffee from the pot on the grill. "You look like you need this, girl."

"Thank you." The scent of the dark brew would wake a hibernating bear.

As she took a sip, she studied her boss. The lines on Angie's face were deeper. Brush scratches reddened her face and neck, and she moved...carefully. She'd been in Shay's wolf pack last night. "How badly did you get hurt?"

"You're such a banfasa." Angie smiled wryly. "A bullet messed up my leg, but Donal mended it. Got some bruises here and there. I'm alive." Sorrow flickered in her gaze.

Deep within, Margery could feel the ache of the broken pack bonds. She'd only known those packmates since spring —not for years like Angie. Margery moved closer to share the grief, to comfort, and Angie leaned against her.

After pulling in a breath, Margery motioned to the

shifters walking toward the road. "I take it the festival is over."

"Aye. The Cosantirs don't feel it's safe to remain."

Approaching, Vicki heard and smiled. "It's always nice when the REMFs are smart."

At Angie's confused look, Margery clued her in. "Rear-echelon motherfuckers."

"Girl," Angie sputtered. "One of those REMFs is your mate."

"Well, that's true enough." Vicki grinned. "He's better than most of them."

Margery laughed. "You're such a fraud." Then she frowned because, although Vicki was moving well enough, she had dark circles under her eyes and a strained expression. "Are you all right?"

"Yeah, fine."

Margery crossed her arms over her chest and tried for a Tynan-authoritative frown.

"You do that well. I'd promote you." Vicki shook her head, and her smile disappeared. "Okay, though it was fun to play with weapons again, the fighting brought back... stuff. It'll take a few days for it to die back down—and yes, Angie, Calum and Alec know."

"That's all right, then." Angie handed Vicki a cup of coffee.

Vicki took a sip before turning to Margery. "Calum told me what you did last night. Thank you for guarding my back."

"Ah, well, you were pinning down a whole bunch of bad guys—there would have been a whole lot more casualties if you hadn't." Mother's breasts, but the female was braver than anyone Margery had ever known. "It seemed only right I should lend a paw."

Vicki bumped her shoulder against Margery's. "Your fur and fangs are welcome to fight with me anytime, anywhere."

A lovely compliment, but Gods, the female thought guns were *fun*. "Oh, let's not."

Angie snickered and helped Margery out by changing the subject. "Since the festival is shut down here, Calum invited everyone to Cold Creek. We'll celebrate in a safer area and have our full moon Gathering. Rainier Territory's also playing host for anyone who wants."

Margery felt her jaw tighten. She'd heard about Pete's blunders. "The Colonel knows there are shifters in Ailill Ridge now."

"And Cold Creek, for that matter," Angie said logically. "But, unlike your Dogwood, our towns have plenty of humans, so a big sweep just can't happen."

"That's why Calum's calling for a street party this evening for humans and shifters alike. The businesses will enjoy it, and so will our human townsfolk."

Margery smiled at Angie. "We'll have food from the diner on sidewalk tables?"

"Exactly." Angie nodded. "Then the Gathering will be at a lake well up into the mountains."

Margery flinched. The *Gathering*. Donal and Tynan had

talked about her staying, but she still had to face the concern that had sent her away. She'd have to watch them mate with other females. Every full moon.

But...she'd manage.

Donal and Tynan loved her, and she loved them.

It was enough. And on that note, she totally needed to go collect hugs and kisses from her mates.

Needy wolf.

CHAPTER TWENTY-SIX

C old Creek, North Cascades Territory - full moon

It was a beautiful night for an outdoor Gathering. The cool air ruffled Tynan's fur as he trotted beside his brother up the forest trail. They were running late. Tynan because he'd had to remove roadblocks from the streets. Donal because a female had sprained her ankle when dancing.

A lot of the shifters at the festival were returning to their own territories today—the Canadians and ones from Wyoming had left near dawn. Other Daonain had accepted Calum's invitation to visit the North Cascades Territory.

Here in Cold Creek, they'd held the ritual to return the fallen shifters to the Mother—and as the bard sang the lost home, those left alive mourned. The broken bonds to his lost packmates still ached inside his chest.

Then the town had put on a street party to restore the balance. All the residents mingled, reminding shifters that not every human was bad, that kindness crossed species— and that life went on.

Food and drink and a sunny day. Music from the humans as well as Emma and some visiting bards. Their irresistible music had pulled everyone into the street to dance. On the sidelines, toddlers and small cubs jumped and bounced to the rhythm. In the middle of the street, some of the seniors had shown off intricate dance steps.

As a precaution, the sheriff had detoured traffic away from the downtown—and no one was allowed past the guards unless they were a shifter or a local. After the Scythe attack, all Daonain territories would heighten security. But that was for the future.

The longest day of the year was over.

Tonight, they'd celebrate the full moon—Tynan glanced at Donal—and possibly the next chapter of their lives.

Anticipation and anxiety created a heady mix in Tynan's bloodstream. His paws caught the urgency and picked up the pace.

The sound of cheerful voices drifted through the night air as he and Donal reached the lake. Someone had already lit the two solstice bonfires on the bank, and the firelight danced over the dark water.

Tynan lifted his nose, sniffing the air, catching the dark, wet scent of the lake and the resinous tang of wood smoke.

There was also the compelling fragrance of females in heat.

Because the Gathering would be held here.

Tonight, rather than restricting the Gathering to single, fertile shifters, the Cosantir also invited the lifemated and those who'd passed beyond their fertile years.

Because today and tonight were about life.

Beside Tynan, Donal dropped the bag containing their clothing. The cat hated wearing mini-packs and, instead, he'd carried the bag up the trail like a dead deer.

"Thanks." Tynan dug out his black jeans and pulled them on. Good enough. He'd stay barefoot and bare-chested for the night.

Dressed the same, Donal grinned. "We ready?"

Tynan did a quick check of his pockets. "We are." In the growing moonlight, his need for a female—for one incredibly special female—simmered like bubbles in his veins.

Where was she?

He spotted Heather moving around the groups as if looking for someone.

Warren raised a hand in greeting.

Breanne, Shay, and Zeb were surrounded by other life-mated members of the pack.

And there was Meggie, near the lake, looking out over the peaceful water. When a male strutted toward her, Tynan and Donal growled and stalked forward.

Near her, Calum was talking to two other Cosantirs. He spoke to the randy male, sending him off, then looked directly at Tynan and Donal.

And grinned.

"The Cosantir is poking his whiskers in again," Donal muttered.

"I'm happy with the results." Tynan headed straight for Meggie.

Tradition said rituals at Gatherings were done in full view of the clan. He'd have it no other way.

Donal strode beside his littermate as unexpected anxiety crept into his gut like mice into the pantry.

Maybe this wasn't the right time. Margery would be exhausted. Stressed. What if she had reconsidered? Planned to take off and join Oliver?

He huffed a breath. "We should have done this before. Last week or something."

Tynan gave him a disbelieving look. "You were the one who told her there would be no lifemating."

"Well, that was stupid. You should have punched me."

"I did."

Donal huffed and touched his bruised cheek. "Good point."

Damn wolf.

As Donal turned his gaze to Margery, anticipation like bright sunlight wiped out his shadowy worries.

By the Gods, she was beautiful, as peaceful as the lake. The moonlight lit her face, rippled over her rich brown hair. Her thin, tight tank top stretched over her full breasts in a way that dried his mouth.

He couldn't imagine a time when her body didn't send lust right through him. Or when her presence didn't fill him with happiness.

She saw them approaching, and the flash of pleasure in her eyes lifted his heart. Then worry tensed her face. Why would she worry?

No, he knew why she was worried. She didn't believe they wanted her, so she'd be bracing herself to keep to the Gathering traditions. No jealousy or being territorial.

It was good they could remove that worry for her.

If she said yes.

Surely, she'd say yes.

As they reached her, Donal breathed in her light floral scent, then took a knee in front of her. Tynan followed suit. Their shoulders rubbed as they looked up at their female. *Ours.*

Her eyes widened. "What are you..."

Tynan took the bracelets from his pocket and handed one to Donal.

Donal set the bracelet in his palm and held it up so the silver moon discs, from crescent to full to crescent, gleamed in the moonlight. He could feel the Mother's blessing that Gawain, the blademage, had called down upon the bracelets.

Tynan smiled and opened his palm, displaying his bracelet there.

Margery stopped breathing.

Hands over her chest, Margery could feel her heart pounding as she tried to breathe, as love swept over her, overwhelmed her.

Donal and Tynan were kneeling in front of her. Holding lifemating bracelets.

Here. In front of everyone.

Tynan smiled slowly, as strong and stable as the mountain behind him. "Margery Lavelle, we are here to tell you that we love you and would have you as our lifemate in this life and all our lives to come."

"We love you, Margery Lavelle. And we know you love us. We belong together." Donal's smile flashed, quicksilver as his personality. "Banfasa, healer, cop—we're perfect for one another. Be our lifemate." His dark brows drew together. "Don't even *think* about refusing."

Tynan's amused snort was her undoing, and she burst into laughter—as did everyone around them.

Then, as she'd come to expect, the entire clan jumped in to offer advice.

"Say yes, banfasa."

"Take the bracelets, Margery. Say yes." Was that Bree?

"They need you, girl." That was Angie's voice.

"Don't make them wait, or the healer will get his tail in a twist."

"Yes, yes, yes. That's the right answer."

The voices around her faded as she fell into the love in her males' eyes. Her own eyes filled with tears.

Because this was every dream she'd ever had and was coming true all at once.

"Yes." Her voice wobbled, and she made it firm. "I love you both so much."

Pulling in a breath, she added the ritual words that would please Tynan's tradition-loving heart. "We will be life-mates in this life and all our lives to come."

Because she couldn't imagine being without them. Ever.

As the clan broke into gleeful shouts, Donal and Tynan rose.

Tynan slid the bracelet on her wrist, and pulled her into his arms for a long, thorough kiss. "I love you, *mo chridhe*," he whispered into her hair and handed her to his brother.

Donal added his bracelet beside his littermate's, pulled her in and whirled her around before kissing her. She could feel the joy bubbling inside him.

Then he stopped and frowned. "Wait. *We* get bracelets."

Tynan laughed and opened his other hand to show two masculine bracelets that matched her smaller ones. "Mark us, Meggie, so all will know we're yours."

Happy tears trickled down her cheeks as she put a life-mating bracelet on Tynan's corded wrist and pulled him down for a kiss. "I love you, Tynan, for this lifetime and into the next and the next..."

His growl of agreement made her heart happy.

She put the other bracelet on Donal's lean muscular wrist. "I love you, Donal, so very much, in this lifetime and all the rest to come."

He purred as he kissed her.

Tracing the lifemating bracelets on their wrists, she smiled. "My mates."

"Yours," Donal agreed.

"Ours," Tynan said.

Whistles and cheers rolled over the forest and echoed off the mountains of the Gods.

EPILOGUE

*C*old Creek, North Cascades Territory – end of summer

Why doesn't she wake up?

In the chair beside Meggie's bed, Tynan held her limp hand in both of his. And waited.

Waited.

Waited.

Her breathing was slow. *Too slow?* No, Donal had assured him—several times—that the rate was to be expected.

Her face was pale. Because she'd lost blood before Donal had gotten it stopped.

Herne's hide and hooves, but he never wanted to live through anything as traumatic as the sound of her bones breaking. Crunching. His guts twisted, and when Meggie stiffened, he realized he was squeezing her hand.

He forced his grip to loosen and stroked over her forearm instead. Too late. He'd disturbed her, and her head rolled back and forth on the pillows. Her hands closed into fists.

Bloody hell, she was dropping into a nightmare again.

So many nightmares over the last day.

"Shhh, lass, everything is all right."

If she would only wake up, everything would be fine. But, feck, she hadn't even woken up during all the construction noise. He glanced behind him at the south wall where all the work had been done. He'd have to close the curtains before he left the room.

"You're safe, sweetheart. I'm here. Nothing will hurt you."

Except them. He'd let Donal hurt her. And Ben.

Gnome-nuts, why the feck did I agree to this?

"I love you, Meggie mine."

Love was such a small word for all that he felt for her. How she'd changed his life—and Donal's, as well. She'd come into his life like the spring sun after a bleak winter, warming his heart, bringing change and new life.

She made a whimpering sound that broke his heart.

"No, no, little wolf. You're fine. You're safe." He opened her fingers and pressed her hand to his cheek, then kissed the palm.

The strain disappeared from her face, and her breathing

slowed again. For the moment, he'd vanquished the nightmares that plagued her sleep.

With a sigh, he kissed her hand again. "It would be fine with me if you'd wake up soon, lass."

Margery could hear a low Irish-accented baritone speaking of love and safety. Telling her she should wake up.

Wake up. But where was she? Pain and terror lingered in her memory. Was she in the Scythe compound?

So many images of fighting, blood, agony, and death were blurred together in one eternal nightmare. What had happened?

She froze. *Don't let them know you're awake.* Sense by sense, she tried to get a handle on where she was.

She lay on her side. In a bed. There was a pillow under her head, a sheet and blanket over her body.

Her eyelids lifted ever so slightly. Shadowy room. To one side, someone was pulling the curtains closed. The room darkened more.

Then he—a big male—walked out the door.

She listened and heard no rattle of gunfire, no screams, no shouting. From somewhere came soft noises and conversation. The voices were familiar.

Remarkably familiar.

Her brows drew together, and she opened her eyes completely. Sat up.

This was *her* bedroom. Her own room that was twice as big as her mates' bedrooms on either side.

The curtains covering the south windows were closed, but the uncovered east window displayed the night sky. A light breeze brought the fragrance of roses from the bushes along the side of the house and an intriguing smell of freshly cut wood.

Another breath brought her the masculine scent of her mates from the linens.

The scent of home.

She was home, where she'd lived with Tynan and Donal since their lifemating over two months ago.

Okay, then.

Pulling in a breath, she tried to figure out what had happened. Why she felt so groggy.

She didn't hurt like after the battle last Solstice. Her head was fine. No knife slices. Her ankle ached...but nothing new about that.

Although an aching ankle might have been what had caused all those nightmares—as well as the urgent need to shift during the horrific dreams.

But each time, someone—several someones—had squeezed her hand and told her no in variations of: "*No, lass. Stay human. I'm here. You're safe.*"

She shook her head. Dreams were funny, weren't they? During some of the worst ones, she'd heard her alpha talking, telling her she was safe. Telling her not to shift—and no pack member could refuse the order of the alpha.

And she'd heard Zeb, too. His harsh voice had been almost a croon as he told her to stay in human form...and that he'd slaughter any Scythe who appeared.

Donal. Of course, Donal had been in her dreams with his resonant voice, saying she was going to be fine, and he was there. To behave and stay human. That he loved her even if she was a stubborn wolflet.

And always, always, Tynan's Irish-accented murmurs ran through her dreams. Reminding he was there. Not to shift because he'd keep her safe. He'd always keep her safe.

"Lass, you're awake. Finally." Tynan walked into her room. His strained expression was replaced by a smile. He wasn't in uniform but wore a loose cotton shirt. Over the summer, his skin had tanned, making his blue eyes seem even lighter.

His smile faded. "Lass, what's wrong?"

"I'm so confused." She looked around the room, and the movement made her head spin. "I don't remember going to bed. And I've had so many nightmares, and I'm *dizzy*."

"Ah, little wolf." After turning on the bedside lamp, he sat beside her on the bed and gently put an arm around her shoulders. He was so solid, so warm, and she cuddled closer. "You're still half-sedated. Do you remember that Donal was after fixing your ankle today?"

"My ankle?" Oh Gods, *that's* what happened. Donal had used human anesthesia on her and re-broke her ankle so he could heal it properly.

"Ah, there, now you're remembering." Tynan tucked her closer.

"Margery, are you ready for some food?" Donal stood in the doorway, holding a glass and a basket.

Tynan frowned. "I thought we agreed you'd clean up the mess in the kitchen."

"Done." Donal gave his littermate a feline's smug smile. "House-brownies have moved in. The kitchen is spotless."

Brownies? "Here? We have brownies?" A burble of happiness escaped her. The small OtherFolk only came to live in homes with happy, established families. "We're a family," she whispered.

Tynan kissed the top of her head. "So we are."

"Aye." After putting the basket and glass on the bedstand, Donal sat on her other side, facing her. His silvery gaze was tired, his color pale.

With fingertips, she traced the dark circle under his eyes. "You look exhausted. What did you do today?"

Tynan chuckled. "Sedation isn't gone yet. She's only half-tracking."

"I'm tracking fine." Wasn't she? Why did he say that?

And why was Donal tired?

Oh, wait.

Then she remembered what Tynan had said before Donal came in. "My ankle!" Her hands closed on the sheets as hope rose. "Is-is it fixed?"

Donal took her hands. "Yes, all fixed, although it took

forever to piece everything together before healing the mess. We had to keep you sedated longer than I liked."

Tynan snorted. "He's irritable because you kept starting to shift, and he knew he'd be your first target."

"Sorry, Donal." At his huffed response, she giggled.

Snuggling closer to Tynan, she rubbed her cheek against his hard shoulder and winced at the ache.

Had she banged her face into something?

She touched her cheek and ran her fingertips over the slightly tender line where the long, bumpy scar *used* to be.

Traced it again. Found nothing. "Donal?"

"Ah...wolflet." Worry swept his face. "The scar didn't bother me or Tynan, but it seemed to remind you of that beating. Of the Scythe."

The memory... *The guard's ring tearing through her skin, ripping her face open. The pain, so much pain.* She swallowed and nodded.

He squeezed her fingers. "After I finished with your ankle, you still slept, and it seemed a shame to waste a perfectly good sedative. So, Tynan and I talked."

"And I agreed," Tynan chimed in.

She had a momentary flash of how their cubs would be, the littermates backing each other up. Standing together. She leaned into Tynan.

Donal took on his healer's smooth tone, the one he used when he was worried. "I cut away the scar tissue. Put the new edges together and healed them. Your skin has good elasticity and—"

"You t-took the scar away." Her eyes prickled with tears.

His expression turned panicked. "Don't cry, Margery. By the Gods, I'll put it back if you want. I can—"

Despite the tears streaming down her face, she was laughing. Donal flustered? Who would have thought? "No, you won't put it back." His face was a blur under the veil of tears. "Thank you.

"She's happy it's gone, Donal. Relax." Tynan chuckled.

Tynan knew her so well.

"Meggie." With tender fingers, he wiped the tears from her cheeks. "Now that you've terrified the healer, tell us how your ankle feels."

Holding her breath, she moved her foot, rotated the ankle. "There's only a bit of aching."

"Normal for that extensive of a healing." Donal flipped the covers back to look for himself. "Between the healing and the sedative after-effects, you'll be sleeping a lot for the next day or so."

Who cared about sleep?

She stared at her leg. The swelling was gone. Nothing grated inside. Hope rose inside her like a huge bubble.

Donal nodded. "Looks good, sweetheart."

It did. It looked *great*. She wiggled it. "I bet I can run on it now—and dance. I want to *dance*."

Donal shot to his feet and pointed a finger at her. "By Herne's holy prick, you are not doing any dancing. Not until I tell you that it's all right. Do you know how fucking scared I was through all this? I didn't do this job on your Gods-benighted, busted ankle to have you ruin all my hard word with pixie-brained idiocy like dancing on a newly healed joint."

Tynan rubbed his mouth to hide his smile...but his shoulders shook. And she burst into giggles.

Donal scowled at his brother then her. "You laugh? *Laugh?*"

Oh Gods, she couldn't catch her breath she was laughing so hard. "I love you, you know." What was he going to do when he had a litter of cubs to drive him crazy?

Huffing, he resumed his seat, leaned forward, and kissed her giggles away. "Bad wolf."

She hugged him, then tipped her head back and kissed Tynan. "Thank you. Thank you both. For the healing and the handholding."

For being there. For loving her.

"That's what mates are for, Meggie mine." Tynan picked the glass up. "If you get some fluids in you, we might let you have something sweet. Maybe."

She took a sip of the apple juice. "One of you actually cooked a dessert?"

"Gods forbid," Donal muttered.

Tynan lifted the basket and set it on her lap. "We have cookies of all kinds, two cakes, scones, and donuts with sprinkles."

As the scent of baked goods wafted up, her stomach rumbled hungrily. "You bought out a bakery?"

"No." Donal smiled at her. "Your clan was worried. All

your friends as well as all the shifters you've treated brought something."

"Sent with love to speed your healing." Tynan stroked her hair.

This time when she burst into tears, her mates just laughed.

Once she'd recovered, she drank down the juice. She ate a muffin—because blueberries made it healthy—followed by a chocolate chip cookie, because...chocolate.

With a sigh, she leaned back against the headboard. "That was awesome. I'll have to thank them all."

Once she was moving again. Which might be a while.

"The carpenter-crew, too," Tynan said.

"Huh?"

He was saying something about a window and changing something out while she was sedated.

Donal laughed. "Brawd, she's not following a word of that."

Tynan chuckled, and she felt him sliding her down in the bed. "Sleep, lass."

"But I just woke up." Her body started to slide back toward sleep—stupid sedation—and her eyelids felt as if pixies were dragging on the lashes. "I can't be tired already."

"Sure, you can." Tynan tucked the covers around her. "It's late, little wolf."

"I don't want to sleep." Tears threatened because... maybe it was the nightmares, but the past seemed too close tonight. The memory of the bare cell, empty of people.

Sitting under the tiny window, longing for the moon. "I don't want to be alone."

"That we can fix." Donal pulled off his clothes and slid into bed beside her.

"I didn't sit with the moon," she protested, even as he pulled her against him. Oh, he was so wonderfully warm she wanted to cry.

"We'll let the moon come to you tonight," Tynan walked over to the south wall.

She shook her head. What was he thinking? To be in the light, she had to sit directly beneath the—

He pulled the curtains.

She stared. The small windows were gone, replaced by three huge windows that took up most of the wall and opened the room to the black sky. And the nearly full moon.

"Oooooh." Nothing had ever been more beautiful. The moon—and the love that had known her need and fulfilled it.

"Looks like we silenced her completely." Tynan grinned at his brother and slid into bed on her other side, pinning her between them.

They tucked her onto her side, her head on Tynan's shoulder, her leg over his thighs. Her hand was on his chest, his fingers laced with hers. Donal curled up behind her, his chest against her back, his arm over her waist...and his palm cupping one breast.

It was their favorite way to sleep.

Their warmth was almost as wonderful as the sense of safety they gave her. The memory of the empty cell faded under the callused hands stroking her, the gentle kisses.

"I love you two so much...mountains and lakes of love."

Tynan's low rumbling laugh told her she wasn't making sense, but the lake of love was there, growing infinitely deep, as her lifemates held her between them.

As she fell asleep, the silvery moonglow poured through the windows, bathing them in light.

GLOSSARY

The Daonain use a conglomeration of handed-down languages from the British Isles. Some of the older villages still speak the Gaelic (Scots) or Irish Gaelic. Many of the more common (and mangled) shifter terms have descended from Welsh.

Errors and simplification of spelling and pronunciation can be attributed to being passed down through generations...or the author messing up. Below are a few of the more common words and terms used by the shifters. And, just for fun, I added pronunciations (good luck with those).

- *a bhràthair*: brother [a BRA (roll the "r" if Shay says it)-her]
- *A brathair-faoirm*: brother in arms [a BRA (roll the "r" if Shay says it)-her] – fwee – a-i-rm]

- *a chuisle mo chridhe*: pulse of my heart [ah hoosh-la muh cwree]
- *dearthair:* brother or birth-mate [Irish – [ghrih-hawr]
- *a leannán*: sweetheart, darling [a le-anan]
- *a mhac*: son [a-machk]
- *banfasa*: wise woman/nurse (Irish Gaelic from bean feasa) [ban-FAH-sa]
- *brawd*: brother [br-ow-d. Don't need to roll the "r"]
- *cahir*: warrior (Irish/Gaelic from Cathaoir) [ka-HEER]
- *caomhnor*: protector/guardian of children (from Caomhnóir) [kuheeoo-NOR]
- *cariad*: lover, darling, sweetheart (Welsh) [core-ee-awt]
- *chwaer*: sister (Welsh) [k-wy-ir like choir only a gutteral beginning and the end almost missing]
- *Cosantir*: guardian or protector (Irish Gaelic from An Cosantóir) [KOSS-un-tore]
- *Daonain*: the shifter race [DAY-ah-nan]
- *dùin do bhuel*: shut up [DOO-in doh viool (oo' as in look, 'i' as short as possible as in view]
- *mo bhràthair*: my brother [muh BRA *(roll the "r" if Shay says it)* her]
- *mo dearthair:* my brother, birth mate [muh ghrih-hawr]

- *mo charaid*: my friend [mo HARd-idge OR mo chaa-ritsh]
- *mo chridhe*: my heart [mo cree]
- *mo leannán*: my darling / my lover [mo le-anan]
- *mo leanbh:* my child or baby [muh LAN-uv]
- *mo thaisce*: my treasure [muh HASH-keh]
- *prìosan*: prison [pree-soon]
- *tha gaol agam ort*: I love you [hah GEUL AH-kum orsht]
- *trawsfur*: transform or shift (Welsh from trawsffurfio) [traws (rhyme with laws)-fur]

Want to be notified of the next release?

Sign up to get a New Release Email at https://cherisesinclair. com/newsletter/

Have you tried the Masters of the Shadowlands series?

Club Shadowlands

Her car disabled during a tropical storm, Jessica Randall discovers the isolated house where she's sheltering is a private bondage club. At first shocked, she soon becomes aroused watching the interactions between the Doms and their subs. But she's a professional woman--an accountant-- and surely isn't a submissive . . . is she?

Master Z hasn't been so attracted to a woman in years. But the little sub who has wandered into his club intrigues him. She's intelligent. Reserved. Conservative. After he discovers her interest in BDSM, he can't resist tying her up and unleashing the passion she hides within.

EXCERPT FROM CLUB SHADOWLANDS

An eternity later, Jessica spotted a glimmer of light. Relief rushed through her when she reached a driveway studded with hanging lights. Surely whoever lived here would let her wait out the storm. She walked through the ornate iron gates, up the palm-lined drive past landscaped lawns, until finally she reached a three-story stone mansion. Black wrought iron lanterns illumined the entry.

"Nice place," she muttered. And a little intimidating. She glanced down at herself to check the damage. Mud and rain streaked her tailored slacks and white button-down shirt, hardly a suitable image for a conservative accountant. She looked more like something even a cat would refuse to drag in.

Shivering hard, she brushed at the dirt and grimaced as it only streaked worse. She stared up at the huge oak doors guarding the entrance. A small doorbell in the shape of a dragon glowed on the side panel, and she pushed it.

Seconds later, the doors opened. A man, oversized and ugly as a battle-scarred Rottweiler, looked down at her. "I'm sorry, miss, you're too late. The doors are locked."

What the heck did that mean?

"P-please," she said, stuttering with the cold. "My car's in a ditch, and I'm soaked, and I need a place to dry out and call for help." But did she really want to go inside with this scary-looking guy? Then she shivered so hard her teeth clattered together, and her mind was made up. "Can I come in? Please?"

He scowled at her, his big-boned face brutish in the yellow entry light. "I'll have to ask Master Z. Wait here." And the bastard shut the door, leaving her in the cold and dark.

Jessica wrapped her arms around herself, standing miserably, and finally the door opened again. Again the brute. "Okay, come on in."

Relief brought tears to her eyes. "Thank you, oh, thank you." Stepping around him before he could change his mind, she barreled into a small entry room and slammed into a solid body. "Oomph," she huffed.

Firm hands gripped her shoulders. She shook her wet hair out of her eyes and looked up. And up. The guy was big, a good six feet, his shoulders wide enough to block the room beyond.

He chuckled, his hands gentling their grasp on her arms.

"She's freezing, Ben. Molly left some clothing in the blue room; send one of the subs."

"Okay, boss." The brute—Ben—disappeared.

"What is your name?" Her new host's voice was deep, dark as the night outside.

"Jessica." She stepped back from his grip to get a better look at her savior. Smooth black hair, silvering at the temples, just touching his collar. Dark gray eyes with laugh lines at the corners. A lean, hard face with the shadow of a beard adding a hint of roughness. He wore tailored black slacks and a black silk shirt that outlined hard muscles underneath. If Ben was a Rottweiler, this guy was a jaguar, sleek and deadly.

"I'm sorry to have bothered—" she started.

Ben reappeared with a handful of golden clothing that he thrust at her. "Here you go."

She took the garments, holding them out to keep from getting the fabric wet. "Thank you."

A faint smile creased the manager's cheek. "Your gratitude is premature, I fear. This is a private club."

"Oh. I'm sorry." Now what was she going to do?

"You have two choices. You may sit out here in the entryway with Ben until the storm passes. The forecast stated the winds and rain would die down around six or so in the morning, and you won't get a tow truck out on these country roads until then. Or you may sign papers and join the party for the night."

She looked around. The entry was a tiny room with a desk and one chair. Not heated. Ben gave her a dour look.

Sign something? She frowned. Then again, in this lawsuit-happy world, every place made a person sign releases, even to visit a fitness center. So she could sit here all night. Or... be with happy people and be warm. *No-brainer.* "I'd love to join the party."

"So impetuous," the manager murmured. "Ben, give her the paperwork. Once she signs—or not—she may use the dressing room to dry off and change."

"Yes, sir." Ben rummaged in a file box on the desk, pulled out some papers.

The manager tilted his head at Jessica. "I will see you later then."

Ben shoved three pages of papers at her and a pen. "Read the rules. Sign at the bottom." He scowled at her. "I'll get you a towel and clothes."

She started reading. *Rules of the Shadowlands.*

"Shadowlands. That's an unusual na—" she said, looking up. Both men had disappeared. Huh. She returned to reading, trying to focus her eyes. Such tiny print. Still, she never signed anything without reading it.

Doors will open at...

Water pooled around her feet, and her teeth chattered so hard she had to clench her jaw. There was a dress code. Something about cleaning the equipment after use. Halfway down the second page, her eyes blurred. Her brain felt like icy slush. *Too cold—I can't do this.* This was just a club, after all; it wasn't like she was signing mortgage papers.

Turning to the last page, she scrawled her name and wrapped her arms around herself. *Can't get warm.*

Ben returned with some clothing and towels, then showed her into an opulent restroom off the entry. Glass-doored stalls along one side faced a mirrored wall with sinks and counters.

After dropping the borrowed clothing on the marble counter, she kicked her shoes off and tried to unbutton her shirt. Something moved on the wall. Startled, Jessica looked up and saw a short, pudgy woman with straggly blonde hair and a pale complexion blue with cold. After a second, she recognized herself. *Ew.* Surprising they'd even let her in the door.

In a horrible contrast with Jessica's appearance, a tall, slender, absolutely gorgeous woman walked into the restroom and gave her a scowl. "I'm supposed to help you with a shower."

Get naked in front of Miss Perfection? Not going to happen. "Thanks, b-b-b-but I'm all right." She forced the words past her chattering teeth. "I don't need help."

"Well!" With an annoyed huff, the woman left.

I was rude. Shouldn't have been rude. If only her brain would kick back into gear, she'd do better. She'd have to apologize. Later. If she ever got dried off and warm. She needed dry clothes. But, her hands were numb, shaking uncontrollably, and time after time, the buttons slipped from her stiff fingers. She couldn't even get her slacks off, and she was shuddering so hard her bones hurt.

"Dammit," she muttered and tried again.

The door opened. "Jessica, are you all right? Vanessa said—" The manager. "No, you are obviously not all right." He stepped inside, a dark figure wavering in her blurry vision.

"Go away."

"And find you dead on the floor in an hour? I think not." Without waiting for her answer, he stripped her out of her clothes as one would a two-year-old, even peeling off her sodden bra and panties. His hands were hot, almost burning, against her chilled skin.

She was naked. As the thought percolated through her numb brain, she jerked away and grabbed at the dry clothing. His hand intercepted hers.

"No, pet." He plucked something from her hair, opening his hand to show muddy leaves. "You need to warm up and clean up. Shower."

He wrapped a hard arm around her waist and moved her into one of the glass-fronted stalls behind where she'd been standing. With his free hand, he turned on the water, and heavenly warm steam billowed up. He adjusted the temperature.

"In you go," he ordered. A hand on her bottom, he nudged her into the shower.

The water felt scalding hot against her frigid skin, and she gasped, then shivered, over and over, until her bones hurt. Finally, the heat began to penetrate, and the relief was so intense, she almost cried.

Some time after the last shuddering spasm, she realized the door of the stall was open. Arms crossed, the man leaned against the door frame, watching her with a slight smile on his lean face.

"I'm fine," she muttered, turning so her back was to him. "I can manage by myself."

"No, you obviously cannot," he said evenly. "Wash the mud out of your hair. The left dispenser has shampoo."

Mud in her hair. She'd totally forgotten; maybe she *did* need a keeper. After using the vanilla-scented shampoo, she let the water sluice through her hair. Brown water and twigs swirled down the drain. The water finally ran clear.

"Very good." The water shut off. Blocking the door, he rolled up his sleeves, displaying corded, muscular arms. She had the unhappy feeling he was going to keep helping her, and any protest would be ignored. He'd taken charge as easily as if she'd been one of the puppies at the shelter where she volunteered.

"Out with you now." When her legs wobbled, he tucked a hand around her upper arm, holding her up with disconcerting ease. The cooler air hit her body, and her shivering started again.

After blotting her hair, he grasped her chin and tipped her face up to the light. She gazed up at his darkly tanned face, trying to summon up enough energy to pull her face away.

"No bruises. I think you were lucky." Taking the towel, he dried off her arms and hands, rubbing briskly until he appeared satisfied with the pink color. Then he did her back and shoulders. When he reached her breasts, she pushed at his hand. "I can do that." She stepped back so quickly that the room spun for a second.

"Jessica, be still." Then he ignored her sputters like she would a buzzing fly, his attentions gentle but thorough, even to lifting each breast and drying underneath.

When he toweled off her butt, she wanted to hide. If there was any part of her that should be covered, it was her hips. Overweight. *Jiggly*. He didn't seem to notice.

Then he knelt and ordered, "Spread your legs."

Get Club Shadowlands now!

ALSO BY CHERISE SINCLAIR

Masters of the Shadowlands Series

Club Shadowlands

Dark Citadel

Breaking Free

Lean on Me

Make Me, Sir

To Command and Collar

This Is Who I Am

If Only

Show Me, Baby

Servicing the Target

Protecting His Own

Mischief and the Masters

Beneath the Scars

Defiance

Mountain Masters & Dark Haven Series

Master of the Mountain

Simon Says: Mine

Master of the Abyss

Master of the Dark Side

My Liege of Dark Haven

Edge of the Enforcer

Master of Freedom

Master of Solitude

I Will Not Beg

The Wild Hunt Legacy

Hour of the Lion

Winter of the Wolf

Eventide of the Bear

Leap of the Lion

Sons of the Survivalist Series

Not a Hero

Lethal Balance

Standalone Books

The Dom's Dungeon

The Starlight Rite

ABOUT THE AUTHOR

Cherise Sinclair is a *New York Times* and *USA Today* best-selling author of emotional, suspenseful romance. She loves to match up devastatingly powerful males with heroines who can hold their own against the subtle—and not-so-subtle—alpha male pressure.

Fledglings having flown the nest, Cherise, her beloved husband, an eighty-pound lap-puppy, and one fussy feline live in the Pacific Northwest where nothing is cozier than a rainy day spent writing.

Printed in Great Britain
by Amazon

80165231R00335